ALSO BY PAIGE TOON

ADVANCE PRAISE FOR *SEVEN SUMMERS*

"With *Seven Summers*, Paige Toon breaks your heart then stitches it back together with expert hands. An emotional roller coaster about second chances, grief, and everlasting love, this book wrecked me in the best possible way."
—Carley Fortune, #1 *New York Times* bestselling author

"Paige Toon's romances are powerful and poignant and never fail to leave me clutching her book to my chest."
—Mia Sheridan, author of *Archer's Voice*

"*Seven Summers* warms your heart, shatters it in pieces, then puts it back together again and again."
—Abby Jimenez, author of *Yours Truly*

"Paige Toon's writing is so beautiful and emotionally resonant that you might not see it coming when she reaches into your heart and pulls it right out. *Seven Summers* is the ultimate love story, the kind with that forever, unshakable kind of love. You've been warned."
—Annabel Monaghan, author of *Same Time Next Summer*

"Paige Toon has spun a deeply layered story of hope and heartache that swept me away. I loved it."
—K. A. Tucker, internationally bestselling author of *The Simple Wild*

"A truly beautiful love story, heart-wrenching and heartwarming in equal measure." —Beth O'Leary, author of *The Road Trip*

"Beautiful, heartbreaking, and hopeful—I don't think I'll ever get over this book. Be prepared to fall in love, cry, and take these characters into your heart. I could not have loved this more."   —Emily Stone, author of *Always, in December*

"Happiness and heartbreak, desperate dilemmas, and delicious descriptions of the Cornish coast. I had no idea how this book was going to end. It's going to be huge!"
    —Jill Mansell, author of *Should I Tell You?*

"This book gave me all the emotions. Heartwarming and heartbreaking in parts, too. I was so invested in these characters and rooted for them the entire time. I dare you to put this book down."   —Jo Watson, author of *What Happens on Vacation*

"Paige Toon makes me fall in love and then breaks my heart every single time! Simply beautiful."   —Giovanna Fletcher

SEVEN SUMMERS

Paige Toon

G. P. PUTNAM'S SONS
New York

PUTNAM
— EST. 1838 —

G. P. PUTNAM'S SONS
Publishers Since 1838
An imprint of Penguin Random House LLC

First published in the United Kingdom in 2024 by Penguin Books.
Penguin Books is part of the Penguin Random House group of companies.

Library of Congress Cataloging-in-Publication Data

Names: Toon, Paige, author.
Title: Seven summers / Paige Toon.
Description: New York : G. P. Putnam's Sons, 2024.
Identifiers: LCCN 2024004173 (print) | LCCN 2024004174 (ebook) |
ISBN 9780593544358 (trade paperback) | ISBN 9780593544365 (ebook)
Subjects: LCGFT: Romance fiction. | Novels.
Classification: LCC PR6120.O58 S48 2024 (print) |
LCC PR6120.O58 (ebook) | DDC 823/.92—dc23/eng/20240202
LC record available at https://lccn.loc.gov/2024004173
LC ebook record available at https://lccn.loc.gov/2024004174
p.   cm.

Printed in the United States of America
1st Printing

Book design by Ashley Tucker

For Lucy

I feel very lucky to have you in my life

THIS SUMMER

P ERFUME EMANATES FROM THE PURPLE AND WHITE wildflowers growing on the grassy banks, and the morning air is crisp and still as I set off to Seaglass, the restaurant-cum-bar on the beach where I work. On either side of me, the hills seem to climb higher and higher as the road cuts down through the valley, and in the far distance, the Atlantic Ocean comes into view, a deep blue where it hits the horizon. I follow the curve of the road past whitewashed cottages, the pub, and the Surf Life-Saving Club before Trevaunance Cove appears in full. The tide is halfway in and the curling, clear aquamarine waves are lapping gently against the creamy-white sand.

Summer has landed and Cornwall is radiant. I feel the hope of it in my bones, as though I might finally be ready to step out of the cold shadow that has lingered over me lately.

My new hair is helping too. I've worn my dark hair long ever since I can remember, but yesterday I went to the hairdresser and told her to do whatever she wanted.

Now it swings in waves just shy of my shoulders and I *love* it. I feel like a whole new person, which is exactly what I need.

My thoughts turn to Finn and my mood takes a nosedive,

but then a breeze catches my hair and blows it back off my face, almost as though Mother Nature herself is reminding me that it's time for a fresh start.

As I head up the external staircase to Seaglass, my attention is caught by something unusual down on the beach below. The stream that leads to the ocean has carved myriad tracks out of the sand and someone has dug a number of the rivulets deeper by several inches so that now they look like tree branches forking outward from a trunk.

I pause so I can better study the art etched into the sand. The tree is leafless, which makes me think of winter. I wonder if it's winter in the artist's imagination too. What tools did he or she use to create the work? As a sculptor, I'm interested.

A wave collapses onto the shore and licks over the highest branches. It won't be long before the tide wipes the canvas clean, and I hate the thought of something so beautiful being stolen away before others have had time to appreciate it.

An idea comes to me and I take out my phone and click off a few shots, posting the best of them to Seaglass's Instagram page, along with the caption How about a little sand art with your brunch?

I'm an artist, not a wordsmith, so that will have to do.

Checking my email, I see that I have a new message from Tom Thornton:

Hi Liv,
Just dropping you a line on the off chance that the cottage will be available earlier than 4—I'm already in Cornwall.
Thanks,
Tom

I sigh. My guests are always trying to secure earlier check-ins.

I type back:

> Hi Tom,
> You're welcome to park your car on the drive, but I haven't had time to clean the place yet, as my last guests have only just left. I'm at work so I doubt it will be ready before 4.
> Cheers,
> Liv

I feel guilty when I see that he sent the message two hours ago. The rules are clear on the website, but I'm so grateful that he booked the cottage for the whole month of June after a last-minute cancellation that I'm thinking maybe I should make an exception for him. I was stressed about how I would fill four weeks outside of the school holidays and then this Tom guy swooped in and saved the day.

I decide to duck out at some point this morning and get the place ready early. I owe him that.

The familiar scent of stale beer and sea-damp mustiness washes over me as I enter Seaglass. I'm the first to arrive, but our chefs, bar staff, and waitstaff won't be far behind. We run food out of the kitchen and restaurant upstairs, the lower-ground floor is the cellar, and this middle level is all about the chilled bar vibe. On the left are French doors that open on to a balcony and face straight out to sea. And on the right is a dark-wood-paneled bar that takes up about half the length of the wall, with space for a winding open staircase and the bathrooms at the far end. A little along from the main door, perpendicular to the bar, is a performance stage.

My stomach pinches as I stare at this small raised platform, and for a moment I'm back in the past and Finn is at the mic, his lips cocked in a half smile, his gaze tangled up with mine.

Will he come back this summer?

Enough.

Behind me, the door clangs open, making me jump. I turn around, expecting to see staff, and instead find a stranger: a tall, broad man carrying a large black rucksack, his hands jammed into the pockets of a dark gray hoodie with the hood pulled up over his head.

"Sorry, we're not open yet," I call.

He comes to an abrupt stop, looking thoroughly fed up. "What time do you open?" he asks shortly.

"Ten a.m."

It's only a quarter past nine.

He mutters under his breath as he turns on his heel and walks straight out again, leaving the door wide open.

Rude!

I go over to shut the door and glance down at the beach in time to see another wave crash onto the sand, erasing a whole section of tree. Despite my determination to stay upbeat today, I can't help but feel a little melancholic as I get on with opening up.

THERE'S NO CAR parked on the drive when I return to Beach Cottage, the aptly named house that has been my home since the age of thirteen. A few years ago, I had it converted into two separate apartments, but from the outside it looks like a two-story cottage. It's built of gray stone with a central door and four symmetrical windows with pale blue frames. Peeking above the high wall enclosing the property are the spiky heads of three fat palm trees. Along the front runs a bubbling stream, which is hugged by a waist-high stone wall with so much lush moss and foliage packed into its cracks and crevices that it looks half-alive. Two bridges, only a meter and a half long, allow access to the driveway and my front door.

I cross the tiny bridge to the main door and let myself into the hall before unlocking the downstairs apartment. My previous guests didn't have children and Tom is coming on his own, so there's little to do in the bunk room and its adjoining bathroom.

Wandering through to the cozy living room, I look around, smiling at the perfectly plumped sofa cushions. The open-plan kitchen and dining area at the back of the cottage are equally spotless. If only all guests were this thoughtful.

Satisfied that I'll have the place ready in no time, I tap out a quick email to Tom, letting him know that he can let himself in at midday. Hopefully, the news will make him happy.

THE NEXT MORNING, when I get out of bed, I go straight to the window and pull back the curtains. *Still* no car on the drive! Did this Tom guy even check in? I haven't seen or heard him and he didn't reply to my email.

An hour later, all thoughts of my wayward houseguest are forgotten as I stand on the balcony outside Seaglass and stare in stationary silence at the *two* trees now etched into the beach.

The first, on the left, stretches outward from the stream in the same style as yesterday's, a span of leafless, elegant branches.

The second has been sketched directly onto the sand in the center of the beach, a tall, slim, spire-shaped conifer that makes me think of the Italian cypress trees I once saw lining the paths of the Boboli Gardens in Florence.

The memory makes me feel hollow.

I find myself being drawn down to the beach and, up close, I notice how the edges of the cypress feather in a way that looks realistic. I think they might have been created with a rake, but the tree that is emerging from the stream seems to have been scored into the sand with a sharper object. I'd wondered if it had been imagined in winter, but next to the tall, strong cypress, it appears starved of life.

I'm desperate to know what my fellow artist was thinking and feeling when they created these pieces. Did the work come from a place of joy or sadness or from somewhere else entirely?

There's an ache in my chest as I walk the length of the cypress and stand staring out to sea and thinking about Florence, a place that once held so much hope for me.

I'd only just left university when I attended the Florence Academy of Art six years ago and I still felt very much like a student playing at being an artist. But during my four weeks there, as I made cold clay come to life under my hands each day, the future felt wide-open and full of possibilities. I was so excited about the next stage of my life: moving to London and getting a job in a studio.

Then it all came crashing down.

I may not have made it to London or back to Italy as I'd once dreamed, but I *am* a professional sculptor now. It doesn't matter that I'm not sculpting full-time—I like working at Seaglass during the summer months.

I smile at the sea and the ache in my chest recedes.

Returning to the balcony, I take a few pics and post one to Instagram with the words: More exquisite sand art gracing our shores this morning . . . We'd love to know who our mystery artist is!

SATURDAYS ARE MY busiest day, what with opening up for brunch, followed by several hours of cleaning and prepping the three other holiday cottages I manage before returning to Seaglass for the evening shift. Before rush hour kicks in, I take a quick look at the post and discover that it's already closing in on fifty likes. I scroll through the comments, hoping for answers but finding none.

One of my oldest friends, Rach, has commented.

Which one's your favorite? she asks.

I reply without thinking: They move me equally, but in different ways.

Somehow, they both speak of loss, even as one thrives while the other falters.

She must be online because she replies within seconds: Wonder if there will be more tomorrow . . .

I tap out: If you're reading this, mystery artist, we'd like a whole forest, please!

At least I remembered to use "we" for that one, instead of "I." It's supposed to sound as though a team of us are bantering away with our customers, when actually it's just my solitary twenty-eight-year-old self.

I'm run off my feet until closing time at midnight, so when my alarm goes off at seven the next morning, I whack the SNOOZE button and almost fall back asleep.

But my desire to catch the sand artist in action supersedes

my exhaustion and I pull myself from bed, hoping that I've timed it right. Low tide was a whole hour and two minutes later today, so there's every chance he or she will still be at work.

When I arrive at the cove, however, I'm once again too late, but my reverence smothers any disappointment I might have felt.

A winding pathway has been carved into the beach, wide where it begins at the boat ramp and narrowing to a single wiggly line where it reaches the shore. On either side of the path are pine trees drawn roughly with sharp, serrated edges. In the forefront they're tall and majestic, but they become smaller and more roughly sketched as the path tapers away.

Suddenly I want to be *in* the picture, walking along that magical pathway leading through an enchanted forest and experiencing it firsthand.

On impulse, I head down the boat ramp and step onto the sand. I follow the curving path, smiling as it shrinks away in perfectly sketched perspective. Soon I feel as if I'm the size of a giant and eventually I have to put one foot directly in front of the other, walking the last section with my arms stretched wide as though balancing on a tightrope. Joy rises up inside my chest and I can't contain the feeling so I spin in a circle, my arms still outstretched.

The smile is still on my face as I make my way back along the winding path toward Seaglass. And then I look up and do a double take. There's a man sitting on a bench up on the cliffs, half-hidden behind gorse bushes bursting with brilliant yellow flowers. I stumble and trip, managing to right myself, and when I look up again, he's gone.

ON MONDAY MORNING, I arrive at the beach to find that it's still a blank canvas.

Am I here in time to catch the artist or have they moved to another cove?

In case it's the former, I slip up the stairs to Seaglass, figuring I'll stay hidden for a while and wait. And that's when I see it: the life-size drawing on the sand that I'd missed.

It's a simple outline of a girl wearing a knee-length summer dress, similar to the one I had on yesterday, with its hem trailing off to one side, caught in an imaginary breeze. Her wavy hair comes almost to her shoulders and her arms are spread wide in a gesture of joy.

A shiver runs down my backbone.

I walk tentatively to the railing and look up at the cliffs.

He's there once again, the man on the bench. Is he the sand artist? Was he watching me yesterday?

I hurry down the external staircase and run up the road, veering left onto the coast path. Gorse scratches my legs with each imprecise step as I climb the narrow, rocky track, my mind racing.

No one who draws that beautifully could possibly be a psychopath, I tell myself.

My compulsion to meet this artist overrides any concern for my own safety.

I know exactly where the bench is because I've sat there many times, watching the tide roll in or surfers riding the waves. My heart is in my mouth as the path opens out onto moorland with far-reaching views, and then I'm looking down at an empty bench, chest heaving, trying to catch my breath.

Where has he gone?

I continue on until the steep path levels out, and *there*! Off in the distance, striding along toward Trevellas Cove, is . . .

A tall, broad man in a dark gray hoodie.

I cast my mind back to Friday morning and the man who was none too pleased when I told him we weren't open yet. I can't remember his face. He's about to crest the brow of the hill when the word flies out of my mouth of its own volition.

"HEY!"

He looks over his shoulder at me and comes to an abrupt stop, turning around to face me. He's too far away for me to be able to make out any of his facial features, but I wave my hands over my head, requesting that he wait as I step up my pace.

I've only gone a few meters when he turns around again and strides away.

"HEY!" I shout again. "WAIT!"

But either he doesn't hear me or he chooses not to listen because a moment later he's vanished from sight.

I feel an unusual mixture of emotions as I make my way back home. I'm elated and frustrated, excited yet disquieted.

It's the most I've felt in a long time.

I'M STILL FEELING all these things an hour later when I'm heading out for the brunch shift. I'm on my way down the stairs to my private entrance when I hear the main front door of Beach Cottage unlocking.

I'm finally going to meet the mysterious Tom.

I heard him pottering around yesterday afternoon, but he's generally been as quiet as a mouse and he never did park a car on the drive. I've been too distracted to give him much thought.

I open up the door, plastering on my warmest, brightest, most welcoming smile, and come face-to-face with a tall, broad man in a dark gray hoodie.

I breathe in sharply, my eyes widening.

At a guess, he's in his early thirties, and up close he's even taller and broader—he practically fills the small hallway. His hood has been pushed back to reveal short, dark blond hair, a strong brow, and a square jaw graced with heavy stubble. His eyes are the color of maple syrup held up to a light, shot through with shards of golden brown.

"You," I whisper as his expression transforms from shocked recognition into a look of weary resignation.

"Ah, fuck," he mutters.

2

SIX SUMMERS AGO

M Y FEET HIT THE ASPHALT IN TIME WITH THE BASS as gravity and momentum send me charging down the hill. I'm on a mission: it's Friday night, I'm home at last, and I can't wait to see my friends.

Amy told me that Dan's band is in residence at Seaglass, and from the sounds of it, tonight's set is already under way.

It's amazing to think that I was in Florence this morning and a month before that I was graduating from my BA Hons in Sculpture at the Edinburgh College of Art. For four years, I trod cobbled streets between historic buildings and fell asleep to the hustle and bustle of a busy, vibrant city. And now here I am in St. Agnes, where the only sounds filling the air are coming from the crashing waves, the sea breeze cooling my sunscorched skin, and the band playing at Seaglass.

Bounding up the external stairs in time to a frenetic drum crescendo, I round the corner to find a packed balcony, cigarette and vape smoke rolling like sea mist across bobbing heads.

A squeal rings out and the crowd parts around Rach as she bulldozes her way toward me. A moment later, we're in each other's arms.

"Where have you been?" she yells right in my face as the song comes to an end and the band launches into another.

"There was traffic coming back from the airport and then my parents wanted me to have a family dinner—I haven't even had time for a shower!"

"You look fine! Come on, you've got catching up to do!"

She yanks me through the nearest set of French doors and makes a beeline for the bar. Her hand is gritty with sand and she looks as though she's come straight from the beach. Knowing Rach, she probably has. Her auburn hair is pulled into a low ponytail and the strands falling loose around her neck are damp from the sea air. I recognize the halter-neck tie of her army-green tankini protruding from her oversize white T-shirt and her trademark baggy board shorts. Classic Rach attire.

I thought I'd gone for casual in jeans and a black top, but my friend takes the description to another level.

"I've never seen it this busy!" I exclaim as she squeezes herself into an impossibly tiny gap at the bar.

"I think Dan invited half of Cornwall. Loads of people from school are here."

I glance toward the band and my eyes alight on Dan Cole, the broad, blond lead guitarist who was the most popular boy in our class at secondary school. Amy used to have a crush on him, but he had a steady girlfriend until his first year at uni, and from what I've heard, he's been sowing his wild oats ever since.

The bassist, Tarek, and the drummer, Chris, were also in our year, as was the band's frontman, Kieran, but he's missing. My eyes snag on the new guy.

His dark, disheveled hair is falling forward into downcast

eyes and his slim hips are jutting off to the side as he cradles the mic between his hands, his lips pressed to the metal.

His voice is good: low and deep, but still musical.

"Who's *that*?" I ask.

"You remember Finn, he was in our art class."

"No way."

The Finn we went to school with was really shy. He always wore beanie hats that he'd pull down so low you could barely see his eyes. I don't remember him being part of Dan's crowd back then. I don't remember him being part of anyone's crowd. From what I recall, he was a bit of a loner.

This Finn is next-level hot in black jeans and a loose black chunky-knit jumper that's riddled with holes—very carelessly sexy rock star.

Suddenly he hollers the lyrics *"I'm lonely,"* followed by a beat of silence from the band that ripples through the crowd. His sharp intake of breath can be heard over the microphone as he launches into the next line and the guitar riff repeats.

The hairs on the back of my neck have stood up.

"What's this song?" I ask, my eyes still trained on Finn.

I recognize it, but can't name it.

I feel Rach's incredulous look. "INXS, 'Need You Tonight'? Honestly, how can you not *know* that?"

"It came out before I was born," I reply dismissively.

"And the last one was Royal Blood, 'Figure It Out,'" she adds.

Rach is an indie chick. I am not. I grew up playing classical music on a piano.

"Oi! AMES!" Rach shouts.

I rip my gaze away from Finn to see a tiny blonde whizz past behind the bar. She glances our way distractedly.

"Hang on, I'll be with you in a—Liv!" At the sight of me, she does a double take, rushing over. "Sorry, it's hell here tonight. We're understaffed."

Amy, Rach, and I have been inseparable since we bonded at a party at the age of fourteen—we were the only ones who didn't want to play truth or dare, so we hid out together in a bathroom.

My friends have seen way more of each other than they have of me in the last four years because Amy attended the much closer University of Plymouth and Rach didn't go to university at all.

My fault for choosing to study more than five hundred miles away.

"I'll come find you later!" Amy promises, reaching past Rach to give my arm a quick squeeze before hurrying off.

"What are you drinking, if I ever manage to flag anyone down?" Rach grumbles loudly.

Seaglass's owner, Chas, comes to an abrupt stop in front of us, looking every inch the weather-beaten sixty-something surfer dude that he is.

"You sure you don't want a job here?" he asks Rach.

"Absolutely not," she replies.

She works part-time at a surf shop up in the village. She'd live on baked beans and spaghetti for a year if it meant that she could spend more hours at the beach. She certainly wouldn't want to fill her spare time with anything as mundane as a bar job.

"I'll take one!" I call, leaning around my friend.

Chas clocks me and his brows lift toward his receding tawny-gray hairline. "Hey, Liv! You back for the summer? You serious? You want a job?"

"Definitely."

"Can you start right away?" he asks hopefully.

"Fuck, no!" Rach interjects. "She's only just got here. *Chill*, Chas! Anyway, she's keeping me company tonight, seeing as you've got our best mate run off her feet."

"All right, all right." Chas holds up his hands placatingly. "How about tomorrow?"

"Okay," I agree with a grin.

"Can you come in at four thirty? This lot are playing again, so it's likely to be another busy one."

The look I cast over at the band hooks once more on Finn.

"I'll be here," I reply, attempting to reel my attention back in.

"In that case, these are on the house. What'll it be?"

"Pint of Rattler, please!" Rach pipes up.

He looks at me.

"Same, thanks." I fancy a Cornish cider.

"And two tequila shots!" Rach calls after him as he pulls down a couple of plastic pint glasses from the rack above the bar.

"What? No!" I whack my friend's arm.

"Come on," she begs. "The last time we hung out properly was New Year's Eve and you'll be working from tomorrow, for fuck's sake. You need to let your hair down. What were you thinking, going straight to Italy after uni to do even *more* studying? Don't you ever want to just put your fucking feet up?"

"Florence was amazing, thank you for asking," I reply with amusement at her outburst as Chas fills a couple of shot glasses and winks at us before going off to serve his next customer.

I love Rach, but we're very different. She still has no idea what she wants to do as a career, whereas I've been forging a path toward sculpture my entire life.

One of my earliest memories is of climbing the giant lions in London's Trafalgar Square. I had a thing for lions for years afterward, until I saw the majestic rearing Horses of Helios near Piccadilly Circus and became obsessed with finding other animal statues.

My parents thought the statues were just a phase, akin to liking unicorns or ponies, but my grandmother paid more attention.

I was eight when she first took me to the Barbara Hepworth Museum and Sculpture Garden in her hometown of St. Ives and I still remember how I ached to touch the chisel marks on the wooden sculptures inside the gallery. Of course I wasn't allowed, but outside in the garden, Gran let me run wild. I was awestruck by the size of some of the sculptures, by the shapes, the colors, and the feel of the different textures beneath my hands.

By secondary school, my interest had begun to lean toward people rather than animals. On a field trip to Paris with my art class, I was almost left behind because I was so caught up in staring at Rodin's *The Kiss* in the Tuileries Garden. I was drawn to the tale that it told of two lovers, to the way their bodies twisted toward each other, clutching one another in the throes of passion. I wanted to bring people to life like that, to catch moments in time and tell my own stories. Figurative sculpture became the focus of my work going forward.

I wish my grandmother was alive to see how far I've come. My parents came to my degree show, which is the pinnacle of a student's achievement, and I know they were proud, even if they mostly seemed relieved that my time in Scotland was ending. It pained them that I'd opted to study so far away, though they've always been generally supportive of my choices. They *literally* supported my monthlong stint at the Florence Academy of Art, which is why I need a summer job: I'm keen to pay them back.

That and I need to start saving so I can move to London. I haven't yet been able to bring myself to tell Mum and Dad that I intend to go away again.

Rach picks up a shot glass and passes it over her shoulder to me with an expectant look on her face.

"Fine," I relent, knocking it back and pulling a face, recovering only to have the second glass offered up.

"You need to catch up," she reminds me, deadly serious.

"Urgh, what are we, eighteen?"

I'm enveloped by a surreal feeling that time in St. Agnes has stood still while I've moved on and grown up. But Rach never left and now she's staring at me expectantly and I don't want to disappoint her. I throw her shot back too and then bask in the warmth of the alcohol and her applause. At least they're free; I don't want to waste money on drinks.

She picks up our pints and backs away from the bar.

It's hard to see the band with all the people in here, but they're on a slightly elevated platform. "Stage" is a stretch.

"What's this one?" I shout in Rach's ear.

"It's '7' by Catfish and the Bottlemen."

"Do they still only do covers?"

"Yep."

Mixamatosis has been knocking around for years. It's a crap name, and spelling it "Mix" instead of "Myx" hasn't helped, but the band itself is popular. They've always played rock songs from a span of several decades, but new or old, I can rarely put a name to any of them. This summer is the first time they've been in residence at Seaglass, which is kind of surprising, considering Dan is Chas's nephew.

"What happened to Kieran?" I ask about their former frontman.

"He wanted to spend some time with his girlfriend at her family's place in Canada. Finn has a band in LA, so when Dan heard he was coming over, he asked if he'd fill in as a favor."

It all comes back to me in a rush: the reason Finn left Cornwall.

"Oh God, I've just remembered what happened to his mum!" I say. "That was so awful."

"Yeah," Rach agrees soberly.

How could I have forgotten? His mother went missing on Christmas Day when we were in year ten. Her clothes were found on a cliff edge not far from here—it was presumed she had jumped with the intention of taking her own life. The sea had swallowed up her body without a trace, so the family couldn't even have a proper funeral. And then Finn had to leave Cornwall to go and live with his biological father in America. This must have been, what, seven and a half years ago?

"So Finn still lives in America?"

"Yep."

"What's he doing back?"

"Seeing his grandparents and his brothers."

"I forgot that he has brothers."

"Half brothers, technically. They all have different dads."

"I didn't even know he and Dan were friends."

"Dan is friends with everyone."

It's true. He's that kind of guy; remembers names, is always willing to stop for a chat on the street. He might be the lead guitarist rather than the singer, but everyone thinks of the band as his.

"How long is he here for?"

"Six weeks," Rach replies. "But he's been here a couple already."

We're almost halfway into July.

She must read something in my expression because she grins. "Obsessed!"

"Shut up. Anyway, you can talk. How do you know all this?"

"Eyes and ears to the ground, my friend. Eyes and ears to the ground."

"No, seriously, how?"

"Sophie and Claire had all the gossip." They're another two of our former schoolmates. "They were all over Finn last weekend when the band did their first gig. Almost slipped over in their drool. You have your work cut out for you if you're interested."

I wave her off. "I'm not interested. *Or* up for it, for that matter."

I have other things on my mind this summer.

RACH AND I dance and shout-talk the next hour away, but through it all I'm hyperaware of Finn. I may have other things to focus on right now, but I can't pretend that shivers don't run down my spine on the rare occasions that he addresses the room.

Toward the end of the night, Amy joins us on the dance floor.

"I'm so happy we're going to be working together again," she says, giving me a hug.

We both did a stint here the year we turned eighteen. It felt like the end of an era then—I was heading off to Edinburgh for four years and she was taking a gap year before starting a three-year course in midwifery—but now it feels like the start of the rest of our lives.

"At least until you get one of these jobs you've been applying for," I reply with a smile, tucking her flyaway long blond hair behind her ears.

"I'm sure I won't. They'll go to someone with more experience."

"Everyone's got to start somewhere."

I feel a flurry of nerves at the reminder that the career path *I've* chosen for myself is far less certain. How many figurative sculptors actually manage to carve out a living for themselves?

But I would sculpt even if I could only do it as a hobby. Sculpting is my passion. Doing it full-time would be a dream, but I have a lot of work ahead of me to make that happen.

For the next couple of months, however, my priorities are saving money and spending time with my friends and family.

I glance across at Rach and Amy and smile. Rach's auburn ponytail gave up the ghost a while ago and Amy is wearing her hair down as usual. I can feel the haphazard bun I fashioned my hair into before I left my hotel room in Florence this morning coming loose. On impulse, I reach up to extract the last few bobby pins and my dark locks come tumbling down, almost to my waist.

"Is there a hidden message in that gesture?" Amy asks with amusement.

"Rach told me earlier that I needed to let my hair down," I reply with a shrug.

"Damn right you do," Rach asserts.

Finn's low, deep voice comes over the mic to announce the last song.

I get full-blown goose bumps.

I have no idea what the song is called, but for the next three minutes, all I want to do is dance the hell out of it with my two best friends.

I NEED THE loo, but I stupidly wait until the band has cleared the stage, a decision I regret once I see the queue snaking away from the women's toilets.

The alcohol charging through my veins leads me past the line of women to the men's. When I put my hand up to push open the door, it whooshes away in front of me and I almost stumble into Finn on his way out.

"Whoa!" he exclaims.

Whoa indeed.

"Did you know this is the men's?" he asks with bemusement.

"I'm desperate," I tell him.

"Ah." He steps back to hold open the door, making space for me to pass through.

I feel the blush rising all the way from my chest to my scalp as I hurry past him and lock myself in one of the cubicles.

I'm desperate?

I'm still blushing by the time I emerge, only to find him standing in the doorway.

"Thought I'd keep the riffraff out," he says casually.

"Thanks," I mumble, averting my red face as I wash my hands, my veil of hair an effective shield.

"I'm Finn," Finn says, making no attempt to leave.

I glance up and meet his eyes in the mirror. "I know."

"And you're Olivia Arterton."

"I know," I say again, shaking off my hands and turning around to face him.

His grin widens.

Holy hell, he has dimples. Big ones. Where did *they* come from? I feel as though the heat lamp beneath my skin has been turned up to the max.

People have always told me that my eyelashes are long, but his are something else. I can't tell what color his eyes are in this light, but they're not dark enough to be brown. His nose is slightly crooked, and the lack of symmetry suits him. I have an overwhelming desire to put my hands on his face and then re-create him in clay. Was he always this beautiful?

I jolt as I realize I'm still staring at him.

But he's still staring at me too.

My eyes dart away, traveling only as far as his holey black jumper. Up close, I can see that he's wearing a gray T-shirt underneath.

He hooks his fingers through a couple of the holes, noticing they have my attention.

"You look as though a moth's been at you," I remark.

He glances down. "Oh no. I was just Jimmied."

"Jimmied?"

"Jimmy, my nephew. He's a year old and got his hands on my jumper. To be fair, it already had a couple of holes in it, but he decided to *enlarge* them. I went with the look."

He gives the word "enlarge" a deliberately American drawl,

but his accent still mostly sounds as though he's from around here.

He looks up from his jumper and grins at me and my stomach flip-tumbles.

Dan appears in the doorway.

"What's going on here then?" he asks suspiciously.

"Nothing. Just talking," Finn replies.

"Great place to have a chat. Hey, Liv," Dan says, "how's it going? First I've seen of you this summer."

"I've just come back from Italy," I reply.

"Nice. Holiday?"

"No, I was on a sculpture course."

"Oh, cool. How was it?"

"Great place to have a chat, mate," Finn interjects dryly. "Why don't you do what you came here to do and we'll see you outside?"

"Yeah, yeah," Dan says, moving away from the doorway and gesturing for me to exit.

I'm intensely aware of Finn walking right behind me as we make our way into the main room. His bandmates call to him from the other end of the bar, where Chas is lining up shots. A few girls are there too, including Sophie and Claire.

Finn saunters straight past me as I join my friends.

"Anything to tell?" Rach asks with a smirk.

"Nope," I reply, but as I turn to see Finn hook his arm around Tarek's neck, he glances my way and our eyes lock.

His lips tilt up at the corners into a half smile and I stare back at him for a couple of seconds until my quickening heart rate becomes too much of a distraction and I have to avert my gaze. I reach for my drink, feeling shaky as I take a sip.

So maybe I'm rethinking my priorities for this summer.

3

THOUGHT IT'D BE HOURS BEFORE WE SAW YOU!" MUM exclaims the next morning when I wander into the kitchen at seven forty-five.

"So did I," I reply ruefully, accepting her offer of a hug.

I'd fully intended to catch up on some sleep, but as I was drifting in and out of consciousness, my mind latched onto my encounter with Finn and after that I was wide awake.

"Tea?" she asks, withdrawing.

"Yes, please." I take in my surroundings with amazement. "I can't get over how much natural light there is in here now."

Our home is an old fisherman's cottage and the original part of the building has lots of character, with thick, uneven walls and deep windowsills. Last autumn, my parents had the 1970s kitchen extension knocked down and replaced with a modern structure that's about three times the size. It comprises a stylish kitchen, complete with an island and barstools, and a large dining area with an eight-seater wooden bench table. This is the section of the room that I'm most drawn to as it has floor-to-ceiling glass doors opening onto a patio area, plus a giant corner window that faces the lush, leafy garden with its tree ferns and succulents. The climate in Cornwall is mild and here we're sheltered in a valley, so it often feels subtropical.

The garden is what sold me on this house when we first came to look at it. I was thirteen at the time and felt torn about leaving London and all my friends—I was only just finding my feet at secondary school and I was very nervous at the thought of being thrown headlong into another. But my parents thought a move out of the city was long overdue for my brother, Michael, and me, and Mum wanted to live nearer to Gran in her old age.

I was on board with the plan because I wanted to live closer to her too. But only two years after we'd uprooted our lives, she was gone.

My grandmother was "my" person, the one soul who understood my artistic hopes and dreams. Before we moved here, I would spend one week every summer in Cornwall with her while Michael remained in London with Mum and Dad. She taught me how to play the piano and read me stories and took me on excursions to theaters and museums and art galleries. Our time alone together meant the world to me.

I sit down on one of the bench seats, facing outward toward the patio. The sun will come streaming through these windows later. What I wouldn't give to be able to sculpt in here.

Mum takes a seat beside me and hands over my first parent-made cup of tea in over six months. I didn't make it home at Easter as I had too much work to do for my degree show.

"Thanks." I lean in to her momentarily, filled with a sudden warmth at being home again, safe in the family enclave.

"It's so good to have you back at last," she says tenderly, pressing a kiss to my shoulder. "It feels like you've been gone forever."

Her words prompt a pang of guilt. I'll be gone again before long, but we don't need to have that conversation yet.

"How was last night?" she asks, oblivious to my worries.

She's quite a bit older than my friends' mums—she was forty-two when she had me—and she's still very attractive: moderately tall and slim, with just-below-shoulder-length honey-blond hair that these days mostly comes courtesy of a bottle.

My brother, Michael, and I have our father's darker coloring, although I did inherit Mum's blue eyes. Mine are more stormy seas than summer skies, though.

"Fun," I reply to Mum's question. "I'm surprised I don't feel more hungover. Then again, I was home by eleven thirty."

"Closer to midnight."

I smile at her. "Were you waiting up?"

She shrugs. "I couldn't sleep."

When I was a teenager and out for the night, she was always on high alert until I arrived home safely. I thought she'd have a more restful time of it now that I'm twenty-two.

"How are Amy and Rach?" she asks fondly.

"They're good." I smile into my mug as I take a sip. "Oh, hey!" My head springs up. "I got a job!"

"Where?" she asks with a frown.

"At Seaglass, behind the bar. I start this afternoon."

"Oh." She sounds disappointed. "At least avoid Sundays," she begs. "It's been a long time since we've had family lunch together."

I frown. "But Sundays are one of Seaglass's busiest days in the summer . . ."

She gives me a look.

"I'll try," I concede.

She sighs. "I guess I shouldn't be surprised that you've walked straight into a job. You take after your grandmother. She couldn't sit still either."

"You can talk. You're exactly the same."

My mum has been juggling work and motherhood all my life. She's employed at the A&E department at the Royal Cornwall Hospital near Truro now, but she used to be a GP like Dad. They're both sixty-four and have *discussed* retirement, but it wouldn't surprise me if they continued working for a few more years.

"I wasn't always like that," she confides. "My parents struggled to get me to do anything. All I wanted to do was lie on my bed and read."

"You literally lived five minutes from the beach!" I slept in her old bedroom when we visited Gran, before we moved here. "You never used to let me lie around and do nothing. You were always shoving me out the door." I'm outraged by her double standards.

"Do as I say, not as I do," she replies irreverently.

We're chuckling when my dad walks into the room.

"I gave up waiting for my tea," he chides, coming over to give me a kiss on the top of my head.

I squeeze his arm affectionately.

"Oh, sorry!" Mum looks contrite, but doesn't get up as Dad flicks on the kettle.

He's wearing the red tartan PJ pants Mum gave him last Christmas. She gave Michael an identical pair.

I still remember Michael's face lighting up when he opened the gift. He'd arrived fully dressed on Christmas morning while we were all still wearing our pajamas, so he changed into his new PJs too.

My brother has Down syndrome and he lives on his own, although Mum and Dad spend a lot of time with him. He's older than me by nine years and was in his mid-twenties when my parents set him up in a tiny cottage just a few minutes' walk from here. He wanted more independence and privacy, but I hated his absence at the breakfast table.

As a child, I was never allowed to eat sugary cereal, but Michael had a sweet tooth and at his age our parents had to respect his choices. So he'd slip me handfuls of Coco Pops when they weren't looking and I'd bury them under my boring cornflakes, then we'd both try not to giggle as they turned the milk chocolaty.

It was a running joke that carried all through my teens. Then, suddenly, he wasn't there anymore. I missed him.

I didn't, however, miss sharing a bathroom. My brother is a self-proclaimed Mr. Messy.

AT 4:25, I leave the house to walk the few minutes down to Seaglass. The French doors have been thrown wide open and people are sitting out on the balcony in full sunshine, chilling with drinks while music plays out of the speakers, not quite loud enough to drown out the sound of the waves crashing onto the shore.

Chas is behind the bar, scribbling something onto a notepad.

"Hey, Chas."

His head shoots up. "Liv!" He comes out from behind the bar, opening up his wiry arms. "I didn't get a hug yesterday."

Chas may be Dan's uncle, but my friends and I have been coming here for years and he's always treated us like family.

"I am so glad you're here," he says as we exchange a brief embrace.

He smells of coconut, probably from the wax he rubs onto his surfboard. He's around the same age as my parents, but the thought of my parents surfing is laughable. It's not that they're lacking in energy, but Chas puts even teenagers to shame. He's very young at heart.

"Where's Amy?" I ask.

"She's not due until five, but she just rang to say that her car broke down so she's going to be late. She's waiting for the AA."

"Oh no! Is she still driving her shitmobile?"

"Afraid so."

I tut with affection. "Where do you want me?"

"Hop back behind the bar and I'll show you the ropes, although you probably remember most of it. Not much changes around here."

AMY SWANS IN nonchalantly at six thirty. When I notice who she's with, it becomes clear why she's seemingly in no rush.

"Dan saw me on the side of the road and gave me a lift," she explains with a giddy grin.

"I thought the AA was coming," I say.

"It was. Hopefully they'll tow my car, but hey-ho, I need a new one anyway."

Judging by the glow radiating from her, I suspect that her crush on Dan is not a thing of the past.

We don't get a chance to chat because the venue is already filling up, and within an hour it's carnage behind the bar, with punters two-deep and crying out to get served. Chas, Amy, and I each have a two-meter section to man and there's also a runner who's bottling, cleaning glasses, collecting empties, refilling ice, and turning over beer in the cellar. The four of us are moving like water, flowing around each other.

When I spot Finn arriving, I forget my current customer's entire order and have to ask them to repeat themselves. My eyes and thoughts are pulled to him onstage throughout the night, but somehow I manage to focus on work. By closing time, my feet are killing me and my back aches, but I am absolutely buzzing.

I look around for Finn. Dan, Tarek, and Chris are still here, along with a few others who managed to avoid leaving when Chas was locking up, but there's no sign of Finn. Has he gone home already?

My adrenaline flatlines and exhaustion hits just as Amy swoops over to me.

"Dan's having people back to his," she says to me urgently, grabbing our things from under the counter. "Let's go."

"I thought we were going to have a drink here?"

"Change of plan. Come on, I want to walk up with them!"

"Oh, do I really have to be your third wheel?" I'm knackered and if Finn's not going to be there . . .

She pauses and stares at me. "Please, Liv?" she begs.

I can never say no to that face.

We set off up the steep road toward the village, passing the Surf Life-Saving Club, the Driftwood Spars Inn, and several houses, including my own, before we leave the last streetlight behind and are plunged into darkness.

I pull out my phone and tap a quick text to Mum to let her

know what I'm up to—there's every chance she's waiting up—and then I use the flashlight on my phone to illuminate the way.

Dan and the band's bass guitarist, Tarek, live together in a two-up two-down, and the dimly lit living room, dining room, and open-plan kitchen feel crowded even with only fifteen to twenty people inside.

I'm dead on my feet and tug Amy toward the sofa in the bay window. Before long, two cold cans of lager find their way into our hands.

Chris plugs his phone into the stereo and turns the sound right up as a rock song pounds out.

More people arrive and cram into the space, pressing up against our legs.

I hug my knees to my chest and chug back a few mouthfuls of lager. Suddenly Amy stands and kicks off her shoes, climbing up onto the sofa to perch on the windowsill. Her bare feet dangle over the sofa cushions and she grins at me, totally at ease and completely up for whatever the night brings.

I smile a small smile and copy her, sitting at her side and scratching the mosquito bites I got on my last night in Italy.

Someone fires up a joint and Tarek leans between us with a "Sorry" as he opens the window, his narrow shoulders brushing against our upper arms.

He's quite a pretty boy, Tarek, with groomed dark eyebrows and warm puppy-dog eyes. He's very different from Chris, whose short dirty-blond hair makes him look as though he hasn't showered in weeks.

I'm yawning when Finn walks in. And just like that, I wake right up.

Over the tops of heads, I watch as he mixes up cocktail jugs with Dan in the kitchen. They're both just over six foot, but Finn is slimmer and has more of an indie-boy vibe compared to Dan, who I suspect lifts weights.

Finn steps up onto a chair and shouts, "Punch!"

Amy looks at me to gauge my interest.

I feel too nervous to waltz right on over there, so I raise my can and say, "After this," before glancing back to the kitchen and catching Finn's eye.

A jolt goes through me as he cocks his head, as though the sight of me here is interesting. We look at each other for a few seconds and then he grins, those dimples appearing as he jumps down from the chair.

He fills a couple of cups and winds his way through the crowd.

"What's in it?" I ask edgily as he offers them up to me and Amy.

"Vodka, rum, Coke. Be careful, it's strong."

We take the cups from him just as "Cotton Eye Joe" by Rednex starts blaring out of the speaker. Trust me to know the name of *this* god-awful song.

"Dude, seriously?" Finn laughs, rounding on Chris.

"I did *not* put that on my playlist!" Chris protests as Finn digs into his jeans pocket and pulls out his phone. "I'll skip it!" Chris yells, scrambling toward the stereo. "My sister must have put it on there!"

"Too late, you've had your chance," Finn replies, manhandling him out of the way.

Amy and I laugh along with others who are watching. "Cotton Eye Joe" is silenced as an indie-rock song begins to play.

Chris looks deflated to have lost control of the music.

Finn, chuckling, whacks him on his stomach and returns to the kitchen.

ABOUT FORTY-FIVE MINUTES later, I'm in the middle of a surprisingly serious conversation with Tarek about architecture when Finn wanders over and hops up into Amy's recently vacated position on the windowsill.

I'm instantly on edge.

My friend is leaning against the wall in the dining area, talking to Dan. He's smiling down at her and I'm not expecting to see her again anytime soon.

Tarek stands up, mumbling something about getting a glass of water, and I turn to Finn, all my senses zinging.

He moves to the edge of the sill and slides down onto the sofa, patting the cushion beside him in invitation. The crowd has gravitated toward the kitchen, so it's not as packed in here as it was earlier.

I pick up my cup and carefully settle down beside him. The sofa bows slightly in the middle, tilting us toward one another, and I'm intensely aware of the heat of his thigh against mine.

"So, what's this about sculpture in Italy?" he asks.

My heart warms that he's paid as close attention to me as I have to him.

"I did a monthlong course in figurative sculpture."

"What did that involve?"

His eyes seem to hold genuine curiosity. I think they're green, maybe with a hint of blue.

"We spent three solid weeks modeling figures in clay and then our last week was focused mostly on making molds." I did some of this at university, of course, but we didn't do a lot of figurative sculpting. Most of my classmates were postmodernist sculptors so I stood out as the only person with a more classical style. It was actually one of the foundry technicians who suggested that I look into the course at the Florence Academy of Art. "It was full-on, but it was without a doubt one of the best experiences of my life. It made me feel like a real artist. We also got to go on some museum tours with experts to see the work of masters up close, like the statue of David, and Bernini's sculptures. That was mind-blowing. Though it probably sounds boring if you're not into sculpture," I finish self-consciously, realizing I've been wittering on.

"Not at all," Finn replies earnestly as I shift to face him and tuck my knees up underneath myself, removing the distraction of his thigh against mine. "There's not much that doesn't intrigue me," he adds. "It's probably why I like writing."

"Songs?" I ask, trying to scratch my mosquito bites discreetly.

"Yep."

"What's your band's name? I heard you have one back in LA."

He screws up his nose.

"What?" I ask with a smile.

"It's a bit crap."

"It can't be worse than Mixamatosis."

"Shh!" He shoots an alarmed look across the room at his bandmates before returning his gaze to me, his smile alight with mischief. "Don't let Dan hear you say that."

"At least he's given up on the idea of deranged bunny masks," I point out with a conspiratorial giggle.

"*What? Bunny* masks?" He looks perplexed.

"They wore gruesome bunny masks for Halloween once," I explain in a low voice, prompting him to lean forward so he can hear me better. His eyelashes are *unreal*. "Fake blood coming from the mouths, and the eyes spray-painted red. Think a sick and twisted Daft Punk. They scared a bunch of kids whose parents complained."

His face lights up with an expression of pure glee and he cracks up laughing. "That's priceless. I can't believe he kept it quiet."

I can't stop smiling as I take a sip of my drink and put it down on the windowsill behind me. When I turn back to Finn, he's regarding me thoughtfully.

"This is more how I remember you," he notes. "With your hair up in a bun. You always looked so neat. Didn't you use to do ballet?"

I reel backward. "When I was *much* younger. How do you even *know* that?"

"I overheard you talking about it in Art once. You used to play the piano a lot too, right?"

"Yes!" My face warms. "I'm surprised you remember me at all."

We hardly spoke when we were at school.

"I used to think that you looked like a ballerina with your hair up like that, and the way you carried yourself, with perfect posture and your chin held high . . ."

"You make me sound like a snob."

"Not at all. You looked elegant. You still do."

His eye contact is unnervingly steady. I try to maintain the connection but can't.

"Well, I was never any good at ballet." I reach for a throw

pillow and pull it onto my lap. "Leaving London gave me an excuse to quit."

"Why did you come to Cornwall?" He's been drumming on his thigh with his right hand in time to the rock song playing, but he's only tapping out half of the beats.

"We moved to be closer to my gran. She used to live in St. Ives," I say, noticing that his foot is catching the other half.

"She's not with you anymore?"

I shake my head. "She passed away when I was fifteen."

He nods, dropping his gaze as his Adam's apple travels up and down his throat. He takes a sip of his drink. His hand and his foot have stopped drumming.

I was in year ten when I lost Gran, which was the same year that Finn lost his mum. I imagine he's thinking of her.

I return to our earlier, safer, subject.

"You were good at art," I say. "I remember your still lifes."

I thought about them this morning when I couldn't get him out of my head.

"Art always was my favorite subject at school."

"Not music?"

"My passion for that came later."

"How?"

"My dad's a sound engineer for a studio. I used to hang out there a lot in my spare time."

It feels like the space between his words holds more than what he's saying. It couldn't have been easy moving in with his dad and his dad's other family, given the circumstances. But I don't press him, noting his tense expression.

"Cool. Do you live with him now?"

"No, I room with one of my bandmates."

"So come on, then, band name." I nudge his leg. "I'm not letting you off that easily."

He grimaces, but I see the edges of his lips twitch as he tucks his dark hair behind one ear.

"Door 54," he reluctantly reveals. "Another of my band-mates lived at number 54 in some random apartment block and he dug that it sounded like a combination of the Doors and Studio 54."

"Are those references bad?"

He releases a small huff and looks me dead in the eye. "Studio 54 was based in New York; we're out of LA. It was peak disco period; couldn't be further from what we are. And anyone who thinks they have a right to compare themselves to one of the greatest rock bands that ever lived is a complete and utter twat."

I burst out laughing and he grins at me.

He's so different from the boy I went to school with, so confident and at ease. How did he recover from what happened, let alone appear to be thriving?

"Why did you agree to it if you hate it so much?" I ask, still smiling.

"We'd been arguing about it for ages and couldn't settle on a name and then he lined up a gig for us at a great venue and told the organizers that's what we were called. By the time the rest of us realized, it was already printed on the flyers."

"That's a bit shit of him."

"He's a bit of a shit," he replies with a laugh.

"You sound as though you don't like your bandmate very much," I say with amusement.

"I don't, but he's a fucking good guitar player."

He turns around and pushes the window open a little wider, letting more air into the hot room.

He's wearing a faded yellow T-shirt that is so well worn it's frayed around the collar and sleeves and is riddled with tiny holes.

"What is it with you and holey clothes?" I ask, daring to prod his shoulder through a small tear in the sleeve.

"Don't judge, it's my look now." He bats me away and takes a sip of his drink, then glances down at his T-shirt. "Maybe the moths really *have* been at this one. Speaking of insects . . ." He nods at my arms. "Fuck me, you have a *lot* of mosquito bites."

"Yeah, I got them in Florence when I was eking out my time in the studio—"

My voice flies up at the end in a dramatic wobble because he's swiped my hand, bringing my arm closer for his inspection.

My heart is slamming against my rib cage when he meets my eyes and says in a low, deep voice, "You must taste really good."

Goose bumps race up my arms, and then shock follows and I don't know who lets go of whom, but his palms spring up in defense.

"I did not mean that to sound so suggestive."

We stare at each other for a few silent seconds and then I keel over and lose it, laughing. A moment later, he joins in.

4

K NOCK, KNOCK, KNOCK!" MUM SHOUTS IN A JOLLY
voice from the other side of my bedroom door the next
morning, accentuating each word with literal knocking.

"Come in," I call in a croak.

The door whooshes open and my mother breezes in and
shoves the curtains back.

"Michael will be here any second and your dad and I have
got something to show you. Can you get ready *pronto*?"

Her Italian accent is adorably terrible. "What's the time?" I
ask, flinching at the light.

"Eleven. At least you caught up on some sleep," she adds
wryly, leaving me to it.

Finn offered to walk me back last night, but Amy wanted
us to go together. It was only as we were leaving that it occurred to me that Finn could have walked us *both* home. Amy
lives up in the village, so I was on my own for the second half
of the journey and I couldn't help imagining what it might
have been like if he'd been there beside me, our arms brushing
together in the darkness.

My brother arrives as I'm getting ready—my windows face
onto the driveway and he's visible in the driver's seat of my

dad's pale blue 1960s Austin-Healey, his head just peeking over the steering wheel.

He loves that car like nobody's business. Dad sometimes lets him take it for a gentle spin at the learner drivers' track at the airfield a couple of miles away, but it's unlikely that Michael would ever get his license.

Mum is standing over the stove when I walk into the kitchen, and the aromas coming from the oven make my stomach rumble. When she sees me, she switches off the heat under the gravy she's been stirring and turns around, her face lit up with excitement.

"Come with me," she says with a grin.

"What is it?" I ask curiously as she ushers me out the back door and calls over to my dad, who's on the driveway talking to Michael.

Michael sees us through the windscreen and presses the horn three times. Dad theatrically flinches and covers his ears as he staggers backward.

My brother is laughing at my dad's antics as he gets out of the car.

"Baby sis!" he shouts, coming forward for a hug.

"Hello you," I say warmly as he rocks me back and forth.

He's in a great mood today. We caught up with each other on Friday night when he came over for my welcome-home dinner, but I was late and he was hungry and extremely grouchy. His ex-girlfriend has got a new boyfriend, apparently. Michael no longer fancies her, but he still considers the act a betrayal.

"Mum and Dad have got a surprise for you," he says in a singsong voice, grinning up at me.

He's only five foot tall to my five foot seven inches. I was twelve when I snuck past him on the height chart stuck to the kitchen wall of our London house.

"Have they?" I glance at our parents.

"Ta-da!" Dad exclaims, throwing his arms toward the greenhouse.

Mum mimics him exactly and then Michael follows suit. It's a sweetly ridiculous picture, the three of them acting like synchronized game show hosts.

I stare at the greenhouse with confusion. It's made of brick with a sloping glass ceiling and French doors, and for a moment, I don't know what I'm supposed to be reacting to.

But then I realize that the old white brickwork has been painted a lovely smoky-green color and the windows and ceiling glass are sparkling clean.

"We finished the exterior last night while you were at work," Mum says proudly. "But we've been renovating the interior for weeks."

Michael bounces on the spot as Dad opens up the French doors, indicating for me to take a closer look inside.

Shelves have been fixed to the bright white walls, and gleaming terra-cotta tiles cover the floor. Cacti and succulents in concrete pots of varying sizes are scattered around the edges of the room.

"We thought you could display your work on the shelves," Mum says.

"And you can store your tools in here," Dad adds, opening one of the drawers of a freestanding metal unit.

"It's a studio," I say in a daze.

My parents have created an artist's studio for me, a place of my very own to work from.

"We modeled it on the one at the Barbara Hepworth Museum. Do you love it?" Mum asks hopefully.

I nod slowly. "It's absolutely beautiful. Thank you."

She claps her hands with glee and Michael beams at her, then at me.

My throat feels tight and my eyes prickle. I'm beyond touched. So much effort has gone into this studio, and I feel the searchlight beams of their love for me shining in my direction. It's blinding. It's too much.

How will I ever tell them about London?

I feel a deep ache inside my chest for Gran. She's the only person who I know would have understood.

5

I WATCH AS THREE GIRLS FLIRT WITH FINN OUT ON THE balcony while I serve a customer at the bar.

One of the girls has folded over laughing at something he's said. Now she's slapping his shoulder and pressing her face into his denim shirt and guffawing, as though she can't possibly contain herself or keep her hands to herself.

He cranes his neck to look down at her, bemused.

Cold lager pours down the side of the pint glass I'm filling and runs over my hand. I flinch and swap out the full glass for an empty one.

It seems surreal, now, that he sat on a sofa with me last Saturday, talking for an hour. Was I just the flavor of the night?

I've been on edge during every one of my shifts this week in case he comes in, but tonight is the first time our paths have crossed, and aside from a jaunty wave hello when he strolled in and accepted the drink Dan had bought him, we've had zero interactions.

That tiny wave alone was enough to make me blush.

I force myself to concentrate on the pint I'm pouring.

"Can I get you a drink?" the guy I'm serving asks.

"Oh, thanks, but we're not allowed to drink behind the bar," I reply, offering him the card reader.

He taps his card against it, picks up his pints, and walks off.

Was he hitting on me? Should I be flattered?

Honestly? I can barely recall what he looked like.

My mood improves slightly when Finn takes to the stage with the rest of Mixamatosis. They launch into the first song, Chris hammering the drums, Dan working his lead guitar, Tarek coolly strumming his bass. Then Finn steps up to the mic and begins to sing in that deep, musical voice of his, his eyes downcast, his dark hair falling forward, and I'm transfixed.

I look for Rach, to ask the name of the song, but can't see her through the crowd of people.

I glance back at Finn and a full-body jolt goes through me when I discover him already looking at me. His lips curl up into a half smile as he holds eye contact for several torturously exquisite seconds, and then he drops his gaze.

I am unbelievably flustered as I get back to work.

A GOOD TWENTY minutes after the set has finished, I'm opening the dishwasher when Finn approaches the bar.

"Hello," he says to me through a cloud of steam.

I try to squash the tiny gymnast cartwheeling around my stomach as I place a couple of dripping glasses onto the rack above the bar.

"Hey. What can I get you?" I'm pleased by how neutral my tone is.

"Straight to business. Two pints of Tribute and a couple of

Cokes, please." He smiles at me, but I remember the girls on the balcony and can't bring myself to flirt.

"Pints or halves for the Cokes?"

"Make them pints. I'm thirsty."

"You're not drinking?" I ask as I get on with the soft drinks.

"Taking a break. Figure it could be another long one. Are you coming to the beach?" He rests his elbows on the bar top.

"Who's going to the beach?"

"A bunch of us, in a bit."

"Oh, right."

"Come," he says simply.

I look at him directly for the first time. His eyes are warm and sincere and hold the same invitation as his words.

"Maybe. I'll see if Amy and Rach are up for it."

"Pretty sure Amy is, if Dan has anything to do with it."

He gives me a cheeky grin and this time I mirror it back, placing his Coke down and reaching for a second glass.

"What was that first song you played?" I ask.

"'Go with the Flow' by Queens of the Stone Age. It's an oldie."

"And the last?"

"'Space and Time' by Wolf Alice."

"Cool. I want to add them to my playlist," I explain casually. "I really liked the fifth one too."

He cocks his head to one side, then shakes it. "I can't remember. I'll pull up the set list later for you if you like."

"Thanks." I smile at him and my insides feel fizzy when he smiles back, dimples showing.

"So what else have you got on this playlist?" he asks, propping his chin on the palm of his right hand and gazing at me.

Maybe his eyes are turquoise, I muse, trying to put a name to their color. They're not dissimilar to the color of the sea around here: Celtic Sea green.

"All sorts," I reply.

"Like what?"

On a whim, I flip off the tap and seek out my phone from my bag under the bar, open MUSIC, and pass it over.

He has a black metal ring on his thumb that glints under the bar lights as he scrolls through. "What *is* this playlist?" he asks with confusion, his brows pulling together as he glances up at me.

"What do you mean?" I'm halfway through filling the first of the two beers.

"It's so random."

"It's my playlist," I reply a touch defensively, not sure what he's getting at.

"You say that like it's your *only* playlist."

I shrug at him and start on the final pint.

"Wait," he says with a frown. "Is this your only playlist?"

"Yeah. It's just a bunch of songs that I like."

"So you don't have a rock playlist or an acoustics playlist or any specific type of playlist?" He's regarding me with open disbelief now.

"How many times can you say 'playlist' in a single conversation?" I ask with a laugh before answering. "No. I don't really listen to that much music, but I know when I like it."

"Who's your favorite band?"

"I don't have one."

"Favorite song?"

"I don't know. I've been listening to Taylor Swift's '22' a lot lately. It suddenly feels relevant." I try to sound cheeky.

He stares at me. Then he passes my phone back.

"I'm making you a new playlist," he mutters.

"What's wrong with Taylor Swift?"

"Nothing. She's a brilliant songwriter, but that's not the point."

I shrug, trying to play it cool as I place the last of his order on the bar, but inside I'm thrilled at the thought of him making me a personalized playlist.

There's a whistle from across the room. "Oi! Finnegan! Get a move on!" Tarek hollers.

"Come get them!" he shouts back, retrieving his wallet from his pocket.

He settles up and grabs his Coke, making no attempt to leave.

Tarek weaves between a bunch of people to reach us, his thick dark brows etched into a scowl, but then he and Finn grin at each other and he gathers up the three other glasses, nodding at me before dodging his way back through the crowd.

Finn meets my eyes, amused.

"I had completely forgotten that your surname is Finnegan," I say, continuing our conversation as I get on with pouring a pint of pale ale for another customer.

"Finn Finnegan," he confirms, pursing his lips. "I keep thinking about changing my name to my dad's surname, Lowe."

"Ah, but Finn Finnegan has such a nice ring to it," I point out playfully, dispensing single shots of whiskey.

"You do know my real name is Daniel, right?"

"Is it?" I ask with surprise as I top up the whiskies with Coke.

"There were four other Daniels in our year—including that

one over there." He nods over his shoulder at Dan. "So everyone called me Finn. I don't think even my mother would be so demented as to call me Finn Finnegan on purpose."

I can't help the small gasp that escapes from my throat.

Finn gives me a flat look. "It's taken years of therapy for me to be able to say that flippantly. What have you been up to this week?" he asks, changing the subject.

"Not much. Working. Hanging out with my family." I ring up the total for my customer and pass him the card reader. "I went to the beach yesterday with Amy and Rach. You?"

"I went to the beach yesterday too—Porthleven, surfing, with Dan and Chris. I've dropped in a couple of times, but I haven't seen you."

Was he looking for me?

"So, will you come to the beach?" he asks, eyes locked on mine.

IT'S LOW TIDE and the sea is a slab of black lined with streaks of white from the surf, visible under the light of the full moon. It makes me think of marble, and that, in turn, makes me think of Italy.

"Penny for your thoughts?" Finn says in my ear, making me jump.

I glance over my shoulder, wondering how he escaped the fangirls who followed us down here. They're still ten meters or so behind, too far to see if they're shooting daggers.

"I was just thinking about Italy," I tell him as he offers me the bottle he's carrying, then chuckles and pats my back as I cough from the vanilla vodka.

Amy and Rach are bantering nearby with Dan, Tarek, and

Chris, but I wandered away from them a while ago, seeking solitude.

"What were you thinking about Italy?" Finn asks as I return the bottle to him.

"Nothing. It's not very interesting."

"I'll be the judge of that," he replies mildly.

I glance across at him in the silvery light. He's waiting.

"I was looking at the water and it reminded me of black-and-white marble and that made me think of this place in Tuscany that I've heard about. It's called Pietrasanta and it's where quite a few international artists live and work. It's a medieval town and it's beautiful—even the pedestrian crossings are made out of marble. The Royal Society of Sculptors arranges trips where you can visit the marble quarries and the old ateliers to watch local marble carvers in action, but you have to be a member to be invited."

"Do you use marble?" he asks.

"No, I don't really see myself as a carver. I feel most at home with clay."

A sudden burst of laughter behind us from Finn's fangirls jolts me violently back into my surroundings.

"Oh God," I mutter, knowing they weren't laughing at me, but they would have if I'd been speaking loudly enough. "I'm lecturing again—sorry. This is what I'm like when I get started."

"Don't say that," he says. "It's fascinating."

"You don't have to be nice about it. My friends' eyes glaze over whenever I talk about sculpture."

"I'm not your friends. How do you become a member?"

I clear my throat, the prickling feeling that's been dancing around my face beginning to ease. "You have to be an established sculptor and you have to have created *works of note*, which feels like a long way off for me."

"It's good to have something to aspire to, though."

I look across at him and realize that I more than fancy him—I *like* him.

He's only here for a few more weeks, I remind myself.

"What do you aspire to?" I ask, ignoring my own warning.

"Seeing if we can get things to take off with the band, I guess. I'd give anything to be able to write songs for a living."

"Have you recorded any? Maybe I'll add them to my playlist," I say teasingly.

He casts me a grin. "Only demos. But we're going into the studio the week after I get back to lay down an EP."

"That sounds exciting."

"What are *your* plans for the foreseeable future?" he asks, and I love the way he speaks in that slow, lazy, almost sardonic way of his.

I feel a familiar thrum of nerves as I think about how to respond. I haven't yet admitted my plan to anyone.

"I'm saving to move to London. I'm going to find a job in a studio." It feels good to say it out loud. "A couple of people who came to my degree show said they would connect me with their friends." I'm a member of a-n, a special organization for artists, and I've also been keeping my eyes peeled on their website for opportunities. "I'm hoping someone might be interested in having a general dogsbody to help out, make lunches, unpack clay, clean up afterward. I'd learn so much watching another sculptor at work, and if they don't want to pay me or even cover my food and board, I could get a bar job in the evenings to get by." I let out a sigh.

His eyes gleam in the darkness with reflected moonlight. "That sounds like a *great* plan. Why the sigh?"

"My parents would like me to stay here permanently," I explain. "They've offered to support me while I find my feet, and they've even turned our greenhouse into a studio, which is so incredibly nice of them, but I don't *want* to settle in Aggie. I want to be around other artists, to keep learning and growing."

My parents are amazing people who have saved countless lives and I'm so very proud of them. All they want is for Michael and me to be our best versions of ourselves, but I'm not sure that my idea of my best version aligns with theirs. In their perfect world, I would have opted to study medicine or law or something more traditional and only sculpt as a hobby. But barring that, their goal is that I stay in St. Agnes.

I know that they love me and don't mean to be controlling, but the conversion of the greenhouse has created a lot of pressure. Its presence in the garden reminds me daily of my selfishness for wanting to leave.

"I love my parents to bits, but I do sometimes feel as though they don't really understand me, not in the way my grandmother did. She would have urged me to put myself out on a limb, to be brave. To see where life takes me."

I miss her so much.

"I'm sorry," Finn says.

His quiet sincerity brings on another wave of embarrassment. I impulsively swipe the bottle from his hand and try to swallow down my discomfort with a large mouthful.

"Why are you even talking to me when you have so many pretty girls at your disposal?" I ask, coughing as the alcohol sears my throat.

He huffs out a laugh and takes the bottle back. "I'm not going to dignify that with an answer."

My insides feel as frothy as the waves crashing onto the shore.

"Is your uni work in your studio now?"

"Yep."

Mum, Dad, and Michael used such care when helping me move the pieces out to the studio on Sunday. Michael was delighted when he found the small model of the Austin-Healey that I'd made for him.

"Can I see it?" Finn asks.

"Seriously?"

"I'd love to."

Nerves flit through me at the thought of showing him my work. But saying that he'd like to see it and actually following through are two different things, so I relax again.

We've reached the shoreline. To our left, high cliffs slice straight into the water and to our right, giant jagged rocks loom dark and foreboding against the starlit midnight-blue sky.

"Ready to start," Finn says.

"What?"

"The fifth song you want for your playlist: 'Ready to Start' by Arcade Fire. I've been racking my brain."

"How does it go?"

He begins to sing the chorus and his voice makes the hairs on my arms stand up as he runs through the hypothetical lines that begin with "If."

When he sings *"If I was yours,"* he glances across at me, holding my gaze in the darkness, but before he can conclude that he's "not," Dan shouts, "Oi, Finn! Stop serenading the girls!"

Finn runs up to a wave that has just crashed onto the shore and kicks water in Dan's direction with one of his big boots.

"You did *not* want to do that," Dan says darkly.

I'm halfway back across the beach, having run away from the water fight, squealing, when Rach joins me.

"He fancies the fuck out of you," she says matter-of-factly as she hunches over and tries to catch her breath.

"Keep your voice down!" I hiss, my stomach bottoming out.

"And you fancy the fuck out of him too."

I glare at her. She is my loudest, most foulmouthed friend by far.

"Even if both of those things were true, he's leaving. I don't want to get too attached. And I *definitely* don't want to have to deal with any morning-after crap," I whisper furiously. "Especially when we're both working at Seaglass."

"So wait until his last night and *then* shag him senseless," my friend says brazenly.

I snort at her comment.

But when I think about the look Finn and I just shared, and the heat of our rare touches, one night with him with no consequences feels irresistibly appealing.

6

S NOW A GOOD TIME?"

I almost jump out of my skin at the sound of the question coming from directly behind me in the darkness. I spin round to face Finn, my hand clutched to my chest.

"A good time for *what*?" I ask breathlessly.

I'm on my doorstep, about to insert my key into the lock. I thought he'd gone on ahead with the others. Dan and Tarek are having people back to theirs again, but Amy has Rach to play her wingwoman and I'm ready for bed.

"A good time to see your greenhouse studio," he replies with a grin.

"What, *now*?" I ask with alarm.

"Why not?"

I stare up at him for several long seconds and he holds my gaze. He's serious. My heart thrills that he's keen—not even Rach and Amy have asked to see my work—but I'm also apprehensive about what he'll think.

I didn't speak to him again after the water fight. In the chaos that ensued, he wasn't exactly available for quiet conversation.

The insecure part of me resolved that I'd been boring him, but now, only half an hour later, he's sought me out again.

"We'd better go in through the gate," I decide, glad of the Dutch courage I've gained by way of vanilla vodka.

I don't want to rouse my parents' interest by entering through the house.

More to the point, I don't want to give my mum cause to spy through the cracks between the curtains, which is exactly what she'd be doing if she knew that I was out here with a boy.

I gently rattle the latch until it comes free and then lift the heavy wooden gate to stop it from scraping along the ground, closing it in the same manner behind us.

"Cool car," Finn says, nodding at the Austin-Healey parked next to my parents' gray BMW 3 Series.

"It's my dad's," I reply in a whisper.

"Does he ever let you drive it?"

"With him, but he won't let me take it out on my own. It's not safe enough."

My parents are quite protective.

We're right outside the greenhouse when I remember that the door is locked.

"Oh. The key is in my room. I don't want to disturb my parents, but look, you can see through the window."

I pull out my phone and switch on the flashlight, then press it right against the glass to reduce the glare.

Finn gasps and recoils.

I stifle a laugh. I should have warned him.

"Whoa," he says, stepping closer. "Who *is* that?"

"My gran," I reply.

He cups his hands to the glass and peers through.

Once, when I was six or seven, I tried to build a sandcastle in the shape of a Trafalgar Square lion. Michael and I had gone to the beach in St. Ives with Mum and Gran and I was completely caught up in what I was doing. I didn't want to take a break to play catch with Michael, but he was so persistent that I dragged myself away. Then he accidentally trampled right through my sandcastle—I was so upset.

"I've got an idea," I remember Gran saying. "Let's go and get you some modeling clay from the art supplies shop. It's not as fragile as sand."

That was my introduction to sculpting and it sparked off a deeper fascination, which Gran always nurtured.

So, for my degree show, I decided to honor her.

Using dozens of photographs as reference points and asking a friend to sit for me, I sculpted Gran's portrait in the round, creating a 360-degree bust out of clay. But when I cast her, I left out certain sections, sculpting them as though the missing parts had broken off and were blowing away on the wind. I was trying to capture my feelings of loss and of life being fleeting.

"You are *unbelievably* talented," Finn declares, turning to look at me.

His words and expression ramp up my internal heat lamp.

"It reminds me of the statue at Tintagel," he adds. "Do you know the one I mean? It looks like King Arthur holding Excalibur."

I nod. The sculpture Finn is referring to is an eight-foot-tall bronze of a king holding a sword, standing right out on a rocky, windswept cliff edge. The king's head, shoulders, and arms are complete, as is his sword, but his cloak falls raggedly to the ground and part of his body is hollow, so you can see the Atlantic Ocean beyond. It's otherworldly and striking—I'm pleased by the comparison.

"I'd love to have this recast in bronze one day, if I can afford it," I tell Finn.

Bronze is an alloy of copper and tin, metals that have been mined here since the Bronze Age. Gran lived in Cornwall for her entire life, so it feels fitting.

"It's really good, Liv," he says seriously.

I still have the flashlight from my phone pressed against the glass door of the greenhouse, the reflection of the light illuminating his features in the otherwise dark night.

"It scared the shit out of you," I reply with a grin.

He smirks. "I'll admit she took me by surprise. She's kind of ethereal, isn't she?"

"She's supposed to be."

"It must have hurt to create her."

"Yeah," I say quietly. "I could hardly speak to introduce her at my graduate show. My mum was in bits."

I'm distracted by the glow of a light turning on in an upstairs window.

"Speaking of my mum, I think she's awake," I whisper, quickly shutting off my phone light.

"I should go," Finn says.

I walk him to the gate and open it as quietly as I can.

"See you around?" he asks over his shoulder.

"Definitely."

He turns to face me and hesitates as though he wants to say more, but then he backs up and walks away. I watch for a moment and then close the gate behind him.

I feel like I'm floating as I go inside via the back door, but my mum brings me down to earth with a bump. She's standing in the hallway.

"Who was *that*?" she asks.

"A friend."

"What's his name?"

"Finn."

"Finn who?"

"*Mum*," I snap, before indulging her. "His surname is Finnegan. We went to school together."

"Danny Finnegan?" she asks with surprise.

Now I'm the one who's caught off guard. "You know him?"

"From my days at Perranporth," she confirms.

She was a GP at the surgery there when I was at school. Finn and his family must have been registered at her practice.

"How is he?" she asks, her brow etched with concern.

"He's good," I reply, her expression making me feel uneasy. "Why do you ask?"

"I know what he went through," she answers somberly, before letting out an audible sigh. "Obviously, I can't talk about my patients, but be careful, Liv. His mother was a very troubled soul."

"Mum, Finn is *not* his mother." It comes out sounding sharper than I had intended.

I do vaguely recall the rumors and the articles in the local papers following her disappearance, pieces that spoke of issues with drink and drugs.

"That's true, but I will say this," Mum starts, tightening her dressing gown in a gesture that I am so familiar with. "You don't go through something like that and come out the other side unscathed. Practice caution, Liv. I'm begging you."

7

MICHAEL LIVES ON STIPPY STAPPY, A QUAINT ROW of eighteenth-century terraced stone cottages that step sideways up the steep hill toward town. His door is robin's-egg blue and there's a bench outside that catches the afternoon sunshine. I'm walking past his place the following day when I see Finn approaching in the opposite direction.

He's wearing navy swimming trunks and a white T-shirt, with beach towels draped around his neck.

"Hello," he says with a broad grin.

"Hello," I reply, my heart cartwheeling.

"Where are you off to?" he asks, coming to a stop.

"Bakery."

I can't help looking at him with new eyes, my mum's warning ringing around my head.

"Careful," he admonishes as two boys roughly shove past him. "Oi!" he shouts as they go to push past me too. "Watch your manners with my friend."

They stop abruptly and look up at me and I vaguely recognize them from around here, but now the similarities between them and Finn jump out at me: the long lashes and bluey-green eyes of the older boy and the dark hair and dimples of the younger, who is grinning at me.

"These are my brothers," Finn corroborates. "Tyler"—he points at the taller boy with the long lashes—"and Liam."

"Hi," I manage before they head off.

"Wait for me at the stream!" Finn shouts after them before returning his attention to me. "Fuck me, they're hard work."

I laugh. "Did you all drink fertilizer when you were younger? Tyler's eyelashes are almost as long as yours."

He looks amused. "My nan wanted them out of the house, so I offered to take them to the beach."

I give him a quizzical look. "How old are they? And where does Jimmy fit in?"

Neither of those boys is anywhere near old enough to have produced a one-year-old nephew for him.

"Liam is ten and Tyler's twelve and Jimmy is my sister's son," he replies with a lopsided smile. "Well, half sister," he clarifies. "She's seven years older than me. My dad was married with two small children when he shagged my mum and got her pregnant."

He says this in a throwaway manner, but his eyes lack their usual sparkle.

I'm saved from responding when the door of Michael's house opens and my brother steps out.

"Liv!" he yells with delight.

"Hey!" I reply, stiffening.

When I was much younger, I never thought twice about introducing my brother to people. But as I got older, I started to notice the different reactions others have to meeting someone with Down syndrome.

If I don't hold them in particularly high regard, I'm less

nervous. The only time I really care is when I don't want to think less of the person because of the way they react to my brother.

In Finn's case, I care. If he turns out to be a twat, I'll be gutted.

Out of the corner of my eye, I register Finn's frozen stance as Michael comes along the tiny garden path, his expression transforming in the blink of an eye from happy to wary when he sees that I have company.

"This is my brother, Michael," I say to Finn.

"Who's that?" Michael asks me bluntly, his eyebrows bunching together in his inimitably expressive way.

"This is Finn," I reply.

"Hi!" Finn lunges forward with his hand outstretched.

Michael hesitates, his eyes narrowing suspiciously. He gives Finn's hand a single perfunctory shake and drops it like a hot potato.

I suppress a small smile as he wipes his palm on his jeans.

My brother takes no prisoners.

"Has Dad finished murdering the lawn?" he asks me.

I've never thought my brother's speech hard to understand, but it can take others a minute. Though Finn would probably look confused regardless.

"Yes," I say to Michael, before explaining to Finn. "In our family we say 'murdering the lawn' instead of 'mowing' it. Years ago, Michael and I played on the grass right after dad had mowed it and got covered in grass stains. Michael thought it looked like the grass had bled all over our hands. Our mum had read something about how some plants can send distress signals to each other and said that Michael might have a point. Apparently, the smell of freshly mown grass that people love is actually a distress signal. Our family has substituted 'murdering' for 'mowing' ever since."

"Ah, I see," Finn replies with a smile. He shifts on his feet. "Hey, I should catch up with my brothers. They've probably fallen in the stream by now."

"Of course. See you later."

He sidesteps me, looking awkward, and once again I worry that I've rambled on too much.

"Bye," he says to Michael.

Michael doesn't reply. His eyes have narrowed once more.

Finn has barely taken three steps away from us when Michael says, "Who was that dick?"

My stomach drops as Finn comes to an abrupt stop. He turns around and looks at my brother.

"Did you just call me a dick?" he asks slowly, raising an eyebrow.

"Oh, you understand me now?" Michael replies, a smile flickering at the edge of his lips.

"*Unbelievable*," Finn mutters, shaking his head as he strides down the slippery path with his long legs.

I stare at Michael and he shrugs at me, visibly entertained.

"You're awful," I chide, unable to hide my own smile. "I'm just going to the bakery to get us some pasties for lunch, but Mum and Dad are waiting if you want to head there now."

I'd planned to grab him on my way back.

"Ooh, good," he replies, clapping his hands and rubbing them together with glee. "Get me three," he commands, coming out through the gate.

"*Three* pasties?"

"Three," he states firmly.

My brother loves anything baked or fried. It's just as well

he chooses to walk to his job as a car park attendant for the National Trust at Chapel Porth.

"You forgot to close your front door," I point out.

He rolls his eyes at me dramatically, but returns to his front door and pulls it closed with a bang. Then he trudges back out through the gate and sets off down the path without so much as a backward glance.

I'm just turning away when he calls over his shoulder: "See you in a bit, baby sis!"

Short, sharp, and sweet, as always.

Those three words do a pretty good job of summing up my brother.

8

'M ON MY WAY DOWNSTAIRS A FEW DAYS LATER WHEN I catch sight of Finn through the front door's glass panels, hovering a few steps back on the road.

My heart skips a beat.

He rakes his hand through his hair as he stares down the hill, and then he glances at my front door and almost jumps out of his skin when our eyes meet through the glass.

I open the door, laughing.

"You scared the shit out of me," he mutters, his palm pressed flat to his chest.

"You weren't expecting to see me at my own house?" I ask with amusement, wondering if he'd been psyching himself up to ring the doorbell.

The thought of this gives me a burst of confidence.

"No, I was, but—never mind." He seems slightly flustered as he digs into the pocket of his ripped black jeans and pulls out his phone. "I made a start on your playlist. Figured I'd grab your number so I can send it to you."

"Oh, cool! Let me see?"

I slip my feet into my VEJAs and step outside, pulling the

door closed behind me. My parents are out back in the garden, but I'd still like to minimize the chances of Mum spying Finn. From what I now know, a face-to-face interaction could be awkward.

"I can literally forward it to you right now," he says with a small smile as I lean against the rough stone wall and waggle my hands at him.

"No, I'd have to go back inside to get Wi-Fi," I reply impatiently, hands still outstretched toward his phone.

A car comes up the road and he quickly steps forward to make room for it, his sudden nearness causing me to take a sharp breath.

"I did want to play this one song to you in person," he admits, staring down at me as my earlier confidence is washed away by an unnerving skittishness.

"It might be a bit noisy here," I murmur.

As if to prove my point, another car comes past, the sound of its engine combining with the rush of water in the stream running beneath the tiny bridge we're standing on.

"Come for a walk with me," he suggests tentatively.

It's late afternoon and the day is overcast and windy, but the air is mild enough that I don't regret not changing out of my denim shorts into jeans as we head down the hill toward the beach. My hands are buried deep in the kangaroo pocket of my navy hoodie, and I feel strangely tongue-tied.

Finn breaks the silence with a violent yawn.

"Gah, sorry," he apologizes.

"Are you all right?"

"I'm shattered. A bit over sleeping on the sofa."

"Whose sofa?" Has he been bouncing around between friends?

"My grandparents'."

"Are you staying with them the whole time you're here?"

"Yep."

"You're sleeping on your grandparents' sofa for six weeks?" I ask with astonishment.

"Yeah, their place is tiny."

I've relaxed a bit by the time we reach the boat ramp, our feet slipping and sliding over the sand as we make our way down the steep incline to the beach. Two lone lifeguards in red jackets stand near the distant shoreline, and the only other people in sight are wet-suit-clad surfers and bodyboarders riding the waves. Any tourists who decided to brave the weather and visit Aggie today are long gone.

We head right toward the rocks that have tumbled down from the cliffs over time. They're fully visible now, but in high tide, they're almost entirely hidden underwater.

As we near the dark cascade of boulders, Finn grabs my arm and yanks me to a stop, his eyes fixed on something ahead. Heart thumping, I follow the line of his sight to a small, furry, cream-colored mound lying about forty meters away.

"Is that—" he starts.

"A seal cub!" I finish his sentence for him.

"No way," he says with glee, dropping my arm. "I thought breeding season was later."

"This one must be early. Do you think it's okay? Should we go and check?"

"No, you're supposed to stay well back. Its mother is probably around somewhere and we don't want to scare her away." He casts me a smile. "Haven't you read the wildlife poster outside the Surf Life-Saving Club?"

I give him a sheepish shrug. "A long, long time ago."

"Clearly I've had too much time to kill," he says dryly.

We scan the waves, looking for the slick body of an adult gray seal.

"What if it's hurt? Should we wait?" I ask. "Watch it for a bit?"

"Sure. Let's find somewhere to sit down."

The rocks are the color of jade shot through with white stripes, like a copse of silver birch trees.

"The trick is finding one that isn't covered in seaweed," Finn says as we navigate the slippery surfaces. "But this looks all right." He slips off his denim jacket, revealing a classic white T-shirt underneath, and lays it on top of a smooth boulder, then gives it a pat, indicating for me to sit down.

"Such a gentleman," I tease as he holds out his hand to help me climb up.

"Does that come as a surprise to you?" he asks in a low voice, but any smart remark I might have hoped to deliver is silenced by the giddiness that comes over me at our skin-to-skin contact.

He lets go of me to climb up himself, then sits down a few inches away.

"Did you have fun with your brothers at the beach on Sunday?" I ask, resentful of the space between us.

"No, it was horrible. They run amok wherever they go," he says in that droll way of his, emphasizing the word "amok." "My grandparents are too soft on them," he confides.

"Do they live with your grandparents full-time?"

I can still feel the ghost of his hand in mine.

"Yeah. Their dads aren't on the scene." He glances at me. "Tyler and Liam are my half brothers. I'm not sure if you knew that?"

"Yeah."

"I guess you knew all about my mum's reputation already." He eyes me circumspectly through lowered lashes.

"Not really, not much at all. I am sorry, though," I say awkwardly. "I'm sorry about what happened to her."

"Life sucks sometimes," he replies flatly, pulling out his phone. "I need to play you this song."

I'm itching to know more about him, but the topic feels closed.

My attention is caught by a name at the top of his phone screen.

"Michael?" I say out loud.

He smiles and presses PLAY and a fast-paced song with a repeating riff begins to spill out of the tiny speakers. His energy levels immediately ramp up, hands tapping, head nodding, his whole body connected to the music. The sudden rush of attraction I feel toward him is intense, but soon the lyrics filter through to my brain and I clap my hand over my mouth.

"I didn't know my brother had had such an impact on you," I say through my fingers, laughing.

The song is about a beautiful boy called Michael who's dancing on a beautiful dance floor.

"He's a character," he replies with a grin as the song continues to play. "Have you not heard this one before?"

I shake my head. "Who's it by?"

"Franz Ferdinand."

"You should play it at Seaglass."

"I will if you want me to."

"Really?"

"Sure."

"What else would you play if I asked you to?" I ask cheekily.

His eyes sparkle. "Try me."

"Taylor Swift's '22'?"

He shrugs nonchalantly and nods. "All right."

"You wouldn't!" I gasp. I was totally joking. "You'd never convince Dan and the others."

"If I do, will you come to Boardies with me?"

My stomach cartwheels.

Boardies, short for Boardmasters, is a big music festival in nearby Newquay.

"It's two weeks from this Saturday," he adds when I don't immediately answer.

"You might find someone else you'd rather go with before then."

"I won't."

The smile that's been dancing about his lips fades as his eyes hold mine, making me feel edgy as hell.

A COUPLE OF days later, Finn saunters into Seaglass just before the band's set, looking sexy and unkempt in his gray T-shirt and ripped jeans, his wild hair caressing his cheekbones and falling into his eyes. He flashes me a heart-stopping grin as he and his bandmates take to the stage and launch straight into their first song.

I can't believe it. It's a rocked-up version of Taylor Swift's "22."

Finn is all over my reaction, while Dan laughs at the sight of Amy jumping around behind the bar, singing along at the top of her voice, hands thrown high in the air.

By the time the chorus comes around again, I'm singing and dancing too.

Luckily, Chas and our customers indulge us, because no one is getting served during those three minutes.

I don't know what this thing with Finn is, or where it can go, but I've never felt so lit up.

9

T'S THE FIRST SATURDAY OF AUGUST AND I'M OUT ON THE
balcony, collecting empties. It was the St. Agnes Carnival today and loads of people ended up here for the after-party. I
could have gone home an hour ago, but Chas did a lock-in and
I decided to stay, even though I'm the walking dead.

I place the stack of cups I've gathered on the ground beside
me so they don't blow away, then lean against the railing, allowing the frigid breeze to cool my hot skin. The tide is on its
way in and waves are galloping toward Seaglass like a herd of
wild horses, gleaming black and shining white. It's windy tonight, and every breath I take feels stolen.

Finn walks out onto the balcony through the only door I
haven't yet locked and looks around, spying me.

He comes over and kicks my feet apart with his big boots.
I laugh lightly at his impertinence and he gives me a small smile
as he steps into the space he's created between my feet.

"Hi," he says, staring down at me.

Ever since I gave him my phone number after our walk on
the beach ten days ago, we've been texting back and forth, and

I've barely stopped listening to the playlist he made for me. He leaves a week from tomorrow, but right now he's right here.

"Look at you two," Amy says, coming out onto the balcony, trailed by Dan.

They're fully seeing each other now. I don't want to jinx it, but Dan seems smitten and I *know* she is.

"What about us?" Finn asks.

He moves so he's leaning against the balustrade next to me, his elbows propped on the wooden railing.

"You look like a beach advert, with your tumbling dark locks and long eyelashes."

We laugh and glance at each other.

My hair was coming loose so I let it down half an hour ago.

"I don't really think you could describe me as having tumbling dark locks," Finn muses, his eyes still resting on mine. "And her eyelashes are way longer."

"No, they're not," I scoff.

"They *definitely* are," he insists.

"So, are we all traveling to Boardies together?" Amy asks, losing interest in our silly argument and moving on to talk about the festival next weekend.

"Sounds like it. Rach is keen too," I say.

I was thrilled when Finn asked me to go with him, but I wasn't disappointed to hear that my friends and Dan are up for it too. It will be fun with a bunch of us going.

"Wonder if we can all get off work for Saturday night," Amy muses.

Dan shakes his head. "It's our last gig before Finn returns to LA. We can't miss it."

My heart recoils at the thought of him leaving. Finn gives

me a sidelong look, as if sensing my inner turmoil. He drops his gaze to the ground and releases an audible sigh.

Kieran returns a few days after Finn goes, so he'll be stepping back into the spotlight as frontman until the end of August. I can't imagine watching the band and not seeing Finn hanging off the mic stand. It's going to be weird.

It's going to be *hard*.

All the more reason to get myself together and head to London, now that I've paid back my parents. I still haven't worked up the courage to tell them my plans.

"Who'll drive?" Dan asks.

"You're the only one of us with a reliable car, so that would be you," Finn replies.

"Aw, man!" Dan looks aghast at the thought. "I can't go to a festival and not sink a few beers!"

"I could ask my parents if I can borrow their car," I offer.

I don't need to drink and I'd be happy to save some money.

"Nice one," Dan says with relief.

Finn gives him a deadpan look as he and Amy head back inside.

I bend down to pick up the stack of cups. Finn takes them from me and puts them back down on the ground.

"What? Why?" I ask.

"Because I've got a moment alone with Olivia Arterton and I'm taking it."

He puts his hands on the railing on either side of me, enclosing me, and I'm surrounded by the warmth of him.

"I had such a crush on you when we were at school," he confesses, suddenly serious.

"*Did* you?" I whisper. "But we barely said two words to each other."

"Yeah, I wasn't much of a talker back then."

"You weren't, were you?"

He shrugs and the indents in his cheeks become less pronounced.

"Oi, where did they go?" I ask.

"Where did *what* go?" He's mystified.

"Your dimples."

He grins and the sight is blinding.

"There they are," I breathe, reaching up to poke one.

He swipes my hand and brings it to his mouth, baring his teeth for a split second before nipping the tip of my finger.

I feel that bite *everywhere*.

His pupils dilate. I stare at him in dazed silence.

"I have to kiss you," he murmurs, his eyes drifting to my lips.

I nod my head in unequivocal agreement.

Shivers roll down my spine as he brings his hands to my face, cupping my jaw, his fingers sinking into the hair at the nape of my neck. I lean into him and press my palms flat against his chest, my pulse speeding up as our mouths meet for the first time. A bolt of electricity goes through me and we begin to move together in a torturously slow dance. His tongue slips between my lips and caresses mine and I feel dizzy with a rush that I have never experienced. Not *ever*.

He tastes of cold sea air and iced cola and I want more. *So much more.*

He slowly draws away, leaving only inches between us.

"I can't believe I've kissed Olivia Arterton," he says in a low voice laced with amusement.

"*I* can't believe I've kissed Danny Finnegan," I reply, sliding my hands down to his waist.

The transformation is instant: he goes completely rigid.

"What's wrong?" I ask with concern as he lets me go and backs up.

"No one calls me Danny."

"Oh." I'm confused.

"Why did you call me Danny?"

"Um . . ." I decide to come clean. "My mum—"

"Your mum?" he interrupts.

"She's a doctor. She used to work at Perranporth."

He takes another step backward so he can see me more clearly. All contact between us has been severed.

"What's her name?" he asks carefully.

"Kay Stone."

"Dr. Stone is your mum?"

I nod. "Don't worry, she didn't tell me anything."

He lets out a brittle laugh, his left temple throbbing. "I should hope not."

"She saw you leaving through the gate a couple of weeks ago. She referred to you as Danny."

"She really didn't say anything else?"

He's perceptive.

"Only that your family circumstances were difficult," I admit reluctantly.

He shakes his head with what looks like disgust and walks away a few paces, halting with his back to me.

I stare at him miserably, wondering how such a perfect moment could have taken this horrible turn. I have a feeling that he's going to keep walking and leave me here alone, but then he turns around and slowly retraces his steps, coming to a stop in front of me.

The wind is brutal, whipping his hair against his face in dark slashes. I've never wanted to lay my hands on clay more.

His gaze falls to my cheekbone and he comes even closer, lifting his hand.

"Stay still," he commands when I pull back reflexively.

I feel his fingers brush my cheek and then he shows me the stray eyelash that he's collected.

"We can solve this once and for all," he murmurs, pincering his own eyelashes and extracting one.

I belatedly realize what he's up to.

"Don't let it blow away!" I say with a gasp, and we huddle together, our bodies forming a shelter from the wind.

"Yours is longer," I say, somewhat indecisively.

"Yours is," he replies, flipping his over so the lashes are spooning each other.

I glance up at him. "Draw?"

He closes his hand into a fist and reaches out, tracing the knuckle of his thumb along the edge of my jaw.

"Sorry," he whispers, making my skin feel charged where he's touched it.

"You have nothing to be sorry for," I reply.

I hear as much as feel his quiet exhale.

You don't go through something like that and come out the other side unscathed . . .

Sorry, Mum. But there's no way I'm walking away now.

10

T'S LATE AFTERNOON AND THE SUN IS SPEARING golden rays through cracks in the cotton-ball clouds. The gusts blowing in off the ocean are cool, but the festival crowd up on the cliff is boiling, a fifty-thousand-strong mass of jumping, happy people having the time of their lives.

I drove us here in my parents' BMW, windows open, sun shining, and music blaring out of the speakers, courtesy of the updated playlist Finn loaded onto my phone this morning. He sat in the front seat, twisted toward me and watching me drive, one hand holding the hair from his face, while Amy, Dan, and Rach sat in the back. I felt the warmth of his gaze on my skin, soaking into my bloodstream, making me feel charged and alive. There has been a current flowing back and forth between us all day, and we've been unable to keep our hands to ourselves—Finn dropping kisses to the nape of my neck, trailing goose bumps along my arms with the stroke of his touch. I've slipped my fingers into the holes in his jumper and felt the sharp intake of his breath. We've reveled in our closeness, the pump of the music, the joyful whoops of our friends, and the energy of thousands of people shouting their happiness to the wind. It's a day I wish I could cast in bronze—a perfect moment in time captured for eternity.

And now we're almost ready to return to Seaglass for one more shift before we can go back to mine. I told Finn earlier that my parents are staying overnight in Bristol for a friend's seventieth birthday party. The look he gave me was loaded.

I glance across at my friends and smile. Rach is giving Amy a piggyback, stomping on a carpet of empty plastic cups littered at her feet as she sings along at the top of her voice to Editors' encore.

Amy's hands are in the air, her pale blond hair flowing out behind her and her cheeks sparkling with pink and purple glitter as she laughs, trying to remember the words to the chorus.

Dan keeps gazing over at her with unmasked adoration. I was worried about him breaking her heart, but he seems to be all-in.

I smile at Finn and he returns my grin, putting his arm around my waist and pulling me to his side, hip to hip.

"What's this song?" I ask him.

"'Smokers Outside the Hospital Doors,'" he replies, his blue-green eyes twinkling. "You'll have to add it to your playlist."

"Or you could add it for me later," I suggest, feeling a deep ache in my soul at the reminder that it's his last night.

Somewhere along the line, my heart snagged on him. A smarter girl might have unhooked it and stepped the hell away before she got badly hurt, but I haven't been strong enough to turn my back on the rush that I feel when I'm with him.

As much as we've touched and as close as we've been, we haven't kissed since our first time last weekend. I know that he's thought about it. His gaze keeps dropping to my lips and every time I notice, I feel as though I'm on fire.

I'M EVEN MORE effervescent with anticipation a few hours later. Mixamatosis are playing their penultimate song and Chas has sent Amy and me to the dance floor, claiming he can manage behind the bar for this last stint.

The song comes to an end and the noise of the crowd dies down as Finn speaks into the mic.

"Thanks for having me this summer," he says to cheers from the audience. His eyes find mine in the crowd. "It's been unforgettable."

He gives me a small smile as he backs away from the mic and a roar goes up as Dan sends feedback jarring through the amps, along with a twanging, super-familiar guitar tune. Chris launches into a fast beat and Finn steps up to the mic, the crowd going wild.

It's "The Boys of Summer," a grittier, faster-paced version than the Don Henley original.

The original is on my playlist. *My* playlist. I wonder if he saw it there.

There's a lump in my throat as I dance along with my friends, singing at the top of my voice. It hurts to push the words out past the swelling.

I'll have to get my hands on some clay this week. I hope it will soothe my pain to create, and then I'll need to tell my parents about London. I'm still struggling with the guilt I feel about leaving them, but I'm planning to stay and work through to the end of September to give us all a bit more time.

Woven into the sadness I feel about losing Finn is excitement for what the future has in store. Even the uncertainty of it is giving me a thrill. I'm ready for my next adventure.

The song builds to a frenzy before ending in screaming feedback. We all go wild as Finn holds his hands over his head and applauds us. He steps back up to the mic and the noise dies down.

"Maybe see you fuckers next year."

And then he's hopping down from the stage, tolerating back pats and hair-ruffling as he pushes his way through the crowd toward me. He's hot and sweaty, his hair falling down around his face and his eyes startlingly dark as he closes the distance between us. My entire body feels electric as his hands land on my waist, his thumbs pressing into the bare skin beneath the lacy white top I wore to the festival earlier. I don't care that we're in a crowded room—when his mouth catches mine, everything around us fades into the background. He deepens the kiss and I feel hot and shivery all at once.

I'm aware of people laughing, but only distantly, and then they're catcalling and clapping and Finn is smiling against my mouth as he breaks away.

I stare up at him, breathless.

This boy can *kiss*.

He turns to Amy. "I'm taking her. Tell Chas," and then his hand is in mine and he's pulling me toward the door.

"Wait! Your bag!" Amy cries after us.

I'm hardly able to think straight as she runs behind the bar and brings it to me.

"Go have fun."

Finn and I don't speak on our way up to my house, holding hands and walking fast, eager. I unlock the door, fumbling with my keys, and then we're inside the dark house, kicking off our shoes, and I'm leading the way straight up the stairs to my bedroom.

He pushes my door shut behind me and I fall against the wall as his mouth crashes onto mine, his hands cutting a path down my thighs and tugging me against him. I gasp at his hardness and he breaks our kiss, pulling back a few inches to stare at me in the moonlit room, leaving the lower half of his body pressed against mine. We hold eye contact for several long seconds, and I almost forget to breathe. Then he gently tucks a stray lock of hair behind my ear, his fingertips skating along my jaw and down the side of my neck to my collarbone, leaving me shivering and wanting.

As his gaze moves higher, I read his mind and reach up to remove the bobby pins securing my hair, letting it fall down across my shoulder. He emits a tortured-sounding moan and sinks his mouth back on to mine, kissing me deeply as his fingers push through my hair.

We kiss for a long time before I begin to lose patience. I want more. And Finn seems to sense it, making space between us as my hands go to the buttons on his jeans. He sees to mine, my breath catching at his brief touch against my skin. He retrieves a condom from his back pocket and pulls me to the bed where we shed the last of our clothing.

When he's ready for me, I reach down and bring him closer, savoring the sound he makes in the back of his throat as we connect in the most intimate of ways. Locking my eyes with his, he pushes into me.

It's only later, after I've gasped his name against his neck, that it occurs to me that we haven't said a single word to each other in hours.

But then I guess we've done enough talking this summer.

"WHY DID WE waste so much time?" Finn asks into the darkness.

His fingers are playing with my hair and it's giving me chills.

"I'm going to miss you too," I whisper, hearing the words he didn't say.

He turns to face me. "I really like you."

"I really like you too," I reply.

As he presses a kiss to my lips, I can feel his smile.

The sound of the doorbell disturbs our moment. I jerk away from him.

"Who's that?" I ask with alarm as the sound reverberates once more through the quiet house.

Finn sits up, frowning, as I jump out of bed and pull on my dressing gown.

"Could it be Michael?" he asks with concern.

"God knows," I reply, hurrying out of the room and down the stairs.

I flick on the outdoor light and my blood freezes over. There are two police officers standing on the doorstep.

11

WAS IN SHOCK WHEN THEY BROKE THE NEWS TO ME.
The police officers asked if I was at home alone, and when I
replied that "my friend, Finn" was upstairs, they suggested
I call him down.

Finn's face was deathly pale and wary as he walked into the
room. He'd dressed in a hurry and it showed. We sat apart on
the sofa, waiting for the words that would bring my whole
world crashing down.

My parents had been caught in a massive pileup on their
way to Bristol, their injuries too severe to be treated. They had
died at the scene.

At first, I felt numb. But when it sank in . . . When I realized
that they would never again walk through our front door,
make Sunday lunch or a cup of tea . . . Never again care about
how much time I spent with them . . . I lost it.

Finn, who had been sitting stiffly beside me, came to life,
clutching me to him as I screamed out my grief. He held me
until dawn as I sobbed and sobbed, long after the police officers had left us, and then he called Rach and Amy.

My friends came with me to break the news to Michael.

Rach had to take over when I couldn't find the words. Then we sat and cried together, the four of us, my brother and I clutching each other as the weight of responsibility pressed heavily on my shoulders.

Mum and Dad did so much for Michael, for us both. How could I possibly step into their shoes?

My brother moved back into his old room for a few days before saying he wanted to go home, so his support worker, Carrie, stepped up her visits to accommodate him.

For almost two weeks, I haven't gone more than a few minutes without one of my friends beside me. If it's not Rach, it's Amy. If it's not Amy, it's Finn. When Amy or Rach have slept in my bed with me, Finn has stayed on the sofa downstairs, but occasionally he has been the one to comfort me during the night when I've jolted awake, unable to catch my breath, weighed down with the most overwhelming sense of darkness. On those nights, he's held me until I've fallen asleep again, joined up in an intimacy that feels acute.

The nightmare that has kept replaying in my mind has been the imagined moment of impact, when the old classic car my parents were driving crumpled, their simple lap belts affording nowhere near enough protection while I was blithely bringing my friends home from the festival in their BMW, equipped with all its modern safety features.

The guilt from knowing that, while I was fixating on having sex with Finn, my mum and dad were taking their last breaths on the side of a motorway makes me feel desperate.

The future appears shadowy. I have already experienced the best day of my life and I am only twenty-two. How could I ever again be as happy as I was on the day of that festival?

When I'd realized through a fog of grief that Finn should have set off for the airport hours ago, he'd shaken his head, his expression grimly determined.

"No fucking way am I leaving," he'd stated adamantly.

He was supposed to record an EP with his band last week, but instead he's here. With me. He's postponed the recording; I heard him discussing it over the phone with one of his bandmates and I sensed they were putting pressure on him to return. His new flight is booked for early next week, three days after the funeral.

He's helped me with everything, from paperwork and registering my parents' deaths to organizing the wake at the St. Agnes Hotel. I don't know what I would have done without him, and I keep remembering that he has experience with all this, that this must be hurting him too. He needs to get back to his life.

I just can't bear the thought of him leaving.

THE NIGHT BEFORE my parents' funeral, we're tangled up in bed together, my throat and eyes swollen with grief, my whole body gripped with despair.

"I don't know how I'm ever going to be okay again," I say in a choked voice.

Finn holds me against his bare chest, cocooning me in his warmth.

"You will be. You *will* be okay. You'll always feel it, and the pain will always be a part of you, but you'll learn to live with it."

"How?"

"One day at a time. This first year will be really hard. But by next year, it will start to feel a bit easier, and a bit easier the year after that. It just takes time, Liv. You can't rush it."

"How did you get over what happened?" Fresh tears have broken out at his words.

"I *haven't* got over it," he replies simply, brushing away the dampness on my cheeks. "I never *will* get over it. But I found a way to survive, to box it up, to compartmentalize. You'll find a way to do that too. One night you'll realize you've gone the whole day without even thinking about them."

"I don't *want* to go a day without thinking about them!" I say on a gasp, and then I burst into full-blown sobs and he apologizes over and over, holding me tighter, pressing urgent kisses to my forehead, realizing that it was too soon for me to hear something like that.

The thought that one day I might not think about Mum and Dad, that I might forget about the things we did together or the way they sounded when they laughed, the tiny freckles on Mum's nose that only came out during the summer or the gray hairs that had just started to appear in Dad's eyebrows—it's too heartbreaking to bear. I'm lost all over again.

"I don't know what I'm going to do without you," I blurt when I'm capable of speech.

I know immediately that I shouldn't have said it, that it's too much pressure to put on one person who has already done so much, but I couldn't keep the words in.

Finn is quiet for a moment. "You can call me whenever you want," he says, rubbing my back. "I don't know when I'll be able to get back over here—money is really tight right now—but maybe you could come to LA?"

"And leave Michael?" I ask with astonishment, my entire body tensing, hardly able to believe that he would even suggest it.

"He'd be all right for a bit, wouldn't he?"

I pull away abruptly and sit up, looking down at him. "Are you joking? I can't leave my brother now, Finn! I can't go anywhere!"

I inhale sharply, but my lungs won't fill. I try again and again, but my body is not cooperating.

"Hey." He sits up, concerned, his hand on my shoulder. "Breathe, Liv. Breathe."

I shake my head violently, panicked.

"Follow me," he coaches urgently. "Breathe in: one, two, three. And out: one, two, three, four, five. Come on, Liv. And again: one, two, three . . ."

I stare into his eyes and eventually I'm able to inhale properly again, but my chest is aching even more because this kind, sweet person who already means so much to me will be gone in three days.

"It's going to be okay," he tries to reassure me again. "We'll stay in touch, try to make this work, FaceTime, text—"

"No," I cut him off.

He stares at me, taken aback.

"No," I say again more softly, shaking my head. "I can't."

"Can't what?" he asks warily.

"I can't do it. This has to end with you leaving. The thought of you going on Tuesday hurts so much. But you'll fly home, I'll stay here, and I've got to try to pick up the pieces somehow. I'll need to find the strength to be here for Michael, to decide what the hell it is I'm going to do with my life if I'm not moving to London. But every time you and I speak, every time we say goodbye, I'll feel like I'm losing you all over again. It will *ruin* me. I can't bear the thought of it. I don't want you to call me. This has to end here," I repeat.

"Liv . . ." He shakes his head, stricken.

"And you have so much going on back in LA," I say, because, of course, this is not just about me. "You need to focus on the band."

He reaches out and grabs my hand, squeezing it tightly. "We could make a plan to speak every week or so."

"But then I'll put my life on hold waiting for your call. I know I will. I know what I'm like." I bite my trembling bottom lip and extract my hand. "I need to focus on life here. You need to do the same."

He looks crushed as he pulls me into his arms, burying his face in my neck. I clutch onto him just as fiercely.

"What if I come back next summer?" he asks in a muffled voice, his lips pressed against my skin.

"I'll be here. But let's not make any promises, okay?"

He nods against my neck and my heart cracks at the thought of him meeting another girl and falling in love with her, of losing him forever. I'm not sure I can do this after all.

Suddenly he shakes his head and pulls away from me. "No. I *do* want to make a promise." His fervent words fill me with light. "I *will* return next summer. And I'm not saying that I expect you to wait for me, because I don't. But if we *are* both single . . ."

His sentence trails off and I nod tearfully, overwhelmed with relief at the compromise we've found as he tugs me into a hug.

For the first time in two weeks, I feel something akin to hope.

12

THIS SUMMER

A ND THEN I SAID, 'YOU MUST BE THE ARTIST!' AND he snapped, 'No, I'm not,' in this deeply grouchy voice, and I said, 'But you're the one drawing the pictures on the beach, right?' and he muttered, 'Not anymore,' and went into the apartment and slammed the door in my face! Can you believe it?" I swipe my wineglass and take a large gulp, my eyes wide with indignation. "Grumpy git."

My friends appear highly entertained as I share the details of my run-in with my downstairs apartment guest on Monday afternoon.

"What does he look like?" Rach asks.

"Very tall and very broad."

"Like, *Dan*-level tall and broad?" Amy checks.

"No, even taller and broader. He must be six foot three or four, I reckon, and his shoulders are like—" I put my hands out to estimate the width.

"Good-looking?" Rach asks curiously.

I pull a face and shrug. "I mean, yeah, he has nice eyes and very, very dark blond hair and a very, very solid facial structure."

They grin at each other.

"What's that look for?"

"Very, very," Rach replies, while at the same time, Amy says, "Facial structure."

Okay, so one is picking on my limited vocabulary and the other is taking the piss out of me for noticing these things. What can I say? I'm a figurative sculptor; I do pay an unusual amount of attention to the shape of a skull.

As for having the headspace to form eloquent sentences, I've been working my arse off and I'm knackered.

"What do you mean by 'very, very dark blond hair' anyway? Isn't that brown?"

"No, it's very, very dark blond," I insist. "If it catches the sun, I'm sure it'll go a lighter shade of blond."

Amy bursts out laughing at my conjecturing.

"Are you sure he's the sand artist?" Rach asks over the sound of our friend's hooting.

"Well, no one else has drawn anything on the sand this week, so I assume so. And he did say, 'Not anymore.'" I put on a stupid deep voice, mimicking him.

"I'm bummed that he's booked the place for the whole month of June," Rach says, irked. "I was looking forward to a few summer barbecues at yours."

I'm relieved he did because I can't pass up that sort of money, but I know what she means—the prospect of being able to use the garden was the only silver lining of the cancellation. The downstairs apartment is booked every week through to the end of September, so we'll just have to hope that early October will be mild and we can have some outdoor parties then. I miss having access to the garden when guests are staying.

"Amy, what do you want doing with the carrots?" Dan calls through from the kitchen.

"Leave them in for a bit longer. I'm going to do them with pomegranate molasses and maple syrup," she calls back.

"Ooh, fancy," Rach interjects.

Amy and Dan are both excellent cooks. Amy is a midwife and Dan is an accountant, but sometimes I plead with them to give up their jobs and come and work with me at Seaglass. Joining them for dinner is always a pleasure and I can practically roll home afterward since they live at the top of a hill on the outskirts of the village.

"Have you sorted out that problem with your photographer yet?" I ask Amy, spearing an olive with a toothpick and popping it into my mouth.

"Yep, she's roped in her nephew to assist," Amy replies.

Amy and Dan are getting married in a couple of months and they just found out that their photographer's regular assistant had double-booked himself.

I'm so happy that two of my closest friends will be tying the knot, but I know that the weekend will be bittersweet when it comes. They set the date for the tenth of August, which is the day before the sixth anniversary of my parents' deaths.

They struggled to book a reception venue, so I don't think the significance of the date even occurred to Amy. I don't usually make a big thing of it, at least not with my friends.

My stomach churns as I wonder, not for the first time, if Finn will make it back this summer. Surely he'll want to attend the wedding, if nothing else . . .

"I'm gutted that he's stopped drawing on the sand," Amy says out of the blue, returning to the subject of our onetime mystery artist. "I was hoping to see his drawings in person."

"They really were beautiful," I reply sadly.

"The pictures you posted were incredible," Rach says.

I never took a photograph of the girl in the sand. She had been washed away when I went back to work later that day and for reasons I don't understand, I couldn't bring myself to tell anyone about her.

Her.

I mean *me.*

At least, I think it was me.

"I still can't believe he sketched out a whole forest," Rach says. "And you requested that on Instagram! Do you think he saw the post?"

"He *must* have," Amy chips in.

I agree.

Dan comes through from the kitchen.

"What are you lot talking about?" he asks, proceeding to massage Amy's shoulders.

She groans, her head lolling back.

"Sand art," I reply as Rach pretends to vomit.

"Pot calling the kettle black!" I exclaim at Rach. "You and Ellie are just as sickening."

"We do *not* do PDAs," she argues. "At least, we don't *mean* to."

Ellie is Rach's girlfriend. Amy and I didn't even know that Rach was bisexual until a couple of years ago. She used to have a crush on Chris, one of Dan's bandmates, and when we were at school, she'd fly off the handle if anyone called her a lesbian. She's always been a surfer tomboy in her baggy T-shirts and board shorts.

Turns out it was more the assumption than the label that bothered her.

"Actually, you're *all* revolting," I declare casually, the only singleton at the table.

Dan removes his hands from Amy's shoulders and her head returns to an upright position.

I didn't mean for him to stop on my account, but I'm distracted by the song spilling out of the speaker.

"Can you skip this one?" I ask.

Dan frowns at me. "It's 'Sweater Weather' by the Neighbourhood. We didn't even *play* this one."

"I know, but it reminds me of him and his holey jumper."

Amy and Rach exchange looks.

"Don't make a big deal out of it," I say a little impatiently. "Can you please just skip it?"

I'm doing well; no need to put hurdles in my path.

Dan reaches for his phone. My relief doesn't last more than a couple of seconds because "Sold" by Liily is the next song to come on.

"Urgh, *no!*"

"This single hadn't even come out when he fronted the band!" Dan exclaims at my reaction.

"Yeah, but he put their EP on at Seaglass a couple of years ago." I added it to my MUSIC app afterward. "Do you reckon we can have a different playlist?"

I'm such a shit dinner guest, but Dan, bless him, doesn't so much as sigh.

"What would you like?" he asks me placidly.

"Um, jazz?"

"I fucking hate jazz, Liv, and you know it."

"I have no clue why I said jazz. I'm not a fan either." But last week we did hip-hop and prior to that it was pop and he vetoed R&B the week before.

"I don't mind what you put on, as long as it's not rock,

alt-rock, indie rock, or anything else that might make me think of a certain someone."

I can't even say his name.

"That kind of rules out all my favorite songs," Dan points out.

"Fuck me, how long is this going to go on for?" Rach mutters. "You'd better be over him by the time these guys do their wedding playlist."

"Billie Eilish?" Amy suggests, ignoring Rach, while I feel a pang of anxiety at her words.

"Fine," Dan replies, and a moment later Billie's new album begins to spill dreamily out of the speakers.

I breathe a sigh of relief and relax.

Rach reaches across and pats my hand brusquely but consolingly. Amy goes one further and tops up my wineglass.

I love my friends.

IT'S LATE SATURDAY morning before I see Tom again. I've just clambered down the stairs with a mop, bucket, and vacuum cleaner and I'm all hot and sweaty because I had to walk up the hill to collect my car first. I leave it on the street outside Amy and Dan's place during the summer because their road is quiet and I don't have to pay for parking.

The downstairs apartment has been deathly silent all week. I have occasionally heard Tom moving about, but rarely. To my knowledge, he hasn't turned on the TV or radio or played any music and I'm curious to know what he's been doing down there.

As I barge my way out the front door, trying not to chip the paintwork around the frame like I did last weekend, I spy him coming up the hill from the direction of the beach. He's wearing light gray shorts with checkerboard Vans and a pristine white T-shirt, and why do I suddenly feel nervous?

"Hello," I call in an attempt to sound friendly, trying to pop the trunk of my blue Honda Civic hatchback.

The head attachment of the vacuum cleaner knocks out of its socket and falls to the ground as I'm wrestling it into the back, then the mop handle slips and, in my attempt to catch both it and the wayward vacuum hose, I drop the bucket carrying all my cleaning supplies.

I swear under my breath as bottles, sponges, and dustcloths scatter.

Tom jogs the last few steps and swoops down to pick up rolling cans of oven cleaner and fly spray.

A car crawls by and the driver glares at me through the open side window.

"Sorry!" I call after them, sliding my tote bag off my shoulder and thrusting it into the trunk.

Tom bends down to collect the dustcloths, handing them over. His muscles are long and lean and exceptionally well-defined.

"Thanks," I mutter, feeling my face growing warmer.

"Why don't you park on the drive?" he asks.

"Because you're staying downstairs." I wipe my brow, wishing I'd tied back my not-quite-shoulder-length wavy hair.

"But I don't have a car," he says as I try to arrange the equipment in the trunk so it all fits.

His voice is deep and there's a subtle lilt to his accent. I wonder where he's from.

"That's a first," I admit, shoving the mop handle through the central hatch between the rear seats.

Where's the furniture polish? I peer under the bumper. The woman who owns the holiday cottages I manage insists on her wooden tables gleaming.

I'm diverted by another car crawling past, hating the fact that I'm holding up traffic. There's only just enough room for me to pull up here and for people still to be able to get past. If an emergency vehicle or a delivery van needed access, I could be in trouble.

"Anyway, there's room for two cars on the drive," he points out.

"My guests usually have kids, a dog, or both, so they don't want me going in and out through the gate all the time," I say distractedly, searching the ground.

"I don't have kids *or* a dog. What are you missing?"

"Furniture polish."

He spins round and scans our surroundings, finding the stray can a few meters down the hill, caught in a fern growing at the base of the rough stone wall.

"Thanks," I say again as he passes it over.

I throw it in the trunk and close the door.

"You can park on the drive, I don't mind," he offers, shoving his hands into his pockets. He's looking toward the house, but he meets my eyes again and once more I'm struck by their unusual maple-gold-brown color.

"Really?" I ask uncertainly, gazing up at him.

He's well-spoken, but I wouldn't describe him as posh. He's polite. Well-mannered. Perhaps not the giant git that I'd pegged him to be.

"Of course. Where do you usually park?" He scuffs the road with his shoe, looking uncomfortable.

"Outside my friends' house, up in the village."

"For the whole summer? That's a pain."

"It is a bit."

"So park on the drive," he suggests simply, pulling his keys out of his pocket and backing away.

"Are you sure?"

"Yes."

He's inside the house with the door closed by the time I drive away.

I THINK TWICE about taking Tom up on his offer. Actually, I go back and forth in my mind about ten times before deciding, sod it, it'll make my life easier.

When I return, I pull up in front of the gates and climb out, jostling them open with more force than I usually need to use. I make a mental note to oil them before my next guests arrive in three weeks.

Driving through the open gates, I tuck the car around the corner so it's as far out of sight from the downstairs apartment as possible. I'm not that successful because when I get out of the driver's door, I can see straight through the kitchen-diner's corner window to where Tom is sitting on the bench facing outward, his elbows resting on his knees and his hands clasped between them. We lock eyes for a moment before I avert my gaze, flustered.

I hear the heavy glass patio doors sliding open with a low whoosh as I'm emptying the trunk.

"Do you need a hand carrying it in?" he calls.

"Oh, I'll be okay," I call back, not wanting to put him out.

He ignores me and the next thing I know he's by my side, lifting the cumbersome vacuum cleaner out as though it weighs nothing.

"Thanks," I murmur.

"Where do you want it?" he asks, taking the bucket of cleaning supplies from my hand.

"The front door would be great," I reply, slightly taken aback by his chivalry.

I follow him with only the mop and my tote bag as he walks out the gates and down to the door, waiting as I search through my bag for my keys.

"How many other properties do you look after?" he asks.

"Three."

"And you've cleaned them all already?"

I pull out my keys, triumphant. "I work fast."

"Clearly."

"And I've got to get to my other job," I say as I unlock the front door and enter the hall.

"The bar on the beach?" he asks as he props open the main door.

"Yes." I glance at him as I tackle the lock to my apartment. Why's he come over all chatty? Is he bored? Maybe he's lonely. He *is* here all by himself.

"I tried to go in there last Friday, but I haven't been back."

"I know." *Why hasn't he been back?* "You came in and I told you we weren't open yet."

"I hoped you'd have forgotten. I wasn't in a very good mood that day. Sorry I was rude."

"Don't worry about it, it was early. Where had you traveled in from? Do you mind bringing that upstairs?"

"Caernarfon," he replies as he follows me.

"Wales?"

"Yes."

He doesn't sound Welsh. I turn into the kitchen and gingerly balance the mop handle against the wall. He places the vacuum cleaner down on the floor, along with the bucket.

This room is part of the original cottage, with thick, uneven walls and only one square window set back behind a deep sill. He seems extra tall and broad in the small space.

"Thanks for your help," I say.

"Not a problem."

He leads the way back down the stairs, glancing over his shoulder at me as he steps outside and probably wondering why I'm trailing after him.

"I need to close the gate," I explain when I reach the hallway.

"I'll do it," he replies, turning on the doorstep to face me.

"It's a bit stiff," I warn.

"I'll manage." His brows pull together, troubled, as he nods past me at my staircase. "You know, you really shouldn't let strange men into your apartment like that."

"You're not a strange man, you're a guest. I have your name and address on the booking form." I lean against the doorframe and fold my arms across my chest.

"That doesn't make you safe," he replies, his tone unexpectedly gentle.

His eyes are full of concern as he stares down at me.

I get the weirdest sensation inside me then. It's as though butterflies are hatching out of their chrysalides and groggily stretching their wings.

"I'm sure I'll be okay."

It feels like a long time since anyone has been protective of me in this way.

How did he go from being rude, blunt, and not even replying to my email to being kind and thoughtful?

"Did you get my email?" I blurt, suddenly desperate to understand his fluctuating personality.

The images he created in the sand were so beautiful. I *want* to like him.

He looks confused. "The one telling me that check-in time was at four?"

"No, the one telling you I'd managed to get the place ready for midday."

His eyes flare wide and he shakes his head. "No, I didn't."

"Oh." My face falls.

"My phone ran out of battery. I came at four, like you said."

"Shit, *that's* annoying," I say.

"I'm sorry."

"No, I meant annoying for *you*. You had to kill almost nine hours."

"Eleven, actually."

"Really?" I'm shocked.

"I got here at five."

"And you didn't drive?"

"No. Trains, buses, on foot."

"How long did *that* take?"

"A while. I don't want to relive it."

"Sorry."

"No, I'm sorry you made an effort to get the place ready earlier."

"Haven't you seen my email since?" I ask, perplexed, still standing in the doorway.

He shakes his head. "I haven't charged my phone."

"Do you need a charger? I probably have spares."

"No, I—" His voice cuts off. "It's deliberate, to be honest," he confides reluctantly. "I'm trying to have a break from it all."

A break from *what*? Friends? Family? A *wife*? I glance down at his left hand, but there's no wedding ring on his finger. Girl-friend? Colleagues? Does he work? He doesn't look like a bum, but a month is a long time to take off. Has he got a job? Has he *lost* a job? Does he work from home?

"Did you see my Instagram post?" I ask curiously.

From the way he's been watching my mind ticking over, I think he's surprised that *this* is my question.

"What Instagram post?"

"On Seaglass's Instagram page."

He shakes his head, confused. "I haven't been online since last Friday morning."

"So the forest was all your idea." I say this quietly.

He stares down at me, his eye contact unnervingly steady. And then he gives me the slightest, smallest nod of confirmation and all my butterflies wake up, all at once, and begin to flap their wings.

He jolts and takes a step backward, as though something has awoken in him too.

"I'll leave you to it," he says. Then he turns and stalks up the road to the driveway gate.

I shakily close the door behind him, wondering why on earth the ground feels so unstable.

13

T HERE'S A MAN UPSTAIRS WHO ASKED AFTER YOU,"
Libby, my new hire, says on Sunday afternoon when I
return to Seaglass with a bag of lemons.

My heart skips a beat. *Finn?*

"What does he look like?"

"Very tall and broad."

A description I'm familiar with.

"What did he say?" I whisper conspiratorially, upending
the lemons into a bowl behind the bar. They were missing
from our regular delivery.

"He asked if you were working today."

I shrug off my raincoat and stash it under the bar.

"He's in the sofa area," she adds.

I feel nervous as I climb the stairs, and even more nervous
when I see Tom at the other end of the room, relaxing on the
sofa with a sea view, one ankle propped up on the opposing
leg's knee. A battered-looking paperback is open in one hand
and a coffee cup is in the other.

It's quite late in the day and he's the only person up here. I
peer through the serving hatch and see that the clean-down is

already underway in the kitchen. I'll probably let the staff go home early.

Tom glances over at me, straightening up and closing the paperback as I wind my way between the tables.

"Hi," he says, giving me a small smile that sets off a baffling chain reaction of fluttering inside my chest.

"Hey."

He's wearing a long-sleeve light gray T-shirt with the sleeves pushed up over his toned, tanned forearms. His faded blue jeans have almost worn through at the knees and his clothes are damp from the rain, as is his hair: I can still make out finger tracks from where he pushed his hand through the slightly longer lengths on top.

"Did you find that on the shelves?" I ask genially, nodding past him to our book-swap display with the cheerful sign I painted myself: *Help yourself, but please return or replace with another sometime!*

"I did," Tom replies, turning the book over so I can see what he's chosen.

"*The Call of the Wild* by Jack London," I read aloud. "Any good?"

"I'm enjoying it so far. Did you get caught in the downpour?" he asks as I comb my hair with my hands, trying to prevent it from frizzing.

I'm still surprised when my fingers fly through my locks and come out into thin air.

"Yeah, I had to nip up to the supermarket. It's brutal out there."

I perch on the arm of the sofa opposite him. There's a damp patch around the hem of the blue-and-white summer dress I'm wearing, but the material is so thin that it will soon dry out.

I have a sudden compulsion to sit down for a chat. I was planning to use the downtime to do social media, but it can wait.

"I'm going to make myself a cup of tea. Do you want another coffee? Or a tea?"

"Sure, I'll take a tea. Thanks."

I stand and he digs his hand into his frayed jeans pocket, pulling out his wallet.

"No, it's on me," I say.

He looks surprised. "Really?"

"Yes."

The nerves are still pulsing inside me when I return with two mugs. I don't know why he makes me feel so edgy.

"I should have asked if you wanted cake," I say, placing them on the coffee table.

"Maybe next time." He looks around as I sit down on the sofa opposite him. "It's nice up here."

"Thanks. This chill-out space has been kind of a passion project for me."

"How so?"

When I took over from Chas at Easter, the restaurant upstairs was still a bit lacking in atmosphere, despite the makeover Seaglass got last year. I thought it could do with some cozying up, so I brought in our comfy old dove-gray sofas from home and purchased new ones for my guests. We'd already stained the wood-paneled back wall a darker shade of coffee brown to match the downstairs paneling around the bar, so I gave the same treatment to a bookshelf and coffee table that I found at a charity shop. The staff and I painted the brick side walls navy blue and fixed up a bunch of randomly spaced silver shelves that we loaded with secondhand paperbacks. I also brought in some succulents in green pots for the sill of the side window and strung up festoon lighting on the walls and ceiling. They're currently bringing a warm glow to the room.

"I did a bit of renovating up here" is what I tell Tom, leaving out the lengthy explanation.

"Have you worked here long?" he asks.

"This is my seventh summer, although it's my first as manager. We batten down the hatches for winter. We've had storms that have almost taken this old girl out."

His eyebrows jump up.

"I watched one of them myself from the cliffs." I point over my shoulder at the panoramic windows facing out to sea. "The swell came right in and spray from the waves hit up here."

It's staggering when you think about it. We're currently three stories up—the lower-ground floor by the boat ramp is our cellar; it has to be cleared out every autumn because it floods.

"So this place is only open for summer?" he asks, reaching forward to pick up his mug of tea from the coffee table.

"From Easter to mid-October."

"What do you do the rest of the time?" He leans back against the sofa, crossing his ankle over his knee again and looking so much more laid-back than I feel.

"I still manage four properties, but it's not hectic, not like it is during the summer. I work every hour this place throws at me so I can take the winter off to sculpt."

"Sculpt?" Once more, his eyebrows jump.

I nod.

"You're a sculptor?"

"Yes," I say, smiling.

"What do you sculpt?"

"People, mostly."

His golden-brown eyes rest on mine, his expression warm and admiring. Now I'm the one who feels shy. I glance at the coffee table, noticing an iPhone sitting there.

"You charged your phone?"

"Yeah, last night." He reaches forward and picks it up. The screen wakes up to reveal a moody blue-gray seascape screen saver. "I've been checking out this place's Instagram account," he confesses, and I'm sure he's trying to suppress a wider smile.

"You saw my pictures?" I ask with a thrill.

"I wondered if you'd taken them."

"I manage the account. I couldn't believe it when I came into work that day and saw your tree—and the next two—*and* the forest." *And the girl* . . . "You're really talented."

He looks embarrassed by the praise. "Nah, I was only messing."

"They were incredible!" I enthuse. "Don't underplay it! But you said you're not an artist?"

He shakes his head. "I used to draw when I was younger. I haven't in years."

"Why not?"

He wrinkles his nose cutely. "I guess because my parents discouraged it."

"Why?" My thoughts divert to Mum and Dad, who always supported my choices, even if they weren't always the ones they would have made for me.

"They wanted me to get a proper job." He doesn't seem upset by this. His tone is accepting.

"And did you?" I can't resist asking.

He gives me a small nod, but doesn't meet my eyes as he opens up Seaglass's Instagram account. "I was in the Navy for a few years and then I moved to search and rescue."

His voice is low as he scrolls through the images on his screen.

"Wow! Doing what?"

"Helicopter pilot."

"That's so cool!" I eagerly lean forward. "Where? Wales?"

He glances up, but his eyes don't mirror my excitement. "Mostly the area in and around Snowdonia and the Irish Sea."

"You don't sound Welsh. Where's your accent from?"

"Norfolk."

"Ah." It's mild, only a slight lilt.

He drops his gaze to his phone again. I move the conversation along.

"We don't usually get that many comments on an Instagram post, so you *are* talented, whether you like it or not," I point out, picking up my mug and taking a sip.

He glances up and full-on *grins* at me. He's *spectacularly* attractive when he smiles.

"Did you write these posts too?" he asks, tilting his phone to show me the second of his sand-art drawings.

"Yes."

"So *you* said, 'We'd like a whole forest, please'?" He reads from his phone and lifts his eyes once more to meet mine.

"Yes."

His expression is incredulous.

"My friends and I thought you must've seen the post."

"No." He shakes his head. And then he chuckles and the sound is warm and deep and *lovely*.

"Did you see me walking along the path you'd drawn?"

I suspect that he was the man sitting up on the cliffs, but he was so far away, I can't be certain.

"I did," he confirms, sobering.

"So the girl you drew on the fourth day was supposed to be me?"

I don't know why I feel so jittery, waiting for his answer.

He nods and averts his gaze, then glances at me again, his brows knitting together. "I realized later that I probably freaked you out."

"No." I shake my head.

"I can't believe you came charging after me like that," he says with a small smile.

"I kind of couldn't help myself," I murmur, staring back at him.

After a few seconds of eye contact, I begin to feel weirdly hot and shivery. I reach for my mug, my face burning.

It's been a long time since any man has made me feel like this, but there's absolutely no denying that this is attraction in its purest form.

14

TOM AND I ARE INTERRUPTED BY BILL, OUR HEAD chef, appearing around the corner from the kitchen. "We're off now, Liv, is that all right?"

"Yes, of course."

I jump up and cross the room to where the sous-chef and KP—kitchen porter—have emerged, putting on their coats.

I follow them down the stairs. It looks dark and foreboding outside, although at least the rain seems to have stopped.

Libby is sitting on a stool at the bar, tapping away at her laptop, while our scruffy-haired runner, Seb, unpacks the dishwasher. Kwame, one of two shit-hot mixologists that I've hired, is at the other end of the bar, looking at his phone. Our waitresses are sitting at a table, chatting. The place is deserted apart from the staff, and Tom upstairs.

It's not quite 5 p.m. and we're technically open until six on Sundays, but I don't think anyone else will brave the weather tonight.

"Do the brush-down and then you can head home," I call over to the waitresses.

They jump to their feet, pleased, and make a beeline for the stairs.

"You too," I say to the bar staff. "I'll lock up."

Seb hastily puts away the last few glasses and Kwame pockets his phone.

Kwame thinks he's doing me a favor by working here, and in all honesty, he is. Seeing him flair as he mixes cocktails is a sight to behold. He's also drop-dead gorgeous with a sleeve of tattoos that drunken women are always trying to get a closer look at.

"Are you sure?" Libby asks me, checking her watch.

"I'm sure. Off you go."

Libby will appreciate the extra time at home. She's a fashion designer and makes clothes for some of the local boutiques. We're kindred spirits, working all hours in hospitality to do the thing we love best. She recently moved to Aggie with her boyfriend, Luke, our second mixologist.

Tom appears with our empty mugs.

"Sorry, I know they're putting chairs on tables up there, but we're still open. You don't need to leave," I say apologetically.

"I'm good, thanks. I was planning to head back to Beach Cottage for an early tea."

"Oh, okay. What are you having?" I ask conversationally.

"I fancy a burger, but it's not the right weather for a barbecue. I might make Mexican and freeze some."

"That sounds nice."

"You're welcome to join me." His smile is genuine, warm, and undoes something in me, but I'm embarrassed to have inadvertently invited myself over.

"Oh, I didn't mean—"

"Have you got plans?"

"No," I admit hesitantly.

"Do you eat chicken?"

"Yes." I give him a shy smile, adding, "I'd love to join you, thank you."

He waits for me while the staff pack up and leave and then I do a final check upstairs before grabbing my coat. It's still dripping wet and he notices, taking it from my hands and holding it open for me to shrug on more easily. It's such a sweet gesture. I couldn't say the last time anyone held a coat or a door open for me, which is the next thing he does.

Back at the cottage, he lets us in through the front door and into the downstairs apartment, leading the way through the living room to the kitchen-diner at the back. He flicks on the lights above the island and the overhead halogens, dimming the latter to a comfortable level. As he drops his phone and keys onto the island, a thought comes to me, along with a feeling of déjà vu: *He looks really at home here.*

"What would you like to drink?"

"Oh, let me nip upstairs and grab a bottle!" I say hurriedly, remembering my manners.

His hand shoots out and snags my wrist, bringing me to a sudden stop. "Don't be silly. I have plenty," he insists, releasing his hold. "What do you feel like?"

"Maybe a glass of wine? Red, if you have it?" My voice comes out sounding a lot steadier than I feel. My wrist is burning from where he touched it.

"Yep."

He goes to the wine rack on the other side of the dining table while I stand and look around, feeling like a spare part. On his way back to the kitchen, he pulls out a stool from under the island unit and gives me a small smile before opening a drawer, looking for a bottle opener.

"Next one down," I say, gratefully taking the seat he's offered.

He follows my instruction and pulls out the bottle opener, eyeing me contemplatively. "This must feel weird, right? Strangers in your house?"

I lift a shoulder. "I'm used to it now."

"I bet you're not. This room is so nice. You must miss it when people are staying."

I'm glad that he doesn't call me lucky, like some of my guests have. I know from the outside it must appear that I am, but this house didn't end up in my possession because I'm *lucky*.

"It is special," I agree, looking around. "Especially compared to my poky kitchen. Which you saw," I add with a smile as he pours a couple of glasses of wine and pushes one toward me. "Thanks."

I track his easy movements as he flicks on the kettle and gets ingredients out of the fridge and cupboards. His long-sleeve T-shirt hugs his body in all the right places, highlighting ridges on top of his shoulders, rippling muscles across his back and clearly defined biceps. His muscles are long and lean, in proportion with his tall, broad frame—he's not built like an ox.

"How long have you lived here?" he asks as he places a frying pan onto the stove and cranks up the heat.

I rack my brain before answering, "Fifteen years."

"How old are you?" he asks with a frown, pouring boiling-hot water over dried ancho chilies to rehydrate them.

"Twenty-eight. You?"

"Thirty-two."

"I was thirteen when we moved here," I reveal as he proceeds to dry-roast the whole garlic cloves and cherry tomatoes that he's just thrown into the frying pan.

"We?"

I swallow. "My parents passed away almost six years ago."

His face falls, his hand stilling on his way to slicing through an onion. "Oh God. I'm so sorry."

"It's okay." It's not okay, of course. "They were killed in a car crash," I reveal to save him wondering.

He looks wretched as he places the knife on the chopping board, giving me his full attention. "Is it just you?"

"I have an older brother. He lives on Stippy Stappy. You might have walked that way to the bakery and the St. Agnes Hotel—the cute row of Victorian terraces that step sideways up the hill?"

"I know the ones you mean. Are they old miners' cottages?"

"I think they were initially built for ship captains."

He shakes the contents of the frying pan and picks up his knife again, slicing the onion. "This area is so interesting."

"What brought you here?" He stiffens. "I mean, why did you choose Cornwall?" I amend hastily, sensing he'd rather not talk about *why* he's seemingly taken a month off work.

"I came here when I was a kid and really loved it," he replies, concentrating on what he's doing. "My granddad lived on the Lizard peninsula, near Helston. He'd take me to watch the Sea Kings taking off from RNAS Culdrose."

"I was sad when they stopped flying," I say of the mighty bright yellow helicopters the Royal Navy once used for search and rescue.

The service is run by a private company now. I wonder if that's who Tom works for.

"Me too," he replies, getting a blender out of the cupboard and plugging it in.

"Can I help?" I belatedly think to ask.

"No, you just relax."

I take a sip of wine and realize I *have* relaxed. I feel strangely at ease in his company, considering the almost constant underlying jitteriness that accompanies me whenever I'm with him.

"So would you say your granddad was your biggest influence?" I ask, sticking with a subject he doesn't seem to mind talking about as he sets about poaching two chicken breasts, adding bay leaves and peppercorns to the water.

I'm enjoying watching him cook.

"Yes. He was in the navy too, actually."

"How cool! My grandmother was my biggest influence."

He glances up, his eyes alight with interest. "Really?"

I tell him about how she used to take me to art galleries and museums when I was younger while he blitzes the tomatoes, garlic, and chilies along with some fresh oregano in the blender.

"I fixed your driveway gates, by the way," he says after a while.

"You did?"

"Yeah, I hope that's okay. The hinges needed tightening. I found a screwdriver in the garden shed."

"Oh! That's amazing. Thank you so much. I thought they might need oiling, but I hadn't got round to it."

"I hope I didn't step on your toes."

"Not at all." I'm struck again by a feeling of being cared for.

"Does your brother help out much?"

"Er, no." I shift on my barstool. "He's not very handy." I feel the need to explain. "He has Down syndrome."

He searches my face while frying up the onions. "Do you have any other relatives?"

"Only an uncle who lives in Spain. But we have friends," I reply. "And Michael has a personal assistant slash support worker who comes most days. She's awesome."

I live in fear of her quitting.

"That's good." I like that there's no pity clouding his eyes. His gaze meets mine frankly, and as our look holds, I feel my face warming.

He pours the contents of the blender into the frying pan and I take a shallow breath.

His phone begins to vibrate, lighting up with a picture of a stunning woman with olive skin, glossy chestnut hair, and an apple-cheeked smile.

Tom glances across at the caller ID, which reads CARA, and freezes.

"Sorry, I'd better take this," he mutters, answering the call. "Hey," he says shortly, wandering out of the kitchen and into the living room. "Yeah, the reception's not great." I can still hear him clearly. "I had my phone turned off." Pause. "*You* were the one who said you wanted space. Now you have a problem with *me* needing some?" He's speaking in a loud whisper.

I hate that I'm inadvertently eavesdropping on his one-way conversation. I feel very uneasy. It doesn't sound as though Cara is a friend. They have history.

But is she history? What if they're just on a break? My stomach lurches at the thought. I distract myself by sliding off the stool and giving the contents of the pan a stir.

"That's good news," Tom says at last, although his tone doesn't match his words. "It's not going to go through in the next three weeks, is it," he points out flatly. "No, I'll sort it when I have to." Pause. "If you *want* to put it in boxes, fine," he replies. "Okay. Okay. Bye."

He ends the calls and walks back into the kitchen, seeing me standing at the stove. "Hey!" he shouts joke-impertinently. "I have a feeling you're someone who can't sit still."

He hip-bumps me out of the way and I laugh at the maneuver as he snatches the spatula from me with a small smile.

"I'm sorry about that," he mutters as he adds some seasoning to the frying pan. "My ex," he explains. "She's had an offer on our house and wanted to run it by me before accepting."

"Recent ex?"

"We broke up a few months ago, but things had been rocky for a while. We've been living together on and off since."

"That sounds hard."

"It hasn't been fun," he agrees, checking on the chicken simmering away in the saucepan.

I'm guessing this is why he's needed to get away.

"No chance of you two patching things up?" I can't help asking as he picks up his wineglass and takes a sip.

"None whatsoever," he replies grimly, pulling out another stool from under the counter and sitting down perpendicular to me. "It's complicated," he says.

"When isn't it?" I reply, thinking of Finn.

I lift my glass before I can think too hard and knock it against his.

"To letting go and moving on."

"I'll drink to that," he replies.

15

FIVE SUMMERS AGO

"YOU CALL THIS A PEELED POTATO?" I HOLD UP THE offending vegetable.

"It'll *do*," Michael snaps, not even glancing my way.

"There's peel all over it!"

"Do you want my help or not?"

"I'm not sure that I do."

"Fine."

He throws the peeler and the potato he's been working on into the sink and stomps out of the kitchen.

"If you want something done, do it yourself!" I shout after him, losing what little patience I had.

"I don't even *like* roast chicken!" he shouts back, picking up the remote control and directing it at the television.

"You can't live off fish and chips forever," I call.

"*I can and I will!*"

He turns up the TV to a volume that renders me incapable of retorting and the sound of Jamie Dornan's Northern Irish accent fills the tiny cottage.

Really? *The Fall* at this time of the day?

Michael loves serial-killer and crime TV series like nothing else. I hate them with a passion. Trying to find something to watch that we both enjoy is a near impossibility.

We were not cut out to be housemates, I think with a sigh.

I thought it was a stroke of genius at first: rent out our parents' house for the summer and make us a killing while I move into Michael's spare room. I knew it wouldn't be a walk in the park, but I'd be popping over frequently anyway. Then Michael went and sacked his last support worker seven and a half weeks ago—not that I'm counting the days—so now he has no outside help, and neither do I.

I finish peeling the potatoes and make a start on the carrots and soon the aroma wafting from the oven begins to work as a balm for my bad mood.

Sunday lunch used to be our family tradition, a way to bring us all together around the table, something that became especially important to my parents once Michael had moved out. They continued with the weekly ritual when I was at university and I'd FaceTime in if I could. I was always expected to attend when I was at home for the holidays, and last summer Mum had made a point of asking me to avoid Sunday shifts at Seaglass. The fact that I grumbled about it fills me with the deepest regret.

My top priority last summer had been working to save up enough money so that I could leave at the end of it. I still feel guilty about that, even though Mum and Dad were none the wiser about my plan to move to London. I'm relieved I didn't tell them before the accident because I know how much I'd regret it now, but I do wish I'd made it clearer how much I loved spending time with them. I would give anything to be sitting around a table with them today, raising a glass, telling them how much I love them.

My eyes prick with tears. The anniversary of their deaths falls on a Sunday two weeks from today and I thought Michael and I could have a special lunch in memory of them. I figured I'd better get some practice at cooking roasts before then as I've never done one before, but I've had a lump in my throat all morning. This will be our first proper Sunday lunch since we lost them. I'd be even more of a wreck if my brother hadn't been winding me up.

I push these thoughts aside. I'm already blinking back tears, but I'll end up in a heap on the kitchen floor if I'm not careful, which is the last thing either of us needs. I try my hardest to hold it together around Michael. He's doing so well, much better than I am, it seems at times.

I'm just starting on the gravy when the doorbell rings, barely audible over the noise of the television. Michael presses PAUSE, but when I glance through to the living room, I discover that he's halfway up the stairs.

"Oi! Can you answer the door?" I ask irately.

"I NEED A POO!" he bellows.

I'm frozen for a second, dumbstruck by the reality of our situation, and then I put down the wooden spoon, switch off the stove, and go to the door.

My hands fly to my face in shock when I see Finn standing on the doorstep.

I'm a mess, no trace of makeup covering the dark circles under my eyes or the zit on my chin, my hair unwashed and twisted into a ramshackle bun on the very top of my head, my too-baggy jeans and white T-shirt smeared with grease because I couldn't find a tea towel, and who cares what I look like anyway?

But, oh. Finn. He looks exactly the same: tall and slim, his pale orange T-shirt washed to within an inch of its life, ripped jeans sitting just so on his narrow hips, black boots, long dark lashes, slightly crooked nose, beautiful blue-green eyes steadily holding mine from beneath those few stray strands of tousled dark hair.

"What are you doing here?" I ask with a gasp.

"I just got back," he replies softly, his eyes scanning every inch of my face.

I feel undone.

"You're visiting your family?" I ask shakily.

He nods.

"When did you arrive?"

"An hour ago."

And he came straight to see me?

I make a concerted effort to pull my hands down from my cheeks. "How did you know where I'd be?"

"Dan."

He and Amy have just celebrated their one-year-of-dating anniversary. I want to be happy for them, but all I can think about is the other anniversary that's fast approaching.

I push the thought of Mum and Dad out of my head with a violent shake because Finn has seen me cry enough tears to last him a lifetime.

"Do you want to come in?" I ask, feeling skittish at being in such close proximity to him again.

"Sure."

I step back into the living room and he pulls the door closed, taking in his surroundings. The cottage may not be at its cleanest right now, but my parents did a great job when they bought this dark little Grade II–listed terrace, updating the old-fashioned decor with a warm, bright, modern interior, stripping the floorboards and accentuating some of the original wooden features while bringing in color with the fixtures, fittings, and accessories. Colorful artwork hangs on the living-room walls, a whitewashed wooden staircase is on the left, and on the right is a yellow coffee table and two pale blue sofas facing a flat-screen TV that is far too large for the space but that Michael deemed "absolutely, definitely necessary."

"Something smells good," Finn says as he follows me into the tiny galley kitchen at the back of the cottage, and to my mind he sounds awkward, trying to carry out a normal conversation with someone who has changed so irrevocably that she might as well be a stranger to him.

"Roast chicken," I reply, opening the oven to give myself something to do and being rewarded with a faceful of steam.

I flinch and close it again. I should probably take the chicken out and let it rest soon, but it won't hurt to leave it in for a bit longer.

"Would you like a cup of tea?" I ask.

"Are you about to eat? I can come back."

"It won't be ready for a while."

"Okay, if you're sure it's not an inconvenience."

"Not at all." I fill the kettle and switch it on.

I'm finding it hard to meet his eyes.

After Finn left last summer, I fell so deep into a black hole that I couldn't imagine ever climbing out. I had asked him not to contact me—a request that was tearfully repeated on the morning of his flight home. I was simply not strong enough to endure loving someone else and losing them, or worse, never being able to have them in the first place. How could Finn ever be mine when he lived so far away? It's not as though I could leave St. Agnes and go and visit him in LA. I had to be here for Michael.

As time has gone on, I've found the will to claw my way out into the light.

I know I did the right thing in asking him not to contact me and I'm grateful that he respected my wishes. But there have also been occasions when I've resented his radio silence.

And I'm shocked that he didn't let me know he was coming.

He leans against the powder-green kitchen counter while I get down a couple of oversize purple mugs from a wooden shelf. He's looking past me at the tiny graveled patio and small lawn. A door opens onto the former, which is currently riddled with weeds, while the grass on the latter is over half a foot tall.

"Your brother's lawn is in need of murdering," he murmurs.

I snort and he smiles at me, not so widely that his dimples appear, but it sends the tiny gymnasts that resided in my stomach last summer into a frenzy of activity.

It strikes me that we were as intimate as it's possible for two people to be, yet we haven't touched since he appeared, let alone hugged.

"How are you?" he asks me quietly.

I swallow and pour hot water over the tea bags I've thrown into the mugs. "That's a big question."

Upstairs, the toilet flushes. I look up at the ceiling and meet Finn's eyes.

"Michael will be here in a moment," I say.

"I hope he had a nice poo."

Laughter bursts out of me, free and unimpeded. "You heard that?"

"It was hard not to."

His dimples are there now. I fight the urge to reach out and touch them.

He suddenly looks pained.

"What's wrong?"

He shakes his head, his eyes brightening with emotion. "You're so fucking thin, Liv."

I tense and get out the milk.

"It's not intentional," I say grimly. "I'm trying to put some weight back on."

"Can I take you out for dinner?"

"To fatten me up?"

"No." He gives me a small smile. "Although that would be a bonus. I just want to catch up properly."

"When were you thinking?"

"Tonight? Tomorrow? Now?"

"I can't go now, I'm about to eat lunch." I point out the blatantly obvious with a smile. "And anyway, look at the state of me," I add, glancing down at my stained T-shirt.

"What's he doing here?" Michael interrupts.

It's a testament to how caught up I was in Finn: I didn't even hear Michael come down the stairs and he's rarely light on his feet.

"Hi," Finn says with a little wave.

Unlike the first time they met, he doesn't offer up his hand to shake.

"What are you doing here?" Michael asks him directly.

"He's visiting his grandparents and he came to say hi," I respond curtly.

"When will lunch be ready?" he asks me.

"In about half an hour. Do you want a cup of tea?"

"No."

"You can carry on watching *The Fall* if you like."

"Are you trying to get rid of me?"

"Yes."

He huffs and walks out of the room. Finn raises an eyebrow at me, amused. Michael presses PLAY on his show and I finish up with our teas and unlock the back door. I indicate for Finn to go ahead and take a seat at the small wooden table for two before closing the door behind us so we have some privacy.

Well, as much privacy as it's possible to get when you're surrounded by neighbors' gardens, but I don't think anyone else is outside.

"How's it going, living here?" Finn asks.

"It's a total fucking nightmare," I reply.

He throws his head back and laughs and it's contagious. We eventually fall silent, but continue to smile at each other. He's so gorgeous, it hurts my heart.

"No, it's not that bad. Most of the time," I add soberly. "It's good for me to be on hand. My parents did so much—I'm a bit out of my depth."

"How long are you planning to stay?"

"Until the second week of September. That's when I've rented my parents' house out until."

His dimples fade as he nods.

It's no longer my parents' house, it's mine. They left it to me in their will, along with a letter asking me to do my best for Michael. They didn't specify exactly what doing my best constitutes—I'm still trying to figure that part out. We had talked about what would happen if they died—I knew that they'd set up a trust fund so Michael and I wouldn't need to worry about money—but none of us ever thought we'd be in this position so soon, or that we'd lose them both at once. They were only sixty-four.

I experience a flashback to the funeral. Finn sat two rows behind me with Rach, Amy, and Dan. I remember seeing him chatting to my uncle at the wake, and the thought of it now feels surreal.

I'm not sure I ever properly thanked him for everything he did.

I add it to the guilt I already feel around Finn.

"How long are you here for?" I ask.

"Just over two weeks."

"That's not very long," I say dispiritedly.

"It was the most I could get off between gigs."

"How are things going with the band?"

"Good. Our lead guitarist is still a dick, but we're beginning to get some traction. We're doing a couple of festivals later this summer."

"That's cool."

"Yeah, we've got a good live agent. We're way down the bill—you need a magnifying glass to make out the band's name—but it's a start."

I smile at him, some of my sadness evaporating. "It's a *great* start. Did you know Mixamatosis is back at Seaglass this summer?"

He nods. "With Kieran, right?"

"Yep, he's singing. They've already been there a month."

"And you still work behind the bar?"

I nod and pick up my mug.

To say that my life hasn't turned out quite how I'd imagined it is an understatement.

I take a sip, staring across the rim at the tall grass.

"You're right, that lawn really does need doing before it's beyond saving."

"Where's your lawn mower? I could do it for you now if you like?"

"You're so sweet, Finn." I give him a tender look, not really needing a reminder of how lovely he is, how surprising. "But Michael lent it to someone and claims he doesn't remember who."

Maybe he gave it away because Dad used to come over and mow the lawn every week in the summer and if Dad wasn't going to be doing it anymore, then he didn't want anyone else to be doing it either.

"How about I bring my grandparents' lawn mower over sometime? They've got a battery-operated one so it would be super easy."

"Really? That would be so helpful, thank you."

"LIV!" Michael shouts from inside. "SOMETHING'S BURNING!"

"Shit!" I jump to my feet, bumping the table hard enough to spill my tea in my hurry.

The carrots are burned to a crisp. I stare at them with dismay.

"I should probably concentrate on getting the rest of this food ready," I say waveringly to Finn, who's followed me back into the kitchen.

"Can I help you with anything?"

"No. Thank you." I gingerly place the tray on a heat-proof mat, fighting back tears. "I'd offer for you to stay, but—"

"Don't worry," he brushes me off, not noticing my expression.

I walk him to the door, blinking rapidly and trying to hold

it together. I don't want him to feel as though he has to stay and comfort me. He's already done more than his fair share of that.

"Are you free tomorrow?" he asks, turning to face me just as I recover.

"Not during the day, but I could do dinner?"

"How about we go to the Taphouse?"

"That sounds good." I'm trying to ignore the creepy-sounding serial-killer conversation spilling from the TV.

"Shall I swing by for you at seven?"

"I can meet you there."

Michael huffs and presses PAUSE.

Finn smiles at me before calling over to him, "See you soon, Michael!"

"Not if I see you first," Michael mutters under his breath, loudly enough for us both to hear him.

"Pardon?" Finn asks innocently.

I snicker and usher him out the door.

His amusement fades as we stare at each other.

"It's good to see you again," he says in a low voice, squeezing the tips of my fingers before setting off. "See you tomorrow," he calls over his shoulder.

That brief touch echoes right through to my heart.

16

FINN IS ALREADY AT THE TAPHOUSE WHEN I ARRIVE the next evening, leaning against the bar and chatting to one of the attractive waitresses, a bottle of beer dangling from his hand.

I stand in the doorway and, for a split second, consider turning around and walking right out again, but then he glances over his shoulder and clocks me, his eyes widening.

I'm wearing a sea-green halter-neck dress, one of the nicest things in my wardrobe.

I wanted to feel human.

No, I wanted to feel *pretty*.

"Hey!" he says, meeting me halfway across the room and pressing a kiss to my cheek. "You look beautiful," he says in my ear.

I breathe him in; it's the closest we've been in a year.

I have to be careful. My heart is still a mangled thing. Finn threatens to bring it to life and I'm not ready.

"Your table's this way," the waitress says amiably, grabbing two menus and leading us beneath a surfboard strapped to the ceiling to the far side of the restaurant.

Potted plants sit on the floor and hang from columns, and

neon signs and artwork adorn the vibrantly colored walls. I sit and order a passion fruit martini, my favorite cocktail on the menu.

The song playing over the sound system is familiar. I point my finger up at the speaker fixed to the ceiling, listening.

"'CCTV'!" I exclaim, thrilled that I can put a name to it.

He smiles. "'Stars of CCTV,'" he gently corrects. "Band?"

I think for a moment and then it comes to me. "Hard-Fi!"

"You've been listening to my playlist."

"A *lot*."

"Well, at least that's something," he says dryly, taking a swig of his beer and giving himself a small shake, as if to gather himself. "How's your day been?"

"Okay. Michael has been interviewing personal assistants," I disclose. "He sacked his last support worker." I laugh under my breath. "To be fair, he was a bit of a, and I quote, 'rooster.'"

"What?" he asks laughingly, leaning back in his chair.

"He once had another support worker who my mum described as a mother hen, always fussing around and bossing him about. A bit overbearing, you know? Michael wasn't comfortable with her, so my parents advertised for a personal assistant and let him choose who he wanted. Carrie was awesome—he loved her—but she moved away a few months ago, sadly, and it's been a nightmare trying to find a suitable replacement. I managed to line up help via the council, but the guy they sent was like a male version of the mother hen, hence 'rooster.'"

He gives me a sympathetic look. "I remember Carrie from the funeral. She was lovely. I'm sorry she couldn't stick around."

"Yeah, it sucks," I say dejectedly.

"So how did the interviews go?" he asks. "Did he find anyone he liked?"

I nod. "There was one woman about his age who seems promising—Hettie—but we've got one last interview tomorrow afternoon. Sorry, this is boring."

"Nothing you say is boring, Liv."

I must visibly wince, because he frowns and adds, "That wasn't a line."

"I know. Just . . . maybe don't be too nice to me," I mutter, wishing I had a drink to sip.

Finn's brows draw together. "Why would you say that?"

"Forget it. How was your day?"

"Hang on." He leans forward, his stare intense. "Why don't you want me to be nice to you?"

Thankfully, we're interrupted by the waitress returning with my drink. "Here we go," she says, putting down a coaster, followed by my passionfruit cocktail. "Are you guys ready to order?"

"Give us two secs," Finn replies.

I bury my face in my menu. I'm outwardly calm, but inwardly on edge. I look up and catch the waitress's eye, but as soon as we've placed our order, Finn leans forward.

"Spill it."

"Urgh. I told you to forget it."

"I can't do that. Why shouldn't I be nice to you?"

"Because I don't want to get too attached, okay?" I reply sharply.

He looks hurt, but I push on. "What I said last summer . . ." I take a steadying breath. "What I said about us still stands."

He frowns and reaches for his beer, taking a swig. "What

about what *I* said?" He replaces his bottle on the table with a small clunk. "Are you seeing anyone?"

"No!" I exclaim. "As if I have time for that! Are you?" My heart gives an unpleasant jolt at the thought.

"Do you think I'd be sitting here with you if I was?"

"I don't know," I reply miserably.

"I wouldn't," he says firmly, leaning forward and reaching for my hand.

I pull away from him.

"Can we not be friends?" he asks quietly.

"Friends don't hold hands," I whisper pointedly.

He smiles and snatches my hand again, lacing my fingers with his. "These ones do."

I shake my head at him, but I can't help but revel in the warmth spreading through my stomach.

17

FINN COMES OVER THE NEXT DAY TO MOW MICHAEL'S lawn. He's gone again by the time my brother arrives home from work, and it's just as well.

"What have you *done*?" Michael exclaims, looking appalled as he steps out onto the patio.

To be fair, the lawn did look a whole lot better this morning. Now it's very short, yellow, and gappy-looking. But it will grow back.

I hope.

"It needed doing," I state reasonably, approaching the woman beside him with my hand outstretched. "Hi, I'm Liv, Michael's sister. You must be Shirley?"

Shirley is the final person to interview for the position as my brother's personal assistant and she's early—she must have bumped into him on his way back down from the village. She's not much taller than Michael at just over five foot and she has a beaky-looking nose, a pointed chin, and thin black hair that doesn't quite reach her shoulders.

"Hello there," she says, tutting as she gives my hand a rough shake. "I'm guessing you didn't abide by the one-third rule?"

"What's the one-third rule?" I ask, mystified.

"Only cut off a third of your grass at any one time."

"*I* knew that," Michael interjects, rolling his eyes at me.

"Why didn't you tell me, then?" I reply a little hotly.

"I didn't know I *had* to," he replies. "I told you I didn't want it to be murdered."

"Murdered!" Shirley barks out with a laugh. "You're right! That lawn has been murdered *epically*. We're talking *Dexter* levels of serial killing, do you know what I mean?"

"Do you watch *Dexter*?" Michael asks her, his face lighting up.

"Fucking love it, mate."

I shoot Shirley a look of alarm before daring to glance at Michael.

He's beaming from ear to ear.

"I LIKED HETTIE," I say once Shirley has left, taking her accusatory attitude with her.

"Nope. Shirley," Michael replies adamantly.

"But Hettie was so warm and friendly."

"She was annoying."

"How can you say that? She was lovely!"

"Annoying," he repeats.

"Shirley seems very dry."

He nods, delighted, his fringe bouncing against his forehead.

He's refused to get a haircut over the last year. He's refused to have a shave too. My brother now has a beard and reminds me of an old-fashioned ship captain. This would amuse me except for the fact that he wouldn't look like this if our parents were still alive. Dad was so well-known for saying "Missed a bit" after Michael had shaved that Michael nicknamed his electric razor "Miss Tabbit."

"I know she'll be happy to sit and watch TV with you, but do you think she'll be good at helping with everything else?"

"What else?"

"Washing, cooking, cleaning, personal care if necessary..."

"I don't need help with any of that."

My jaw hits the floor. What have I been doing all this time, then?

"Come on, Michael. What about helping you to manage your money?"

"I don't need help with that either," he states.

"How can you—" I start with frustration. "You *do* need help remembering to pay bills!"

"No, I don't."

"Well, no, maybe not since I moved them to direct debit, but what about staying on top of the money in your account? Mum and Dad aren't around to advise you if you decide to go on a spending spree."

"I don't even *like* shopping."

"You bought your new friends—what are they called? Ronnie and Tina? Didn't you buy them a TV?"

"They're not my friends anymore," he replies, entirely missing the point. "Shirley. I like Shirley. She's *brilliant*. She can start next week too, which is good."

I'm not sure if it *is* a good thing that she has no other job to give notice to, but I know when the battle is lost.

ON FRIDAY NIGHT, I'm behind the bar at Seaglass when Finn walks in and the déjà vu makes me feel weak at the knees.

Amy and Rach are on the other side of the bar along with Dan, Tarek, and Chris, and the moment they see Finn, all five of them swarm around him, greeting him with warm hugs and enthusiastic back slaps.

The strange quiet that settles over the group when Finn presses forward to say hi to me is unnerving.

Am I that much of a buzzkill?

"Hey," he says, leaning across the bar to give me a brief squeeze.

"How are you?" I ask, aware that we still have our friends' attention.

"Good."

"Did you make it to the beach today?"

"No. Tyler wanted to go surfing at Perranporth and I didn't, so he flipped out and refused to move from the TV."

"Sounds fun."

Chas comes over to say hi.

"Is this one bothering you again?" he asks me jokily, nodding at Finn before shaking his hand.

There's a girl in my area waiting to be served, but when I make a move toward her, Chas pats my back to let me know that he'll handle her order.

He has really looked out for me since Easter, when I returned to work at Seaglass. I guess you could say that I was over the worst of my grief by then, but it still knocks me off my feet sometimes and Chas is always sympathetic. I've often found myself having a chat with him after service. He's been a rock. I always used to think of him as being like a cool uncle to the young people around here, but in the last few months, he has genuinely felt like family.

"Did Shirley say yes?" Finn asks me.

Finn and I caught up two days ago for a coffee and I filled him in on the situation with Michael's personal assistant.

"She starts Monday," I reply with a resigned smile.

"Have you two seen each other already this summer?" Amy interjects, joining us.

"Yes," I reply.

She looks taken aback. "When?"

"A few days this week. Why?" Finn asks.

Amy's eyebrows jump up and she glances at Rach, who's looking equally surprised.

"No reason," Amy replies with a bright smile.

I frown at her before turning back to Finn.

"Can I get you something?"

"Déjà vu," he replies with a grin.

"You're telling me."

Out of the corner of my eye, I see that Amy and Rach are still glued to our exchange. I flash them a perturbed look, wondering why on earth they're looking so pleased with themselves.

Rach is still working at the surf shop up in the village and spending most of her free time swimming and surfing, so not much has changed where she's concerned, but at the end of last summer, Amy landed a job on the neonatal unit at the Royal Cornwall Hospital.

It felt strange agreeing to come back to Seaglass when Chas asked me—especially when I knew Amy wouldn't be joining me behind the bar. But I like it here. I feel safe with Chas and I enjoy the buzz of being rushed off my feet; it doesn't allow time for thoughts.

I haven't felt any compulsion to sculpt since losing my parents. I still remember those hours I spent with my grandmother at the kitchen table, creating creatures out of Plasticine. I used that type of non-drying modeling material and wax for years, but the first time I pushed my hands into a mass of soft, real clay straight out of the earth, it was as though something inside me settled.

Sometimes I have an inner restlessness, a snake that slithers and twists and can wrap me up in knots. But when I'm sculpting, when my fingers are enveloped by this cool material that I can manipulate and bend into shape and press into form, that snake coils itself up and goes to sleep.

Clay will help soothe my soul when I'm ready, but I don't want to rush it. Art isn't something that you can force. Sculpting is my passion, not my duty; it will come back to me when it's ready.

In the meantime, I plan to work as many hours as I can and save enough money to see me through the winter once the tourists pack up and go home.

It's not a long-term plan, but it's the only plan I'm capable of forming right now.

18

PUSH THE KEY INTO THE LOCK AND TURN, ENTERING with a loud exhale. The silence and stillness are unnerving. There was a family of four staying here at Beach Cottage this week, and for a moment I allow myself to picture what that must have looked like: the sunshine spilling through the window onto the kitchen table, a mother and father and their children eating their breakfast, beginning their day in the most mundane of ways. Showers running, people getting dressed, the sounds of talking, giggling, and complaining reverberating along the corridor and hallway.

I need to get this over and done with as quickly as possible.

Stripping the beds and setting the washing machine going, I move on to tackle the bathrooms. I'm scrubbing my third toilet of the day when my phone buzzes.

It's probably Amy. I've been dealing with a Spanish Inquisition from her all morning. She can't seem to accept that Finn and I are just friends, that I don't want to take things further. I'm not even sure *he* would, given half the chance. My life is messy and complicated and I'm not the same girl I was a year ago. Who would want to get caught up in *that*?

Despite my protestations, my heart leaps when I pull out my phone and see that the message is from him: Coffee break?

Smiling, I tap back: I'm at my parents' place.

I know. Open the door, he replies.

I rush downstairs, grinning at the sight of him standing on the doorstep with two takeaway coffee cups in his hands.

"Where did you get those?" I ask with delight.

"Café next to Seaglass."

"You're so lovely. Thank you."

"Can I come in?"

I step back, disconcerted by the way my insides have lit up.

"What are you doing here?" I ask, accepting a coffee.

"I wondered if you wanted any help."

"Don't you have anything better to do?"

"Not really."

I smile and lead the way into the kitchen. Of course, in reality, the sun only streams through the window in the afternoon; my imagination conjured up something impossible when I pictured that happy family of four eating breakfast. It's a tendency I've always had, leaning toward the things that feed my pain.

"This is such a cool room," Finn says, looking around at the extension.

He saw it in the aftermath of my parents' deaths, but that was hardly the time to appreciate it.

"Have you done much to the house to get it ready for rentals?" he asks.

"You want a tour?"

"I'd love one."

We carry our coffees with us as I show him the spare room, which is tucked around the corner of the stairs and has a window facing onto the street, and point out the laundry and cloakroom, which opens up onto a second hallway and a side door that accesses the garden and driveway.

The main hallway used to be the living room in the original cottage and it still has a fireplace, but it's no longer in use and my piano is backed up against it.

Finn runs his fingers across the keys.

"Do you play?" I ask, pausing.

He nods. "Only self-taught, though. I bet you did grade exams, didn't you?" he asks with a smirk.

"Yes," I admit.

"How far did you get?"

"Eight." I stopped taking lessons when I was fifteen, when Gran died.

"Play me something."

"No, *you* play *me* something. I'm the one who needs cheering up."

His eyes widen and his dimples appear. "Emotional blackmail!"

I laugh and pull out the stool, perching at one end and patting the space beside me.

"Do you want to hear something I've been working on?" he asks a little hesitantly, sliding onto the stool beside me and passing me his coffee cup to hold.

"A song?" I ask excitedly. "For your band?"

"No, for me."

"I didn't realize you wrote."

"Of course I write. I write for the band first and foremost, but I also write for myself, the sort of stuff we wouldn't play."

"Like what?"

He places his long, slender fingers on the keys and after a moment's pause begins to play a lilting, melancholy tune. I can barely breathe as I sit there soaking it up. He stops playing abruptly just as my nose begins to prickle.

"Why did you stop?" I ask.

"That's as far as I've got."

"It's beautiful."

His eyes are cast downward, and I'm mesmerized by the glint of turquoise beneath his dark lashes.

"Does it have lyrics?" I ask.

"A few. But I'm not going to sing them." He casts me a bashful grin. "Come on, show me upstairs." He nudges my leg and stands up.

We head up the stairs to Michael's old bedroom, which faces onto the street; it's neat and tidy, with twin beds for holiday rentals. Opposite, on the other side of the corridor, is a large family bathroom, and then I'm opening my bedroom door.

"Still looks pretty much the same," he notes, and suddenly the space feels very small.

I close the door and move on to the last room at the end of the corridor, which used to belong to my parents. It has the best light of the upstairs rooms, with windows facing out to the garden on three sides.

"It must have been so hard, clearing everything away for rentals," Finn murmurs, looking around.

"You have no idea." I pause. "Or maybe you do."

We've never really talked about what it was like to lose his mother at the age of fifteen.

He sighs and nods. "I probably have a better idea than

most, but we didn't own our place. And I had some help clearing out Mum's things."

"Your grandparents?"

"Yeah. Did anyone help you?"

"My uncle offered when he came from Spain for the funeral, but I wasn't ready to do it then."

"Of course you weren't."

"And Michael came over a few times, but I don't think either of us is very good at handling the other's grief. If I got upset about something, it would set him off and vice versa. In the end, I figured it would be easier if I just cracked on by myself. He didn't seem to mind." I tilt my head to one side. "You said you didn't want to go to the beach at Perranporth yesterday. That's where you used to live, right?"

"Yep," he replies tersely, walking over to the window and staring down at my converted studio. "I keep trying to psyche myself up."

"Do you want someone to go with you?" I ask.

He looks over his shoulder at me. "Who?"

"Me?" I slide my back down the wall and sit on the floor, patting the space next to me in invitation.

His lips curve into a small smile and he shrugs, sitting down opposite me instead, his back resting against the bed. "I don't know. Maybe next year."

"You're coming back again, then?" I ask with a grin.

"Guess so." He smiles and stretches out his legs so they lie on either side of mine. "Do you reckon you'll be here?" He knocks back the last of his coffee.

I let out a snort. "I'm not going anywhere."

"Why not?"

"How can I?" I reply with a frown. "Who would look after Michael?"

"Shirley?"

"No, he needs family around. I can't desert him."

We fall silent.

"So what will you be doing next summer?" he asks, looking around the room.

"God knows. I can't imagine living with Michael again. He lost it with me this morning after I walked in on him in the kitchen, doing his laundry in his underpants. I squawked and told him to put some clothes on and he shouted that it was his house and if he wanted to do his laundry in his underpants, then he bloody well would."

Finn chuckles.

"My parents always said that he liked his independence, but he was over at our house so much that I didn't really believe it. Now I'm grossly aware that I'm in his space, getting in his way. He's so cross with me all the time. The sooner I can come back and live here, the better. But I don't need all this room, and yet I couldn't bear to sell this house. I don't know what to do."

Downstairs, the washing machine beeps to let me know it's finished its cycle.

"I need to put the next load in or the sheets won't be ready in time," I say, getting to my feet.

Finn follows me back downstairs.

"Have you ever thought about converting this place?" he asks.

"In what way?"

"You could convert it so you only rent out the downstairs space and then you could live upstairs during the summer, only using the rest of the house when you don't have people here."

"But then it would only be a one-bedroom for rentals."

"Do you really need this side-door access?" he asks as we head into the wide corridor off the laundry. "If you could fit a washing machine in the kitchen and make the kitchen door your main access to the garden and driveway, you could lose the laundry and cloakroom and turn this whole space into a kids' room with bunk beds."

I take a moment to look around.

"And you could convert the big main hallway with the front door into two entrance spaces, one that goes straight up the stairs to your apartment and another that works for guests. Upstairs, you could convert the big bathroom into a kitchen and turn Michael's or your parents' room into a living room."

My mind is spinning at the possibilities he's opened up.

"Did you ever think about becoming an architect?" I ask, beyond impressed.

"I never allowed myself to dream about that sort of thing," he mutters, averting his gaze. "But you should ask Tarek."

"Tarek?" I'm caught on the look on his face a moment ago, echoes of what Mum told me playing in my mind: *His mother was a very troubled soul.* I hate that he didn't feel he could dream when he was younger. I want to wrap my arms around him, but I resist the impulse.

"He's at university doing his Architecture Part 2, and he works part-time for a practice in Truro."

"I forgot that he was training to be an architect," I say. "We had a whole conversation about it at one of his and Dan's house parties."

The washing machine starts to beep again and Finn reaches past me to turn it off.

"Thank you," I say, squeezing his arm and prompting him to look at me. "You've really given me something to think about."

Something positive for a change.

19

I'S SATURDAY, ONE WEEK LATER, AND I'M AT WORK, GLAD
to have a distraction from the swiftly approaching anniversary of my parents' deaths.

I'm cooking Sunday lunch tomorrow to mark the occasion
and I'd hoped that the experience I'd gained might mean that
Michael and I would be able to relax together and share some
fond memories of Mum and Dad.

But then he went and invited Shirley, as well as Timothy, a
friend he met years ago at a social club for people with special
educational needs. My parents used to take him three times a
week, but he hasn't wanted to go since we lost them. He's still
in touch with a couple of his friends, though, and of them,
Timothy is the closest.

Tomorrow is going to be tough no matter what, but it will
be even tougher if I have to entertain people I hardly know,
though I'm glad Michael is reaching out to his friends. I just
want to climb into bed and spend the whole day with my head
under the covers. I'll be relieved when it's over.

Sometimes I wonder how Michael is experiencing his grief.
He cried when Mum and Dad died, and I've seen him cry
many times since, but he seems to bounce back from bouts of

sadness very quickly, so his periods of anguish seem shorter and more transient. He lives in the present, concerning himself mostly with what's happening today or tomorrow or next week. He looks forward, not backward, and he has an enviable ability to leave the past more or less in the past.

But occasionally he'll say something that reminds me that of course he is hurting too.

This evening, as I was leaving the cottage, he told me that he misses the Austin-Healey.

It was the classic car our parents were driving when they were killed.

His statement knocked the air out of my lungs. Even now, as I think about it, I'm fighting back tears.

"Why don't you call it a night, love," Chas says to me, rubbing my back. "Go on, we can manage here."

"Thank you." I'm blinking rapidly as I grab my bag and sling it over my shoulder.

Mixamatosis are performing their last song and the space around the stage is packed. Finn is somewhere in the middle of the crowd, watching them.

I try to swallow the lump in my throat as I push my way to the front door. I'm halfway down the steps before the despair welling up inside my chest becomes all-consuming. I want to go home, but I can't. *My* home, I mean. I don't want to return to Michael's.

On impulse, I veer right toward the beach, the sounds of Seaglass carrying through the night air behind me. A cheer goes up as the last song comes to a raucous end, and a few moments later the stereo begins to pump out another rock song.

My phone vibrates in my bag.

"Where did you go?" Finn asks when I answer it, his voice muffled by the bass thumping around him.

"I'm at the beach," I reply.

He ends the call and I turn around, watching with tears in my eyes as he jogs down the stairs and strides in my direction.

"It's the anniversary of their deaths tomorrow," I tell him in a choked voice as he reaches me, pulling me to his chest.

He cradles the back of my head with his hand and holds me close as I cry.

"I told you not to be nice to me," I mumble against him after a while.

"Shut up," he mutters, releasing me.

We walk in silence toward the shoreline.

"How's Michael feeling about tomorrow?" he asks.

"It's hard to know. He answers 'fine' to everything. Well, no, sometimes he'll tell me that he's 'not great,' but in the past 'not great' has meant that he's in terrible pain and needs to be hospitalized for a chest infection, so that says it all, really."

I still remember my parents relaying to me how much he'd downplayed that chest infection. It's another warning I know I need to heed in case it happens again.

Finn takes my hand and squeezes it, giving me encouragement to go on.

"Earlier he told me that he misses Dad's Austin-Healey."

He glances across at me. "That's the car they were driving?"

I nod, my face crumpling. He comes to a stop and tries to pull me into his arms again, but I wrench myself away.

"If they'd been driving their BMW, they probably would have survived."

A stillness comes over him.

"What are you trying to say?" he asks warily.

We never spoke about it. I couldn't bring myself to voice my suspicions out loud, but then I read the police report and did some research and my worst fears were confirmed. The guilt has intensified, poisoning me.

"They weren't driving their BMW." I bite back another onslaught of tears. "*I* was. I took us to the festival in it."

"Please don't tell me you blame yourself," Finn says with horror, and then his expression transforms into shock. "Do you blame *me*?"

"I blame us," I whisper. "If I hadn't been so into you, they'd still be alive."

He shakes his head fervently. "Fuck, Liv, no. Please don't say that. Please don't *do* that."

"I can't help it!" I cry.

"Fuck!" he says again, stepping away and raking his hand through his hair. He stares at the ocean with a bleak look on his face.

I should send him away to punish myself, but all I've done in the past two weeks is get closer to him.

I'll pay my penance in the pain I'll feel when he leaves.

I walk forward and slip my arms around his waist, resting my cheek against his back. He slowly places his hands over mine.

"I'm so lonely, Finn. My grief is so big and I feel so small and there's no one to share it with."

He hangs his head.

"Will you stay with me tonight?" I whisper against his soft T-shirt, almost too scared to ask.

"I fly back to LA on Monday," he replies hoarsely.

"I don't mean to . . . I just . . . I don't want to be alone. Will you hold me? Please?"

I sense his hesitation, but I'm gratified when he nods.

MICHAEL'S COTTAGE IS dark and quiet when we enter. I'm conscious of every beat of my heart as we creep upstairs and into my room. I gather my pajamas and head to the bathroom while Finn sits on the edge of my bed.

He's under the covers when I return to the room, and when I pull them back and slip inside, I see that he's stripped down to his boxer shorts. He opens up his arms and I snuggle in close, and after a while, some of my sadness seeps away.

20

I WAKE UP ON THE ANNIVERSARY OF MY PARENTS' deaths feeling as though I've drunk down grief and it's solidified inside me like plaster, setting in a twisted, mangled form. There is nothing beautiful about it; it's pure pain.

Finn starts awake beside me.

"Hey," he whispers, reaching out to me.

I swallow and swallow, emotion gathering like a storm inside my chest. I need to cry, but once I start, I don't know if I'll be able to stop and the last thing I want to do is wake Michael.

"Get dressed," Finn orders, climbing out of bed and reaching for his jeans. "Let's go for a walk."

TEARS STREAM DOWN my cheeks as I follow him along a narrow path banked on either side by tall, prickly brambles and feathery ferns. We round a curve in the track and up ahead is the ocean, steel gray under the lightening sky. Heading off on the left-hand fork, we walk in silence past trees so bent and broken by the wind that their insides look as though they've been scooped up and spat out.

I feel like one of those trees: hollow, but still living. Half-dead, half-alive.

The line between the sea and sky is almost indecipherable and it's so still I can barely make out the swell of rolling waves far below.

But the farther we walk, the higher the sun rises above the horizon and the more vibrant the world around us becomes. The last time I was here, the dying ferns had turned the cliffs to the color of rust. Now it's a landscape of undulating moorland carpeted with a jewel-like crust of golden gorse, amethyst heather, and emerald bracken.

When the water's color fluctuates from aquamarine to teal and the wind picks up, Finn slows to a stop. Up ahead is a rocky outcrop, and beyond it the green cliffs roll down to an expanse of creamy-white beach.

I cast a look at Finn. He's staring straight ahead, his jaw clenched, the wind whipping his dark hair into a frenzy.

And it hits me: this is where they found his mother's clothes, where she took her own life, jumping from the cliff.

I'm *not* alone in my grief.

Is that why he's brought me here? To share my pain?

"I promise you it will get easier, Liv." He repeats what he told me last summer, his voice sounding low and tortured.

"How did you cope?" I ask with anguish at his pain—and mine. "You were so young."

"I'd already lived every day in fear, wondering how she was next going to hurt herself, hurt us. In some ways it was a relief when she chose to leave." He swallows hard and glances at me before staring at the ground. "I've never said that out loud to anyone."

I loop my arm through his and press against his side.

"Have you been back here since that day?"

It'll be nine years as of this Christmas.

He shakes his head. "I couldn't bring myself to come up here last summer."

"Why *did* you come back to Cornwall after all this time?"

"My grandparents had been begging me to for years. They've brought Liam and Tyler to the States twice, but they wanted me to get to know them, really get to know them, on their own turf. And I'm still not sure that I have," he confides.

"What do you mean?"

"Liam's all right, but Tyler . . . He's so angry. I think he's angry at *me* for leaving, as though I abandoned him too, after Mum did. But I didn't have a choice," he says jaggedly. "My grandparents didn't have room for me—their place is *tiny*. My dad was the only one who was willing to step up and be a father." He sighs. "I guess if my nan and granddad passed away anytime soon, Tyler and Liam would come and live with me."

"Wouldn't you move back here if that happened?" I ask with surprise. "If they're still at school?"

I watch his Adam's apple bob up and down as he swallows, and then his gaze reluctantly travels to mine.

"I couldn't, Liv," he says to me heavily.

"Why not?"

"It hurts, being here."

I stare at him, my heart contracting.

His eyes are dark as he implores me to understand. "I have so many bad memories of this place. My life is in LA. My dad's there, my older brother and sister, nephew, my friends and my band . . . I was broken when I left Cornwall, but LA is home now. I'm happy there."

I suddenly want to cry again. I bite my lip, fighting the impulse as he unloops our arms and puts his around my waist.

"Have you sculpted anything lately?" he asks softly.

I shake my head, swallowing. "I don't have the heart. I know it will help at some point, but I'm still too raw. I think I need to sit with the pain for a while, let it work its way out of me. Or learn how to let it become a part of me, learn to live with it."

"Will you sculpt them, do you think?"

I hesitate before nodding. "One day."

LATER THAT AFTERNOON, I'm sitting on the floor of Michael's living room with my back against the wall, laughing at a story Amy is telling us.

Today has turned out nothing like I'd imagined it. Instead of being seated alone with Michael at a table, reminiscing about Mum and Dad and trying to hold it together, we're surrounded by our friends.

When Rach and Amy heard that Michael had invited Shirley and Timothy for lunch, they asked if they could come too and insisted on bringing fish and chips from the shop in the village.

Finn is also here, and because there's not enough room for everyone at the table, we've pushed back the sofas and are all crammed together on the floor around the coffee table, even Shirley.

"Get off!" Michael snaps, batting away Rach, who has just nicked a chip from his plate.

"Sorry, that one looked particularly crunchy," she replies cheekily.

Michael cranes his neck to look at her plate. "I'll take . . . that one!" he declares, picking up a fat chip.

"Oi, that was much bigger than the one I stole," she complains.

My heart expands as I watch them. I've always loved the way my friends interact with Michael. They adore each other. The hugs Michael gave both Amy and Rach when they arrived were full of warmth.

"Shall I bring some more chips through from the kitchen?" Finn asks, knowing that we're nowhere close to consuming our quota.

"No need," Michael answers before anyone else can, stealing another chip from Rach.

I can't believe I'm actually having a good time.

This morning helped colossally. I needed to be able to grieve and now I feel an overwhelming relief because the day is almost over.

I catch Finn's eye and smile.

FINN IS THE last to leave. Michael has already gone upstairs to bed, utterly exhausted. Amy and Rach left only a short while ago, with Shirley offering to drop Timothy home to Perranporth, where he lives in an assisted living accommodation.

I'm curled up on the sofa, my head on Finn's lap. He's running his hand through my hair.

"I guess I should probably go," he says with regret.

He flies home to LA tomorrow.

I lift my head to look at him. "Stay," I request quietly.

He looks down at me, tucking a lock of hair behind my ear, and desire pulses through my lower body.

I sit up and face him.

"Stay," I whisper again, with meaning.

"I want to," he confesses, and I know from the look in his eyes that neither of us is thinking about sleep. "But if I do, it's going to make it even harder for me to go."

"I don't have the willpower to care."

He examines my face for a long moment before caressing my jaw.

"Are you sure?"

I nod.

My skin tingles as he guides me onto his lap. We stare at each other and then our mouths come together, our lips joining for the first time in a year.

It is the sweetest kiss, slow and searching, and it causes shivers to rush down my spine.

I rock against him and feel him harden beneath me. His hands drop from my waist to my hips and he pulls me closer, gasping into my mouth.

"Upstairs," I whisper.

I have no idea how we manage to keep quiet.

"I STILL DON'T think we should be in touch," I say in the cool gray hours of the early morning.

Finn rolls onto his back and stares at the ceiling, two frown lines etched between his brows.

"It's too hard," I say, sounding slightly desperate. "I don't want to be waiting around for your calls or messages, it will only prolong the pain. I'd rather know for certain that I'm not going to hear from you—a quick ripping-off of the bandage."

He pauses and then nods, turning his head to meet my eyes. "If that's what you want."

"It is." It's not. But it's for the best. "And I think you need to know that I'm not going to wait for you on the off chance that you'll come back."

"I *will* come back, Liv, but, as before, I don't expect you to wait for me."

"I don't expect you to wait for me either."

He doesn't answer, but his gaze is cool, assessing, wondering if I mean what I'm saying.

It would be unrealistic to think that he'll turn down all the girls who will be throwing themselves in his path once his band starts taking off—and I have no doubt that it will.

"But . . . if I'm single and you're single . . ." I say, letting my voice trail off.

He smiles at my attempt at flippancy and leans in, catching my mouth in a kiss. "I'll see you next summer."

21

THIS SUMMAR

"TAREK IS ILL," AMY CALLS TO TELL ME.

"What's wrong?" I ask with concern.

"He's got stomach flu."

"Poor guy."

"He can't make the pub quiz. I wondered if Luke or Libby might be up for it?"

"I doubt it. They see enough of me, working at Seaglass." I pause before saying, hesitantly, "I could ask Tom."

"Who's Tom?" she asks, and I can perfectly picture her baffled expression.

"The guy who's staying downstairs."

"The grumpy git?" she asks with alarm.

"He's actually really nice."

"*Since when?*" she squawks, her pitch climbing up several notes.

"Since Saturday when he insisted that I park my car on the drive and then helped me carry all the cleaning supplies in. He cooked me dinner last night too."

"*What?*"

I laugh and bring her up-to-date.

"He sounds positively dreamy," she remarks. "Definitely bring him."

"I'll ask him," I reassure her, smiling as I end the call.

I go downstairs and knock on the apartment door. My butterflies were half asleep when I mentioned Tom's name to Amy. They woke up fully on my way down the stairs. And when the apartment door opens and Tom's maple-brown eyes flare with surprise and pleasure at the sight of me, they fly into a kaleidoscopic frenzy.

He's had a shave. I liked his stubble, but he looks out of this world clean-shaven.

"Hi!" I say.

"Hey!"

"Are you still in the mood for a burger?" I ask brightly, giving him a hopeful smile.

TELL ME ABOUT your friends," Tom says as we climb the hill half an hour later.

"Well, there's Rach and Amy, who are my closest, oldest friends. We went to school together in Truro and they've been with me through thick and thin."

"I like them already."

I grin at him and continue. "Dan is Amy's fiancé—they've been together since we graduated from uni. He's great. And Ellie is Rach's girlfriend. They work together at Surfers Against Sewage HQ and met a couple of years ago."

"Cool," he says. "So who am I stepping in for?"

"Tarek."

He glances at me, and I can see the question in his eyes.

"He's just a friend. Dan's best mate. We all went to school together. His girlfriend hates quizzes."

I don't think I imagine the glimmer of relief on his face at my answer.

There are high winds again today, but thankfully the rain has held off for our walk up here.

He's wearing the same jeans he had on yesterday along with a navy brushed-cotton shirt that's hanging open over a white T-shirt. His sleeves are rolled up to just below his elbows.

I'm also wearing light blue jeans and a white T-shirt, but my jeans are more of a slouchy fit, sitting lower on my hips, and my T-shirt is a loose-fitting crop top, so we're hardly twinning it. A faded black boxy cropped jacket completes my look.

I'll admit, I put an unusual amount of effort into my outfit tonight. I'm hoping I look casual but sexy. I even spent time curling my dark hair into glossy, loose spirals.

We're shown to a table for six, the first to arrive. Candles are already burning on every tabletop and the atmosphere is buzzy, with lots of people tucking away food before the quiz starts.

"Thanks for coming with me," I say.

"Thanks for asking."

"I'm glad you said yes."

He moves the candle a little closer to him, his attention fixed on the flame.

"I'm not very used to my own company, to be honest," he admits.

"Have you been lonely?"

His eyes lift to look at mine and he gives me the smallest shrug. "A bit."

"You can knock on my door for a cuppa anytime. Or pop down to Seaglass—I'm never far."

His lips tilt up at the edges. "Thanks."

My attention keeps getting drawn back to his toned forearms and I almost jump out of my skin when Amy calls, "We're here!"

Her eyes rove between Tom and me. She looks like the Cheshire Cat.

"Hello!" I slide out from the table as Dan appears.

Tom stands up and waits to be introduced while I quickly hug my friends and turn to them.

"Guys, this is Tom. Tom, this is Dan and Amy."

"Hi!" Amy gushes, standing on her tiptoes to embrace him. She shoots me a look of pure glee as she withdraws.

Before we can sit down, Rach and Ellie arrive, so we go through another round of introductions.

"Fucking hell," Rach growls in my ear as I give her a brief squeeze.

I flash her a warning look before greeting Ellie.

Ellie is so pretty. She's not much taller than Rach at about five foot five and she has dead-straight jet-black hair, courtesy of her Japanese heritage on her mother's side.

For a long time after she and Rach started going out, Rach looked as though she wanted to pinch herself every time she glanced at her new girlfriend.

Ellie gets a similar look on her face when she watches Rach surf. My friend is spectacular on the waves.

She's spectacular always.

We take our seats. I forgot to warn my friends not to delve too deeply into Tom's reasons for coming to Cornwall, as he's seemed reluctant to talk about it, so I'm on edge as they ask him about what he does and why he's here. He gives them more or less the same explanation he gave me, managing to avoid a more in-depth interrogation. By the time our burgers arrive, we've all relaxed into our usual casual banter.

Eventually the quiz master's voice comes over the sound system to welcome everyone and the loud chatter around the restaurant quietens to a hushed murmur. Tom is opposite me and gives me an amused smile that zips straight down my spine.

Amy has her pen poised. The bar falls quiet as the first question is read out.

"What is the sinus node and what is its function?"

Everyone around the table stares at each other blankly, except for Tom, who leans forward and whispers to Amy: "It's the heart's natural pacemaker. It generates electrical impulses to set the rhythm and rate of a healthy heart."

She furiously scribbles it down.

"How did you *know* that?" Dan asks Tom with astonishment.

"You pick up things when you work in search and rescue," he replies with a shrug.

"I'M SORRY, BUT *how* hot?" Amy asks aloud when Tom and Dan have gone to the bar to restock our drinks during the break.

She gives me a meaningful look. "You need to tap that, right now."

I snort. "I don't think so."

"Why not? The man is sex on legs—*and* he's smart. I think this might be the first time we'll ever get into the top three."

"He *is* smart, isn't he?" I wriggle with pride.

"I mean, a search and rescue fucking helicopter pilot, Liv?" Rach interjects. "Could there *be* a sexier job?"

Ellie grins at her. "I can't think of one."

"Does this mean we can start playing good songs again?" Rach asks.

"You're getting carried away," I reply.

"Am I? I bet he's a tiger between the sheets."

"I doubt he'll be jumping into bed with anyone anytime soon," I say, involuntarily squeezing my knees together. "He's only quite recently come out of a serious relationship. Plus I saw a photo of his ex-girlfriend. She was a stunner."

"You're a stunner," Amy points out loyally.

"It can't have been that serious," Rach says. "And he's clearly over it now."

"Why do you say that?" I ask.

"Because he can't take his fucking eyes off you," she points out.

I feel myself growing hot as I glance at Amy and Ellie.

"It's true," Amy says with a grin, while Ellie says, "She's right."

Rach leans forward. "And you seem to like him too."

"How could I not? He's gorgeous."

And kind, and caring, and oddly protective of me, even though we've only known each other for a few days.

Rach turns to Amy with a smug look. "You might be able to put Brit Easton on your wedding playlist after all."

"Shush!" Amy snaps at her, throwing an awkward glance in my direction.

I'm plagued by a sudden bout of nausea at the mention of the pop star's name.

"What's this?" I ask warily.

"Amy has been playing 'We Could Be Giants' on repeat," Rach reveals. "She loves that song and is too scared to tell you."

"Stop causing trouble," Ellie berates her girlfriend with a frown, while Amy looks as though she wants the floor to swallow her up.

Tom and Dan come back with our drinks and I try to force a smile onto my face, but I can't stop thinking about the song.

Or the woman who sings it.

And especially not the person who wrote it.

22

IT'S FAIR TO SAY THAT I AM VERY TIPSY INDEED. I HIT THE prosecco after Tom and Dan came back from the bar and then we won the drinks voucher and they went and got a second bottle. The bubbles have gone straight to my head.

"I can't believe we won!" I exclaim as I try to walk straight on the steep hill down to Beach Cottage.

"I can't believe you knew which Mr. Men characters wear shoes," Tom replies.

I laugh. "Mr. Silly and Mr. Noisy were easy, but I was pretty pleased with Mr. Chatterbox." We only had to name three out of nine. "How did you know that Edinburgh was farther north than Vancouver and Moscow?" I reach over and shove his arm, proud as punch.

"It's bloody close."

"Still, I went to Edinburgh and I never would have guessed. Did you go to university?" I ask.

"Leeds," he replies.

"To do what?"

"Aviation."

"Did you always know you wanted to fly?"

"It was my only passion other than drawing."

I may not be at my most coherent right now, but it's impossible to miss the melancholy in his voice.

As soon as we fall silent, my head begins to spin.

"Are you all right?" Tom asks.

"Gravity really, *really* wants me to cartwheel."

"Do you want to take my arm?" he asks with a small laugh.

I cast him a look and screw up my nose, not wanting to embarrass myself.

But embarrass myself is exactly what I do because the sideways glance throws me off-balance.

"Shit, Liv, you almost fell in the stream!" he gasps, grabbing my arm and hauling me back onto the road.

"Oh God," I mutter, mortified. "I don't usually drink that much."

"You obviously needed to let your hair down," he says with a chuckle.

The comment brings back memories of the summer after I'd left university.

Tom puts his arm around my shoulders and suddenly that's *all* I'm thinking about.

"Is this okay?" he asks cautiously, peeking down at me.

"More than," I reply, leaning into him a little. I steady myself further by putting my arm around his waist and my free hand on his chest. He's so solid and strong and steady. I feel very confident that he'll keep me upright. "Do you go to the gym?"

I'm going to regret blurting that out tomorrow.

He huffs out a laugh. "There's equipment at work. There wasn't much else to do while we were waiting for a call."

"So you just sat there and lifted weights all day?"

"Not quite," he replies with amusement. "During quiet

spells, if we weren't team training, I'd cook, sleep, read, work out, sometimes even play the piano."

"There's one at your work?"

"Our building is like a home away from home. You have to be on call for over twenty-four hours at a time."

"I have a piano upstairs!"

"I know. I've heard you playing."

"Have you?" I pull a face at the thought.

"What? You're good."

"No, no." I shake my head. "I won't be able to play now that I know someone's listening."

"Don't stop. I like it."

"You haven't even turned on the TV. What are you doing down there? Sorry, that was rude. I'm a rude, rude landlady."

I feel his low laugh vibrating against my palm. We're walking like we're a couple, and I feel oddly safe. I'm surprised by how much I'm allowing myself to enjoy this simple contact without spinning out, but then, I have sunk a quarter of my weight in fizz.

"I've been doing a lot of reading since I've been here," he confides. "I don't know why, but I haven't really felt like watching TV."

"You don't listen to music or the radio either."

"I listen to you playing the piano."

"Sorry, the sound really carries, doesn't it? But I'm not playing it that much."

"No, you're not," he agrees.

"And usually my guests are out of the house a lot more."

"I've gone out for loads of walks!" he protests.

"Did you take lessons?" I ask with a smile up at him.

He nods down at me. "You?"

"Yep."

"Grade eight?"

"How did you know? Where did *you* get to?"

"Same."

"Oh my God, we have so much in common!"

I feel his low laugh against my palm again, but it's true, we do.

Finn and I also had playing the piano in common, and Finn used to draw when he was at school. I wonder if I'm attracted to Tom because of his similarities to Finn or if it's his differences that I like.

I'm too drunk to go down that particular rabbit hole. I'm not sure I'll ever be sober enough, actually.

"Why have you stopped drawing on the beach?" I ask out of the blue.

We walk a few more paces before he answers. "It was easier when it was anonymous. A bit like you playing the piano when you thought no one was listening."

My face falls. "I can't believe I ruined sand art for you."

He glances down at me with a smile.

"Please don't stop drawing on the sand because of me," I beg. "If you want a more secluded beach where fewer people are likely to watch, you could walk along the cliff to Trevellas Cove."

The beach is a bit pebbly, but there's more than enough sand to create something meaningful, if not a forest on the scale of his last one.

"Maybe I'll go in the morning if the rain holds off."

"Can I come and watch you at work?" I ask eagerly.

He throws his head back and laughs and it's as though someone has upended another bottle of prosecco directly into my stomach.

I love the sound of his laugh, and his smile is glorious. Lovely lips and nice teeth: straight and white but not completely uniform.

Shit, I've been staring at his mouth and he's noticed.

"What's the point of me going to another beach if you're going to watch me anyway?" he asks, looking down at me.

"Oh. I didn't think of that. But I'd really love to watch you at work. What do you use? I mean, what tools?"

"I borrowed a rake from your garden shed, actually."

"You *definitely* have to let me watch you then!" I exclaim, slapping his hard chest. "I'm part of your process!"

"We'll see," he says gently, lifting his chin to indicate something up ahead.

I'm gutted to realize that it's Beach Cottage.

"Are you going to be all right?" he asks, releasing me and opening the front door with his keys before holding it back for me.

"Yeah, I'll fall straight into bed," I reply, feeling dejected as I duck under his arm.

"Drink a pint of water first."

I dig out my keys and salute him, unlocking the door.

He waits until I'm over the threshold of my apartment before entering the hall.

"Thanks again for coming," I say, turning to face him.

He gives me a warm smile, his golden eyes shining under the ceiling light. "It was fun. Ask me again sometime if anyone drops out."

"I will. Night, Tom."

"Night, Liv."

I close the door on the crushing thought that "sometime" will probably be "never." He'll be gone in less than three weeks and then I'll have new guests staying in the downstairs apartment.

I walk up the stairs feeling cold and miserable and oddly untethered without the weight of his arm around my shoulders.

Why do I keep doing this to myself? Why can't I meet a nice local boy, someone who isn't going to up and leave me at the end of their holiday?

23

FOUR SUMMERS AGO

W HAT THE FUCK?" RACH SAYS WHEN I SHOW HER the latest creation to be etched onto the foam on top of my latte.

"Elephant?" I ponder, sounding dubious as we carefully wind our way between holidaymakers, trying not to kick sand onto their patchwork of colorful beach towels.

Where have all these people *come* from? Where have they *parked*? They surely can't all be staying in St. Agnes.

"That's not a fucking elephant, Liv. That's a cock and balls."

"Shh!" I say, unable to keep from laughing, even as I flash a concerned look at some nearby children.

Thankfully they're too caught up in their sandcastle to pay my foulmouthed friend any attention.

"He's trying to show you what you're missing out on," Rach teases, shoving my arm.

"If this is it, I'm not sure I want it."

"I don't know. I mean, that's a hefty length."

"Stop!" The tears collecting in my lower lashes finally break free.

It's been about two weeks since the good-looking, blue-eyed barista at the café next to Seaglass started getting artistic with my coffee. He began with birds—simple seagulls flying in the sky—but my face must've lit up as he slid the cup toward me because he gave me the sweetest smile and I felt his eyes on me the whole time I was paying up.

When I next went in, he drew the profile of a plump little bird on top of my latte.

"Sparrow?" I asked with a smile.

"I think it might be a robin," he replied in an Australian accent.

"Cute."

From birds, he graduated to an outline of a cat, following it up with a dog.

"You should have started with a fly and a spider," I joked.

He cocked his head to one side, amused but perplexed.

"The old lady who swallowed a fly?" I prompted. "You don't remember that rhyme?"

"Oh, yeah!" he exclaimed, full-on grinning at me. "My nan used to sing it to me."

"Was this back in Australia?"

"Accent give me away, did it?" he asked, his eyes full of humor as he pushed his beach-blond hair back off his face.

Total surfer vibes.

"Just a bit. Where are you from?"

"Sydney."

"Are you here for the summer?"

"At least. I'm on a year out, but so far I'm liking Cornwall." He grinned and folded his arms across his chest, an action that made his biceps pop.

I felt oddly unstable as I walked out, as though the concrete floor had turned to sand.

Yesterday, he asked me what my favorite animal was. I said

a giraffe. He took a bit longer with that one and it wasn't a complete success—he went with a face instead of a whole body and it looked more like a cow than anything—but we both had a bit of a laugh and I left saying that I couldn't wait to see what he came up with tomorrow.

"Something good, I promise," he called after me.

And lo and behold . . .

"What did you do when he handed it over?" Rach wants to know as she lays her towel out on the sand.

"Blushed."

"And then what?"

"That girl he works with burned her hand on the panini-maker so he rushed over to help," I reply as she removes her Sam Fender tour T-shirt, revealing her army-green tankini top underneath.

She's worn the death out of that tankini.

"Go back and ask him what it is," she suggests as I balance my coffee cup on the sand.

"No! It's an elephant! Of *course* it's an elephant."

I pull my yellow summer dress over my head and kick off my flip-flops, looking around for my hot-pink beach bag.

I realize I've left it in the café at the same time that I spy the barista striding toward us with it clutched in his hand.

"Sorry! Thank you!"

"No worries," he replies, handing it over and shielding his eyes from the sun.

"How's your coworker's hand?" I ask, wishing I hadn't been quite so quick to strip down to next to nothing. I'm in a lilac bikini, but still.

"She'll live."

"Hi," Rach calls over.

I whip round and pin her with a look of warning.

"I'm Rach," she says, avoiding eye contact with me as she leans back on her hands. "I've been admiring your artistry."

"Oh, thanks," he replies.

"Are you an artist in your spare time?" she asks.

He chuckles and scratches the sandy-blond stubble on his jaw. "Er, no. Not much of one, anyway, as Liv can probably confirm."

"How do you know my name?" I ask with surprise.

His tanned face takes on a pink hue as he replies, "I might've asked around."

Rach looks as though she's about to spontaneously combust.

"I'm Brendan," he introduces himself.

"Hi," I reply shyly.

"Are you up to anything later?" Rach interrupts.

Rach! WTF?

"No," he replies, glancing at me.

"We're having a surprise birthday party for a friend. The more the merrier—bring a mate if you like."

"Oh. Okay, cool." He's taken aback, but not unpleasantly surprised.

"Liv will text you the details," she adds, lying flat out and turning her sunglasses-clad face up to the sun.

I laugh under my breath at her tactics and get my phone out of the zipped pocket inside my beach bag. "What's your number?"

I'M TOO AMUSED by my friend's brazenness to give her much stick, but later that day, my stomach is writhing with nerves as we pull into the Chapel Porth car park. It's been a long time since I've had anything close to a date and I'm not even sure if that's what this is.

"Relax," Rach says firmly, yanking my hand away from my face.

"I can't!"

I really want to bite my nails.

"You need this," she states.

"Do I?" I ask uncertainly, fighting the urge to fidget.

"Yes, you do."

"How old is he anyway? He said he's on a year out. Does he mean a year out after university?"

"Who cares? So what if he's younger than you? That boy is all man."

"What?" I glance at her with bafflement.

"You know what I mean. You like him, otherwise you'd be getting your coffee for free from Seaglass."

"Yes, but Beach Café does pastries."

As my increasingly curvy waistline can attest to.

"*And* eye candy," she adds pointedly. "Don't tell me you haven't been enjoying a hit of *that* along with your morning croissant."

"I prefer the pain aux raisins."

"Shut the fuck up and get out of the car."

It's Dan's birthday and Amy has arranged for a bunch of us to hide out in a cave while she takes him for an early dinner at Blue Bar in Porthtowan, the next village along, after which they'll go for a romantic stroll along the beach. We'll leap out and scare the living shit out of him and then get very drunk together.

It's a solid plan, apart from the fact that we only have a window of about three hours before the incoming tide will cut off our escape route. The tide comes in very fast here and is extremely dangerous, so someone had better keep their wits about them.

Rach and I intend to walk home and collect the car in the morning before the car park charges kick in.

"Is Michael working tomorrow?" Rach asks as she pops the trunk to release the party paraphernalia we brought with us.

"Yes, but I wouldn't rely on him to do a Pay and Display for you, if that's what you're thinking."

"That's exactly what I was thinking."

Michael still works for the National Trust at Chapel Porth as a parking attendant, a job he loves because he's a total car nut and he gets to see all sorts here. Plus, his boss organizes a vintage car run sometimes—Michael adores him.

"Maybe I should just drive home," Rach mutters, and I feel bad because she's taken up the torch as my personal taxi driver ever since I sold my parents' BMW.

It felt like a step along the road to recovery—I no longer have to deal with the pang of guilt I felt every time I saw it parked in the driveway—but I should probably think about getting another car. I'm only resisting because it's better for my guests to have the whole garden to themselves, and I have nowhere to park a car if not in the driveway.

"Have a few drinks with me," I beg Rach. "We can stumble home in the dark later—it'll be fun with a bunch of us."

"Stumble would be about right. The last time I walked home to Aggie from Chapel Porth, I fell in the bloody stream."

"At least you didn't take the cliff path," I joke, and

immediately regret it because it makes me think of Finn and his mum, but Rach is too busy getting out of the car to notice my pained expression.

We're just hauling the last of our bags from the trunk when Tarek pulls into a space beside us with his girlfriend, Gaby, in the front seat. Chris, Kieran, and Kieran's girlfriend, Hayley, slide out of the back.

Tarek has a portable cooler filled with ice, plus several six-packs, none of which he'll drink himself since he's Muslim and alcohol is haram in Islam. I've gotten to know him quite well over the last eight months. He submitted the planning permission to convert the house and oversaw the work, and I'm thrilled with the results. Currently, there's a young family of four staying downstairs and the sound of the children's giggles traveling up through the floorboards has been making me smile. The little boy and girl are a far cry from last week's raucous ten-year-old twin boys who play-fought all day, every day, and broke two plates and three glasses, plus the living room lamp. I can't lie: I was glad to see the back of the little buggers.

A few more old school friends arrive, so we have plenty of hands to help carry everything down to the beach. Luckily Dan's birthday falls on a full moon, because if this was next Friday's neap tide, we might not be able to get around to the caves at all.

Grass-carpeted hills roll up and away on either side of us, vibrant green beneath the candy-floss-blue sky, but as we navigate the large pebbles that lead to the beach, the soft curve of hillside gives way to sharp-edged cliffs, which seem to tower ever higher as we make our way downhill. The sand feels thick and claggy underfoot and a light sheen of sweat coats my skin as we trudge on, trying to find a shallow spot in the stream where we can cross without getting our shoes wet.

We decide to make the cave itself our party palace and set about stabbing tall solar-powered lights into the sand. Hayley brought decorations, but Rach confiscated her balloons, giving her a lecture about the damage they could do to wildlife. Recently Rach has been working as a part-time surf instructor and also volunteers at the local Surf Life-Saving Club, but she has just applied for a full-time job at Surfers Against Sewage HQ. I hope she gets it.

Now Hayley is in a bad mood, trying to stuff the ends of paper streamers into cracks and crevices and swearing every time one tears off because the walls are so damp.

"How about we rope them around the solar lights?" I suggest, trying to appease her.

We've just finished stringing the streamers from solar lights around the perimeter of the cave when Brendan rocks up. I catch sight of him outside the wide, jagged opening and do a double take. The sun is hitting him from behind and making his hair glow with a golden hue.

He looks like an angel, I think as I go outside to say hi and meet the mere mortal he's brought with him.

"How lucky are you with the weather?" Brendan exclaims, after introducing me to his mate, Darren, a lanky-limbed guy with a shaved head.

"I know. We couldn't have picked a more perfect evening if we'd tried."

This heat wave we've been experiencing has been unbearable, but no one is complaining tonight.

The retreating tide has left behind rock pools that sparkle

and glint under the sun's rays, and the black mussels clinging to the colorful rocks look especially smooth and shiny.

"Where does the red color of the rocks come from?" Brendan asks me.

"Depends on who you ask," I reply. "Mineral deposits is the scientific answer, but the people around here will tell you that it's the blood of the evil giant, Bolster. You might hear about the legend at the carnival tomorrow, if you're going?"

"I'd planned to," he says. "You?"

"Of course."

Ooh, maybe we could go together . . .

It's a big day in the village calendar, as is Bolster Day, in May.

"Everybody inside!" Rach yells, holding her phone aloft—Amy said she'd text when they were setting off.

Brendan's halo is snuffed out once he enters the gloom of the cave.

"That sight is making me itchy for my surfboard," he says, hovering by the entrance with me while his mate raids the cooler.

"Have you surfed this beach yet?" I ask.

He nods. "Actually, the two of us went kitesurfing farther along the coast yesterday. Cheers," he says to his friend on his return.

They knock their cans together and crack them open, chugging back a few mouthfuls. I tug my gaze away from the long expanse of Brendan's tanned neck and peek out of the cave, trying to spot Dan and Amy. Off in the distance, I catch him swinging her up into his arms to carry her over the Porthtowan stream. She throws her head back, her long blond hair streaming out behind her, and I can imagine her laughing.

Two years in and still madly in love. They're talking about getting a place together.

"They're almost here!" I call over my shoulder.

Everyone backs up into the cave. Looking out, the ceiling hangs down to form a jagged line framing the sea straight ahead. Frothy waves thrash at the shore.

It's hard to make out the turquoise color of the sea from this level. Up on the cliffs is where the colors of the landscape really sing. The beach looks whiter, the water appears greener, and the moorland all around is carpeted with glittering wildflowers.

A memory comes back to me of being up there with Finn last summer, but I push it away, along with the reminder that it's the anniversary of my parents' deaths on Monday. I don't want to think about that now, nor about Finn.

It's been hard to put him out of my mind, with Door 54 opening for All Hype on the North American leg of their tour and several famous people posting pictures of them on Instagram. Buzz is building and everyone around here has been talking about it.

It's only a matter of time before they make it over to tour the UK. The last time I stalked them online, I saw that they were playing four festivals this summer. I keep checking the Boardies lineup, just in case, but I would have definitely heard about it if that was in the cards.

Finn didn't stay in touch when he left, not at all. I know I asked him not to and I should be glad that he kept his word to me, but in all honesty, his silence over this last year has been even harder to handle than it was the previous year.

I texted him a stupid joke at Christmas, just to cheer him up, to let him know that I was thinking about him, an acknowledgment of the difficult memories he must have to endure.

He wrote back Ha ha and then followed it up with another message that said, You broke the rules.

I texted back, Doesn't count at Christmas, to which he replied, I hope you're having an ok one.

It's fine! I tapped back, and that was the extent of our exchange.

I fought the urge to text him again, to go into more detail, to *ask* for more detail, but I reminded myself of all the reasons why I need to keep him at arm's length. I've already lost too much to fall in love with someone who can only be a peripheral part of my life.

DAN HAS HAD his wits suitably frightened out of him and now we've all spilled out of the cave onto the beach to catch the last of the day's rays.

"What's that building?" Brendan asks me, looking toward the old ruins up on the cliff, the tall chimney stack of the iconic enginehouse, hazy in the evening sunshine.

"It's part of the Wheal Coates tin mine. The shaft used to go down something like six hundred feet before heading out to sea. The miners would hear the waves thundering right over their heads as they worked."

"I think I might've seen it on *Poldark*," he remarks blandly.

"You watch it?" He doesn't seem like the period dramas type.

"My mum is obsessed."

I inwardly groan as "Dummy," one of Door 54's more popular songs, starts to play out of the stereo Tarek brought with him.

"I heard somewhere that the lead singer of this band used to play at Seaglass," Brendan says.

"He did." So much for avoiding thinking about Finn. "He was covering for Kieran, over there." I point out Kieran, who's laughing about something with Chris and Dan. "Those guys and Tarek had a residency at Seaglass for a couple of years in a row, but they've all got proper jobs now."

Dan is working as an accountant in Truro—he and Amy commute to work together sometimes.

"The band that's played the last couple of Saturdays is good, though," he comments.

"Have you been in?"

"Yeah."

"I haven't seen you."

"I've seen *you*, pulling pints like a pro." He grins. "How old are you?"

"Twenty-four. You?"

"Twenty-two."

The lyrics of Taylor Swift's "22" start playing in my head and once more my thoughts have led me back to Finn.

"So what are you going to draw on my latte tomorrow?" I ask, trying really hard to focus on the here and now.

"I think I might keep it simple. That elephant today was a bitch."

"I *knew* it!" I cry, looking toward Rach, who's standing by the cave entrance with Chris.

I'm sure she fancies him—they often end up chatting at parties—but she's been very coy when I've grilled her about it.

"Why, what did you think it was?" Brendan asks with alarm.

My brightening cheeks give him his answer.

He cracks up laughing. "You are kidding me. Really? You think I'd be that obvious?"

I shrug. "I don't know."

"So you don't want me to draw you a snake?"

I laugh. "Please don't."

"How about a heart? I'm pretty good at those."

"Are you now?"

"Yeah."

"How many hearts have you drawn onto other girls' coffees then?"

He laughs, caught. "A few."

"And where does that get you?"

"It can get me pretty far, if I'm honest."

"And where are you hoping your little foam hearts are going to get you with me?"

"I wouldn't dare to dream."

I laugh. "You're a smooth talker."

"Pillow talk is where I really excel."

"Oh, is that right?"

His blue eyes are twinkling and I can't say I'm not enjoying having a bit of a flirt.

"Who's the hottie?" Amy asks me, draping her arm around my neck when I go inside to grab us some more beers.

"His name is Brendan. He works at Beach Café."

"He's the guy who drew a dick on top of her coffee," Rach interjects casually.

"What's this?" Dan asks with a grin, overhearing.

Rach takes it upon herself to explain while I stand there,

rolling my eyes and adamantly repeating that it was an elephant. Not that anyone is listening to me.

"Poor old Finn," Dan says teasingly. "No more 'If you're single and I'm single' stuff, then," he adds with a grin, making double quotation marks in the air with his fingers.

I reel on Amy accusatorily. "How much have you told him?"

"She tells me *everything*," Dan chips in.

"I'll remember that."

"Oh, shut up," Amy says to Dan. "I do not. Your secrets are safe with me," she insists, trying to seem sincere.

I don't believe a word of it.

"Have you heard from Finn?" I ask Dan edgily.

"Yeah, he's on his way."

My heart does a somersault. "What do you mean?"

"He'll be here in a bit."

And another somersault.

"Wait. He's coming here? Tonight?"

Dan frowns at me. "He didn't tell you?"

"No. Did you know?" I ask Amy.

"He only texted half an hour ago," Dan interrupts. "He just flew in today."

Okay, now I'm getting heartburn.

"I'd better take this to Brendan," I say shakily, walking out of the cave with the cans of beer I scooped out of the cooler.

The sun creeps around the edge of the tall rock we're standing beside and a shaft of light hits the pool of water at its base, making the ripples on the surface twinkle like a billion tiny diamonds. I look north and my attention alights on a tall, slim, achingly familiar figure making its way toward us across the damp sand.

And just like that, Brendan is blasted right out of the water.

24

T WAS ALL GOING SO WELL. I COMPOSED MYSELF SO my face didn't give away how violently my heart was hammering and I managed to pretend for several seconds that I hadn't seen him, directing all my attention at Brendan. But then I overegged acting surprised when Finn was only a few feet away, and staggered straight into a rock pool on my way to hug him hello.

Now I'm standing here shivering, in soaking trainers, with Finn's denim jacket wrapped around my shoulders.

"How am I going to walk home in these?" I moan as Rach and Amy recover from laughing their arses off at me.

"I'll drive you home now," Finn offers, materializing beside me. "Not to leave," he speaks over the sound of my friends' protests. "You can get changed and I'll bring you back."

"Are you sure?" I ask, teeth chattering.

"Of course I'm sure," he replies, briefly meeting my eyes.

Goddammit, he's so good-looking. He's had a haircut. He can no longer tuck it behind his ears, but it's still shaggy and unkempt and falling haphazardly into his blue-green eyes. It's the sort of hair you just *have* to run your hands through.

And I really shouldn't be thinking things like this when my sort-of date is standing a few feet away, watching us.

"That'd be great, thanks," I tell Finn. "Just give me a sec."

I go to let Brendan know what I'm doing, promising that I'll be back soon.

He doesn't seem too fussed, but he's over two beers in.

"Who's the dude?" Finn asks as we walk away.

Well, *I'm* walking, *he's* striding. His legs are so long that it's an effort to keep up with him.

"Brendan. He works at Beach Café."

He doesn't say anything else, doesn't ask if I'm seeing him. I kind of wish that he would because the thought of him no longer caring suddenly feels too painful to handle.

"Wait, do you have a car?" I think to ask as we approach the car park.

He nods. "Rented it for the week."

"You're only here a week?"

"Most time I could get—"

"—off between gigs," I flatly finish his sentence for him.

He glances at me, his eye contact sliding away again. "Actually, I have a couple of meetings I need to get back for."

He pulls a car key out of his pocket and directs it at a dark gray SEAT Leon.

"I had no idea you were coming over," I say when we're safely buckled up.

"I thought about texting you," he replies, looking over his shoulder as he reverses out of the space.

"I wish you had."

He frowns at me. "You said—"

"I know what I said. That was my head speaking."

"Well, you're right. It probably was for the best."

"Yeah. I mean, goodness knows how you could have possibly resisted all the attention you must've had from fangirls over the last year."

I mean to sound breezy, but my tone comes off as bitter.

He pushes the gear stick into DRIVE, but doesn't set off.

"Can we just . . . *not*," he says, glancing across at me, his dark eyebrows pulled together.

He sighs and stares out the windscreen, driving us out of the car park.

We head back to St. Agnes in loaded silence, but my brain is close to short-circuiting. It's weird seeing him drive. I keep glancing over at the length of his arms as he turns the steering wheel, noticing his casual flicks of the indicator lights and occasional glances in the rearview mirror. He has a confidence behind the wheel that I find alarmingly sexy.

"Are you staying at your place or Michael's?" he asks on our way round the one-way system.

"Mine."

He turns down the long road that leads to Trevaunance Cove and finally pulls up in front of my house.

"I won't be long," I say, reaching for the door handle.

He stares out his side window. "You did the work," he notes with surprise, spying the new hallway through the front door's window panels.

"You didn't know?"

"Honestly, I thought it was easier to not even ask after you."

He meets my eyes—again, very briefly—before averting his gaze.

Easier for *whom*?

Has he been hurting too?

"Do you want to come in and see?" I ask him impulsively. "You could leave this in the car park?"

There's a small one just across the road.

"Don't you need to rush back?" he asks, and yes, there it is, that slightly dry, sarcastic edge that lets me know he *didn't* like seeing me with another guy.

"Nothing's happened yet," I blurt, which warrants another sharp look. "With Brendan, I mean."

This time, when he turns his head away, an air of defeat seems to settle around his shoulders.

"I really *didn't* expect you to wait for me," he says gruffly as I watch the shadowing of his jaw, the hard press of his lips.

"I didn't even know if you were coming back . . ."

"We said—"

"Yes, I know, but God, Finn! Couldn't you have warned me, like, a month ago? I would have waited that long, for Christ's sake."

He grins at me.

My heart flips again.

And then his hand is cupping the back of my neck and he's pulling me close and kissing my lips.

That's the moment where every ounce of my self-control flies out of the window.

"I'M A LITTLE upset that I'm not going to be able to get my pastries from Beach Café anymore."

Finn's laugh is low and deep, reverberating from his smooth, toned chest right into my ear cavity. We are completely naked—it was a struggle getting my wet clothes off, but well worth the effort. It is beyond blissful being in my bed with him.

"I've probably had a few too many of those lately anyway," I say dolefully.

"Stop," he mutters, running his hand over my hip. "You look so much better."

I've put on the weight I lost, plus a bit more.

"Would it be bad if we didn't go back to the party?" he asks sleepily.

"Yes, it would be terrible. But I'm not sure I care," I admit.

"Would it be bad if I fell asleep here?" he asks.

"Not so terrible," I reply.

"Would it be bad if we had sex again?"

I lift my head to look at him, detecting mischief in his tone.

"That wouldn't be terrible at all," I whisper, sliding my hand down and feeling him wake up in my palm.

He yanks me up his body and attacks my mouth in a greedy, all-consuming kiss, sending shock waves across my skin as our tongues mesh and tangle.

I guess we are definitely not going back to the party.

FINN IS SNORING lightly beside me when I slide out of bed and grab my phone, intending to send a quick message to the group chat I have with Rach and Amy. There's a string of messages from them already, wondering where we are, whether we're coming back, if I plan to let poor Brendan know that I've been otherwise detained . . .

I bite my lip, feeling bad as I tap out, I'm sorry. I had unfinished business to attend to. How did the party go?

No shit, Rach replies. I've just left Dan and Amy's—a few of us went back after the beach.

Was Brendan okay?

Let's just say I don't think you'll be getting any more phallic symbols in your coffee anytime soon.

I'll text him now.

I look up his number and type: Hey, I hope you had a good time tonight. I'm sorry I didn't make it back.

Three flashing dots show me that he's reading my message, then they disappear.

I sigh and put my phone on charge before climbing back into bed with Finn.

A potential year with Brendan or a week with Finn?

I have no regrets.

FINN IS STILL asleep beside me in the morning when I come to. He was awake in the night—jet lag, probably. I rolled over and saw him scrolling through Instagram on his phone. I stroked his arm to let him know that I was glad of his presence, but I was too exhausted to keep him company.

I'm pleased he fell back asleep again. And I'm thrilled that he's still here.

I get out of bed and pull on my dressing gown before heading next door to my new kitchen. It's nothing like the kitchen-diner downstairs with all the windows that my guests get to enjoy, but it's fine for now. And it was a brilliant idea of Finn's to do this to the house in the first place.

I'm smiling, my internal radiator turned up to full power as I make two mugs of tea and take them back into the bedroom. Finn is still asleep, but he stirs when I put his mug down on the bedside table beside his pillow.

"Morning," I say, marveling at how dark his lashes are, how blue-green his eyes. "Tea?"

He groans and sits up in bed, giving me a smile that only just brings out the indents in his cheeks.

"Thanks."

"Did you get much sleep?" I ask.

"A bit. Your bed is a darn sight more comfortable than the sofa."

"I still can't believe you sleep on the sofa at your grandparents' place. No wonder you don't stick around for long."

"I might change my mind if you let me crash here."

"You can crash here," I say flippantly.

"Really?" He seems surprised and I experience a severe pang of anticipatory grief at the thought of him leaving.

I should be keeping things casual between us, not inviting him to sleep in my bed.

"Are you working today?" he asks, reaching for his mug.

"Later. It's the carnival, remember?"

"I completely forgot it was this weekend. I guess I should take the boys."

"It's also changeover day. I have a family due at four, but I'll try to get organized earlier. I'm at Seaglass later for the after-party."

"You still like working there?"

"Yeah, it's fun," I reply, sounding a touch defensive. "And it's easy. And I love working with Chas. And when I start sculpting again, it will be the perfect job because I can work all hours during the summer and sculpt when Seaglass shuts up shop for winter."

"So you haven't started sculpting?" he presses gently.

"I haven't really had a chance," I reply sheepishly. "Not with all the work I've been doing on the house."

"Inspiration yet to strike?"

"I guess so."

He gives me a sympathetic look and takes a sip of his tea, his downcast eyes creating fan shapes where his long eyelashes connect with his skin. They look as soft as butterfly wings.

"I wondered if you'd be up for coming with me to the Barbara Hepworth Museum," he says, resting his mug on his chest. "I've never been."

"I'd love to," I reply, glad that we're not still talking about the lack of direction my life has had. "I haven't been in years. I used to go there all the time when I was younger. When were you thinking?"

"Monday?"

My stomach dips. "Oh, I'm not sure about Monday."

"Have you got other plans?"

"Only to wallow. It's the anniversary of my parents' deaths."

"Don't spend the day on your own," he implores, reaching over to take my hand.

"Shouldn't you be hanging out with your family?"

"I'll see them plenty. Come with me," he urges.

"Okay," I whisper.

He places his mug on the bedside table and reaches forward to pull down the collar of my dressing gown, gently biting my shoulder. I shudder, desire coursing through me as I set aside my own mug and return to his arms.

It's another forty minutes before we make it out of bed.

25

FINN TURNS UP ON MONDAY MORNING WEARING A cream-colored 1970s terry-cloth T-shirt with a red-and-blue stripe across the front. It's either shrunk in the wash or is two sizes too small for him because if he lifts his arms, I'm pretty sure he'll expose the whole flat expanse of his stomach.

"Where do you *get* your clothes?" I ask as I buckle up, the sadness that has been overwhelming me this morning ceding to amusement.

"This was a charity-shop purchase. I like your dress."

"Thanks." It's a floaty, ditsy-print one. "Our style could not be less alike, could it?"

"Wouldn't have it any other way," he replies.

I pop my sunglasses on top of my head and search through my bag for a packet of headache tablets, swallowing two without water.

"Are you okay?" he asks.

"I will be."

I had breakfast with Michael this morning. I kept getting teary and this seemed to make him uncomfortable, so I managed to contain myself until I could get back home and have a proper cry.

I slide my sunglasses back into place, knowing that my eyes are still tinged red. "Best if we don't talk about it. What have you been up to?"

He fills me in on yesterday as he drives us to St. Ives. He took his brothers to a theme park and last night they ordered takeaway pizza. He wanted to come over afterward, but I really did need some time to wallow. We'd already spent Saturday night together after he rocked up at Seaglass while I was working, and on Sunday morning he left just as Michael arrived.

Michael's eyebrows have always been extremely expressive, but they drew together with horror when he saw me kissing Finn goodbye on the doorstep.

"Are you her boyfriend now?" he demanded, glaring at Finn.

"No, he's not!" I exclaimed.

"That was a very violent rebuttal," Finn commented mildly.

"Well, you're not, are you?" I looked at him.

"I guess not," he replied in that same mild tone, before catching my chin between his thumb and forefinger and pressing a chaste kiss to my lips.

"Urgh!" Michael erupted, pushing past me to get through the door.

"Bye, Michael!" Finn called over his shoulder chirpily as he walked away.

Michael and I still do Sunday lunch. Sometimes it's at mine, sometimes it's at his, sometimes we have company, sometimes it's just the two of us, sometimes it goes well, sometimes it's a disaster. It's completely unpredictable, but I've grown to kind of like that.

FINN AND I return to the conversation about what we look like when we're walking through the streets of St. Ives on our way to the museum. I've just glanced across at him and laughed at his T-shirt again.

"Are you embarrassed to be seen with me?" he asks, pursing his lips, but not quite managing to suppress his dimples.

"It'd more likely be the other way round," I reply.

"*Whaaat?*" He staggers sideways, pulling a comedy face.

"I bet I'm a total nerd compared to the people you hang out with back in LA."

"Shut up, you're perfect." He hooks an arm around my neck as he adds, sweetly, "Way out of my league."

I snort and he lets me go because it's too difficult to walk these hills conjoined and not stumble.

"You are," he insists. "You always have been."

"Rubbish. It's totally the other way around, especially now you've gone and got famous."

I reach over and punch his arm and he rolls his eyes.

When I've been in a dark place at various points over the last year, I've found myself obsessing over Door 54's Instagram feed. It's full of grungy shots of four boys on tour, falling over drunk onstage, crowd-surfing, stumbling out of sleek SUVs, frequenting cool-sounding venues with names like the Fonda and the Roxy . . . And then there are the reels. There's one in particular that shows Finn and his lead guitarist, Dylan, standing on the rooftop of a low-slung bungalow, throwing random objects into a bright blue swimming pool. The backdrop is a brilliantly blue sky, complete with a tall, skinny palm tree.

It made me feel oddly small, watching that video.

The Finn I knew—or at least, the Finn I *thought* I knew—didn't seem to fit in with the Finn on Instagram at all.

"How *is* band life?" I ask. "Are you getting on better with your guitarist now?"

I don't call him by his name, I'm not sure why. Maybe because I don't want Finn to realize how much I've been learning everything there is to know about Door 54 and its members.

Fun facts: the baby-faced drummer, Gus, is the son of a country-and-western star, and the bass guitarist, Ernie, was photographed recently at a club with Selena Gomez.

"Not really," Finn replies. "Things are a bit strained all round, to be honest."

"In what way?"

"We want different things. They're all on the same page, but I'm not."

"What do they want?" I ask with a frown.

"To move away from alt-rock into a more aggressive metal-core, electronic sound. But I like the way we sound now."

"I like the way you sound now too."

"Have you heard our album?" He glances at me.

"Of course."

"Aw." He grins and hooks his arm around my neck again.

"Argh, Finn, you're going to pull me over!"

"No, I'll keep you upright," he bats back. "Is that the sculpture garden?" He releases me to look through an arched gateway built into a high stone wall.

"Yep."

I step closer and peer through the bars of the black wrought-iron gate at sculptures that are barely visible among the thick tree cover.

"The entrance is around the corner," I say, leading him away.

I'm still holding his hand when we arrive at the museum.

We linger in the entrance hall, reading information about Barbara Hepworth and her life as an avant-garde artist. I've been here so many times, but there's always something new to discover.

"Do you still want to become a member of the Royal Society of Sculptors?" Finn asks me as he reads through a list of Barbara Hepworth's key achievements.

I lift my shoulders in a small shrug and nod toward the staircase. "Right now, I just need to focus on getting back into sculpting."

"Any ideas for what you might make?" he asks as we come out at the top into a gallery space with white walls and wooden floors.

Sunshine is streaming in through large windows carved out of the sloping roofline.

"*Who*, you mean. I'm most interested in people." I stand and stare at the stylized Burmese-wood sculpture of an infant. "I'll have to rope someone in to sit for me."

"I'll sit for you if you like," he says, following me as I move on.

"You're leaving on Friday." But it's sweet of him to offer.

"Can't you just do a little one of me before I go?"

"A titchy person?" I say over my shoulder with a grin.

"Or a body part," he suggests, his lips curving into a significant smile.

"What sort of body part do you have in mind?" I ask in a low voice.

"I'm open to suggestions," he replies in a tone that sends a frisson shimmering down my spine.

I come to a stop in front of a life-size bronze sculpture of Barbara Hepworth's hand. It's so detailed, down to every last vein and wrinkle.

"Hand it is, then," I say, and he smirks at me. "No, I'd probably do your nose."

"My *nose*?"

I giggle at his reaction. "I like how it's not completely symmetrical."

"Er, yeah, that would be because—"

He cuts off mid-explanation.

"Because what?" I ask with a frown, my laughter dying on my lips.

"Never mind," he mutters, moving on. "I like this."

He pauses in front of *Pierced Form*, which is one of the pieces I used to love most as a child, with textured chisel marks that my fingers itched to touch. It's a large abstract shape made of smooth, polished light brown wood with a white-painted interior. It looks like a giant nut that has been cracked open, only to find a worm has chewed a hole through the middle.

I step closer to Finn's side and take his hand, the lines of our arms pressing firmly together. I'm giving him space in my silence, but not in my actions.

"Tyler's dad broke my nose when I was twelve," he reveals after a long moment of us quietly standing there.

My breath hitches and I lean into him a little harder. "I'm so sorry."

"'S okay. He's in prison now. Not for punching me in the face," he clarifies, sounding more like his old self. "He's been in and out of prison on various assault charges for half his fucking life, waste of space that he is."

"Does Tyler ever see him?"

"No, thank God. He's not interested in being a father."

"What about Liam's dad?"

He shrugs. "Who knows? Mum never said who he was. I'm not sure she knew."

He squeezes my hand and leads me outside to the garden. I take the hint and follow him in silence.

Ahead is *Four-Square (Walk Through)*, a giant bronze sculpture that you can literally walk through. It has square edges and smooth round holes and I like it because I used to play hide-and-seek around it with my grandmother.

I also like it because it showcases two of my favorite patinas: verdigris and penny bronze. The emerald green of the verdigris and the golden tones of the penny bronze are offset beautifully by the darker glossy chestnut patina used on the remaining surfaces.

"Is this bronze?" Finn asks with a perplexed look on his face, running his finger around the shiny interior of one of the round window holes.

"Yep."

"How do you get it to go gold?"

"That's actually the natural color of bronze. The surface has been polished and lacquered, but it takes a lot of maintenance to keep it that way."

"What about the green?"

"That's a hot patina, done with heat and chemicals."

"I don't really understand how it works with clay. You make something and then what?"

"You build a mold and then cast it."

"But how do you do that?"

"The method I use is very traditional, but combined with some more modern materials: first you take a silicone mold of the clay and then you pour in liquid wax. Once the wax has solidified, it's released from the mold and covered in a ceramic shell mixture. When you heat this up, the wax pours out—which is why they call it the lost-wax method of bronze casting. The void that's left behind is filled with molten bronze."

"That sounds like a right faff."

"It is a bit, but it's worth it."

"Do you still want to do your gran in bronze?" he asks me.

"How do you remember everything I say?"

"Because you're interesting." He flashes me a playful look. "If you were a book, I'd highlight half your lines," he adds cheekily, causing me to burst out laughing.

"You should put that in a song," I say.

He smirks. "Yeah, my bandmates go all in for cheesy."

I take it from his tone that he's being sarcastic.

"I *have* written about you in one of our songs, though," he says offhandedly.

"Have you?" I shoot my head round to look at him. "Which one?"

"Track three off the album."

"'Leah'?"

"You know it?"

"I told you, I've listened to your album. Many times," I admit coyly. "Am I supposed to be Leah? I assumed she must be some girl you fancied."

"She is," he replies with a knowing look before grinning. "Nah, she's mostly made-up, apart from all that *'when she talks, I listen'* stuff."

His cheeks pinken and he wanders away.

"I can't believe I'm in a Door 54 song." I catch up with him, my glee bubbling over.

"Make the most of it. It'll probably be the one and only time."

"Yeah, I don't really think metalcore, whatever that is, would suit my personality."

He comes to a stop in front of one of my favorite pieces, *Garden Sculpture (Model for Meridian)*, a tall aquamarine structure that looks like a distorted spiral with ribbons of bronze forming triangular loops.

"I doubt I'll be in the band for much longer," he says.

"You're quitting?" I ask with surprise. "Just as you're taking off?"

"They'd be better off with a frontman who's happy to scream their lyrics. I want to write more of my own stuff, but I can't pour my heart and soul into something I don't believe in. There's no compromise to be found when you're putting out music. Artists who compromise fall out of love with their songs and you play them too much to risk that. I don't want to burn out before I'm twenty-five."

"Sounds as though you've made up your mind."

He looks dejected. "Does, doesn't it? I'll do the festivals, then think about going solo. That's why I have to get back—I've got a couple of meetings lined up with record labels."

"Wow. Good luck, Finn," I say seriously.

"Thanks."

The heat wave is easing off, but I'm grateful for all the shade provided by the trees. We wind our way along a path to the highest part of the garden, brushing past flower beds humming with bumblebees. The property is secluded and private, surrounded by the high wall we passed on our way here and banked by the house and studio. Above the trees in the lowest part of the property, a cream-stone church tower rises into a blue sky dotted with clouds, and across the slate-gray rooftops dusted with yellow lichen is the cold blue sea, hugged on the other side of the cove by the sprawl of St. Ives.

"What a place to have lived and worked," I murmur.

"One day I'll become a successful songwriter and buy you a place just like this," Finn jokes. "Or otherwise you'll become a famous sculptor and buy it for yourself, whichever comes first."

I smile at him with his wild dreams and am hit with another pang of preemptive grief at the thought of him leaving.

Up ahead is the greenhouse. I inadvertently squeeze Finn's hand and he glances at me questioningly.

"Do you want to go inside?" he asks.

"I'm not sure."

He senses my hesitancy and gently pulls me to a stop.

"No, it's okay," I say impulsively, starting forward.

The moment we step into the cool interior, my face crumples. This is the greenhouse that Mum and Dad modeled my studio at home on, with its white walls, red-tiled floor, and sloping ceiling complete with roof lights. They even potted up a multitude of succulents and cacti to sit on the floor around the inner walls.

Those plants have died because it hurt too much to go in there and water them. All I've managed to do is throw dust sheets over my work and lock the door so none of my guests attempt to investigate.

"I feel like I have a lump of marble in my throat," I say in a choked voice.

"You won't be able to swallow it, so cry it out," Finn replies softly, drawing me close.

"I wish I'd told them how much I appreciated them, how much I loved the studio they created for me. I don't think I ever expressed it enough."

It's the last thing I say before my body begins to quake with quiet sobs.

"Of *course* you did, Liv. Of *course* they knew how much you loved and appreciated them," he says urgently into my ear. "You wear your heart on your sleeve—it's one of the things I love most about you."

I clutch him tighter and give myself over to my pain for as long as I'll allow before pulling myself together, lowering my sunglasses, and leaving the garden to its peace and quiet.

26

S THIS GOING TO BE *VERY DIRTY*?" FINN ASKS IN A
vaguely seductive manner as he saunters into my small
kitchen.

"If you try anything while I've got clay all over my hands, I
won't be impressed."

"I can't imagine clay feeling too good on specific body
parts anyway. Today's mud bath was grim enough."

He took his brothers quad-biking earlier and sent me a pic
of the three of them, completely splattered.

I pull the damp cloth off the skull that I've been working
on this morning and Finn does a double take.

It was surreal unlocking the door to my garden studio. I
had to wait until my downstairs guests had gone out before
letting myself in through the driveway gate, and maybe knowing that I didn't have long helped me to focus, but I didn't get
upset, not like I thought I would.

When I took off the dust sheets, I felt a pinch in my chest,
but as I sorted through the drawers to retrieve the tools and
materials I needed, my overriding emotion was excitement. I
was preparing to do something that once came as easily to me
as breathing and suddenly I couldn't wait to get started.

What Finn said yesterday about my parents knowing how much I appreciated them helped. I've since remembered a few more details about the day we set up my work in the studio. At the end of that evening, after Michael had gone home, I went back in to look at the space and was racked with worry about how to tell my parents I didn't plan to use it for long, that I wouldn't be staying past the end of summer. My mum walked in behind me and she spotted the shine in my eyes and gave me a hug. I breathed "Thank you" into her neck, and in that moment, I know that my mother and I were wrapped in love.

I feel more at peace, remembering this.

"How have you made that already?" Finn asks with astonishment, staring at the basic skull on the table.

This morning, I built an armature, which is like a metal skeleton made out of iron piping and aluminum wire that holds the clay in place. Then I packed clay into the metal to fill it out. Having my hands surrounded by the soft material again made me feel as though I'd come home after a long time away. Now I'm ready to start sculpting in detail.

"What can I say? I guess you inspired me."

He looks touched.

"Take a seat."

He pulls up a chair next to the small table that's pushed against the back wall. There's only just enough space for furniture in here. The kitchen is the one room upstairs that doesn't have carpet, so it's the best place to work.

I'd love to be doing this downstairs in the kitchen-diner, but the apartment has barely had a week free since the Easter holidays.

The family I've currently got staying leave the TV on *all* the time. It's like living with Michael only I can't ask them to turn it down.

Not that my brother ever listened to me on that front anyway.

I tell this to Finn conversationally as I get stuck in, which prompts him to ask after Michael.

"How's he doing these days?"

"He's well. He was funny on Sunday when he saw you kissing me goodbye."

"Yeah, he really doesn't like me, does he?"

"He's always taken a while to warm up to new people. Except for Shirley. He loved her from the moment he met her."

"Is she still working for him?"

"Yep! Predicted that wrong, didn't I? They get along like a house on fire—and luckily *haven't* set the house on fire or done any other lasting damage, as far as I know. She's actually really great at encouraging him to look after himself. Much better than I thought she'd be. And she doesn't just stick to her working hours, either. Sometimes I'll pop round for a cuppa and she'll still be there, sprawled out on the sofa, watching the latest gory crime thriller they've got stuck into. They look so annoyed at the interruption that I never stay for long. But it's good. She's nice to Timothy too—Michael's friend."

"Has Michael ever had a girlfriend?"

"He's had a couple. He stayed friends with his last girlfriend, but they fell out because she kissed someone else at a club dance night. Michael refused to go back to his club for ages. Dad eventually persuaded him not to cut off his nose to spite his face, so he started going again."

"When you say 'club' . . . ?" Finn says with confusion.

"Not a *club* club," I reply with a smile. "He goes to a social club for people with learning disabilities." He stopped during the year after our parents died so I was relieved when he recently started attending again. "It's where he met Timothy."

I've been working away as we've been speaking and Finn's face is beginning to take shape beneath my hands. It feels unbelievably good to be sculpting again.

"I'm loving this," I say quietly after toiling away in silence for a while. I've been pinching off small pieces of clay and smoothing them onto mini-Finn's cheekbones to build them up.

That feeling I had earlier, when I was packing the clay into the armature to fill it out, that feeling of coming home, is even more concentrated now I'm in full sculpting mode. Small waves of euphoria keep passing through me.

"I'm enjoying watching you," he says. "The look of concentration on your face is intense."

I meet his eyes. "I'm never going to be able to do your eyelashes justice."

He lets out a low laugh.

"Or your hair. I like it shorter, by the way."

I've been enjoying running my hands through it every time we've been in bed together.

He enjoys it too, judging from the noises he makes.

"What are you thinking?" he murmurs.

"Naughty things," I reply.

We move at the same time, and a moment later, I'm straddling his lap and my lips are locked with his. His hands grip my hips to hold me in place because my hands are filthy and I'm keeping them aloft and out of the way.

I doubt I'll finish this sculpture.

A FEW DAYS later, Finn and I say our third goodbye, and it's agonizing.

"Will we stay in touch this time?" he asks.

I hesitate. "I don't know."

Right now, I can't imagine how I'll ever resist reaching out to him.

"I'm sorry I came back at the wrong time," he says.

"What are you talking about?" I lift my head from his shoulder, my vision blurry from tears as we stand at the top of the stairs, embracing for the last time. "You came back at exactly the *right* time."

"I'm glad you think so," he murmurs.

I realize he's referring to my missed opportunity with Brendan. I *still* have no regrets.

He presses a kiss to my forehead and takes a step backward, briskly rubbing my upper arms as if to warm me up.

"Goodbye, Liv."

He turns and walks determinedly down the stairs and my heart leaps into my throat, almost as though it's trying to chase after him. I nearly call out to stop him from leaving before we've agreed to give this thing between us a shot, but I clamp my mouth shut.

My head knows what's best for me; what's best for us both.

These next few years are when people typically meet the person they want to spend the rest of their lives with. We'd be foolish to hold back.

That's not to say that he doesn't take a piece of me with him when he goes.

And I have a feeling he's left a piece of himself behind too.

27

THIS SUMMER

I WAKE UP VERY EARLY ON THE MORNING AFTER THE PUB quiz and stare at the ceiling, my head pounding. After downing a full glass of water, along with some painkillers, I climb out of bed and go and sit at the piano in the living room.

I play one song pianissimo—very softly—but if Tom's up and awake, he'll hear it.

And hopefully he'll hear my hidden message: if I show you mine, will you show me yours?

I'm in the kitchen, halfway through a piece of toast, when there's a knock on my downstairs door.

I jump to my feet, the remnants of my breakfast discarded, and jog down the stairs, beaming. I know it's him, because anyone else would have to ring the doorbell.

As I swing the door wide open, my heart skitters at the sight of Tom in the hallway, fully dressed in jeans and a muted-blue long-sleeve T-shirt, his hair still damp from the shower.

"You've made your point," he says, eyes dancing. "You ready?"

I spy the rake he's holding in his right hand and let out a squeak of excitement.

"Just let me put on my shoes!"

WE HEAD IN the opposite direction of Chapel Porth, taking the coast path toward Trevellas Cove. The air carries a chill and the wind is whipping my hair all over the place as we hug the rugged coastline. A bank of low clouds flirts with the horizon, but the sky overhead is pale blue and far-reaching. Tom has checked the tide times and we should arrive as it's almost fully out.

"How's your hangover?" Tom asks as the narrow track we've been treading widens, the ruins of the old Blue Hills tin mine coming into view.

"It's not too bad, actually," I reply.

The bracing wind and fresh air have cleared my head. If anything, I feel invigorated.

We don't speak much, but it's a comfortable silence as we make our way down into the valley. Gravelly tracks and patches of naked stone have been scored out of the weathered hills on the other side of the cove, making me think of the marks I sometimes make in clay. The heather is not yet in bloom.

"Pretend I'm not here," I say to Tom as we approach the beach, looking for a ledge to perch on while he heads to the middle of the empty expanse.

He glances over at me as I sit down, his eyes resting on mine for a few seconds before he returns his attention to the sand.

It makes my heart sing, watching him work. The beach is his canvas and the rake is his pencil. Working with a smooth stretch of sand about eight by twelve meters, he begins to draw. A picture forms of a gnarly tree in the foreground with branches leaning off to one side, its shape elongated as though caught in a relentlessly blowing gale. Behind it, he draws mountains climbing into the distance, and to its left, a dry stone wall.

He sets the rake aside and uses his hands to sketch out a curvy shape at the base of the wobbly trunk. I laugh as a sheep emerges.

He looks over at me as he straightens up, grinning. Cocking his head to one side, he lifts his broad shoulders in a half shrug.

He's finished.

I stand up and climb the rocks toward him. He comes over and holds his hand out to help me down the last section and the heat of our palms connecting spreads halfway up my arm.

"I love it," I say, reluctantly letting go of his hand and going to take a closer look. "Where is it?" I ask over my shoulder.

"Snowdonia," he replies, and the light in his eyes seems to dim.

"HOW DID YOU get into sand art?" I ask on our return home.

"Remember how I said that I used to draw all the time when I was younger, but my parents didn't encourage it?"

I nod.

"They tolerated me doing GCSE art, but vetoed it at A level. To be fair, I needed math and physics for my aviation degree, so I didn't resent them for steering me away from creative subjects, but I no longer felt comfortable sketching around them at home. We lived in Norfolk, near a beach, so I used to go for walks on my own and sometimes I'd find myself drawing on the sand. It relaxed me, but I only ever did it when no one else was around. It felt like a dirty secret."

"That's sad."

"It doesn't feel like that anymore," he says with a sideways glance at me.

"Good. Art shouldn't ever feel sordid. So why trees?"

He thinks for a moment before answering. "You know when you see a pattern or an image of something in an unexpected place? Like a shape in the clouds or a face in the rock?"

"Yes."

"I used to see lots of shapes in nature. My granddad was the same. We'd lie on grassy hilltops and watch the clouds roll by and point out shapes that reminded us of things. So when I got here in the early hours of Friday morning and saw the stream running out to sea, carving its way through the sand . . . It made me think of the old apple tree we used to have at the bottom of our garden. And I couldn't stop myself from trying to re-create it."

"Were you picturing it in winter?"

"No, in its last stages of life. My parents had our apple tree cut down years ago. I used to climb it when I was a boy, so I was gutted."

"What about the Italian cypress?"

"My granddad had one in his garden. They always make me think of him."

I smile softly. "And the forest?"

He chuckles. "I can tell you now, hopefully without it weirding you out, but *you* gave me the idea for the forest."

"So you *did* see my post on Instagram!" I exclaim.

"No! I really was offline for a few days." He hesitates. "I saw you on the beach that second day. You walked the whole length of the cypress tree and then stood there on the sand, staring at the ocean, and for some reason it made me think of a beautiful girl walking through a forest." He lets out a self-conscious laugh while my insides fizz at his use of the word "beautiful."

"I wanted to give you a path to wander along."

"And then I did exactly that," I say with amazement.

We stare at each other for a few seconds.

"I couldn't believe it when, a few days later, I read what you'd written on Instagram," he admits, his gaze returning to the horizon.

"That was such a weird coincidence," I agree.

But inside, I'm thinking it felt a lot like fate.

"DID YOU COME to Cornwall much when you were a kid?" I ask on our descent toward the road.

We're walking single file now, along the narrow track.

"On and off. I spent my whole summer holiday here once, when I was eleven. That's the trip I really remember, when it was just my granddad and me. My parents were going through a tough time," he confides over his shoulder. "My dad had an affair and they were trying to patch things up, so they sent me off to stay with my granddad for six weeks to give themselves some space. And me, I guess. The arguments were messing with my mind."

"I'm sorry, that must have been really unsettling."

He doesn't disagree. "It was, but it was also the best thing they could have done for me."

"Are you an only child?"

I'm not sure he's heard my question because he doesn't answer at first, but then he replies.

"Yeah. And it was lonely at times, but I loved that summer. Hanging out with my granddad, building sandcastles, painting pictures . . . He was retired, so he had all the time in the world for me. Except he didn't have all the time in the world, as it turns out," he says somberly. "He passed away soon afterward."

"I'm so sorry."

"You sound as though you were close to your grandmother too."

"I was. I was distraught when we lost her. She lived until she was ninety, but it was still hard to see her go."

"My granddad was only sixty-one."

"That's so young. What happened?"

"His heart went." He looks toward the ocean and I see him swallow. "I'd just started secondary school. In a weird way, I think his loss helped bring my parents back together. He was my dad's dad."

"Are your parents still married?"

"Yep. Thirty years now."

"That's heartwarming to know."

"Yeah." He agrees so quietly his words are almost carried off by the wind.

We come out by the Driftwood Spars Inn. Smoke is spiraling from the chimney and the lights are on inside. It hasn't been open long.

"That looks very cozy," Tom comments, glancing through the window.

"Fancy a pint by the fire?" I suggest.

"Hair of the dog?" He raises an eyebrow.

"Why not?"

"I'd better run this back to your place first," he says of the rake.

I take it from him. "I'll prop it up round the side of the building."

He's leaning against the bar, looking toward the door, when I walk inside.

"What are you having?" he asks me.

"Um . . . tea, please," I decide, telling it straight to the girl behind the bar.

"After all that bravado," he teases me gently, ordering himself a bitter shandy.

We sit at a table by the cast-iron fireplace. It might be June, but it's a cold morning and I'm glad of the warmth as I rub my hands together and hold them up to the flames. Tom looks all around at the objects fixed to the rough stone walls and dark wooden ceiling beams: old-fashioned lanterns, guns and swords, ship wheels and brass tide clocks.

"Does this place have rooms?" he asks me.

"Yes, it's a B and B. Why, you thinking of moving?" I joke.

"I'm thinking of *staying*," he replies meaningfully.

"In Aggie?" My heart jolts.

He nods. "Another two and a half weeks doesn't seem nearly long enough. Is your place booked out for the rest of the summer?"

"Afraid so," I tell him with regret.

"And the other places you manage?"

"They're all fully booked. You should ask at the bar, though. You might be lucky." I can't suppress my grin. "I'm so pleased you want to stay."

He seems heartened as he reaches for his pint. "I *really* love it here."

"Once I couldn't wait to escape, but now I can't imagine leaving."

"Where did you want to escape to?"

I tell him about my plans to move to London, and how I'd hoped to return to Italy someday.

"And you don't want to do that anymore?"

"I'm still keen to do a residency someday, or take part in a sculpture symposium, but I wouldn't want to be abroad for any length of time."

"What's a sculpture symposium?"

"It's when a group of sculptors are invited to come together to create public art with a central theme. They take place in different countries all over the world."

"I'd love to see some of your work."

"Most of it is commissions, so I don't get to keep it, but my latest is public art," I say with a twinge of pride. "It's still at the foundry, having the finishing touches put to it. I have to go check on it tomorrow."

"Where's the foundry?"

"Near St. Ives. You're welcome to come if you fancy a day trip," I say before I can overthink it.

I haven't even extended an invitation to Michael or my friends. In fact, I'm not sure I've ever willingly shared an unfinished piece with anyone since my student days. I don't know what it is about him that makes me feel able to lay myself bare.

"I'd love to." His maple-brown eyes hold mine as his lips tilt up at the corners.

"Have you heard anything else about your house sale?" I ask, topping up my tea as my face warms.

"No, nothing."

"You haven't switched off your phone again, have you?"

"No, but it's tempting," he grumbles as he lifts his pint.

"Is it very strained between you and your ex?"

"It's not great. We were together for three years, so it was always going to be messy unpicking that."

"Three years is a long time."

"Yeah, I thought that was it for me."

"You were ready to settle down?"

"Marriage did seem like the most likely next step," he admits bleakly.

He would have married her? And there was Rach, assuming it hadn't been serious.

"All our friends were tying the knot and everyone was saying it would be us next, but we were just coasting. It felt like the right time to settle down when we got together, but we weren't that well suited. I didn't want to face up to it at first, but it's blatantly obvious now. We'd always wanted different things."

"Was your breakup mutual?"

"She was the one who called it quits in the end. I'm still trying to get my head around it all, to be honest."

That's code for "time to stop fishing."

I wonder what the tipping point was between them.

"Is there anyone significant in *your* life?" he asks casually.

"No," I reply.

It feels like the truth when I say it.

28

THREE SUMMERS AGO

This is your one-month warning

My heart leaps as I read the text that I woke up to. I quickly tap out a reply, hoping Finn's still awake.

Have you booked your ticket?

It's a quarter past eight in the morning here. What time is it in LA? It must be after midnight. I hold my breath as three flashing dots show that he's reading or replying.

Yep. Are you single?

I'm laughing as I reply: What do you think?

Please keep it that way for the foreseeable future.

I send him back a smiley face and bounce out of bed.

When Finn left last summer, I barely managed seven days before I sent him a Missing you message, to which he replied, I miss YOU. So fucking much.

I rang him the moment I received it.

"Well, *this* is a pleasant surprise," he answered with what I knew was a grin, although I couldn't see him, as I hadn't Face-Timed.

"I don't want to go a year without speaking to you," I admitted, beyond happy to hear his voice.

"I'm glad you've come to your senses," he replied.

I *hadn't* come to my senses. I'd lost them.

We texted and called *all* the time. I lived through the ups of his meetings with record labels and through the downs of his split with his band. He shared in my happiness when I started sculpting again properly and in my pain when I found myself desperately missing Mum and Dad.

Whenever I had something to say, some news to share, Finn was the one I wanted to call.

But therein lay the problem.

There have been times when I haven't felt present in my life here. I forgot Rach's birthday, turned up an hour late to Amy and Dan's housewarming party, almost missed a meeting that Shirley had called to talk about a falling-out Michael had had with his best friend, Timothy. They made up again before we intervened, but that's not the point. I wasn't there when my friends and family needed me.

I told Finn when I forgot Rach's birthday. He sympathized, but when I next messed up, I was too embarrassed to confide in him.

At around the same time, I began to realize that he was holding back from me too. He had an argument with his dad that he played down, a run-in with one of his former band-mates that he brushed off.

And when I rang him on Christmas Day, he kept things

light and cut our call short because he had to go for lunch at his dad's place. I mentioned how much I'd like to meet his family and hinted at the idea of him FaceTiming me once he got there, but it was three days before he called again and we didn't even speak on New Year's Eve or New Year's Day because he'd gone to a swanky party and was so hungover afterward that he didn't answer my call. Eventually, he confessed that he'd been feeling low and hadn't wanted to bring me down.

It *has* made me wonder if his happy-go-lucky life in LA is all it's cracked up to be.

WHEN FINN WALKS into Seaglass a month later, I see him right away. I observe the way he searches the bar until he finds me, register the warm joy that spreads across his face, a reflection of my own. I'm in the middle of serving a customer and he's swamped by friends, but the second I'm able to, I rush out from behind the bar and he immediately breaks away, swooping me up in his arms and hugging me tight.

"I've missed you," he growls in my ear.

I pull away to look up at him, beaming, and he lets go of my waist, cups my face, and kisses me, right there in the center of the room.

"Just as well my boyfriend isn't here tonight," I murmur when we break apart, slipping my hands over his shoulders and looping them behind his neck.

He looks alarmed for a split second before wrinkling his nose and play-punching my arm. "Don't joke about it."

I grin and kiss him. "I don't want anyone else," I say seriously. "At least, not for the next two weeks," I add casually, before erupting into giggles against his shoulder.

"Actually," he says, and the way he leaves the word hanging makes me sharply look up at him.

"I might have managed to shift some things around." He's smiling down at me.

"Tell me," I demand with excitement.

"I'm staying for a month."

I gasp. "Really?"

He nods, eyes sparkling.

"Oh my God, Finn!" I give him the hardest hug.

It's going to hurt so much more when he leaves after four whole weeks together. But the simple fact is, no other guy has ever come close to making me feel the way that Finn does. And recently, I haven't been short of offers. I've been asked out more times in the last few months than in the past few years.

I know I can't remain in this limbo state with Finn forever, but for now, there's no choice to be made. For this summer at least, I'm his. I'll deal with the consequences later.

I WAKE UP on Sunday morning feeling groggy. I've been up half the night—we both have. I thought I'd keep Finn company in his jet lag, but I'm going to be sore today . . .

I pull on my dressing gown with a smile and go downstairs to the hallway, unlocking the door to the downstairs apartment. My guests who were supposed to arrive yesterday had to delay their trip until tomorrow, so we have rare access to the whole house.

I'm in the bright, airy kitchen, making us a cup of tea, when Finn drives through the gate in his rented SEAT Leon, moving it from the car park across the road. I open the back door and call to him as he's climbing out of the car.

"I'm in here!"

He gives me a thumbs-up and then pops the trunk, getting out a battered army-green rucksack, followed by a black hard-shell suitcase. I laugh as he wheels it across the drive toward me.

"You really *are* moving in for the summer."

"I hope that's okay," he replies with a cheeky grin.

"Do your grandparents mind that you're not staying with them?" I ask as I step aside to let him in.

"Nah. Anyway, you might change your mind yet and kick me out."

"Unlikely."

As he takes me in his arms and kisses me, I imagine for a moment that this is our life. An ordinary moment in an ordinary day, kissing in our kitchen as the kettle sings.

I back away from the precipice—that way only heartbreak lies. Because this beautiful thing we have will once again be put on ice when he returns to the other side of the world.

I try to push these thoughts aside and live in the moment with him, but I can't escape the fact that our time is limited.

29

"Wow!" Finn exclaims when I show him what I've been working on.

It's a sculpture of David Schulman, my first commission, given to me by his wife, Arabella.

I never did finish Finn's sculpture. To have him sitting for me in person was magical—it made me feel alive and connected to the process. But once he'd gone back to LA, I had no interest in it.

What my fingers itched to feel was fresh, untouched, untainted clay. I lost myself in the material for a while, creating weird and wonderful shapes that soothed and healed my heart. And eventually I felt that pull back to figurative sculpture.

In autumn, once Seaglass had shut up shop and most of the visitors had left our peninsula, I turned to museums, galleries, and artists' studios for inspiration.

I met Arabella at an art exhibition in St. Ives back in January. She was on her own and held herself with incredible poise. In her early eighties, with gray hair secured in a neat bun, she was wearing a long black dress and a diamanté-studded comb in her hair that kept catching the light, sending sparkles bouncing off the dark walls. My attention was repeatedly drawn back to her, but she was the one who sought me out as I was staring at a huge painting of a flower.

"I'm not keen, are you?" she said bluntly.

"Um . , ." I looked around for the artist, hoping she wasn't in earshot.

"Too much color," she added before assessing my floral-print dress and long red cardigan. "Color looks good on *you*, dear. Just not on that painting. And certainly not on me."

I smiled at her, feeling tongue-tied. I tried to think of something to say that would keep her with me—I was finding small talk tough as I was suffering from a severe case of impostor syndrome.

"I'm still in mourning," she offered up.

"I'm so sorry. Who have you lost?"

"My husband, David, one year ago. Cancer."

"I'm so sorry," I repeated.

"Are you an artist?" she asked me.

"I'd like to be."

"There's no 'like' about it, either you are or you aren't."

"Then I am," I decided, finding her attitude refreshing.

"What sort of art?"

"Sculpture."

"A sculptress! How interesting. We need more sculptresses. Far too many men win the big public art commissions—it's depressing. What do you sculpt?"

"Mostly people, but it's been a while since I've created anything half-decent."

"Why's that, then?"

"I've had some setbacks." I paused, but she seemed to be waiting for me to go on and I found myself telling her. "My parents died a few years ago and I lost the love of it for a while. I'm only just starting to get back into it."

"How old are you?" she asked, not shying away from my tragedy.

"I've just turned twenty-five."

"You're very young to have lost them," she said, and it felt like her way of saying that she was sorry without actually using the words. "Tell me about your favorite piece," she prompted. "What have you created that you're proud of?"

So I told her about Gran. She gave me her details and asked me to email her pictures, which I did the following morning, and within half an hour of my sending them off, she replied to ask if she could commission me to create a similar piece of her husband. She wanted it cast in bronze.

I still can't believe my luck.

"It looks finished," Finn says of David's portrait.

"It is. I finally stopped tweaking it a few days ago. I'm taking it to a foundry on Monday."

"And then what?"

"Then they'll make a mold out of it and cast it in bronze."

He shakes his head, awed. "You've done it. You're earning a living as a sculptor."

I smile. "I'm not quite earning a living yet—I still need to work at Seaglass—but I'm happy. I have the best of both worlds: lively summers and peace and quiet the rest of the time so I can sculpt."

He leans forward and kisses my lips. "Sounds perfect. So is

this your permanent studio now?" He looks around at my parents' former bedroom.

"I guess so, yes. The kitchen really wasn't big enough."

I've tipped the bed up onto its side and pushed it against the wall, covering all the furniture and carpet with big sheets of plastic.

"When Michael walked in, he said it looked like Dexter's kill room," I say with a laugh.

I didn't know what that meant, but I looked it up later and felt squeamish.

Finn chuckles. "Does he still like watching serial killer stuff?"

"More than anything else."

"How is he these days?"

"He's all right. He had a nasty cough last month that wouldn't shift, but he seems to be on the mend. People with Down syndrome are prone to infections, so I was worried. I live in fear of him ending up in hospital."

"Hasn't he already been in hospital with an infection?" Finn asks, his eyebrows pulled together with concern.

"Yes, with a chest infection. Have I told you that before?"

"A couple of years ago."

"But he had Mum and Dad the last time he was admitted, and they were doctors. I'd have no idea how to handle his needs in that situation. I'd be so scared. Obviously not half as scared as Michael." I sigh. "Sometimes I think my parents only had me so that Michael wouldn't be alone in the world once they left it. There's such a big age gap between us." I stare at the studio photograph hanging on the wall of us as a family. "I used to think that my conception must've been an accident, but now I wonder if my parents were actually being strategic."

"Your parents had you because they wanted *you*, Liv," Finn says gently as he squeezes my hand.

"Is it strange that you and I can fall into such easy step with each other after so long apart?" I ask out of the blue.

"I think it's miraculous," he replies with a sweet grin, pulling me into his arms.

"Miraculous," I repeat into his neck, liking the sound of it as I stare past him at the garden and the three fat palm trees on the top terrace. "I'm already dreading how much I'll miss you when you're gone," I murmur.

"Me too. I was a mess when I left you last summer."

I pull away so I can study his face. "Were you?"

He frowns. "Completely."

I'm still not alone in my pain.

"How are things with the band? Have they forgiven you for going solo yet?"

"No, they're still livid. Now they're not even speaking to me."

"Well, Dylan seems happy to scream the lyrics instead of sing them," I say wryly of the band's guitarist, who has stepped in as lead singer.

"Hey, shall we go out for lunch?" he asks on a whim.

"Michael's coming over for Sunday lunch, but you're welcome to stay."

He looks unsure, but then he nods, agreeing.

"Ooh, we could have a barbecue! Make the most of the outdoor space while I don't have guests staying! We could invite Amy, Dan, and Rach?"

"Sounds great," he replies, looking tickled by my enthusiasm.

I send a quick text asking our friends and then give Michael a call, suggesting he invite Timothy.

"Ace!" he exclaims.

WHEN MICHAEL TURNS up at the house later, however, he's not happy to see Finn.

"What's *he* doing here?" he asks grouchily.

Here we go . . .

"Michael, please stop being rude to Finn," I say reasonably. "I'm going to be spending a lot of time with him over the next few weeks and I'd like you both to get on."

"He *is* your boyfriend, isn't he?" Michael says reproachfully, side-eyeing me.

I look at Finn and find I'm not sure how to answer this time. "Well, maybe he is. For the next month."

Finn grins.

"You'd better be nice to my baby sister," Michael warns him.

"I'm always nice to her," Finn bats back.

"You'd *better* be."

"Okay, okay, that's enough now," I say. "Is Timothy coming?" I ask Michael.

He shakes his head grumpily. "He *was* going to come, but he missed the bus."

"Oh no."

"Where does he live?" Finn asks.

Michael frowns at him. "Why do *you* want to know?"

"Maybe I could give him a lift if it's not too far away."

"Perranporth."

Finn's jaw twitches.

"You don't need to do that," I say hurriedly.

He shakes his head. "No, I can. Do you want to come with me?" he asks Michael. "Show me where his house is?"

"He's this side of town, not in the center," I tell him, hoping he won't have to drive past his old house, something he's avoided doing for years. "But call him first to see if he's still keen," I suggest to Michael.

HALF AN HOUR later, when Finn returns, Michael is in a *much* perkier mood.

He leads the way inside, Timothy hot on his heels. The pair of them are wearing identical baggy red T-shirts.

"We saw Finn's old house," my brother says happily.

"Did you?" I flash Finn a quick look.

"It was a shithole!"

"Michael!" I gasp.

"It's okay," Finn interjects, coming in behind them. "He's not wrong."

"There were weeds everywhere!" Michael says with unbridled glee. "And it was tiny!"

"It's a caravan," Timothy chips in, buoyed by Michael's enthusiasm.

"A mobile home," Finn clarifies for my benefit.

He says it flippantly, but the way his gaze lingers on my face makes me think he's not as indifferent to my reaction as he makes out.

"You sound as though you've all been on an adventure. Michael, can you get Timothy and Finn a drink please? The others will be here soon."

As soon as Michael and Timothy have turned away, I

grab Finn's arm and step forward to plant a single kiss on his lips.

He doesn't meet my eyes as he pulls away.

"TYLER ASKED ME to take him to the spot where they found Mum's clothes."

I open my eyes and look at Finn, barely able to make out his features in the darkness of my bedroom later.

I was just starting to doze off after a fun day with our friends when his voice brought me back to consciousness.

"How do you feel about that?" I ask, sensing that he's been in two minds about saying anything.

"I haven't been back since you and I went." He lets out a heavy sigh. "He wants to see where she jumped."

"Oh," I say tentatively. "Has he asked your grandparents if they might go with him?"

"I don't think so. He told me that he didn't want to upset them."

"So do you think you will?"

It's a moment before he speaks, his voice strained. "It feels like a lie to take him."

"What do you mean?"

"I don't believe she jumped off that cliff."

Full wakefulness comes over my body. I reach over and turn on my bedside lamp, needing to see his face for this conversation.

He flinches from the light but recovers, squinting at me as he folds his pillow to prop himself up against the wall.

"When I packed up her things after she'd gone, I noticed

some of her clothes were missing: a couple of her favorite out-fits and her old cowboy boots that she used to love. I asked my nan about them, but she said Mum must've thrown them out. But what if she didn't? What if she took them with her, wher-ever she went?"

I sit up and lay my hand on his smooth, warm chest, feeling his heart thudding beneath my palm. I don't know if he's try-ing to find an alternative to the devastating fact accepted by the community that his mother took her own life, or if there may be some truth to his conjectures.

"Have you got any theories about where she might have gone?"

He stares up at the ceiling for a few seconds before answer-ing with a shrug. "She always used to say that she wanted to go to Goa for a fresh start. Maybe she did."

"Did you ever speak to your therapist about this?"

He gives me a sharp look. "How do you know that I've had therapy?"

"You told me once when we were talking about your real name."

"So I did," he replies broodingly. "It's not something I shout about. But no, I've never talked about it."

"What will you do about Tyler?" I ask after a moment.

"I don't know."

"Could you show him the spot where her clothes were found—avoid saying that she jumped?"

"Maybe. I guess I could say it's where she left us."

"Or where she made the decision to leave?"

He shakes his head. "She made the decision to leave us well before that. She must've had the whole thing planned for months. Do you know, she spent more money on our presents that year than any of the previous few combined. She wanted to see our faces when we opened them so she could give herself a nice memory of us looking the happiest we'd been in ages. And after she'd got that kick, she fucked off, forever ruining Christmas for each and every one of us, including my grandparents."

"I'm so sorry, Finn." My heart hurts at the thought of the pain and suffering that he and his brothers and his grandparents had to endure. At the pain they must *still* feel every single year at Christmas, when it would be especially hard to forget.

He sighs and takes my hand off his chest, pulling me into the crook of his arm. "Turn the light off."

I lie there, my mind ticking over as his breathing begins to settle.

30

FINN JOLTS AWAKE, MOMENTARILY CONFUSED AS HE looks around, bleary-eyed.

"My latest guests have arrived," I whisper.

"Jesus," he exclaims groggily.

"Tarek did urge me to put in better soundproofing, but I didn't have the budget."

I've been awake for about fifteen minutes, listening to my newest arrivals boisterously unpacking their car. They must have driven through the night to get here this early. It's only six forty-five, but they were supposed to arrive on Saturday and have paid for the full week, so I can't complain. I'm just relieved I cleaned up after everyone had left last night.

"It's noisier here than at home," Finn complains as a child with a high-pitched voice talks nineteen to the dozen.

"You're welcome to leave anytime," I say dryly.

He turns his head and looks at me. "Do you want me to leave?"

"No!"

"I'm being a grump, aren't I?"

"Just a bit."

"I didn't sleep well."

"You fell asleep before I did."

"Well, I woke in the night when you were fast asleep and snoring your pretty little head off."

"I do not snore!"

"My ears beg to differ."

I pull my pillow out from behind my head and thump him with it.

"Oi!" He laughs.

"Are you okay?"

The gravity of the previous night's conversation has come back to me.

He screws up his nose and shrugs. "Meh."

"I do like having you here," I whisper.

He stares at me for a moment and then grins, pinning my wrists to the mattress as he rolls on top of me.

"If we can hear them, do you think they can hear us?" he asks flirtatiously.

"I don't want to risk finding out!"

"Well, in that case, you'd better be quiet."

I'M NOT WORKING until later, so we decide to go to Blue Bar for breakfast, but first we have to walk up to Finn's grandparents' house to collect his car—he parked it on their street after dropping Timothy home yesterday evening.

Finn's grandparents live in a small, tidy bungalow high up on the hill with a view over the rooftops to the ocean in the distance. The garden at the front is simple, with one large coral-colored rosebush in the corner of a small, neatly mowed lawn.

"Do you want to meet my grandparents?" he asks neutrally as we approach the house.

"I'd love to!" I say with delight.

This is a good sign. I still haven't met any of his American family—not even over FaceTime—and I've been worried Finn has been holding back parts of his private life.

The door is opened by his granddad, a short, stout man in his late sixties. He has thinning gray hair and a bulbous red nose and he doesn't resemble Finn at all, but I like the way his eyes light up at the sight of us.

"Who's this then?" he asks in a jaunty manner, and *now* I can see his grandson in him.

"This is Liv," Finn says serenely. "We've come to pick up my car. Thought we'd say hi."

"Come in! Come in!" He backs up into a small hallway and waves his hand toward the living room. "Trudy!" he calls over my shoulder as he follows us inside. "Finn's here and he's brought his lady friend!"

I hear clanking and a yelp from what I assume is the kitchen and a small woman bustles out, hastily drying her hands on a tea towel.

"Hello!" she cries, her eyes roving between our faces, but settling solidly on mine.

"Nan, this is Liv," Finn says. "Liv, my nan."

"Hello!" she gushes again. "It's so good to finally meet the famous Liv."

"*Nan,*" Finn mutters, looking uncomfortable.

"Tyler! Liam!" she hollers off to the side before stepping forward and giving me a cuddly hug.

She looks nothing at all like my own grandmother, who was tall, slim, and stylish, but she has unmistakable grand-motherly vibes.

Liam mooches into the room looking none too pleased to

have been interrupted from whatever he was doing on a Monday morning in the summer holidays. He must be thirteen now and his features are a lot rounder than they were a few years ago, his hair longer and straighter and not a little greasy.

"Hello, Liam, it's good to see you again," I say.

He mumbles something that sounds like "All right."

"Tyler!" Finn's granddad bellows.

I hear a low groan of annoyance and the sound of gunfire that has been spilling out of a nearby room is silenced. Finn clears his throat and raises one eyebrow as his other brother saunters in to join us.

Tyler is fifteen now and nearly as tall as Finn, but much skinnier. His face is all angles: high cheekbones, slightly narrow-set eyes, and a sharp jaw.

They've grown so much. They're almost unrecognizable from the boys I met outside Michael's place on Stippy Stappy a few years ago.

"Would you like a cup of tea?" Finn's nan asks us hopefully.

Tyler and Liam hover in the living room with us, looking like they'd rather be anywhere else.

I glance at Finn.

"We're heading out for breakfast," he replies.

"We could have a quick one?" I suggest, hoping to wipe the disappointment from his grandparents' faces.

Finn gives me another sidelong look before agreeing with a nod. "Sure."

"Take a seat, Liv," Trudy insists, scuttling back into the kitchen.

Finn strolls after her and Tyler and Liam slink away, leaving

Finn's granddad standing in the middle of the room with me, looking awkward.

There's a photograph of Finn's mother on the side table. I saw it straightaway, my eyes drawn to her dark hair and dimples, her stunning bluey-green eyes. She looks to be in her late teens or early twenties in the photograph and she seems happy.

How on earth did it all go so wrong?

"MY GRANDPARENTS ARE worried that Tyler is going off the rails," Finn reveals later as we walk along the beach after breakfast.

"Oh no." I shoot a look at him. "In what way?"

"He's been drinking and smoking and getting into trouble at school. They want me to stick around, to be a better influence on him."

"Will you?" Hope sparks.

He shakes his head and the spark goes out just as quickly. "This trip has already been too long for me."

"You've only been here three days!"

His comment has made me feel ill.

"I don't really mean it," he growls, hooking his arm around my waist for a rough squeeze before taking my hand. "Anyway, my feeling that way has nothing to do with you. You're incredible." He stops and turns to me, catching my chin so I have to meet his eyes. "You make coming back possible. You must know that." We start walking again. "I get dark when I'm here for too long. It's different in LA."

"Are things that good in LA, though?" I ask tentatively.

His eyes cut to mine. "What do you mean?"

"Well, you know, like you've fallen out with your band-mates and had arguments with your dad—"

"*Everyone* has arguments," he interrupts bluntly.

"I'm just saying that I get the feeling life in LA is not all it's cracked up to be sometimes," I try again.

He frowns, his grip tensing. "It's not perfect. That doesn't mean that it's not a damn sight better than it would be over here."

I hate it when he says stuff like this.

"What's so good about it?" I ask irritably, letting go of his hand.

"Come on, Liv," he says impatiently.

"No, really, I want to know. What am I competing with?"

"That's not fair. It's not about you, it's about me, about what I want from life. LA has a proper music scene, gigs, connections to the music industry. Cornwall is out on a limb—I'd never get anywhere if I stayed here. And yeah, things might not have been perfect with my dad late last year, but he's my dad. I love him. It's taken us years to build up a good relationship—I'd miss having a beer with him in front of the telly or popping into the studio to see him at work."

"Why haven't you introduced us over FaceTime?"

He glances at me. "Is that what's bothering you?"

The hurt on my face gives him his answer.

"If it matters to you, I will. It's just a bit weird, that's all, doing it on a tiny screen. I'd be on edge, my two worlds colliding. That sounds melodramatic—sorry."

"It's not melodramatic if it's how you feel. But *is* that how you feel? That this life is so separate from your life over there?"

He thinks about it for a moment before nodding. "You've

got to remember that I had to put this life behind me when I moved to America. I was a mess after what happened, having to leave my grandparents and my brothers. The only way I could survive was by focusing on the present. I barely knew my dad when I went to live with him, but he was there for me; he helped me through it, lining up a therapist so I had someone to work through all my shit with. He *cared*. I mean, fuck, my existence alone probably caused the breakdown of his marriage. He could have been resentful. My older brother and sister could have made my life hell. But they didn't. They're good people. They looked out for me. I owe them a lot."

"Your dad probably already had problems with his wife if he cheated on her, so I don't believe you could have been the cause of their divorce, but I hear what you're saying."

We fall silent.

I let out a long breath, which releases some of the tension in my shoulders, but my hurt remains. It doesn't sound as though Finn is even the slightest bit open to the idea of leaving LA. How can we sustain a long-distance relationship if there's no end in sight?

We've just passed the caves where we celebrated Dan's birthday last year. It's a spring tide today too, and not far away, half-buried in the sand, is the boiler from SS *Eltham*, a steamer that was wrecked on this beach in the late 1920s. I remember Dad reading facts about it to us when Michael was going for the job at Chapel Porth. He hoped it might help him to secure the position. Perhaps it did.

I glance toward the car park, thinking we should go say hi to my brother. I turn to Finn to suggest this and see that he's staring ahead at the cliffs, a pained expression on his face. I follow his line of sight and can just make out a rocky outcrop in the far distance, beyond the old Wheal Coates enginehouse.

I feel a chill as I think about what Finn said last night, about his suspicion that his mother *didn't* take her own life, that she faked her suicide to have a fresh start. As Finn pointed out, her body was never found.

But then the eleven-strong crew of the SS *Eltham* were never found either. Two empty lifeboats were washed ashore, but the entire crew had been lost to the rough seas. Michael was fascinated with the mystery of the missing people.

"I saw a photograph of your mum at your grandparents' place," I say.

"I hate that photo," he mutters.

I glance at him. "I thought she looked beautiful."

"She does. She used to be a total stunner. She didn't look like that when she left us. She was haggard, wasting away. That photo feels like another lie. I turn it to face the wall when I'm staying in that room. It does my grandparents' nuts in."

"I guess they miss her."

He chews his lower lip, scowling.

"Talk to me," I implore. "You never talk to me about her. You never speak about your childhood."

"That's because I've spent my life trying to forget it."

"But it might help you to work through these things. Not just with a therapist, but with a friend."

"Argh, Liv!" he snaps with frustration. "What do you want to know? That my mum used to do crack at the kitchen table right in front of us? That I'd sometimes walk in on her fucking strangers in the living room? That she hit me once because I asked why we had no food in the fridge? *What do you want to know?"* Anger has exploded across his face and his voice has grown increasingly irate with every question that has flown from his mouth.

"I'm so sorry," I say with shock.

I didn't realize how close he must have already been to his threshold because it seems I've just pushed him over it.

I reach for his hand, but he reels away from me.

"My childhood was fucked up and my mum was fucked up and Tyler and Liam are probably going to be fucked up and there's nothing I can do about it because I'm fucked up too!"

"Finn." I breathe out his name, desperately wanting to comfort him.

His chest is heaving, his expression wild, and I ache to lay my hands on his body and soothe him, put out the fire that's raging deep inside.

You don't go through something like that and come out the other side unscathed.

My mum's words come back to me.

And then, suddenly, he deflates. He presses the heels of his palms roughly to his eyes and when his hands come away, all the wind seems to have been sucked out of his sails.

"We should get back," he says flatly.

I step forward and engulf him in my arms, but his returned embrace is lacking in strength.

31

'M VERY GENTLE WITH FINN AFTER OUR TALK ON THE
beach, but he seems to have no intention of dwelling on it
and is soon back to his old self. I try to follow his lead because it's clearly what he wants me to do, but the memory of
his pain is difficult to shed. I feel closer to him, even though I
suspect that he'd turn back time and avoid our ever having
had that conversation if he could.

We fall into a rhythm as the weeks pass. He often comes
into Seaglass while I'm at work, chatting to me at the bar, and
then we go home and kiss and cuddle and talk late into the
night, followed by lazy mornings and breakfasts in bed. It feels
natural, a vision of what life could be like, though when
thoughts like that surface, I tamp them down.

We have an unspoken understanding to stick to safe subjects like our friends and our careers. He confides that he's
been writing a lot, and when we hear the downstairs guests
going out for the day, he plays some of his compositions to me
on the piano, which has been relocated to my living room. I'm
beyond proud to hear that his meetings have finally come to
something and that a major label wants him to put out a solo
album. But he's unhappy about their terms and conditions

and doesn't want to be tied down to a multi-record deal. He hates the thought of someone having control over his career, dictating what he does and even what he wears, when he could be a relatively anonymous songwriter. He's thinking about recording something with a small indie label to give himself a bit more freedom.

Eventually, he does begin to confide in me about his family and friends in America. I drink in every detail, learning more about his brother and sister, as well as his boisterous little nephew, Jimmy, who has just turned four. He tells me about his dad and his dad's new girlfriend, and it warms my heart to look through photographs with him and see the people who mean something to him.

He also fills me in on the outings he goes on with his brothers. I give him space to talk about his childhood, but I won't pry again, not like I did that day on the beach. I hate the thought of him associating his bad memories with me—he said I was the only thing that made his trips here bearable and I don't want to jeopardize that.

I do wonder how we can have a future if he can't stand the idea of living here. Though I suppose that's the truth I've been shying away from—we can't.

IT'S WITH THIS new headspace that I decide to spend the morning of the anniversary of my parents' deaths on my own. Finn is still asleep when I wake up and I manage to pull on clothes and leave the house before he comes to.

But he finds me sitting on a bench on the cliffs west of St. Agnes, not far from the place where he brought me the first year after they died.

"Hey," he says, his expression grim as he approaches.

I've become better at living with my grief, but on this one day, it hits me like a ton of bricks and I just need to cry it out.

I'm not sorry to see him.

He sits down next to me and opens an arm. I don't ask how he knew where I'd gone and he doesn't ask why I left without telling him. I slide closer and rest my cheek against his shoulder, breathing in shakily.

A gray shadow hangs over the sea in the distance, a bank of rain creeping toward us. Soon we'll be engulfed by it and I don't even care.

"Are you doing anything with Michael to mark this anniversary?" he asks.

I shake my head, tears sliding down my face. "No. He didn't even want to talk about it last year. I don't really speak to anyone about it either now, other than you."

He rests his head against mine.

"Are you okay?" I ask him, sensing his reflectiveness.

"I was just thinking about Tyler."

I brush away my tears and take his hand, giving him my full attention.

"I *will* bring him here and show him where Mum's clothes were found," he decides. "I won't tell him my theory or screw with his mind. But I can feel him drifting away from me and this might bring us closer."

"Have the boys been out to LA to see you?"

"Not for a few years, but I thought I'd see if they want to come over for Christmas."

"Have they ever been there at Christmas before?"

"No," he replies, squeezing my hand.

I give him what I hope is a supportive smile. "I think that would be so good for you all."

Finn has resisted bringing his two worlds together, but maybe that's exactly what he needs. He's currently divided in two, one foot here, one foot in America. Maybe spending a Christmas with his brothers and grandparents in LA, along with the rest of his family, would help him to feel whole.

He searches my face. "Your eyes are the same color as the sea today."

"I always thought Mum's eyes were summer skies and mine were stormy seas."

"Come back to LA with me," he whispers.

A stillness comes over my body. "For a holiday?"

"To live."

I shake my head. "Finn, I can't. You know I can't."

His expression hardens. "Why not?"

"I can't leave St. Agnes. I can't leave Michael. He needs me."

He pulls his arm out from behind my body and hunches over, his elbows resting on his thighs, staring out to sea as the first of the rain begins to hit.

"I don't know what to do," I say. "This time with you has felt different."

We've moved up to another level, which has made it both better and harder.

"It's going to be fucking unbearable when I go home," he says miserably. "I miss you when I'm gone. I think about you all the time. I hate leaving you."

"Then *don't* leave," I implore desperately, rain streaking down my face and washing away my tears. "You're needed here. Couldn't we make it work?"

I know I'm being unfair, putting this pressure on him. He's made his feelings clear. But I can't help it.

"Don't ask me to stay, Liv." He sounds desolate.

"Then don't ask me to leave," I counter.

A schism opens up in my heart as he looks at me and nods in silent agreement.

I have a devastating feeling that we've just marked the end of us.

"We can't keep going on like this," I say wretchedly. "Not indefinitely."

"What else can we do?" he asks.

"We should have stuck to our rules," I say with sudden bitterness. "At least then we'd stand a chance of getting on with our lives, of not feeling so torn."

"Is that what you want to go back to?" he asks reluctantly.

I *know* it's what we should do. I knew it from the very beginning. But pain sears my chest at the thought of severing all contact.

"Maybe we just need to cut down on the amount we speak. Make it once a month or so, just to touch base, not be so caught up in each other's lives."

He thinks about this for a moment, his lips pressed into a thin line, and then he gives me a single curt nod.

THE WEEK AFTER he leaves, I find my solace in clay.

32

THIS SUMMER

THE WARMTH OF TOM'S GAZE MINGLES WITH THE
heat that's already shimmering over my skin as I speak
to one of the foundry team about a joint that needs further fettling. My nose is prickling with the smell of ammonia
and my throat is catching on the burning scent of the molten
metal in the furnace, but it's not unpleasant. I love being in
here. This is where it all comes together, where the vision of my
hard work is realized.

We move on to talk about patination and the shade of
green I'm hoping to achieve, and when we're done, I smile at
Tom and beckon him over. He's been hanging back, not wanting to get in the way, but as the foundry worker leaves us to it,
Tom joins me, his golden-brown eyes glimmering.

He shakes his head, awed. "Your first public art. I can't
imagine how you feel right now. You must be so proud. It's incredible, Liv. I'm genuinely blown away."

His reaction is so lovely that my eyes unexpectedly sting
with tears.

"Aw," he says softly, tenderly squeezing my shoulder as I
brush away the moisture that's collected in my lower lashes.

"You should have seen me a couple of years ago when I

sculpted my parents," I say with a small laugh. "I was completely overwhelmed when they were broken out of their molds. The foundry workers gave me a wide berth." My smile wavers. "I'd give anything for them to be here now, sharing this achievement."

The tears that have been brimming in my eyes spill over, and Tom's expression is full of empathy as he reaches out and tugs me into his arms.

"I'm so sorry," he murmurs against the top of my head.

My chest is flush to his and my nerves are jangling at our close physical contact, but somehow it feels natural to be in this moment with him.

"It's okay," I choke out as he rubs my back. "Some days I go hours without thinking about them and other times it's as though I lost them only yesterday." I withdraw much sooner than I'd like to because I desperately need a tissue. "My mum and dad weren't at all creative, but I know they'd be proud," I say as I find one in my bag and sort myself out. "And also, I think they'd be thankful that I have art in my life. Does that sound strange? Sculpting has helped me to process my grief since I lost them. It's been good therapy."

"It doesn't sound strange at all." He lets out a small sigh. "I wish my granddad had been around to see me fly," he confides. "I know he would have got such a kick out of it."

"Your parents must be proud, though?"

His smile warms. "My mum used to ask me for details of our hairier rescue attempts and then she'd completely freak out about how dangerous it all sounded. That's her, though. She'll claim she hates horror movies and will then sit through two hours of one, peeking through her fingers and jumping out of her skin."

"What about your dad?" I ask with a smile at the mental picture he's given me.

"I guess you could say that he's quietly proud. He's not very vocal, but I've overheard him telling friends about my job." His smile fades and he averts his gaze.

"I'm sorry they didn't encourage your artistic talent," I find myself saying.

He shakes his head and throws me a wry smile. "I'm a far cry from being anything like you."

I frown at him. "That's not true."

"Liv." He stares at me and it's meant to be pointed, but his expression makes my insides swoop. "I draw pictures in the sand."

He's so self-deprecating, it's infuriating.

"Art is art," I state.

"No, you're right," he agrees, suddenly serious. "Just because my drawings wash away every six hours while your bronzes will last for an eternity doesn't make them any less important."

I roll my eyes at his teasing and he grins at me, his eyes alight with humor.

"Do you fancy going to the Tate gallery after this?" he asks.

"Sure!" I'd love to spend the day with him.

"I've been dying to check out some of Barbara Hepworth's famous sand sculptures," he adds glibly, trying to keep a straight face.

I reach out to playfully smack his arm before saying, "One day, you really must visit Florence to see Michelangelo's spectacular pavement art. It's really something."

He throws his head back and laughs at me, and we're both still grinning as we leave the foundry.

"YOU MUST HAVE been here so many times," Tom says almost apologetically as we walk down the steep hills of St. Ives in full sunshine, the sounds of summer at the seaside carrying through the air toward us. The beach is just across the road from the gallery.

"A few," I admit. "But it never gets old. Tate Modern in London is somewhere I really want to revisit."

"When was the last time you went?" he asks.

"When I was sixteen, seventeen? I know I could go to London on my own. I *should*. I'm desperate to check out some sculptures."

"Any in particular?" Tom asks with interest as the Tate's striking round white entrance foyer comes into view at the end of the road.

"There's a life-size Virginia Woolf bronze in Richmond upon Thames that I'd love to take a closer look at. The artist, Laury Dizengremel, sculpted her sitting on a bronze bench, looking very serene. People can actually sit beside her and watch boats drifting past on the river." I like the interactive nature of it. "Did you know there are more monuments in London that depict animals than there are in honor of named women?"

Tom pulls a face. "Really? That's bad."

"I know! Another statue I want to see is Emmeline Pankhurst standing on a chair, holding court, but she's in Manchester, which is even farther away."

Hazel Reeves, the sculptor, has another public artwork, installed in King's Cross station, but I'm less interested in the subject, Sir Nigel Gresley. I'd still like to see her work up close, though: half a ton of clay was used to create the scaled-up, seven-and-a-half-foot statue.

Sculpting is a tough profession to break into if you're female, so Hazel and Laury give me hope.

"Rach or Amy wouldn't be up for a city break?" Tom asks as we make our way up the external staircase to the entrance.

"Nah, my friends aren't interested in art and culture."

"Well, if you want some company, you can always give me a shout," he says casually, opening the door for me.

The balloon that presses against the inside of my rib cage is punctured by the realization that he's already almost halfway into his monthlong stay at Beach Cottage.

"You're going back to Wales soon," I remind him over my shoulder.

"So? They have trains to London from Wales too, you know," he teases, touching my lower back as we approach the ticket desk.

My insides glow at the thought that he'd like to stay in touch.

And we could . . . Wales is not LA.

As we wander from room to room, pausing to stare at the art, I have a surreal feeling that Tom and I are on our first date. When we come to a stop in front of a colorful abstract by Patrick Heron, his arm brushes against mine. I fight a natural instinct to edge away. But I stay put and so does he, and then I'm no longer thinking about the painting; I'm entirely consumed by the skittish feeling in my stomach.

It occurs to me, as we stand there for what feels like an age, that Tom came to St. Agnes on the very day I'd decided I was ready for a fresh start.

Maybe it's fate, or maybe it's a coincidence. It's beautiful either way.

33

T HE FOLLOWING EVENING, TOM COMES INTO SEA-
glass while I'm behind the bar, mixing up cocktails for
sunset seekers.

The vibe is perfectly chilled. Lorde is spilling from the
loudspeakers and the sun is streaming in through the open
balcony doors onto tall round tables surrounded by people on
barstools. I'm glad Tom gets to see it like this. It was practically empty the last time he came in, when it was tipping it
down.

"Hello!"

"Hey," he replies, seeming as happy to see me as I am to
see him.

He's wearing an olive-green T-shirt that fits perfectly across
his broad shoulders, and his skin is the color of golden honey.

"I'm just finishing these up and I'll be with you."

He smiles and props his elbow on the bar top while I pour
the contents of my cocktail shaker into three coupe glasses. I
can feel him watching me as I pinch three tiny lilac violas off
the plants on the counter and lay them gently on the foamy
tops of my passion fruit martinis.

My customer carries them to her friends at a nearby table

and I hear them gushing over how pretty the edible flowers look.

"It's nice to see you in here again," I say to Tom as I wipe down the bar top.

My insides feel practically balmy.

He's regarding me with equal warmth and Rach's words come to mind: *He can't take his fucking eyes off you.*

I thought of those words yesterday at the foundry too.

"Would you like a drink?" I ask him with a smile.

The girls nearby are getting out their camera phones.

"I'd love a pale ale. Which local ones do you recommend?"

"Lou's Brew? It's named after the landlady at the Drifty. Have you been into the Driftwood Spars' microbrewery?"

"I went in a couple of days ago. God, I love it here."

Every time he says it, I like him a little more.

Finn could never seem to get away from St. Agnes fast enough.

"You planning to exchange that for another one?" I nod at the battered paperback copy of *The Call of the Wild* that he's put on the bar top as I decant his bottle of beer into a glass.

"Thought I might, if that's okay?"

"Absolutely. That's what they're there for." I'm pleased that he's using our book-swap service. "At least you won't have to carry a bunch of books home with you."

"I'd have to leave them here. I only brought a rucksack with me."

"The rucksack you were carrying when you came in that first time?"

He nods.

"You fit all your belongings into that one tiny bag?" I'm astonished.

"It's actually kind of a big rucksack," he replies with a chuckle. "Will you have one?" he asks me hopefully as I ring up his order.

"I can't drink back here, but hang on. Libs?" I call down the bar. "I'm taking my break now, okay? You good?"

"All good," she replies with a nod.

"What'll it be?" Tom asks me.

"I want one of those," I reply with a smile, nodding over at the girls with the passion fruit martinis.

It'll have to be a nonalcoholic version, since I'm working, but it's still my favorite cocktail.

The dinner rush hasn't yet started as it's five o'clock, and there are only a few covers at the upstairs tables. Tom and I wander over to the sofas and sit down opposite each other.

"I've had no luck finding somewhere else to stay," he says conversationally, and my heart jumps because I hadn't known how serious he was about sticking around in Aggie for longer.

"The Driftwood Spars had a few days here and there, but not a long stint," he adds.

I screw up my nose at him, disappointed.

He mirrors me exactly.

We both laugh.

TOM IS READING out the blurbs for Harlan Coben and Lisa Jewell novels, trying to get my opinion on which book to read next, when footsteps on the stairs make me turn my head.

My stomach lurches at the sight of Tyler sauntering toward me, all long legs and arms, thick dark lashes and disheveled hair. I jump to my feet, rattled.

"Hi, Liv," he says.

He's so like Finn. I haven't seen him around town in the last year.

"Hi!" I exclaim. "Is everything okay?"

My voice comes out sounding weird, all high-pitched and panicky.

"Yeah, fine," he replies, casual as anything. "I was wondering if you've got any bar work going."

I'm shocked. Finn's brother working here with me at Seaglass? I'm not sure I could cope.

"Oh," I say regretfully. "We're kind of okay for staff right now. Anyway, you have to be over eighteen," I add hastily.

"I *am* eighteen," he states.

"Are you?" I squeak.

"Last month."

"Oh, wow! Congratulations!"

He stares at me, probably wondering why the hell I'm acting so oddly. Am I being unfair? It's not his fault Finn has moved on.

I feel a pang, but notice that it's muted.

"Gosh. Um. I don't know, Tyler, maybe?" I'm starting to rethink my knee-jerk reaction. "Bill could probably do with some help in the kitchen. Does it have to be bar work?"

"I'd prefer to mix drinks, but I guess I could help out in the kitchen." He sounds his usual surly self.

"Let me ask. Do you want to give me your number?" I remember that my phone is downstairs behind the bar.

"Why don't you give me *your* number?" he suggests bluntly before I can go with option number two: hunting out a scrap of paper in the kitchen to write on.

"Er, okay."

I reel it off and he inputs it into his phone, then calls me, hanging up after a few seconds.

"You have my number now," he says.

"Great. Thanks. I'll be in touch soon."

He's so confident. So sure of what he wants.

Not at all like his brother in that respect.

He wasn't always that way, my mind whispers.

"Oh, Finn said to say hi," he calls over his shoulder as he's leaving.

My face is on fire as I watch him go.

When I turn around, Tom is regarding me quizzically.

"I'd better get back to work," I mumble.

LATER THAT NIGHT, I return home after one of the worst shifts I've had in a long time. I can't stop brooding over the fact that Finn told Tyler to say hi to me. I still have no idea if he's coming back for Amy and Dan's wedding in August—Amy said he hasn't RSVP'd. She's promised to tell me as soon as he does, but not knowing is unsettling.

As I approach my front door, I can see light through the curtains of Tom's bedroom window. For a moment I wonder if he's waiting up for me, but I dismiss the thought. I haven't had anyone wait up for me in years.

The memory of Mum makes me feel suddenly and desperately alone as I enter the hall, closing the front door behind me. Tom's door whooshes open and I jump.

"Sorry, I didn't mean to startle you," Tom says. "I just wanted to check you were okay?" Concern is shining in his eyes even before he notices the tears in mine. "Oh God, you're not, are you?" He starts through the door and abruptly halts.

I wince and swallow, but the lump in my throat is going nowhere.

"Do you want to come in for a drink?" he asks.

I should probably head straight upstairs and try to sleep off my mood, but my body is already turning toward Tom's.

When I'm nestled into the corner of the sofa in the living room, a glass of red wine in my hand, Tom tells me that he was worried about me. He's sitting at the other end of the sofa, facing me.

"You seemed a bit shaken when that guy came in," he says. "Do you want to talk about it?"

The swelling in my throat hasn't completely gone down, so I know it'll be a struggle to speak without sounding upset, but I decide to try.

"I have history with his family," I divulge. "Specifically, his brother."

"Finn?"

It feels surreal to hear Finn's name coming out of Tom's mouth.

I nod.

"Is he your ex?" he asks.

"He was never really mine in the first place," I reply flatly.

"Where is he now?"

"In LA. Where he's always been. We kind of had an on-and-off relationship for a few years, but it was impossible to maintain it long distance."

Tom sighs and looks away, scratching his lower lip with his thumbnail. He appears contemplative.

"Yeah, that's tough," he says eventually. "I wouldn't blame you for not wanting to see his brother at work every day."

"It threw me," I admit.

He flashes me a grin. "He was quite self-assured, wasn't he?"

"*Wasn't he?*" I erupt, leaning forward, my eyes wide, a smile suddenly breaking out on my face.

He smirks. "Wouldn't surprise me if he proved to be a bit of a handful."

"I thought the same thing! I'm not sure how well he'd take orders." As soon as I say it, I feel bad. "He's had a lot of shit to deal with in his life," I reveal, staring down at my hands. "I don't know. Maybe I should give him a trial run."

"Do you have any work for him?" Tom asks, and when I meet his eyes, I see that his earlier amusement has faded to a more serious expression.

"We actually do have a position opening up soon. Our sous-chef is moving to London in a few weeks, but obviously that's far too experienced a role for him. But our KP is off on Saturday, then on holiday from Wednesday, and I still haven't found any cover." I experience a flurry of panic at the thought. "I don't think Tyler would enjoy the work, though—there's *some* food prep involved, but it's mostly washing pots and pans, keeping the floors clean, and sanitizing food prep areas. Bill doesn't suffer fools gladly and he'd blow his top if Tyler slacked off. It's a bit too much of a baptism of fire for someone with his temperament, I think. I'll see if I can juggle some bar shifts. That's where he really wants to be."

Maybe we could bring him in as a runner. Although the thought of Tyler racing around, collecting empties, cleaning glasses, refilling ice, and changing barrels is a bit of a stretch too.

"That's very kind of you," Tom says sincerely, giving me a significant look. "I'm sure he'll attract lots of female attention shaking the shit out of cocktails."

I burst out laughing and his lips curve up at the corners, his gaze steady on mine. The olive green of his T-shirt brings out the golden highlights in his eyes.

"He probably *would* make a good mixologist. I can just imagine him flairing like Luke and Kwame and winning all the girls over."

We only introduced cocktails last year after I urged Chas to glam up our drinks menu. I argued that it should be more in line with the great new food our kitchen was putting out. Before that it was all pints and shots.

I feel a pang of nostalgia for the old days. I can't imagine a band like Mixamatosis thrashing out at Seaglass since it's had its makeover.

But Dan, Tarek, Chris, and Kieran have long since hung up their instruments anyway.

Unlike Finn.

I release a long drawn-out sigh. Everyone and everything has moved on, even Seaglass.

"What are you going to do about your KP's cover?" Tom asks.

"I don't know." I push my hand through my hair and try to detangle it. "Being a manager is really bloody difficult."

The schedule is my least favorite part of the job, trying to juggle shifts with people wanting this or that day off. And then there are the sick days, holiday cover, hiring and firing, training, dealing with useless people who refuse to follow the systems—*and* the occasional cocky dickhead who thinks he or she knows better than me. Plus, there's the ordering and stock-taking. At least Bill does all that for the kitchen.

"Well, if you're stuck, let me know," Tom says.

I smile at him, assuming he's joking.

He *can* cook—I've seen him in action and it was hot as hell—but the kitchen porter is far too junior a role for someone like Tom.

"I'm serious," he says.

I lean forward and look him in the eye. "Tom, did you hear the job description?"

"Yeah, but I don't mind mucking in. I'm itching to do something other than sit here and read."

"Can't you find a better way to occupy your time? You *are* on holiday."

He gives me a wry look. "I'm not really sure what this is."

What *is* he doing here? Why doesn't he seem to be in any rush to get back to his job in Wales? Does he even still have a job in Wales? Maybe he's on an extended sabbatical.

My expression softens. "Do you want to talk about it?" I turn the tables on him.

He lets out a low groan and scrubs his face with his hand. "Not really. But I am bored out of my brain. I'd be happy to help you out."

"I'd be very grateful if you did," I say with a grin, loving the turn this night has taken.

"Then consider it sorted," he says.

34

BARELY SLEEP OVER THE NEXT COUPLE OF NIGHTS, AND thanks to our current heat wave, we're even more run off our feet than usual. I'm shattered, but I think part of it is emotional exhaustion. My mind keeps circling back to Finn telling Tyler to say hi. It was such a throwaway comment, but surely Finn knew that it would set my head spinning.

When Tom opens the door to me late Saturday afternoon, there's something new in his eyes, and for some reason, I find it hard to look at him directly. As we walk down to Seaglass for the evening shift, I notice that my tiredness has been replaced by a strange anticipation.

He doesn't put a foot wrong in the kitchen, according to Bill. When Bill and the sous-chef head home, Tom sticks around for a drink at the bar, and after the clean-down, we have a lock-in. There's been so much camaraderie between the staff tonight and it's a pleasure to sit down with everyone, but by twelve thirty, they've all gone home and only Tom and I remain.

We've been making our way through a bottle of rosé and cracking each other up with silly anecdotes. From the way we keep losing it laughing, I think we're both pretty tipsy. Alcohol has conquered my earlier shyness, and he seems completely chilled, half twisted toward me, his foot propped on the foot-rest of my stool. Occasionally his knee knocks against mine, and every time this happens, my skin seems to vibrate, but neither of us has moved away to gain more room. He's wearing jeans and I'm in a flirty-hemmed, thigh-length summer dress, so I'm sure I'm feeling the effect of our contact much more than he is.

I've been telling him about how I set my skirt alight with a Bunsen burner once when I was at uni and I realize that his attention keeps drifting to my lips. Now that I've noticed, I'm intensely aware of it. The next time his knee grazes mine, it stays there.

I feel heat radiating from the spot, soaking into my blood-stream and warming me through from head to toe. Our con-versation dries up and we sit there for a long moment, simply staring at each other.

"I guess we should go home," I murmur when I become a bit more conscious of the silence.

He removes his long leg from between mine and languidly gets to his feet as I slide off my stool.

"I'll just check everything's in order upstairs."

He follows me up, seemingly without thinking. That's what he's like, I've found: if something needs doing, he wants to help.

"Can you switch off the lights?" I call over my shoulder as I head into the kitchen. Satisfied with what I see, I come out again to find that the ceiling lights are off, but the festoon lights are aglow.

"Sorry, I couldn't find the switch," he says apologetically, looking around.

"Behind you." I nod at the navy wall by the sofas, but I'm already crossing the room toward him.

I lean past him to flick off the switch they're wired to, and when I straighten up again, I realize just how closely we're standing. For a moment, I can't even breathe.

My eyes travel up to his. They're glinting in the light from the full moon outside the panoramic windows. The darkness around us feels intimate.

Neither of us moves a muscle as he gazes down at me. I know that he hasn't long been out of a serious relationship and I'm clearly not over Finn, but from the way we're staring at each other, nothing else matters right now.

As though in slow motion, he reaches out, his hand skating lightly along the curve of my waist. The heat from his fingers sears straight through the thin cotton of my dress to scorch the skin beneath.

My breath hitches and I inch a little closer, touching my hands to the waistband of his jeans.

He inhales sharply. I tilt my face up to his, and a moment later he lowers his mouth onto mine.

My whole body is rocked with a jolt of electricity as our lips connect, and then goose bumps are shivering into place all over me as we begin to kiss, slowly at first, and then with more pressure. Both his hands come up to hold my waist and I take this as an invitation that it's okay for me to touch him in turn, so I do what I've been fantasizing about for the last week and slip my hands under the hem of his T-shirt.

I'm heady at the feel of his perfectly flat stomach, the soft hair that travels up from the top button of his jeans, the ridges and contours of his chest.

I can barely catch my breath as I explore his smooth, firm skin and hard muscles. I want to explore every inch of him, and as he pulls me flush against his hips, I figure he might just let me.

His breathing has become ragged, his kisses more demanding as his tongue caresses and probes, but the deeper contact is making my legs feel shaky. I edge us toward the sofa, lightheaded and dizzy. I think I could live on his kisses alone. He's phenomenal.

He falls down to the cushions, bringing me with him.

"Fucking hell, Liv," he mutters into my mouth, his voice thick and heavy with desire as he jerks me roughly against him. I'm losing my mind. "Shall we take this back to the cottage?"

"No. I don't want to wait," I reply.

I'm done with waiting.

35

TWO SUMMERS AGO

T'S THE FIRST SATURDAY OF AUGUST, THE DAY OF THE ST.
Agnes Carnival, and I'm upstairs at Seaglass, snatching a mo-
ment of peace before the madness hits. It's only lunchtime—
I plan to go and watch the parade later with Michael.

My friends are taking part this year—Rach is riding on a
float for surfers and Amy has joined a comedy dance troupe.
Dan, meanwhile, is one of about eight puppeteers who will
be working the giant Bolster. Shirley took Michael and Timothy earlier to help decorate the giant effigy with fresh flowers. It's always a fun day and Aggie is buzzing—the whole
village comes out for it. I can't wait to see my friends in
action.

We're hosting an after-party at Seaglass. We have a fantas-
tic new head chef called Bill who's been doing great things
with our menu. Chas has always been so chilled, but he's
stepped up his game this year. He's even started an Instagram
page for Seaglass, posting regularly.

I figured I should probably do the same for myself, now
that I'm getting commissioned, so a few weeks ago I set up an
account of my own. It's a bit alien to me, self-promotion, but

it's the way the world works these days so I've got to get on board if I want a career as a sculptor.

On a professional level, it's been a great year. After Finn left last summer, I threw myself headlong into sculpting and from October, when Chas battened down Seaglass's hatches for winter, it was pretty much all I did.

Arabella Schulman, the woman who commissioned me to make a sculpture of her late husband in the style of Gran's, asked me to create a similar piece of her late son.

It was fun to sculpt her husband, who'd lived a long and happy life, but I found the process of working on her son emotional. He'd died in a motorbike accident decades earlier, and it made my heart squeeze to study photographs and imagine his mother's pain when he'd been taken in such a sudden and tragic way at the age of nineteen. I poured a lot of my own sadness into that clay, and I often found myself thinking about Mum and Dad. I realized I was approaching a time when I'd feel able to sculpt them.

I expected Arabella to well up when I presented the piece to her, but she simply stared at her boy for a long time before saying, "I'd like you to do me now. But I want a straightforward figurative portrait," she declared. "I haven't gone yet."

Sculpting Arabella was a different experience entirely. She sat for me throughout most of January, February, and March, and toward the end of our intensive time together, she said that she would arrange a space for me to exhibit my work. I hadn't realized how influential she'd been in the art world, having owned a gallery in London for many years, and she's still well-connected.

Once Arabella's portrait was finished, I was ready to sculpt Mum and Dad.

The process was exquisitely heartbreaking and I was consumed at times, occasionally working right through the night and into the next day.

When Seaglass threw open its doors in April, I didn't return immediately. I was too caught up in what I was doing.

In May, Arabella came through on her promise, arranging a space at a gallery in St. Ives for me to exhibit my "bereaved" series, which now included her late husband and son as well as Gran, whom I'd had recast in bronze.

When I was thinking about what to call the pieces, I was inspired by something Arabella herself had said when she'd asked me to sculpt her.

I want a straightforward figurative portrait. I haven't gone yet.

The label I requested to be etched onto the plaques was GONE.

Rach, Amy, Chas, and Dan came to the exhibition, as well as Michael and Shirley. Rach even brought a new friend from work.

It was one of my proudest moments to stand there among friends and family in my section of the gallery, talking to art enthusiasts. I got one more commission after that night, and there could be another on the cards.

But in June, once the fervor of sculpting my parents had begun to settle, I decided to return to Seaglass. I wasn't sure how I'd feel about stepping behind the bar again after so many months of working as an artist, but I found that I loved it. Seaglass is a second home to me, and Chas and the staff are like a second family. Plus, I still crave the adrenaline rush I get from a busy service.

In the evenings and on my days off, I continued to put the

finishing touches on Mum and Dad, and last month, they were finally ready to be cast in bronze.

I wept when they were broken out of their plaster molds at the foundry. I'd had to cast them in sections, and there was a lot of work to be done sandblasting the bronze and welding each of them together, a job the foundry team is still seeing to, but in their rawest state, they were beautiful. It had taken me almost four years to get there, but I felt an incredible sense of achievement.

I also felt at peace. I couldn't wait to take them home.

More than that, I couldn't wait to show them to Finn.

I *still* can't wait to show them to Finn. But I have no idea when or if he's coming back.

We did stay in touch after he left and we tried to stick to our new once-a-month rule, but even that proved to be too hard.

To begin with, it was obvious to both of us that we were holding back, trying to protect ourselves from the hurt of our cyclical separations.

And then, in early February, our rule went completely out the window when Michael was admitted to hospital with a respiratory infection.

He was there for three weeks, and every time I had to go home, he'd clutch my hand and beg me not to leave. But I wasn't allowed to stay overnight.

The doctors and nurses were mostly great, but there were a few who weren't clued up about how to deal with his needs, leaving Michael worried and unsettled.

At least I could go and see him every day, which I wouldn't have been able to do if I'd lived farther afield. Thankfully,

Shirley was able to visit too, as well as some of his friends from his social club, but it wasn't enough. Michael told me, sobbing, that he missed Mum and Dad, and it crippled me. I ached for them too. It was around then that I started sculpting them.

I called Finn more often throughout all of this, but the contact actually made me feel worse. I'd ring, crying, and discover that he was out at lunch or in the studio and I'd clam up, not wanting to disturb him. He was recording his first solo album for an indie label and sometimes he simply wasn't available. I know it hurt him too, not to be able to comfort me.

In the end, I told him, tearfully, that it was too hard, that it would be better to have no contact at all than to experience what felt like rejection, even if it wasn't intentional. It was a torturous decision to make, but I think he understood.

We haven't been in touch for over four months and now that we're into August I'm close to cracking and reaching out to him. So far, my pride has kept my curiosity in check. I feel as though I'll lose something if I'm the first of us to make contact after all this time. I can't explain it.

He usually returns during Tyler and Liam's school holidays, but the boys went to LA at Christmas so there's a chance he won't even visit this summer. The thought of him not coming makes me feel ill, but the agony I'll feel if he does return and then leaves again will be worse.

I focus on my phone and post a couple more pictures of the progress the foundry workers have made with my parents this week. I have ten new followers, I realize, clicking on NOTIFICATIONS. My attention zeroes in on one name: *Finn Lowe*.

My heart skips a beat.

There you are . . .

Finn changed his surname to Lowe for his solo album. I guess he decided that Finn Finnegan didn't have a nice ring to it after all.

He's liked all of my posts and has commented on a couple.

Stunning he says simply of a close-up of my mother's face.

Beautiful is what he says of another.

After skipping a beat, my heart is now racing.

I do follow his Instagram feed, but I never comment. It doesn't make me feel good to look at it, so I tend to avoid it. Seeing pictures of him and his happy-go-lucky life in LA makes me feel horribly disconnected from him.

But now that he's written, I can't resist replying.

I feel nervous as I send him a DM: Well, hello, stranger. Visiting our shores anytime soon?

I doubt he'll be awake yet, so I force myself to close the app and go downstairs to the bar.

Chas is standing in the corner, facing the wall, one elbow propped up against the bar top. There's something about his body posture that doesn't seem right. He looks smaller. He looks *older*, I realize, and he is, of course. He'll be celebrating his seventieth birthday next year.

"Are you okay?" I ask him.

He glances over his shoulder at me, his usually deeply tanned face seeming a little pale.

He wrinkles his nose. "Not feeling that hot."

"What's wrong?" I ask with concern, as Chas hasn't taken a single day off for ill health in all the time I've known him.

"I don't know," he replies. "Maybe I'm coming down with something."

"Symptoms?"

"Nausea. A bit of light-headedness."

"Go home," I insist, walking over to him and rubbing his back.

"No, I'll be fine." He brushes me off.

"At least go and sit down on the balcony for a bit, get some fresh air."

The fact that he obeys worries me.

CHAS CLAIMS HE'S feeling a bit better by the time I leave Seaglass to walk up to the village via Michael's house. It's a windy and overcast day, though thankfully no rain is forecast, and when Michael and I reach the bakery on the corner, we see that the colorful bunting lining the buildings along the high street is straining against its fixings, fluttering wildly. The streets are already packed with people waiting for the procession to arrive.

Michael's face is radiant with expectation. He loves the carnival. I keep encouraging him to take part, but he shakes his head violently at every suggestion, which is why I'm standing here on the sidelines, keeping him company.

That's what I keep telling myself, and it's what I tell my friends too, when they try to bully me into joining one of the floats, bands, or dance troupes, but the truth is, the thought of all those eyes on me brings on a cold sweat.

It's why I was surprised at how much I enjoyed exhibiting my art back in May. It was the first time I'd shown my work since university. I guess talking about art is the one thing I can do.

"Here comes Bolster!" Michael exclaims as the sound of far-off drumbeats fills the air. I'm standing behind him and he's jumping on the spot, his head turned excitedly toward the street where the procession will appear. I can hear anticipation in the chatter of the children and adults around us.

When two hands cover my eyes, I almost jump out of my skin. I spin round, bashing slightly into the offender's chest, and almost keel over when I see Finn standing there, his dimples out in force.

"Oh my God!" I squeal. "What are you doing here?"

"Thought I'd surprise you," he says as Michael turns around, spies him, and does a dramatic eye roll before returning his attention to the street.

"Hey, Michael, how are you doing?" Finn asks affably.

"Bolster's coming," he replies in a monotone voice.

Last summer, after Finn left, Michael came over and saw me in tears.

It wasn't the first time this had happened.

"I don't like the way he upsets you," he said.

"Who?" I asked, because I hadn't offered an explanation as to why I was crying.

"Finn."

My brother is more astute than I sometimes give him credit for and suddenly it made sense why he still had it in for Finn after so much time. We had a bit of a heart-to-heart about it and I tried to reassure him, but he's clearly still feeling protective.

"Ty! Liam!" Finn shouts out across the heads of the people packed outside the bakery. He waves enthusiastically, trying to get his brothers' attention. "Come here!"

Satisfied that they're making their way over, he turns back to Michael and me.

"When did you get here?" I ask.

"Last night."

Why didn't he give me any warning?

"Look, look, look," Michael interrupts, tugging on my sleeve.

Bolster appears around the corner behind the drum band, a lumbering twenty-eight-foot-tall puppet, and I let out a laugh at the sight of Dan, dressed in what appears to be an old potato sack, manhandling one of its arms at the end of a long pole.

"Priceless," Finn mutters with a grin, placing his hands lightly on my hips from behind. "Missed you," he says in a low, deep voice, directly into my ear.

My insides are a crazed, jittery mess.

"I missed you too," I reply, but I can't meet his eyes. "I take it you're single?"

He stiffens. "Yes. You?"

I nod.

I went on a date last month, but there was no spark. Or at least, if there *was* a spark, it was so muted compared to the burning desire I feel for Finn that I simply couldn't be bothered. I've been too busy to date, anyway.

I feel him relax again as he steps a little closer, splaying one hand across my stomach.

I can barely breathe at the contact.

FINN BRINGS HIS brothers to Seaglass for the after-party. They sit at a table by the balcony. I pop out from behind the bar to say a quick hi.

"What have you got playing?" Finn asks me with a frown, clearly disapproving of our music choices.

"I don't know. Would you like to take over the playlist?" I ask, syrupy sweet.

"Damn right I would." He jumps to his feet and sets off toward the bar.

I watch him give Chas a hug before turning back to his brothers with a grin and an eye roll. What is he *like*?

Liam purses his lips at me. Tyler is nonplussed. They're fourteen and sixteen now. Tyler has grown a little taller since last year, but Liam has gone outward as well as upward. I wonder if he plays rugby.

"How are you two?" I ask them while Finn's otherwise engaged.

Now he's chatting to Chas, who I know will indulge him, music-wise.

"Good," Liam mumbles.

"Fine," Tyler replies.

"Did you have a good time in LA at Christmas?"

Tyler shrugs and nods, but Liam's expression thaws by several degrees. "We went to Disneyland."

"Awesome! Was that fun?"

I know this already. Finn mentioned it, but didn't go into detail.

"Yeah," he says.

"Did your grandparents go with you?"

"Yeah, but not to Disneyland," Tyler chips in.

"It must've been nice seeing where Finn lives." I'm a little envious because I haven't, but the thought of being on Finn's home turf also makes me feel strangely nervous. "Do you think you'll go back?" I ask.

"We are. This Christmas," Tyler replies.

"Cool!"

"Maybe we'll make it a regular thing, right, lads?" Finn says, overhearing as he returns.

I cock my ear to the speaker. "Who's this?"

"Liily," he replies.

"Sick," Tyler proclaims.

"I'd better get back behind the bar," I say.

Finn reaches over and squeezes my hand as I start to walk off. "See you later."

HE TAKES THE boys home at 10 p.m. I happen to be looking toward the door when I see them leave, and the darkness that washes over me at the realization that he didn't even say goodbye impacts me for the next forty-five minutes.

Then he waltzes back in again and all is right with the world.

He smiles as he comes over to the bar where I'm pulling a pint, resting his elbows on the top and leaning right over.

It takes me a second to realize that he's after a kiss.

I flip off the tap and lean toward him, feeling effervescent as his lips meet mine in a brief, gentle press. I withdraw, blushing, and he smiles at me, his eye contact steady as I carry on filling the pint.

"I thought you'd gone home," I say after my customer has settled up.

He frowns. "Without saying goodbye?" He suddenly seems so familiar to me with that affronted expression.

"Do you want to come back to mine later?" I have to pluck up the nerve to ask, so I'm gratified when he nods.

Gasps and yelps from farther down the bar wrench my attention away. My heart is in my throat when I see what's caused the commotion: Chas has collapsed.

I fly over to him while our new bar girl stares in shock.

"Chas? Are you okay?" I ask urgently.

His eyes are open, but his face is ashen and he's clutching his chest.

Rach muscles in behind the bar next to me.

"He was complaining of light-headedness and nausea earlier," I tell her.

She shouts to Amy, "Call 999!" and then over the bar top to her friend Ellie: "Go and get the AED!"

She's referring to the portable defibrillator that has been hanging on the wall of the Surf Life-Saving Club for the last few years, ever since the community fundraised enough money to buy it.

To me, she says, "I think he's having a heart attack."

36

THE ONLY PEOPLE LEFT WITH ME AT SEAGLASS ARE Finn, Rach, and Ellie.

Dan went with his uncle in the ambulance and Amy is following behind in their car. The rest of us are sitting here, reeling.

I simply can't imagine this place existing without Chas behind the bar. I'm in shock.

Ellie was so cool and collected when she ran back with the defibrillator. She and Rach both volunteer at the Surf Life-Saving Club and are trained in resuscitation, so they knew exactly what to do. Rach had already cut Chas's T-shirt open and she and Ellie fixed the two pads to his chest. Chas was awake—he hadn't gone into cardiac arrest—but the AED would have delivered an electric shock to try to restart his heart if needed.

I felt completely useless, standing by. Dan and Finn were the ones to clear people out of the bar so that the paramedics had good access once they arrived.

"I think it's time to make a move," Rach says wearily, patting Ellie's thigh.

"Yeah," I agree, looking around.

The rest of the clean-down can wait until morning—I sent the staff home twenty minutes ago.

I walk Rach and Ellie to the door. "I'll see you downstairs in a sec," Rach murmurs to Ellie after we've said goodbye and I've added another thank-you to the ones I showered on her earlier.

Ellie leaves and Rach turns to me, apprehension gleaming in her hazel eyes.

"Thank you so much—" I begin to say, but she interrupts me.

"Liv."

"Yes?"

"Ellie's my girlfriend."

I stare at her for a moment, uncomprehending. And then I get it, all at once, and my chest inflates. I pull her in for a fierce hug, hating that she would ever doubt that this would be my reaction.

"I thought you fancied Chris!" I exclaim in a whisper as we break apart.

"I did," she replies with an amused shrug, before her expression sobers. "I wanted to tell you earlier, but with all that happened . . ."

"I'm glad you still did," I say, rubbing her arm.

"I was about to leave and then I thought, fuck it, life's too short. Tonight proved that."

"Let's catch up soon," I say meaningfully.

She nods and looks past me at Finn, who's sitting at the table where we left him, scrolling through his phone.

"Have a good night," Rach says with equal significance.

It's after 1 a.m. by the time Finn and I make it back to Beach Cottage.

He looks shattered and I realize he must be horribly jet-lagged.

"I don't know how you're still standing," I say as we climb the stairs to my bedroom.

"I think I'm running on adrenaline," he replies.

"Me too. Do you want water or tea or anything?" I ask over my shoulder as I reach the top.

"I just want you."

I come to an abrupt halt and turn around, my blood warming in my veins at the heated look in his eyes.

He takes me in his arms and lowers his mouth to mine, kissing me slowly, deeply.

My knees tremble as I clutch his slim waist, and then everything speeds up and we're stumbling into my bedroom and landing on my bed.

We shed our clothing quickly, desperately, but just as I think he's about to take things up a notch, he hesitates, staring so deeply into my eyes that emotion begins to gather at the base of my throat.

"Finn," I whisper in a choked voice, cupping his face with my hands.

He bends down to gently kiss my lips and then slowly sinks into me, our bodies connecting for the first time in almost a year. The sensation feels raw and not just physically. I don't know why it hurts so much.

"YOU DIDN'T BRING a suitcase over this time," I say the following morning as I lie in the crook of Finn's arm, our heads resting on the same pillow.

"I left it at my grandparents' place."

"Will you bring it over later?" I tilt my face to look at him.

"I'm not sure," he says, and his indecisiveness sounds strange, as though he might be putting it on.

"Why does this feel so different to last year?"

He doesn't respond for a moment. Maybe he's pondering my question, or maybe he's just trying to work out how to give me his answer.

I'm all ears when he speaks.

"I think last year was a little too hard," he admits quietly, nestling his head against mine. He pauses. "I had reservations about coming back, if I'm honest."

"Reservations about being here in Aggie or reservations about seeing me?"

"Both."

My heart aches as he lifts my hand from his chest and presses his palm against mine in the space between us, linking our fingers. I stare up at our hands and my vision goes blurry.

"I'm glad you came back," I say thickly, and I feel his grip on my hand tighten a fraction. "How long will you stay?" I turn my head to look at his face.

"Ten days." He's still staring at our entwined hands.

"Oh." *That's no time at all.*

"How's Michael?" he asks. "He seemed back to his usual self yesterday."

"He is."

It pains me to remember how distant I felt from Finn when I was suffering through the trauma of Michael's hospital stay. I thought I might lose my brother at one point, and I'd realized that a world without him in it would be intolerable.

"He's the most resilient person I know."

Finn's expression has grown serious. "I'm sorry I couldn't be there for you."

I nod, needing a moment to swallow the lump in my throat.

"What are your plans for today?" I ask after a while, changing the subject.

"I don't have any. You?"

"I've got to go back to Seaglass this morning and clean up."

"Will you open today? After last night?"

"I don't know."

We woke to a text from Amy saying that Chas is stable, but I have no idea when or if he'll be able to return to work. What if he can't? The future of Seaglass suddenly feels uncertain, as does the future of everyone who works there.

"Could you cover for Chas, do you think?" he asks me.

"As manager?" I reply.

He nods.

"Yeah, I think so. I mean, I've worked there long enough. I know the ropes now."

I decide to text Dan and ask what he thinks. He happens to be with Chas at the hospital when he replies only a minute or so later.

The Unc says please open for brunch but feel free to close early. Been a rough night!

How is he? I reply, glad to hear that he's awake and capable of discussing work. That's a good sign, surely?

Already talking about getting onto a surfboard.

I smile with relief, although I know we're not out of the woods yet, and then I set about texting the rest of our staff.

"No Sunday lunch with Michael today then?" Finn asks me once I've discarded my phone and returned to his arms.

"We don't do it every weekend anymore."

"No?" He seems surprised by this.

"We catch up often enough during the week that it doesn't really feel like it has to be a thing. I probably do a roast for us maybe once a month."

"That's nice."

"It is. It works well. And it means he can do more Sunday shifts at Chapel Porth. He likes those. It's the day he's most likely to see classic cars come in."

We fall silent.

"*Well, hello, stranger,*" he says with amusement.

I glance up to see that he's on his phone and has found my message on Instagram.

"Yes, that was a surprise, seeing your comments on my posts," I say dryly.

He kisses my temple. "I'm so proud of you," he murmurs against my hair.

I pull away and look at him.

"You did it," he says. "Your parents. Sculpture. Everything's taking off."

I'm full of warmth as I smile back at him. It means so much to me, his acknowledgment.

"Tell me about you," I prompt.

"Later. I want to know how all this came about."

I fill him in about the exhibition in May and then have a freak-out when I realize the time. I leave him in bed while I get ready to go down to Seaglass.

When I come out of the bathroom, he's buttoning up his jeans.

"You off?"

"Yeah, I should probably get back."

"When will I see you again?"

The nervousness that has been plaguing my insides ramps up. I suddenly feel as though I'm on shifting sands, not really sure where I stand with him anymore.

"Later?" he asks.

"Tonight?" I check.

"If you're free."

"I'm free." I'm sure I've failed to hide my relief.

He smiles at me, but his dimples are suppressed.

37

WITH EVERYTHING THAT'S HAPPENED OVER THE last twenty-four hours, I completely forgot that I'd told Michael I'd drive him to a dance at his social club tonight. I'd made do without a car for so long, but it was all getting a bit ridiculous, and when Arabella commissioned me to make a sculpture of her, she asked if she could sit for me at her place. With the amount she was paying me, it was the least I could do—and it proved a pleasure to get out of the house each day. It also made me long to sculpt in my garden studio again. I'm determined to use it this autumn, once my guests have left, although I'm not sure for how long. I suspect it might not be warm enough once winter hits.

When I tell Finn about Michael's dance night, he offers to come with us for the drive.

"Maybe we could grab a bite to eat in Perranporth."

I'm surprised he's suggested it, but I'm pleased, considering he's steered clear of his hometown over the years.

We take a shortcut up past Michael's terrace of nine tiny cottages and knock for him, figuring he can walk up to my car with us. I've taken to parking it on the quiet street where Dan and Amy live.

Michael bursts through the door in high spirits, wearing a smart black shirt that Shirley must have ironed for him because I know from experience that *he* certainly wouldn't have. At the sight of Finn, his happy expression morphs into one of mild repugnance.

He has the most expressive facial features of anyone I know.

"Is Timothy going to be there?" Finn asks him as we walk up the hill together.

"Yeah," he replies grouchily.

"Any of your other friends?"

"All of them."

"Any girls?"

He side-eyes Finn. "Yeah."

"Cool."

"You can come if you want."

My eyebrows jump up. I shoot Finn a quick look, but he's staring at Michael.

"Am I allowed to?"

"Yeah. Anyone's allowed."

"Don't you have to have tickets?" I ask, wondering how we're going to get ourselves out of this.

"You can buy them there."

"Looks like you and me are going to a dance tonight, baby," Finn says cheekily, grabbing my hand and swinging it high.

Michael looks at our hands and rolls his eyes, but not as dramatically as usual.

I drive us while Finn sits in the front seat of my blue Honda Civic, his long legs stretched out. It's only a short journey, but he's plugged his phone into the car's stereo and is trying to decide what to play to get us in the mood.

"Hang on, Mikey, you're going to love this song," he says.

"Don't call me Mikey!" my brother snaps.

"He hates it," I say as an aside to Finn.

"Hang on, Michael, you're going to love this song," Finn says in exactly the same neutral tone as before, not taking the slightest bit of offense.

He puts on Franz Ferdinand's "Michael."

I glance in the rearview mirror at my brother in the back seat and see him staring out of the window. His head begins to bob.

"Oh, I like this one!" he gushes, his face riddled with excitement as he uses our headrests to haul himself forward.

"Put your seat belt on!" I scold him.

He flops back and nods his head along to the beat as he fastens up, singing the odd word here and there.

When the chorus kicks in, Finn belts it out and Michael's face lights up with glee. Then he joins in too and I try to concentrate on driving while laughing at the pair of them.

We pull into the car park opposite the social club, and as soon as I've turned off the ignition, Finn jumps out of the car and jogs around the front to hold up his hand to Michael. My brother grins and high-fives him.

Finn has tried time and again to be friendly to my brother—his persistence is one of the things I admire about him. I'm thrilled that Michael finally seems to be thawing.

Lots of Michael's friends live in Perranporth and loads of them are already at the social club when we go inside. P!nk is blaring from the sound system, and red, green, and blue disco lights are swirling around the wooden dance floor. There are lots of people here, and not just those who regularly attend Michael's club—the crowd is full of friends, family, and support workers.

Michael has made a beeline for Timothy, so Finn and I go over to say hi. They're chatting excitedly about something, but they come to a sudden stop when they see us.

"Hello!" Timothy says cheerily, and he and Finn share a hug complete with back slaps.

"I'll go to the bar!" Finn shouts over the music after I've also had a hug. "What do you guys want?"

He takes their orders for two pints of Tribute and turns to me expectantly.

"I'll come with you."

I decide to leave my brother to it, not wanting to cramp his style.

It's the reason I haven't come to one of these social dances before, but there are so many other family members here that now I feel guilty.

I follow Finn through the crowd to the bar, which spans from one side of the room to the other and has colored fairy lights fixed to the bulkhead. In front of it, several tables and chairs have been set out on the carpet.

Finn leans over the counter to order.

I can't believe he's up for this. I adore him for it.

We deliver Michael and Timothy's drinks to them and then take ours to a table, huddling close so we can hear each other over the music.

"Tyler and Liam seemed well yesterday," I say in his ear.

He smiles. "It was great having them in LA at Christmas."

"Liam said he had fun at Disneyland."

He laughs. "Yeah, that was eventful. Tyler got friendly with a girl and went on all the rides with her, but Liam and I had a laugh together."

"How is Tyler generally?" I ask.

"Pretty good, I think. He's done better at school this year. Hasn't got himself into as much trouble. We speak on the phone a fair bit."

"And your grandparents? Did they enjoy the trip?"

"They loved it."

He's been staring at the dance floor, a small reminiscent smile on his face, but now he looks at me and smiles properly, happiness radiating from him.

"I hope we can do it every year," he says, returning his gaze to the dance floor.

"I'm so glad it went well."

He nods, reaching under the table to hook his hand around the inside of my thigh. I'm wearing a short summer dress with a floaty hemline and I'm hyperaware of his thumb brushing my bare skin.

I love that he's being tactile. I've been unsettled by the way he didn't text me to say that he was coming, and how he didn't even let me know that he'd arrived. He sought me out at the carnival, but he hesitated to put his arms around me, and it wasn't until later that he kissed me. We went back to mine after and I thought perhaps we just needed to warm up, but even this morning he seemed pensive.

The fact that he had reservations about coming back this summer unnerves me. If his family continues to regularly visit him in LA, it won't be as necessary for him to come here. Will the day finally arrive when he'll decide not to return at all?

The thought of it makes me feel cold.

I decide to do what I've always done and try to enjoy the time we have, but things feel different, like we've both put up walls.

I don't like it. I want him to be here with me fully, body and soul.

I reach out and push his dark hair behind his ears. It's grown out since last year—it's almost as long as it was that first summer.

He turns to look at me, his blue-green eyes gleaming beneath those dark lashes. I bend down and gently kiss his lips, my blood warming as he moves in deeper. He breaks away after a few seconds and glances toward Michael and Timothy.

"You're going to get me in trouble with your brother," he murmurs.

"Tell me what's been happening with you," I prompt, edging closer. Really, I'd be happiest sitting on his lap. "How's the songwriting going?"

"Good," he replies, pursing his lips in a bit of a smirk. "I could have some news to share at some point."

"What?" I press.

He glances at me. "I don't want to jinx it."

"Shut up, just tell me."

"Have you heard of Brit Easton?"

The beautiful pop star with dark corkscrew curls and brilliant green eyes?

I stare at him, my eyes growing round. "Are you kidding?"

"Well, if *you've* heard of her, she must be big," he says facetiously.

"I've got two of her songs on my playlist," I tell him, shoving his arm.

"Your *playlist* playlist?"

"Finn!" I ignore his teasing. "What's happened?"

"Jessie, the lead singer of All Hype—the band we went on tour with—passed my solo album on to her, thought it was something she might like. Brit reached out a couple of months ago and asked if I'd be up for meeting. I think we kind of hit it off." He shrugs. "I recorded the album because I thought it might help me to go down more of a songwriter route, so, yeah, it's pretty cool." He hesitates. "She says she'd like to put out a cover of 'We Could Be Giants.'"

"No way! I love that song!"

"Thanks." He squeezes my thigh under the table again, his fingers sliding farther down to tuck beneath my knees. "I mean, I'll believe it when she signs on the dotted line, but she seems kinda keen."

Brit Easton is a pop artist, whereas Finn has more of a rock background. His solo stuff, however, falls somewhere in between. I could imagine Brit putting her twist on it.

"She also said that maybe we should write together," he adds casually.

"Shut. Up."

This is *major* news.

"Like I say, I'll believe it when it happens."

"So you liked her? When you met?"

"Yeah, she was nice," he says diffidently.

"She wasn't a diva?"

He groans. "Don't believe everything you read on social media. Just because someone knows what they want and how to go about getting it doesn't make them a diva. You should see her in a room, directing an orchestra. She's ridiculously talented."

His passionate rant makes me uneasy.

"Should I be worried?" I ask, trying to sound jokey but probably coming off as needy.

"No," he scoffs lightly.

"How many times have you met her?"

"A few."

I am definitely worried. It sounds as though he might like and admire her on a scale that's potentially even more personal than professional.

"Brilliant," he says with a grin, his eyes on the dance floor. "Michael and Timothy are going for it."

I look over to where my brother and his best friend are po-going around with about five of their mates. "Come On Eileen" is blasting out of the speakers and loads of people are dancing.

"That looks like too much fun to pass up," Finn says, letting me go.

He scoots his chair out from under the table and grabs my hand, leading me into the throng.

I laugh until I cry that night, but I can't ignore the niggling feeling in my gut that everything's about to change.

38

O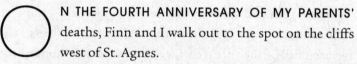N THE FOURTH ANNIVERSARY OF MY PARENTS'
deaths, Finn and I walk out to the spot on the cliffs
west of St. Agnes.

"You seem to be in a much better place this year," he says as
we sit side by side on the bench, his arm draped lazily around
my shoulders.

There's no view to speak of. A sea mist is rolling in off the
ocean and we're shrouded in white fog. But there's nowhere
else I want to be.

"I am," I agree.

Grief still pulls the rug out from under me, and it's there
right now, a heavy stone in my gut, but most of the time I can
think about Mum and Dad without getting upset, especially
since finishing their sculptures.

"What are your plans for the foreseeable future?"

I remember that it's exactly the same question he asked me
during our first summer together, but his tone is even and
straightforward, less dry and sardonic-sounding than it was
back then.

It occurs to me that our relationship has leveled out and
matured.

"I've got to get this summer out of the way first," I reply with a smile.

I've been working harder than ever over the last week, covering for Chas, but Bill, our head chef, has helped me with stocktaking and ordering and between us we seem to be running Seaglass relatively smoothly.

Chas has wanted to be kept in the loop. He's out of hospital and doing well. He expects to be back at work the week after next, which seems far too soon to me, but he's promised us all that he'll take it easy.

"But I think I'll say yes to the rental properties," I say.

A couple of days ago, one of my neighbors who lives in the terrace of old fishermen's cottages down the hill stopped me on my way to work and asked if I'd be interested in taking over three of the properties she manages. She's getting older and thinking about cutting back on work—she said she could put in a good word for me with the owners if I was keen. I asked for a little time to think about it.

"I think I could manage the extra workload, especially over the winter. It'll probably do me good to get out of the house occasionally once Seaglass closes, otherwise I run the risk of becoming a mad artist, squirreled away in her studio."

He smiles. "And sculpture? What's next on the cards?"

"I've got one *Gone* piece to get cracking with from a lady who came to my exhibition. She's asked me to do her late husband. And then I'm hoping to be commissioned by a couple of Arabella's friends."

"To do what?"

"They'd like a life-size statue of one of their ancestors for their sculpture garden. They have a country house over near

Bodmin. Apparently, their family has links to royalty," I add with a smile.

"Wow," he says. "That sounds like it could be a big deal."

"It should open more doors for me if it happens."

"Why haven't you told me about this before?"

"I didn't want to jinx it." I repeat his words about Brit back to him.

We haven't spoken of her since that night at the social club, but that doesn't mean I haven't thought about her.

"When will you know?" Finn asks.

"They've asked me to make a scale model," I reply. "If they like it, hopefully they'll commission me to make a full-size replica."

It's been such an exciting process. I met the lord and lady of the house at the briefing six weeks ago, when they took me to the site where the statue would be erected. It was quite something to imagine one of my creations on a plinth sur-rounded by rosebushes within a stunning walled garden.

If they decide to commission me, it will be the largest piece I've ever done. I'm trying to keep my excitement in check, even though Arabella claims that it's a done deal. Lord and Lady Stockley like to support upcoming, emerging artists, she said. I'm thrilled to think that I may be considered one.

Perhaps I'll be taking on too much, managing these three other holiday cottages as well as my own, but the art world is fickle. Who knows if or when the work will dry up? I'd rather be too busy than not busy enough, and I figure I can make Friday the changeover day for my place so I have more time on Saturdays to clean the others.

The mist is evaporating, dissolving like spirits leaving the land. The sea stretches out before us, swathes of muted blue linen rippling in the breeze.

"I hope everything works out for you back home with your music," I say, leaning a little closer to Finn.

"Thanks," he murmurs.

"It's going to be strange if things do take off. Hearing about you on the internet or through the grapevine . . ."

"So you don't want to revert to the one-month rule?"

I swallow. "I think that was also a little too hard. Don't you?"

"It wasn't easy," he agrees with a sigh.

We've been doing so well. We're making things happen for ourselves now; we probably need to focus on our careers without added distractions. It's not as though we're ever going to be able to truly support each other, not when we're so far apart.

Finn has been watching me sort through my feelings. And now he nods and looks away.

A strange calm settles over me.

Ahead of us, sunshine spears down through a crack in the clouds, a brilliant ray of gold lighting up the sea.

"*Here comes the sun*," Finn sings, adding the little *doo-doo-doo*s at the end.

"Sing the whole song to me," I request quietly, resting my head against his shoulder.

He does. And as he sings about coming out of a long, lonely winter, I feel as though he could be singing about us.

39

THIS SUMMER

'M LYING ON MY SIDE IN THE DOWNSTAIRS BEDROOM, too wired to fall asleep. Tom is flat out on his stomach beside me, one arm pushed beneath his pillow, his handsome face turned in my direction. The broad expanse of his back and shoulders is just visible in the low light and I can barely resist reaching out and tracing my fingertips across his warm skin.

He deserves his rest after what he's accomplished tonight, I think with a smile.

After having hot, urgent sex on one of the sofas at Seaglass, we came back here for a slower, more exploratory round two.

It's hard to pick a favorite time—this man *really* knows what he's doing.

He's the first person I've been with since Finn and I kissed almost six years ago. I recoil from memories of him, trying to stay here with Tom, but I can't control the way thoughts of Finn envelop me.

Let him go, Liv, I urge myself as emotion builds inside my chest. *Enough is enough.*

I want to get back to the afterglow I was enjoying as I think about what Tom and I did, the feeling of our bodies pressed together, how connected we felt during those moments.

I like the way he looks at me, how *seen* he makes me feel. I've lived with a hollowness inside my heart for so long, but I don't feel empty when I'm with him. My heart feels full.

Finn and I have history, but so much of it is tainted, so many of our shared memories are tinged with pain. Tom hasn't seen me broken, and I'm glad of the clean slate we have to launch from. This thing with him feels clean and fresh and *good*, and I hope that the only way from here is up.

As I focus on Tom's steady breathing, slowly matching my own to his, the thoughts of Finn gradually drift away.

THE SOUND OF the doorbell wrenches me from my dreams and for a few seconds I'm in the past, fear pressing in on me from all sides.

But then the bed creaks and Tom rests a warm hand on my shoulder as he stands up, telling me that he'll get it.

It's probably the postman, I think sleepily, as I hear him dragging on his jeans and pulling a T-shirt over his head.

I snuggle languidly under the duvet, my eyes falling shut again, in no rush to leave this lovely cocoon. Maybe we can go for round three this morning . . .

"Who are you?"

The sound of Michael's forthright question causes my eyes to spring open and I remember that it's *Sunday*. There *is* no postman coming today. But my brother can't already be here for lunch, can he? *What's the time?*

"I'm Tom. Hi, you must be Michael," I hear Tom reply genially. "I've heard a lot about you."

I sit bolt upright.

"Are you Liv's boyfriend?"

And freeze.

"Er, well, no, not quite, but maybe—"

"Good, because she already has one," Michael interrupts. "And his name is Finn."

Shit! I scramble from the bed and wildly look around for my clothes. Where are they?

"Oh. Okay," Tom says placidly.

"And you have big shoes to fill!" Michael declares.

Where the hell is my dress? I find it near the en suite. It's inside out, so I hurriedly thrust my hands into the sleeves and try to turn them the right way out again.

"I see," Tom says as I hastily pull it over my head, forgoing a bra and knickers.

"He's *really* famous," Michael adds.

Oh God.

"His songs are on the radio and everything!"

He's now right outside the bedroom, having clearly sauntered straight past Tom without an invitation.

"And he'll be back soon because he comes here every summer, and she's my baby sister and you'd better watch out!" he warns as I burst from the room.

"Michael!" I snap.

He looks so small next to Tom's towering frame—his head barely reaches Tom's pecs.

"Oh, there you are!" my brother says cheerfully.

"What are you doing here?" I demand to know.

Michael seems to realize something, his dark eyebrows knitting into a look of confusion as he glances straight past me at the room I've just exited, his attention zeroing in on the rumpled duvet.

"No, what are *you* doing here?" he asks emphatically. "That's not your bed."

"Would anyone like a cup of tea or coffee?" Tom interrupts weakly.

"I'M SO SORRY," I mutter once my brother has left.

He didn't stay long; he was just dropping by to tell me that he couldn't make lunch today. One of his coworkers is ill so his boss asked if he could cover for him.

"Finn is *not* my boyfriend," I state resolutely, fighting the urge to squirm as Tom places a bowl of granola, berries, and yogurt in front of me.

We're in the downstairs kitchen. The sun hasn't hit this part of the house yet, but it's such a bright day that light is flooding in from all sides. I wish I had a pair of sunglasses, but I'm too lazy to go upstairs.

"You don't owe me an explanation," Tom says calmly, taking a seat opposite with a bowl of his own.

"I feel that I do. Especially after the way I reacted to his brother coming into Seaglass on Thursday. You must think I was trying to mislead you. I wasn't."

He shakes his head dismissively.

"Finn and I ended things for good last summer and Michael hasn't caught up," I explain. "He knows. I've told him. But it's going in one ear and out the other."

"Sounds as though he doesn't want to listen," Tom agrees.

I let out a huff. "He couldn't even stand Finn until relatively recently. Michael sometimes takes a while to get used to new people."

"He's protective of you," he notes.

I slide my hand across the table toward him and brush his fingertips with mine. He takes my hand and gives it a squeeze.

"How are you feeling this morning?" he asks, lifting his eyes from his breakfast and studying my face.

"I was feeling really bloody lovely until that rude awakening."

His face breaks out into a grin and suddenly I want to climb across the table and attack his sensual mouth. Day-old stubble graces his jaw and he has bedhead hair, all sexy and rumpled.

His thumb brushes over my knuckles and I have a flashback to his hands last night, how skilled they were, how thoughtful.

His eyes darken.

"Have you got any plans for this morning?" I ask, heat flooding my lower body.

"Taking you back to bed?" he replies.

I can't think of a single thing I'd like more.

40

D ON'T LET ON, BUT WE'VE SLEPT TOGETHER. I'M only telling you now because I don't want you seeing something on our faces and blurting—"

Amy cuts off my sentence with a squeal and claps her hands while Rach tilts her face to the ceiling and exclaims "YES!" with her hands pressed together in what looks remarkably like a prayer. I know for a fact that she's not religious.

And *then* they throw their arms around *each other* and start jumping on the spot.

I stand and stare at them, flummoxed.

It's Monday night and we're back at the pub quiz. I was with Tom earlier when a text from Amy came in, asking if I wanted to bring him.

Tarek is a bit over quiz night, she claimed.

I don't know if that's the truth or if my friends are meddling, but Tom seemed glad of the invite.

He's at the bar with Dan, while Amy, Rach, and I wait around the corner for our usual table for six to be cleared. Ellie is running late.

"What are you doing, hugging *each other*?" I ask my friends in disbelief.

"We're so happy!" Amy cries.

"You know he's going home in less than two weeks, right?" I whisper, confused. "It's just a holiday fling."

Immediately, those words feel wrong. This does not feel like "just a holiday fling."

"Yes, but this is *you* moving on," Rach says earnestly, her eyes shining.

Her expression and tone are so unlike her that for a moment I feel as if I'm in a parallel universe.

The waiter interrupts to tell us that our table is ready and Tom and Dan appear around the corner with our drinks, so I take a seat, feeling very surreal.

Tom sits down opposite me and gives me a warm smile. Beneath the table, our knees knock together. Neither of us moves away.

AFTER AMY AND Rach's reaction, I find myself paying more attention to the dynamics around the table. I notice Dan reaching forward to brush a crumb off Amy's nose and how she doesn't even flinch, and the way Rach draws infinity symbols on Ellie's wrist when she thinks no one's watching. I see the small displays of affection between them, the unrestrained love in their gazes.

Usually it hurts to watch my friends interacting so intimately with the people they want to spend the rest of their lives with, so I've tended to look away. But not tonight. Witnessing Amy and Rach's joy at the idea that I'm moving on from Finn makes me realize even more acutely how much my heart has been on standby the last six years. I've never had a no-holds-barred, permanent, happy relationship with anyone. Looking at my friends, I realize I want one. Very much.

"YOU WERE QUIET tonight," Tom comments on our way home.

I should be over the moon. We won again, largely thanks to his knowledge of geography and random medical facts. It turns out his father was a doctor. Something else we have in common.

"Contemplative," I reply, hooking my arm through his as we walk along the dark road cutting down through the steeply wooded valley.

The gesture is meant to be reassuring. I don't want him to think I'm having second thoughts about us. I've slept in his bed for the last two nights and I'd like to make it a hat trick.

"Are you okay?" he asks.

"I'm good. I just had a bit on my mind."

He falls silent.

Wales is not LA, I remind myself. What's to say that this couldn't be the start of something permanent?

We're on the narrowest stretch and a car is approaching from behind us. I move over to the side to make room for it and feel Tom's strong hands on my shoulders, using his own body as a shield.

My heart expands at the protective gesture.

No, it opens.

ON WEDNESDAY MORNING, we walk down to Seaglass together, having spent most of yesterday in each other's company. I made a few noises about leaving him to his own devices, not wanting to overstep or encroach on the space that he's paid good money for, but somehow we kept ending up back in each other's arms.

He's filling in today for our KP, who's on holiday. When I double- and triple-checked he really was happy to help out, he replied, "When I say something, I tend to mean it. You don't need to doubt me."

I found that statement unbearably sexy. I love his straight-forwardness, his steadiness. I could fall in love with a man like Tom.

"It's going to be funny being at work with you for the next week and a half," I muse with a smile as we walk up the external staircase.

"Sleeping with the boss," he replies playfully. "Are *you* all right with that?" He leans his shoulder against the wall and watches me as I get my keys out.

"More than. Although I probably won't let on to the staff."

"I'll try to keep my hands off you if anyone's watching," he vows as I unlock the door.

I already know that I'm going to hate it.

He helps me get the place ready for customers and we finish up by pinning back the balcony doors.

It's a sunny day with very little wind. The deep water of the sea beyond the cove is especially blue and the waves curling onto the shore are a pale crystal green.

Chas used to love the view on days like this. It's when he could relax and really enjoy it. Whenever there was a swell, he'd want to be out there.

We were all so pleased for him when he finally decided to set off on the round-the-world trip he's always dreamed of. But I miss him. And from the sounds of it, he's missing us too. Last week, we received a postcard from him in Maui. He's having a brilliant time, but he's looking forward to coming back in August. Dan really had to persuade him to take a chunk of the summer off. June, July, and August are always so brutal—we make pretty much all of our money for the whole year in those three months, so there was no way Chas would put his feet up if he was here.

Tom shakes his head in awe as we stand together at the balcony railing, soaking up the view.

"I can't believe you get to live and work here."

"So move," I joke.

"It's tempting."

I laugh.

"I mean it," he says, and the hairs on my arms stand up at the look on his face when he casts me a sidelong glance, because there's a chance he's serious. "I know I haven't even been here three weeks yet, but I feel so at home in Cornwall. Maybe it's the time I spent here as a kid, but the thought of leaving . . ." He looks shell-shocked. "It actually makes me feel sick. Sorry, that's fucking weird, but it's the God's honest truth," he mutters, straightening up.

I prop my elbow on the railing, facing him. "*Could* you stay?" I pry.

He gives me a small nod and mirrors my body language. "I have nothing in Wales to go back to."

"What about work?"

His brow furrows and he turns his head to look at the sea, his expression pensive. "I'll get a job here."

Search and rescue operates out of Newquay, only a half-hour drive away, so it's more than possible.

"Does that freak you out?" he asks carefully, returning his gaze to mine.

"In what way?"

"The idea of me sticking around."

I let out a small laugh. "Are you kidding?"

It's only when his shoulders relax that I realize they were riddled with tension a moment ago.

Tom studies my face before saying, "The manager at the Driftwood Spars thinks she can shuffle things around and put me up for a week or so at the beginning of July. She also has a few more days here and there, so I'm on a waiting list."

"That's great news!"

He looks pleased at my reaction.

We're interrupted by Tyler appearing around the corner of the balcony.

"Oh, hey!" I exclaim. "You're early."

"No, I'm not," he replies with a frown.

I check my watch. "Whoa, it's that time already. I need to open up," I say to Tom, reaching out to squeeze his arm before thinking better of it.

I gave Tyler a call on Monday after deciding that he shouldn't miss out just because I'm still sore about Finn.

Am I still sore about Finn?

Not at the moment, I'm not. But that might have something to do with the gorgeous man who's just gone upstairs to the kitchen.

41

T'S FRIDAY AFTERNOON, A LITTLE OVER A WEEK LATER, and I'm on my way back to Seaglass after getting Beach Cottage ready for a family of four. This morning, Tom moved out and into the Drifty and I hated being in the downstairs apartment without him. I was gutted watching him pack up, even though he wasn't going far. If he'd returned to Wales today, as he'd initially planned, I would have been a wreck.

This time with him has been magical. We've spent every night together in his bed and have had breakfast opposite each other every morning in the kitchen-diner. He comes with me down to Seaglass, and even though the kitchen closes before the bar does, he waits for me to finish my shift before walking me home. He's been back to the foundry with me to check on the patination work and I've sat on the beach a couple of times and watched him draw in the sand. I feel as though I've been given a sneak peek at a life that suddenly feels attainable, a future with someone to have and to hold, someone to wake up with, someone to share a home with.

Our KP returns tomorrow, but our sous-chef has asked for a few days off to prepare for his big move to London in ten days' time, so Tom is going to step into his role and work at Seaglass for a bit longer.

We still haven't found a replacement sous-chef. I thought the KP might be promoted, but he's only been working with us since Easter and Bill needs someone with more experience.

TYLER IS OVER by the stereo when I walk into Seaglass, and Beach House is no longer filtering out of the speakers.

"Don't mess with the music, please, Tyler," I call as Arcade Fire's "Ready to Start" begins to play.

He looks annoyed. "That shit was so dull."

"It's in line with the chilled vibe we're going for," I argue, feeling twitchy at his song choice as I walk over to the bar.

"I thought you liked rock."

He's so confident for an eighteen-year-old. He doesn't even seem to care if he gets an order wrong or mucks up while pulling a pint. Yesterday he put so much head on a pint of beer that Luke asked if he wanted a Flake in it. But he just takes it all in his stride.

"I'm not in the mood for it right now. Can you change it back, please? Or put, I don't know, Cigarettes After Sex or The xx on?"

He huffs. "*Or something from this decade,*" I hear him mutter, selecting another artist entirely.

At least it's not rock, so I let it go. I'm going to have to pick my battles with this boy.

I look past Tyler to see Tom standing by the partition wall to the bathrooms. He gives me an amused, knowing look, and then returns to the kitchen.

"HOW'S TYLER GETTING on?" Tom asks later that night.

"On the whole, pretty well. He needs to speed up a bit, but I think he'll get there."

I spent ages training him that first morning, but Libby and Luke have helped too, although Kwame has no patience for him after he dropped his precious cocktail shaker on the floor.

"Did I imagine it or did Michael say that his brother is famous?"

Urgh.

"You don't have to tell me." He good-naturedly waves away the question when he sees the face I've pulled.

"No, it's fine," I reply dully.

Everyone else has cleaned up and gone home, but he and I have found ourselves having a last drink together in the sofa area upstairs, where the festoon lights are casting the room in a warm glow.

I'm in no rush to get home and he's apparently in no rush to go back to his room at the inn.

"He's not really famous as such. But he's had a few hit singles with someone who is. He's a songwriter."

"Ah. Michael said his songs were on the radio. I assumed—"

"He did use to be in a band and then he put out a solo album with an indie label, but all he ever really wanted to do was write, so now he works with other artists."

"Anyone I'd have heard of?"

"I don't know what sort of music you listen to. You never played any while you were staying downstairs."

Which made a welcome change.

I decide to stop being cagey because, really, what's the point?

"He cowrote Brit Easton's new album."

His eyebrows jump up. "Okay. So a big deal then."

"Do you follow celebrity gossip?" I ask reluctantly.

He shrugs. "Not particularly. Why?"

I sigh. "Finn and Brit fell in love while writing her album. They're a couple now—their pictures have been everywhere."

He gives me a sympathetic look. "It wouldn't be easy seeing your ex with anyone else, let alone someone who's famous."

"He's not really my ex." I hope I don't sound as hurt or as bitter as I feel.

He takes a sip of his whiskey and leans back against the sofa, his gaze calmly trained on my face.

"Michael said he comes back every summer."

Goddammit. Why did he commit to memory every word my brother said?

I nod slowly. "He's come back every summer for the past six years. And somehow, I found myself putting my life on ice for him," I confide wryly.

My head didn't want me to, but my heart's been running this god-awful shitshow.

"But I've stopped now. I've moved on," I state firmly.

Just like Finn has.

"Thanks for telling me," Tom says quietly.

"I mean, it *is* starting to feel a *little* off-balance between us," I say with a small laugh, but my words are pointed.

"I'm sorry," he replies awkwardly. "I came here trying to get away from my life."

"Whereas you've crashed headlong into mine."

"Is that a problem?" he asks cautiously.

"No, I like it."

He smiles. "I love how honest and open you are."

"I'm embarrassed now."

"No, please, it's refreshing. Cara was so closed off."

"You can talk." I'm only half teasing.

"I'm not usually." He sits up straighter. "Cara and I had talked ourselves to death. I thought I was done. I wasn't expecting this."

"What?"

"This." He indicates the two of us.

He maintains eye contact for a few seconds before looking away toward the kitchen.

"What do you want from life?" he asks, turning back to me.

His out-of-the-blue question momentarily stumps me.

"I guess I'd like to carry on doing what I'm doing, working here through the summer so that I can sculpt in the winter. Maybe one day I'll have so many commissions, I'll need to sculpt full-time, but I like the balance of the way it is now."

I take a sip of my rosé and smile across at him. He's still gazing at me.

"What about family?" he asks.

I tilt my head to one side. "I'd *like* to find someone to spend the rest of my life with." I'm thinking of Dan and Amy and Rach and Ellie, if I could ever be that lucky.

"Kids?" he asks frankly.

"One day, if I can."

His eyes drop to his whiskey.

"What about you?" I ask.

"I like the sound of *your* life," he confesses, his voice sounding oddly gravelly.

I notice the shadows of his jaw muscles clenching and unclenching.

"Tom, are you okay?" I have a feeling that he's not.

He lets out a long, heavy exhale and eventually he meets my eyes.

"I can't have kids," he says with regret. "I thought you should know."

My head is reeling. *He thought I should know?*

That says a lot. We've only known each other for a few weeks, but I keep feeling a compulsion to look to the future.

And Tom has just made it clear that he feels the same. He can also imagine a future for us—*if* I can get past the fact that he can't have children.

We stare at each other and I sense that we're trying to read one another's thoughts. My stomach lurched at his revelation, but the idea of having a family with anyone still feels like a long way off. If Tom *is* the right man for me, we'd find a way to make it work.

I react instinctively and get to my feet, joining him on the sofa.

"Have you known for long?" I ask gently, sitting very close with my knees resting against his thigh.

"A few months."

I run my fingers lightly over the back of his head, hoping to soothe him. His hair has grown out a bit since he's been here, and it's lightened a little under the sun.

"Did this have anything to do with why you and Cara—"

"It was part of it," he confides.

My heart fractures at the sight of tears shining in his eyes.

"I'm so sorry." I nestle into his shoulder and lay my hand across his chest. "But there are other ways to have children."

"I know," he replies, placing his hand over mine. "We could have done IVF or considered adoption, but . . ." He shakes his head. "It wasn't meant to be between us, anyway," he says, falling silent.

I lift my head to kiss his cheek and give him a soft smile. "See? You *can* talk to me."

He lets out a small laugh. When he looks at me, his eyes are still shining, but with some other sentiment I don't understand.

A moment later, he dips his head and catches my lips in a gentle kiss.

We withdraw after a couple of seconds and stare at each other. And then we set about closing all other physical gaps between us.

He doesn't make it back to his room at the Drifty that night.

42

LAST SUMMER

CAN'T THANK YOU ENOUGH," I SAY TO ARABELLA AS WE stand in the sun-drenched rose gardens of Lord and Lady Stockley's manor house, sipping chilled champagne from cut-glass crystal flutes.

The statue was unveiled a short while ago—I had to do a speech and everything—and tonight there will be a dinner to celebrate.

"This was all you, dear," she replies, giving me one of her meaningful looks.

"That's not true, but I appreciate you saying so."

She's dressed up for the occasion, a navy gown with a black shawl and pearls draped around her neck, her long hair rolled up into its usual topknot. Her look reminds me of when we first met at the art gallery in St. Ives two and a half years ago. That meeting changed my life.

Her eyes return to the statue. The Lord Stockley of past times is wearing a tweed coat and is leaning against a rake with his back to the house, looking out across the gardens. He was a keen horticulturalist in his day.

"Have you any ideas about approaching town councils or

charities about a public art commission? It's been a while since I've fundraised, but I'm game if you are," Arabella says.

She knows that I'd still like to become a member of the Royal Society of Sculptors. We've grown quite close—she's the person I most like to talk to about art and sculpture.

"I'll give it some thought," I reply, squeezing her arm affectionately.

"Do," she says. "You're on a roll now. Don't let the momentum go to waste."

IT'S LATE BY the time I've driven Arabella home to St. Ives and carried on to St. Agnes. I have guests staying, so as usual, I park my car up on the hill outside Dan and Amy's house. It's even more of a pain getting it from here now that I have three more properties to manage—and I hate pulling up on the road outside my house to pick up all my cleaning supplies. Most cars can get by, but wider vehicles struggle, and after Chas's heart attack last summer, not to mention an incident a few years ago when a stray firework set the gorse alight behind the Drifty and parked cars caused access troubles, I'm always on edge in case an emergency vehicle comes.

But Dan and Amy's road is nice and quiet. They live close to Finn's grandparents and I've bumped into them a few times, once when I had rare winter guests staying. On that occasion, Trudy was falling over herself to tell me about how well Finn and Brit Easton's songwriting sessions were going.

Finn and I actually did manage to stick to our no-contact agreement when he left last summer, but he broke the rules when he signed his publishing deal with a major record label—the deal that would later enable him to write with Brit.

I can't not share this with you, he texted, attaching a press release.

I was blown away for him and I wrote back to tell him so.

I later heard from Dan that he'd been paid a big chunk of money so he could focus on writing. A publishing deal like that would get him into rooms with all the right people.

The only time *I've* been the one to instigate contact was at Christmas when I sent him a funny meme and Thinking of you x.

He sent me a funny one back, along with a simple text that said, Happy Christmas x.

It was such a glib exchange. I hoped that he'd read between the lines to see how much I was thinking about him, as it felt wrong to leave it like that.

I did, though. My willpower has been monumental over the past twelve months. I have been determined not to break.

I glance down Finn's grandparents' street out of habit and do a double take at the sight of a dark gray SEAT Leon parked outside their house.

My stomach turns over.

Is he home?

And if so, why hasn't he told me?

I come to a stop and stare down the road at the house. Lights glow dimly in the windows, but it's eleven thirty—I can't go knocking at this hour. Even if it was the middle of the day, I'd hesitate. If Finn wanted to see me, he'd reach out. But why wouldn't he want to see me?

Maybe he's just flown in. I try to convince myself that this must be the case, but I still feel shaky as I walk the rest of the way home. I suppose it's possible that he called into Seaglass earlier. I'd normally be working on a Friday, but I was at Lord and Lady Stockley's statue unveiling and dinner party.

An idea comes to me as I'm heading up the stairs to my bedroom. Getting out my phone, I tap out a text, using similar phrasing to the one Finn used for me when he told me about Brit.

Couldn't not share this with you . . .

I attach a picture that Arabella took of me standing next to the Lord Stockley sculpture and then sit for a minute, staring nervously at my phone.

My heart flips as three dots appear.

So impressed, he writes back. Are you around tomorrow?

I decide to play ignorant. Yes. Why?

I'm here but whacked. Been up talking to Ty and about to hit the sack. Brunch?

I'd love that. Welcome home!

Thanks. Blue Bar? 10 am? I'll pick you up.

Can't wait.

He sends me a thumbs-up emoji and I sit staring at my screen for another twenty seconds.

Have I made a mistake, keeping him at a distance?

43

BRIT EASTON IS ONE OF THE MOST BEAUTIFUL PEOPLE I have ever seen. The photograph I picture when I think of her was taken on the pink carpet at the Billboard Women in Music Awards earlier this year. She's dressed in smart black trousers and is wearing a black crop top that exposes her perfectly flat caramel-brown midriff. Her hair falls to her shoulders in glossy black braids secured with golden beads, 1940s red lipstick graces her full lips, while eyeliner flicks and what I hope to God are false eyelashes—because no one can be *that* lucky—accentuate her piercing green eyes.

When I saw this photograph, I felt ill. Finn had been working with her for one month.

So it should come as no surprise to anyone that I'm keen to try to make myself look as nice as possible on Saturday morning, but despite my best efforts, I look drawn and tired. My sixth sense has kept me awake half the night.

I'm wearing a midi dress in classic green—Finn once told me that I looked beautiful in green, so my attention was drawn straight to this item in my wardrobe.

I'm leaning against the waist-high stone wall that runs alongside the stream outside my house when he pulls up, and

I notice through the glass that he has a strange look on his face. His lips are pressed together in a straight line and there are creases between his brows. As he peers out the windscreen at me, his expression seems tormented.

But his lips tilt upward into a reasonable-size smile when I open the front passenger door.

"Hey!" he exclaims, leaning across the center console to give me a hug. It's brief—just enough for me to get a hit of cold sea air on his skin—but the way he clutches me for those two seconds feels almost . . . desperate.

"You're a sight for sore eyes," he comments casually. "Nice dress. You looked like something out of a fairy tale, leaning there against the mossy wall amid all those ferns."

I let out a laugh, tickled by his description.

"Thanks. You look nice too."

His dark hair falls at its longest lengths to the nape of his neck, but around his face it's slightly shorter, caressing his jaw and cheekbones in a windswept look. His eyes are as lovely as ever, but they carry an emotion that I'm struggling to make sense of as he gazes across at me. It's almost wistful, edged with longing. I'm hyperalert.

"Is Michael working today?" he asks, and to anyone else he'd sound normal.

But not to me. To me he sounds strained.

"Yes, I think so."

"I was just wondering about doing it the other way around: parking at Chapel Porth and saying hi, then walking to Blue Bar from there."

"That's a good idea."

"Are you very hungry?"

"No, I'm not actually."

I don't have an appetite at all, but I'm sure I'll feel better once I know what's going on with him.

Or maybe I won't.

THE DRIVE TO Chapel Porth isn't long, but we manage to cover his flight and I also get an update on his UK family. Tyler, Liam, and his grandparents went to LA for Christmas again last year. I had already had this relayed firsthand by Trudy, who was so proud to say when I bumped into her that Finn had flown them all over, but it was nice to hear it from Finn's perspective. It sounds as though they all had a good time. It must be a relief for them to spend Christmas together away from St. Agnes and the memory of what happened all those years ago.

The Chapel Porth car park is already almost full, but a couple of surfers are just climbing into a van on the seafront so we luck out and drive straight in. Michael is busy directing the car in front of us and misses our arrival. He's halfway down the other leg of the car park when we get out of the car, but we can see him in his red T-shirt and hi-vis jacket, directing a driver into a free space. He looks so in his element, and I can't help smiling as he gives the driver a thumbs-up along with a cheerful smile.

A canary-yellow Lotus convertible turns into the car park and Michael almost spontaneously combusts with excitement. As the driver pulls to a stop to await instruction, Michael lifts up his hand in a high five.

"Oh my *God*!" Finn blurts with sudden outraged incredulity. "Look at how nice he is to total strangers! He usually treats me as though I'm something unpleasant he's stepped on."

I burst out laughing, but when I realize that, actually, I think he might genuinely be a little hurt, I reach out to squeeze his hand.

"Aw," I say.

His hand remains limp and my stomach clenches as I relinquish the contact.

Michael has his back to us as we approach, but when he turns around and sees me, his face lights up. And then he looks past me to Finn and I expect his expression to morph into his typical repugnance, but it doesn't. If anything, he looks brighter still.

"Finn!" he shouts, opening his arms for a hug, and my heart swells at the sight of Finn as he looks over Michael's shoulder at me, all wide-eyed amazement and glee.

"What are you doing here?" Michael asks him as they break apart.

"I was just taking your sister for brunch."

"Come and have a cup of tea!"

"With you?" Finn asks.

"Yes, I can take my break now."

"Okay, if you're sure."

We sort out a parking ticket and then I go to the café to order while Michael insists on introducing Finn to his boss. They're in the shelter by the café now, chatting, while I wait for our drinks to be prepared.

Finn looks different, and at first I couldn't pinpoint why, but now I realize that he's filled out a bit since last year. He's twenty-seven, the same age as me, and he's not a super-slim indie boy anymore. But that's not the only thing that's changed about his appearance. When did he stop wearing ratty T-shirts and secondhand clothing? He's wearing black jeans and a pale blue T-shirt, but there's nothing well-worn about them. My heart squeezes and I turn back to the counter, readying my card to pay.

"I got you a muffin," I tell Michael when I go over to them.

"Thanks, baby sis!" he replies chirpily. "You want some?" he asks Finn.

"Nah, I'm good, thanks. Don't want to spoil my appetite."

We sit there and talk until Michael has to return to work, and then we set off toward the beach so we can walk to Blue Bar. But I can't shake the feeling that something's wrong and I can't imagine eating a single thing until I get to the bottom of it.

"Finn, wait." I tug on his wrist as we're passing his car.

"What is it?" He turns around.

"I need you to tell me what's going on."

"What do you mean?" he asks warily.

"Something's changed. Between us. You've put walls up. Why?"

He stares at me for a moment and then his shoulders slowly drop.

"It's Brit, isn't it?"

He bows his head, and when his eyes return to mine, they're full of regret.

A wave of darkness crashes over me.

He pulls his keys out of his pocket and unlocks the door, indicating for me to climb back into his car.

We sit in the front, our bodies twisted toward each other.

"Have you slept with her?" I ask in barely more than a whisper.

I know I have no right to ask this—that was our deal: *If you're single and I'm single . . . I don't expect you to wait for me . . .*

We made no promises, even *I've* been on dates. It's not his fault that they never went anywhere.

But Finn may have made a connection with someone on a deeper level.

He doesn't speak. His slight nod and pained expression say it for him.

"Oh God." I face forward and hunch over, burying my face in my hands.

"I'm sorry," he whispers.

"Is it serious?" I ask into the footwell.

When he hesitates, I straighten up and look at him.

He swallows, his face ashen. "It might be," he admits.

"Oh God." I bury my head in my hands again. "Is this it for us?"

"Liv," he says wretchedly, placing his hand on my back.

That's all he says, so I force myself to look at him again. His face is racked with agony.

"Do you love her?" I almost can't bring myself to ask it.

He shakes his head, but it's not an answer to my question, more a reluctance to even go there.

"I care about you, *so much*," he says. "I miss you. You're never far from my mind, but I want someone to share the highs and lows with all year round, not just in the summer. Until I met Brit, I didn't realize how much I needed that."

"So you really talk to her? You open up to her?"

He nods and I think it hurts even more than knowing he's had sex with her. If he's not already in love with her, it's definitely heading in that direction. Her hand has snaked around his heart and I want to reach in and prize off her fingers.

"Why did you even come back?" I ask, tears breaking free from my eyes.

"Because I wanted to see you."

"Just to tell me that it's over?"

"Not necessarily."

Hope fills my heart at the look in his eyes.

"But we can't keep going on like this," he says. "Something's got to give."

"Are you moving back to Aggie then?" I don't know where my sarcastic tone has come from, but I can feel anger simmering in my gut.

"You know I'm not," he replies quietly.

"Well, you know I can't leave."

"Why not?" he asks me, and his question comes out sounding so reasonable that it makes my anger bubble up a little more.

"What do you mean, why not? You've just seen why not! Your answer is right over there, in the car park!"

"Michael doesn't need you as much as you claim he does."

"You don't know what you're talking about," I mutter.

"He's got more friends than *you*, for fuck's sake!" he erupts, irked himself now. "He'd be absolutely fine if you spent more time away from this place!"

"No, he wouldn't," I argue.

"You can't keep using Michael as an excuse not to leave. I think the truth of it is that you're scared. You're scared of being out of your comfort zone. You've been using this place as a crutch since your parents died."

"That's not true."

But he's not finished.

"I think that you might even *relish* the feeling that you get when I leave. You've told me yourself that you throw yourself into sculpting. You harness the hurt. You need it to work."

He's not telling me anything I don't already know, but I'm incensed he has the gall to say it.

"I haven't seen you sculpt a single thing that comes from a place of joy. I was glad when I saw that statue of Lord What's-His-Face because his expression is peachy, but then I remembered that he's *dead* and that it probably killed you to sculpt him too."

"How dare you say that to me!" I cry. "You're such a hypocrite! Your songs are riddled with lines about your upbringing, about this place, about your tragic childhood . . . You've written songs based on your own pain and suffering for practically as long as I've known you! You've written songs based on *my* pain and suffering! And how many songs have you been inspired to write after leaving *me*? You use the pain to your advantage too—you're exactly the same!"

"I don't want to feel like that anymore!" he yells. "I want to be *happy*, Liv! I want a peaceful life! A proper girlfriend! A wife and kids someday! I want *you*, but you're not fucking available!"

Banging on the window jolts us both to attention. Michael is peering in at us, a thunderous expression on his face.

I open the door. "What's wrong?"

"Why are you arguing?" he asks in a raised voice.

"We're not."

"*I heard you!*" he shouts.

"We're having a discussion," I say, trying to compose myself.

Finn leans across the console to speak directly to Michael.

"Your sister thinks she can't leave St. Agnes," he says.

"Finn!" I snap.

I thought he was going to back me up, not haul my brother into our mess.

"Why not?" Michael asks.

He's no longer shouting but it's not far off.

"Because she's worried about leaving you here on your own," Finn explains remarkably calmly.

"I'm not on my own," Michael replies with a frown, shifting on his feet, and he looks so small standing there, at only five feet tall, drowned by the size of his hi-vis jacket.

Finn gives me a pointed look. "See?"

"Don't you do this," I warn him furiously.

"Where do you want to go?" Michael asks me, perplexed.

"I don't want to go anywhere," I reply.

"She's lying," Finn calls across from the driver's seat. "She won't come to LA, she won't go back to Italy, she won't even go to London. She won't leave St. Agnes and she won't leave *you*. She thinks she has to look after you."

"You don't have to look after me!" Michael interjects with a scowl. "I don't want you to stay here because of me."

He's getting irate and I could kill Finn for putting him in this position.

"It's okay, Michael," I say, reaching out to take his hand. "It's okay. I'm not going anywhere. I don't *want* to leave you."

"No!" Michael replies, infuriated, wrenching his hand away. "You don't look after *me*." He enunciates every word slowly and meaningfully, just as our parents taught him to. "*I* look after *you*!" he states. "YOU'RE. MY. BABY. SISTER."

I stare at him in shock.

Is that the way he sees it? That he's been the one looking out for me all along?

Could there be some truth to it?

He hated me living in his house, but he tolerated it. And when I think about all those times he dragged himself over for

Sunday lunch, complaining about not really feeling like it or wishing he could be in front of the telly or at work, watching classic cars roll into the car park instead, I wonder if I've had it wrong all this time. Was he the one doing *me* a favor? Was *he* supporting *me*? Because he thought I needed him to?

The world around me shifts, forcing me to look at this situation from a different perspective.

But even if Finn and Michael are right, how can I consider going to LA now? Even if I wanted to up and move—which I *don't*—Finn has already fallen for someone else.

44

THE CORNFLOWER-BLUE SKY IS LITTERED WITH PUFFY white clouds as I approach the bench at the edge of the cliffs that I've come to think of as ours. A lone figure sits there already, his shoulders hunched over, his elbows resting on his knees.

I wasn't sure if I'd see Finn again. I demanded to be dropped straight home after Chapel Porth—I was so angry at him for bringing Michael into our argument that I couldn't even look at him, let alone spend a morning in his company.

Over the last couple of days, I've shed a lot of tears as I've tried to make sense of everything that was said. Even if I can see where my brother and Finn are coming from, I'm not sure what it changes. Things are finally taking off for me as a sculptor—I don't want to start all over again in LA, a place that I feel no connection to. Maybe Michael—and Rach and Amy—would be okay with me leaving, but *I* wouldn't be. It feels like too much of a sacrifice to make right now. And why *should* it all come down to me? Where are the sacrifices *he's* made? Where are the compromises?

Finn slowly straightens up at the sight of me, his expression bleak but relieved. He reaches out his hand, his distraught eyes imploring me to take it.

I do. It may be the last time.

We sit beside each other and stare out at the sea, emerald green melting away into icy blue. My cheeks are already wet.

It's the anniversary of my parents' deaths, but the tears I'm shedding today are not for them.

"Liv," Finn says in a hoarse voice, slipping his arm around my shoulders and pulling me close.

I am *aching* for him. It hurts so much. How will I ever feel this way about anyone else?

"You could have come back any time of the year, couldn't you?" I say in a small voice. "But you've always chosen to return so you're here for the eleventh of August. I thought you were coming back for the school holidays."

"I've always come back for you. For this anniversary. You don't go through something like that with someone and sever ties lightly."

I have a flashback to that night, remembering Finn sitting with me on the sofa as the police officers delivered the news, the way I clutched him and screamed out my grief, and how he canceled his flight, staying by my side until after the funeral, helping out in any way he could. I've never fully contemplated what that must have been like for him, to witness someone else's pain on such a raw and emotional level. He can't not have been affected by it. We formed a bond during that time, a bond that can never be broken. We will always have this link to each other.

But I don't want to be tangled up with him if he's in love with someone else.

"Tell me about her."

He goes rigid beneath my fingers. He doesn't want to have this conversation.

"I need to know, Finn. How did it happen?"

He sighs and lets me go, avoiding my gaze. "When you're working with an artist, you have to find out what makes them tick, so we spent a lot of time together before we even started writing, chatting over coffee at her house, about life and dating and the breakdown of previous relationships, trying to find concepts for songs. It's intimate and it felt organic, and Brit allowed herself to be vulnerable with me. She had a rough childhood too, so we had that in common. It's hard not to feel something when someone is pouring their heart and soul into their lyrics."

I want to catch the cotton-wool clouds from the sky and stuff them into his mouth to keep him from saying any more. But I know I was the one who asked.

I bet he felt starstruck too—a hugely successful artist like Brit opening up to him.

"Does she know about me?"

He swallows. "Yes."

"Does she know you've come home to see me?"

"Yes."

"And how does she feel about that?"

"She was very upset when I left her."

This feels surreal. To think that Brit Easton is worried about Finn's feelings for *me*.

"But you still came."

"I couldn't not."

"Is this the end of us?" I whisper.

"That depends."

"On what?"

"On what you've been thinking about since Chapel Porth."

"If I moved to LA, would you call it off with her?" I ask hypothetically, brushing my tears away.

He nods, his expression tortured.

"So it's an ultimatum. Move to LA or we're over."

He hesitates, looking torn as he holds my direct gaze.

And then he answers. "Yes."

"And what if I said to you, move to St. Agnes, or you lose me forever? What would you do?"

"Is that what you're saying?" he asks, his blue-green eyes wary.

"I don't know!" I'm not sure I can put it on the line for him like that. What if he chooses her? "I can't believe we're giving each other ultimatums!"

"This was *always* going to end in ultimatums, Liv," he says darkly. "You thought we'd just *fizzle* out? What we have doesn't just *fizzle out*. I was *never* going to fall out of love with you."

My eyes widen and I stare at him.

"Of *course* I fucking love you, Liv," he tells me in anguish.

I burst into tears, hunching forward, my body heaving with sobs.

He pulls me into his arms and I bury my face against his neck, feeling him shaking beneath me as he also gives in to his emotion.

"I love you too," I tell him, and he clutches me tighter, our skin wet with each other's tears.

But as our sobs die down and our breathing stabilizes, I think about the road stretched out before me, one fork veering off toward Finn and an uncertain life in LA, and the other looping straight back here to Michael and my friends and Seaglass and St. Agnes, a place I've come to love with all my heart, and I realize something.

Love is not enough.

45

THIS SUMMER
THE SEVENTH SUMMER

STILL REMEMBER THE FIRST TIME I SAW A PICTURE OF Finn and Brit together. It was in December, several months after he'd returned to the States, and according to the caption, they'd just been to Variety's Hitmakers Brunch in LA, which celebrates the twenty-five biggest songs in America—one of which was Brit's cover of "We Could Be Giants."

They were walking down a littered, graffitied backstreet in Downtown LA. Finn was out in front, his long arm stretched behind him, Brit's hand firmly encased in his. Their expressions were taut because there were paps around. I could see how hard Finn's jaw was clenched as he stared straight ahead, but the action made his cheekbones seem even more pronounced, and with his dark lashes and wild hair, he looked heart-stoppingly gorgeous. Brit's eyes were on the ground, her dark ringlets half hiding her face as she allowed herself to be led by Finn. She was wearing his denim jacket draped over her shoulders.

It was the same jacket he'd laid on a boulder for me to sit on, the same jacket he'd lent to me when I stumbled into a rock pool.

It hurt acutely, seeing that picture, but anyone who paid

attention to celebrity gossip would have been intrigued. Who was this hot twenty-something guy who'd snatched Brit Easton's heart?

Throughout January and February, more pictures emerged online: photographs of them at the beach in Santa Monica, eating ice cream cones; Finn backstage at Brit's Madison Square Garden gig, watching from the sidelines, his face gleaming with pride; caught at the traffic lights while driving, Finn behind the wheel; coming out of bars, restaurants, night-clubs, and gig venues.

On each occasion when Finn knew he was being watched, his expression would be guarded, but when caught unawares, it was impossible to miss the adoration on his face.

Journalists and bloggers followed the story of their romance, unveiling facts about how they'd fallen in love while writing Brit's last record.

In March, when her first single was released, it went straight to number one, and when her album landed a month later, it hit the top spot in five countries.

The first time I saw dimples fully indented in Finn's cheeks as he gazed down at Brit, I sobbed. And all throughout May I couldn't listen to a single song that reminded me of him.

In early June, Brit, who had been as tight-lipped as Finn about their relationship, finally spoke out.

"We're very happy," she said. "We're just seeing how things go right now and enjoying spending time together."

Those words made me go and get my hair cut.

I want to say that I'm over Finn. I've had a year to move on. But in the months after he left, when I'd heard nothing about him and Brit in the press, I couldn't help but hope that he'd be coming back to me after all.

Now that hope has been crushed.

I wasn't ready for him to leave me behind. I didn't think I'd ever be ready for it.

But then along came Tom.

"I MISS OUR kitchen," Tom murmurs as we lie side by side in my bed, staring up at the ceiling and listening to two small children squealing like banshees in the downstairs apartment. Their father shouts at them to keep the noise down, his booming voice echoing right up through the floorboards.

I smile at his use of the word "our."

"Me too."

"What would you do if you did have a family one day?" he asks. "Would you convert this back into one house?"

"I'd love to, if I could afford it."

Tom has only spent three of the last thirteen nights in his room at the Drifty. Somehow or other, he keeps ending up in my bed.

I thought it would feel strange having him here in my apartment, in my bedroom, which contains so many memories of Finn, but Tom seems to fit wherever he goes. It feels natural to be sharing the same space with him. It's as though I've known him for months, not six weeks.

It's why I was so surprised at the revelation Bill sprang on me last night . . .

"I think we might have found a replacement sous-chef," he said in an upbeat tone.

"Who?" I asked, delighted to hear of another problem solved.

"Tom!" Bill exclaimed with a look like he thought it was obvious.

I was taken aback, and when I mentioned that we'd still have to find a permanent replacement at some point, Bill couldn't believe I didn't know that Tom planned to stay in Cornwall.

I thought he was the one who was confused, until he revealed that Tom had found somewhere to live in Perranporth. He also told me that Tom had chef experience from his time in the navy, another thing I'd been clueless about.

There's so much about him that I still don't know.

I roll over in bed and look at his profile. A moment later, he turns to face me.

"I need to go back to Caernarfon on Sunday."

My heart jumps at his words, and for a second, I'm scared Bill got it wrong, that he's leaving.

"Why?"

"I have to pack up my stuff. The house sale looks as though it's going through."

"And then you'll come back?"

"Yes."

My relief must be as evident as my fear was a moment ago.

"How will you get there?" I ask.

"Same way I came."

"Will you bring a car back with you?"

"No."

"What about all your stuff?" I ask with concern.

"I'll have to get it sent separately. Cara is taking the furniture."

"Would your things fit in *my* car? I mean, do you want a lift?"

He stares at me. "Really?"

"Would that be weird?"

"In what way?"

"Will Cara be there?"

"No, she's already moved out."

I smile at him, but his own smile fades and he sits up and swings his legs out of the bed.

"Are you okay?"

"Yes, fine," he says over his shoulder as I stare at his smooth, muscled back. As I reach out to touch him, he gets up and goes into my en suite, closing the door behind him.

He's *not* fine. I'm not sure why he lied.

A COUPLE OF days later, he changes his mind.

We're having breakfast at the small table in my kitchen and he's just told me that he'll be taking the bus and train tomorrow after all.

"If you don't want me to drive you, then how about I put you on my car insurance?"

I'm trying to sound chilled and reasonable. I'm guessing he'd rather I didn't witness the wreckage of his broken life, or maybe Cara's going to be there after all. Or perhaps he just feels bad about putting me out.

"No, Liv, it's fine," he replies.

"Tom, it's a nightmare journey. It must have taken you close to ten hours to get here. Why would you do that to yourself when you could do it in half the time and bring all your stuff back with you?"

His facial features are taut and he seems to be avoiding eye contact.

"Is it me?" I ask in a small voice.

"No, Liv, it's definitely not you," he promises adamantly, reaching across the table to take my hand.

Now he meets my eyes and I'm relieved to see that he's sincere.

"Then why won't you let me drive you? We could go after lunch tomorrow and come back Tuesday night. I have those days off anyway."

"Thank you, but no," he replies firmly, extracting his hand and picking up his spoon. "I need to do this by myself."

"Well, in that case, I'm putting you on my car insurance," I state firmly, trying to ignore the sting.

I think I'm helping him by insisting, but he slams his spoon down.

"I don't *want* you to put me on your insurance," he says sharply, his eyes sparking as he shoves his chair back.

"Why not?" I find the courage to ask as he begins to pace the room.

"Because I don't drive," he snaps.

I stare at him as he rakes his hand through his hair, frustrated.

I'm lost for words. But he's a helicopter pilot!

Isn't he?

How can he *not* have a driver's license?

And then it occurs to me: he's lost it.

What happened?

Did he drive too fast?

Drink too much and get behind a wheel?

Did he hurt someone?

Kill someone?

Has he lost his job because he killed someone?

Is that why he's here?

Wait. *Is he on the run?* He turned up with just a rucksack . . . *Who does that?*

He lets out a long, heavy sigh as he watches all these thoughts racing around my head.

"I very much doubt it's any of the things you're thinking," he says heavily, his voice sounding extremely weary as he sits back down at the table and rubs his jaw.

"Why can't you just tell me?" I ask quietly as he looks away.

A moment later, he returns his gaze to mine, his golden-brown eyes full of resignation.

"Because it will change things. And I'm not ready for that."

I am so confused.

He sighs and reaches his hand out, a peace offering. I stare at it for a few seconds before placing my palm in his. He traces his thumb over my knuckles.

"I've found somewhere to stay in Perranporth."

Finally, he's telling me!

"Bill asked if I'd be interested in the sous-chef position. I said I'd speak to you."

"He's already mentioned it," I confess, staring at his thumb making its slow tracks back and forth.

He cocks his head to one side. "You didn't say anything."

"I was waiting for you to."

Five seconds pass before he speaks. "Just let me get Wales out of the way."

"And then what?" I ask.

"And then we'll talk."

I swallow and nod, then get up and clear my plate from the breakfast table.

I haven't eaten a thing.

46

WHILE TOM'S AWAY, I DO SOMETHING I QUICKLY come to regret: I look him up online.

I can't find a single thing that offers any clues as to why he might have lost his driver's license, but I do find an article about him at work. And the thought that I ever doubted his claim of being a helicopter pilot makes me feel deeply ashamed. I feel as though I've broken his trust and I'm still none the wiser about any dark secrets he may or may not be hiding away.

Now it's Wednesday morning and I've woken up in the early hours, my mind ticking over.

Did something bad happen when he was out on a job? The article referred to the difficult terrain he has to navigate around Snowdonia National Park and out at sea, winching to cliffs and boats and landing in tight spots on mountains. Any number of things could have gone wrong, and maybe plenty did. Could he be suffering from post-traumatic stress disorder?

I wish my mind would give it a rest. He will talk to me when he's ready, and until that day comes—and I have to resign myself to the fact that it may *never* come—I need to respect his privacy.

Over on the side table, my phone lights up. I slip out of bed and check the message that's just come in, my heart jumping when I see that it's from him.

I'm back. Will you text me when you wake up?

I tap out: I'm awake! Where are you?

It's only five thirty in the morning. When did he arrive in Cornwall? Late last night? He said he'd head straight to Perranporth to get himself settled. He's booked to stay for three weeks in a mobile home in a holiday park, which is not quite the permanent accommodation Bill had thought it was, but they had availability so it will get him by until the first week of August.

Beach. St. Agnes, he replies.

I'll be there in ten!

My phone begins to ring. It's Tom.

"Hello?"

"Or I can come to you," he suggests, and the sound of his warm, deep amusement curls itself in and around my rib cage.

"Is that an option?" I ask breathlessly.

"I'll be there in ten," he repeats my words back to me.

I go straight to the bathroom and brush my teeth.

In the couple of minutes that I spend waiting by my open apartment door, listening for Tom's footsteps, I experience the surreal feeling of struggling to remember what he looks like.

But then I see his gorgeous face appear through the glass panels on the front door and my stomach does backflips.

He gives me a small smile, his maple-syrup eyes regarding me with slight wariness as I step forward to let him in. He hasn't shaved since he left me three days ago, his dark blond hair is disheveled, and he's wearing the black rucksack and charcoal-gray hoodie that he had on when he was no more than a stranger to me. I should feel daunted by his height and breadth—he's so tall, so strong. I should be practicing caution, knowing how closely he guards his secrets. I still don't know why he's in Cornwall, why he's not currently working as a helicopter pilot, and why he has no driver's license. I still don't fully understand why his relationship broke down or why he seemingly wants to leave Wales. He's an enigma in so many ways, and yet, as he stands here before me, I can feel my heart reaching out to his, aching to eradicate the space between us.

It feels like a physical wrench to back away without touching him, but I move into the area at the bottom of my staircase to allow him to close the two doors quietly behind us.

I don't go straight up the stairs as I usually would, perhaps because I *crave* being in a too-small space with him. In the darkness, with no lights on and no windows, the air around us feels charged.

I slide my hands up over his chest and shoulders and he brings his own to my waist, gradually drawing me flush to his hips. My heart takes off at a sprint as he lowers his mouth onto mine.

Our kiss is slow and deep. Shivers roll up and down my spine and my legs turn to jelly. I try to push the rucksack straps off his shoulders, but it's too heavy. He breaks away from me abruptly in an action that feels like a magnet being pried apart from another and shrugs his bag onto the floor. Then we're sucked back together again, our two bodies aligned.

There's barely enough room for me to attack the buttons of his jeans, but I'm determined. As his hands glide up my thighs, gathering up the hem of the summer dress I threw on, I'm vaguely aware of grit on his fingertips, but then I'm only aware of his fingers and his hot gasp into my mouth at the realization that I'm not wearing any underwear.

He takes full advantage of the situation and after surely no more than a minute I'm uttering a desperate cry into his mouth: "*I want you.*"

"I don't have any protection." His reply is guttural, jagged, and he's still touching me.

"I'm clean. Are you?" My words come out sounding garbled. I'm losing my mind.

"Yes. What about birth control?"

"I'm covered."

It vaguely occurs to me to wonder why he asked if he can't have children, but then I'm distracted by his strong arms lifting me up and turning me and laying me gently on the stairs. A moment later, we are one.

I STRUGGLE TO catch my breath afterward. That was so hot, so unexpected. He's still inside me and I feel as much as hear his quiet laugh against my neck.

"I hope your guests wear earplugs to bed."

"Oh shit!"

The staircase runs right over the end wall of the master bedroom, so my guests are directly beneath us.

"That'll get them back for all the early-morning wake-up calls we've had to endure," I whisper, stifling giggles.

The family who has been staying for the last ten days have two particularly noisy youngsters, but it's their dad's booming voice and sudden bellows that have set my teeth on edge.

"Shall we go upstairs?" Tom murmurs.

I nod against him. I don't want him to let me go and to my surprise he doesn't. He picks me up and carries me right up the stairs and into my room, leaving his rucksack where he dropped it. His strength is such a turn-on.

"I could do with a shower," he says, kicking the door shut behind us.

"Me too."

So he takes me into my en suite before placing me gently on my feet and reaching past me to the tap.

In the minutes that follow, I take great pleasure in soaping up his body and washing the sand off him. He seems to get just as much pleasure in taking care of mine.

"THAT'S NOT HOW I imagined seeing you again," he says to me afterward, when we've returned to bed, naked, our limbs entangled.

His voice is surprisingly quiet and contemplative.

"No?"

"I was going to go straight to Perranporth and get myself sorted."

"You didn't?" He'd planned to stay there last night.

"No, I came straight here."

"You couldn't keep away."

"I couldn't," he agrees.

"Did you feel compelled to draw on the sand again?" I haven't forgotten the grit on his fingers.

"No, I felt compelled to see *you*. Drawing on the sand was just killing time."

I smile against his shoulder.

He reaches down and caresses my cheek, gently lifting my chin so I'm looking at him.

"I'm falling in love with you, Liv," he says softly, earnestly.

My heart almost bursts from my chest as I stare into his eyes, shining with emotion. Before I can open my mouth to reply, he continues.

"And it scares the hell out of me."

"I'm falling in love with you too," I say, hoping to reassure him that we're in this together.

"That's even more terrifying."

His admission, along with the sudden haunted look on his face, makes me go still.

"Why?" I ask warily.

"We need to talk."

47

Y OU'VE MOVED ON FROM TREES," I NOTE WITH SUR-
prise when we arrive at the beach.

Tom asked if I'd be willing to take a walk with him,
even though it's still only about 7 a.m.

If he's finally ready to open up to me, I'll go with him when
and wherever he wants me to.

"They were never supposed to be my 'thing.' I just like
drawing," he says with a sweet smile, holding his hand out to
help me step down from the boat ramp.

The tide has washed away a lot of the sand, so the level of
the beach has dropped. Right now, the stream is spilling out
onto rocks and pebbles so the tracks that will forever make me
think of Tom's apple tree are missing.

"Any reason for the alphabet?" I ask as we walk across varying versions of *A*, *B*, and *C*. Some are uppercase, others lower,
some seem to be in bold while others are in italics. All look as
perfect as anything you'd see in print.

"It's not the alphabet," he replies.

Erm, it looks like an alphabet to me, I think, looking ahead to
*D*s, *E*s, and *F*s, and even farther afield to *L*s, *M*s, and *N*s stretching out and interlinking with each other around us. But then I

begin to notice other symbols etched into the sand, symbols that look like an *x* that has been joined up at one side to appear almost like an *a*, another symbol that's a cross between an *8* and an *S*, and another that looks like a *T* that's fallen over, drunk.

"What *are* these?" I ask, puzzled.

"Aeronautical symbols."

I grin at him and point at an italicized uppercase *V*. "What does that stand for?"

"Velocity."

"And that?" A slanting lowercase *h*.

"Altitude above sea level."

God, I fancy him.

Maybe he can see the heat in my eyes, because his voice becomes low and seductive. "And that," he says, totally playing to his audience, "stands for *thrust*."

I begin to giggle.

He smiles at me, but I can see worry residing in the depths of his lovely eyes. He nods in the direction of the old harbor ruins that look like toppled Jenga blocks and we begin to walk across his canvas.

"I'm no longer a helicopter pilot, Liv," he says quietly. "I quit my job a few months ago."

My chest contracts because I don't think it's what he wanted, judging from his wrecked expression. I wait for him to tell me why.

We sit down beside each other on a section of the old harbor wall. The flat wide rock is cold and damp from the sea air and I'm glad of the jeans and jumper I threw on before we left the house.

He looks at me directly. "Do you remember asking me if I was an only child?"

"Yes."

It was when we were talking about how he used to come to Cornwall as a boy, and about that one time he stayed with his grandfather for six weeks while his parents were going through a rough patch in their marriage. I have no idea how it's relevant to why he's quit his job, though.

"It wasn't the full truth. I had an older brother who I never knew. He died in his sleep when he was ten months old. The doctors said it was SIDS. Sudden infant death syndrome."

"Your poor parents," I murmur, shifting so I'm more turned toward him.

"Late last year, my dad suffered a cardiac arrest. He survived, but he'd had fainting episodes leading up to it, which is exactly what happened to my grandfather before his own cardiac arrest."

My brow furrows as I wait for him to go on.

His expression is grave. "Turns out, my dad has a heart condition that affects how his heart beats. This condition can cause arrhythmias—fast, erratic heartbeats—as well as blackouts, fainting, and, in some cases, seizures. Normally, the heart's rhythm will reset after a couple of minutes and the person will regain consciousness. But in my grandfather's and father's cases, it carried on beating abnormally and they went into cardiac arrest. My granddad was on his own, but my dad was with a friend who thankfully knew how to perform CPR and they managed to get his heart going again. He was later diagnosed with long QT syndrome—LQTS."

I've never heard of it.

"It's rare," he continues, pausing before adding, "It's also hereditary."

I stare at him, my blood running cold. I reach out and take his hands, my nerves stretched to breaking point.

"It's likely to have been the real cause of my brother's death," he reveals.

"Do you have it too?" I ask the question on a sharp intake of breath, suddenly overwhelmed, as if I might cry.

"I don't know for certain," he admits gently, allowing me to bring his hands closer, onto my lap. "But I think that I might."

"Have you had any symptoms?" It's hard to even get the question out with the sudden swelling in my throat.

"I blacked out five months ago."

I gasp.

"And I stopped flying that same day," he continues. "The thought of fainting in the cockpit while we were on a call-out . . . I didn't need to be diagnosed to know that I could never risk flying again."

"But you've been diagnosed now?"

He shakes his head.

"Why not?" I ask with alarm.

"I'm not ready. It's another reason why Cara and I split up."

I'd opened my mouth to speak, but this renders me silent. I let it be a lesson to me.

"She also couldn't handle the fact that LQTS is hereditary. As far as I'm aware, I *can* have kids, but I told her that I wouldn't risk passing this on to a child. Lots of people still have children and that's their choice, but I couldn't."

"Is there any treatment for it?"

He nods. "My dad's on beta-blockers and at some point he will probably get an ICD."

"What's that?"

"An implantable cardioverter defibrillator, which is a small electronic device that's connected to the heart and monitors your heartbeat. It can restart your heart if it goes into sudden cardiac arrest."

Didn't he have some random answer to a question about the heart's natural pacemaker at our first quiz night? Was the clue staring me in the face all along?

"Could you also have one of those?" I ask hopefully.

He shakes his head. "They're mostly only implanted in people who have already suffered cardiac arrest."

"So your heart could just *stop*?"

I feel as though I could throw up.

He nods. "Stress or exercise or shock could trigger it. It could even be caused by a sudden noise like an alarm going off, and it can happen in your sleep if your heart slows down."

I'm going to be watching him so closely from now on. And I'm canceling all my alarms.

"It can also happen when you're swimming," he says. "And obviously you run a greater risk of drowning if you black out in the water."

"You're never going in the water again," I state firmly, glad that he hasn't been in the sea since he's been here, at least not to my knowledge.

His expression softens. "Luckily, I'm not a fan of cold-water swimming."

I breathe out a small sigh of relief.

"I don't want to change my life, though, Liv. I don't want to avoid exercising or even swimming if I want to, and I don't want to live in fear of loud noises and shocks. Life is too short at the best of times and I intend to live it as fully as possible.

And plenty of people with LQTS *do* live long, full, and happy lives. I can't do my dream job anymore, and that's taking a lot of getting used to." His eyes begin to shine and he looks away and clears his throat. "But I want to live how I *choose* to live, without anyone telling me differently. I could die tomorrow, regardless of whether I have this condition."

His words make me think of Mum and Dad.

"Cara and my parents and my closest friends have all been on and on at me to get diagnosed and to take medication and to change the way I live. That's why I needed a break. I needed space from them all just to have some peace and quiet and to think. And then I met you. And it scares me that I'm bringing you into my mess, Liv. I understand if you want to walk away."

I lean forward and kiss him on his lips to shut him up.

"I'm not walking away," I say firmly, hot tears pricking my eyes. "Maybe they can't understand how you want to live every day as if it were your last. But I can."

48

S O, THE THING IS . . ." I SAY IN A TONE THAT SOUNDS as though I'm talking to a very small child, when in fact I'm straddling Tom's lap on the sofa in a deserted Sea-glass and looking down at his greatly amused face. "The thing is, I love you. And you love me." I tilt my head to one side and he indulges me by nodding his assent.

We said the words properly to one another a week ago and my feelings for him have only grown stronger since.

"And I want to spend every minute with you that I can and you want to spend every minute with *me*!" I say brightly. "So it really makes no sense at all that you're looking for somewhere else to live right now when you have the perfect place at your fingertips."

His three-week stay at the holiday park in Perranporth is coming to an end.

He raises one eyebrow. "Are you asking me to move in with you, Liv?"

"Why not? You're practically living with me anyway. That mobile home has been a terrible waste of money."

He smiles, but his eyes are serious. "We've only known each other for two months."

"So? Life's for the taking, right?" My heart squeezes as I say this and he can't have missed the flicker of pain that I'm certain crossed my face just now, but I try to cover it up with a breezy smile.

I've been doing this for the last three weeks. You'd think I'd be better at it by now.

"I love you," he murmurs, pressing a gentle kiss to my lips to let me know that he appreciates my bravado.

The last thing he wants is a hysterical woman in his life reminding him that he could—*Oh God!*—literally drop dead at any second.

My blood runs hot and cold as this fact hits me once again. The stress of trying to hide my fears from him may well be the end of *me*.

I pull back from his lips and look at him. "So let's go get your stuff and bring it back to mine."

He smiles and dips his head, saying into the hollow at the base of my neck, "I've got other things I want to do first." His hands cut a slow path up my thighs, causing goose bumps to race down my arms.

I decide to let him have his way with me. He could get away with pretty much anything these days.

I STRUGGLED TO leave Tom's side once he told me the whole truth about why he's here in Cornwall. He came for peace and quiet, but he's staying because he's fallen in love with the place.

And he's fallen in love with me.

It fills me in a way I didn't know I needed, that he wants his fresh start *here*, that he's chosen St. Agnes, out of all the villages, towns, and cities he could have chosen.

It hurt so much every time Finn turned his back on Cornwall, on me.

I'd mostly been managing to put him out of my mind, but for some reason he's often in my thoughts recently. It isn't from a place of heartache, although it still hurts to know that he's moved on, but I have become more analytical about our relationship.

Finn helped me through the darkest, bleakest stage of my life. He was strong for me when I was at my lowest ebb, returning year after year and helping me to stand tall. He was the Italian cypress to my withering apple tree, and I will always love him for it.

I'm so proud of his achievements. He's doing so well and he deserves to be happy. And he deserves to be with someone else who's happy too.

It does strike me as slightly ironic that I'm doing the best I've ever done, both mentally and in my career, just as he's no longer around to witness it. He helped me to fly, only for another man to see me soar.

Part of what I love about my relationship with Tom is that it started from a place of strength. I'm no longer a shadow of myself, crippled by pain and grief, and we're not pulling in different directions. I like that I'm strong enough to support him if he needs me to.

I hope that Finn knows how much I appreciate the love and support *he's* showered on me over the years. I hope he knows that I will always be grateful.

One day I'll tell him, although I'm not sure when. He's finally RSVP'd to Amy and Dan's wedding to say that he can't make it—he's currently in the studio with another artist and he's unable to get away.

I feel such conflicting emotions about this. On the one hand, I don't want to be anywhere near him—I'm still hurt and I'd hate things to be awkward at the wedding, especially with Tom being there.

On the other, I can't imagine going a whole summer without seeing his face.

I'M STILL THINKING a lot about Finn when I attend the unveiling of my public art.

It was Finn who gave me the idea for my subject, that day at Chapel Porth. His words rang around my head for weeks: *I haven't seen you sculpt a single thing that comes from a place of joy.*

And then one day, it hit me.

It was a nightmare to get him to sit for me for hours a day, months on end, and afterward he swore that he never wanted to see my face again, but now, as I stand beside my brother with his life-size bronze effigy on my other side, I can say that every second of it was worth it.

At least on my part. Michael is looking thoroughly nonplussed.

A Down syndrome charity commissioned the public artwork, after I'd had the idea to approach them. They agreed with my argument that we needed more memorials to represent minority groups and gave me the go-ahead to start fundraising. Arabella helped and Lord and Lady Stockley made a generous donation. Now Michael's statue has been erected in a green space right outside the charity's headquarters. And because "joy" was a word that I kept returning to, I decided to sculpt him at his happiest, with a great big smile on his face.

Which is funny because he's currently tutting with disgust and shaking his head at the official press photographer.

"Say cheese, Michael!" I prompt chirpily.

"Cheese!" He delivers his heavy sarcasm with an exaggerated eye roll.

"Imagine an Aston Martin DB5 has just pulled into the car park at Chapel Porth," Tom calls out.

Michael laughs at Tom's prompt, and that sets me off too. The official photographer quickly clicks off a few more shots.

Michael has moved on from serial killer thrillers to spy action movies now and is presently making his way through every single James Bond film that was ever made. The films are much more my scene than the gory stuff he usually binge-watches, so Tom and I have been joining him on occasion, and it amuses me to see their reactions to all the cool cars.

Michael has really warmed to Tom over the last few weeks. It helps that Tom's a car enthusiast too, plus he also knows every single model of aircraft that appears on-screen.

A couple of weeks ago, we all got together to watch *Spectre*. The baddie, played by Christoph Waltz, was flying in a sleek black helicopter when Michael paused mid-chomp of popcorn, his head shooting around comically to silently question Tom.

"Eurocopter AS365 Dauphin N2," Tom replied without missing a beat as Daniel Craig and Léa Seydoux chased it down the Thames in a speedboat. "Formerly known as an Aérospatiale SA 365 Dauphin 2," he added.

"How do you *know* that?" Michael erupted with amazement.

"I used to be a helicopter pilot," Tom replied with a shrug.

We were cuddled up together on one sofa while Michael had the other to himself. I tensed, but Tom's chest was relaxed under my palm, his long legs stretched out and crossed at the ankles, his feet resting on the coffee table.

Meanwhile, Michael had shot upright, his jaw hitting the floor. "You used to be a helicopter pilot?" he asked with astonishment.

"Yep."

And then Michael paused the TV and demanded to know about every single model of aircraft that Tom had ever been in.

Later, when we finally made it home to bed, Tom confessed that it had been nice to talk about flying without feeling the pressure of having to explain why he no longer can.

It was a lovely bonding moment between them.

WE'RE DONE WITH the photos, but I still need to give a couple of short interviews to journalists from the regional press. Out of the corner of my eye, I see Rach giving Michael a hug. He's all smiles and cuddles now that he no longer has to pose for the photographer.

I'm so grateful to my friends for making the trip to Middlesex with me. Dan and Amy are here too, even though they're only three days out from their wedding. Tom is chatting to them, probably offering to help with any last-minute jobs, knowing him.

He catches my eye and smiles and I momentarily lose track of what I was saying.

As soon as I'm released from my duties, I go to him.

He tugs me into his arms and says in my ear, "I'm ridiculously proud of you."

I pull away and kiss his cheek, noticing that Dan and Amy are watching us, smiling.

Amy was so pleased when she heard that Tom and I have booked to go to London for a couple of nights next week. It feels like a big deal as it will be the first time I've been away from Michael in years, although it made my heart melt when Tom asked if I wanted to invite him. I absolutely did not.

One, Michael wouldn't have enjoyed it—the last time I dragged him into a gallery, he stood and loudly declared that it was "*Borrrrring!*"

And two, I want a couple of nights away with Tom on our own. The thought of being able to wander around galleries and museums hand in hand, sharing my passion with someone who understands and appreciates it . . . I can't wait.

I'm glad of something to look forward to, something to take my mind off the fact that it's the anniversary of my parents' deaths this Sunday and now I know for certain that Finn won't be coming back for it.

Year after year, for five years, he returned unfailingly, but now he's fallen head over heels in love with another woman. And not just any woman. How could I have ever hoped to compete with Brit Easton?

I used to dream about Finn leaving Brit, coming back to me, begging for my forgiveness, telling me that he'd move to St. Agnes for me.

When I imagine that scenario playing out now, a cold flush comes over me. What *would* I do if I was faced with a choice between Finn and Tom? Finn and I have so much shared history—would I really be strong enough to turn my back on him?

I decide there's no point in getting stressed contemplating a scenario that's never going to happen.

49

A FEW DAYS LATER, AMY AND DAN TIE THE KNOT. Rach and I are Amy's bridesmaids and I struggle to hold it together as they say their vows. It blows my mind to think that they've known each other since high school and that one summer fling at the age of twenty-two led to them declaring their undying love.

They've chosen to marry in St. Agnes Parish Church, and for the most part I'm able to set aside my memories of my parents' funeral six years ago. At least the reception is not being held in the same place. Chas has closed Seaglass's doors to the public tonight so he can host his nephew's wedding reception, which is a huge deal considering it's a Saturday in August. He returned from his round-the-world trip a few days ago and was straight back behind the bar.

"Christ, I've missed this old girl," he said, standing there with his hands propped on the bar top. His face was full of love and wonder as he looked around before staring across the room at the sea with a wistful expression.

I thought he'd feel less nostalgic once he reexperienced the carnage of Friday-night cocktails, but he seemed to enjoy the adrenaline rush last night.

I hope he takes it easy, but I do feel better knowing that I can administer CPR now. I went round to Rach's house in the days after Tom opened up to me and asked her to teach me. She also explained how to use the community defibrillator.

I shed a lot of tears on my friend's sofa that day.

Tom is sitting with Ellie in the church—we were at the quiz night a couple of weeks ago when Dan and Amy invited him. Dan had just pulled me to one side and given me a quick hug, whispering in my ear: "It's good to see you happy."

I'd had a surreal moment shortly before that when I'd noticed Amy and Rach throwing each other wary looks as I was laughingly relaying an anecdote. Tom and I had been to the beach earlier that day and he'd been drawing small pictures of animals on the sand between us. I'd just told him about Brendan and his coffee-foam creatures, so he was jokily trying to compete. When he came to drawing an elephant, he made the trunk so long that I fell about in hysterics.

For some reason, Rach and Amy weren't finding my story as funny as I'd thought they would—and then I realized: "The Boys of Summer," the rockier, grittier version by the Ataris, was playing over the sound system. It's very similar to the version Mixamatosis played on their last night with Finn as their frontman. My friends had been waiting for me to notice.

"I'm going to be fine with whatever songs you pick for your wedding playlist," I reassured Amy with a smile, squeezing her hand.

"I'll avoid Brit Easton," she promised.

"Well, that I *would* appreciate."

WE SPILL OUT of the church to clear blue skies. The church bells are ringing and can be heard all over St. Agnes. Passersby pause to watch as we shower the beautiful bride and handsome groom with rose petals. Amy is wearing a simple white gown with an elegant cowl-neck, and Dan looks gorgeous in a dark gray suit.

Rach is also in a gray suit, although in a lighter shade than Dan's, the same color worn by the groomsmen, Tarek and Chris. She was so grateful to Amy for not requesting that she wear a dress.

I'm in a long, flowing emerald-green number with very high-heeled gold sandals, and Tom is rocking a navy suit. I went with him to buy it and almost feel embarrassed about how hot he looks right now. He's toweringly tall and the slim-fit cut of his jacket makes his shoulders look ridiculously broad.

I wasn't thinking of the steep hills when I chose these heels, but Tom keeps me steady as we set off toward Trevaunance Cove, my grip firmly in his.

He's been so calm since he told me about his suspected heart condition. He really doesn't seem to give his health much thought, but I have found myself resting my head on his chest when we're in bed together, listening to his heart thumping in the silence. He's so strong in so many ways, both physically and mentally. It's reassuring. I hope that I'll worry about him less as the days and weeks, and hopefully months and years, go by.

We have to walk single file once we reach Stippy Stappy and I smile when I see Michael sitting on the garden bench outside his cottage.

"Hello!" he shouts, waving happily at us.

"See you later?" I call, waving back.

"Yep! I'll be there!" he replies cheerfully.

He's coming to the post-reception party. Amy and Dan are putting on a seafood buffet for their closest friends and family. Once the dinner service is over, the tables downstairs will be cleared to make room for other friends to come and help them celebrate.

With all the people coming in, I have no idea how Chas plans to keep the general public out, but I doubt Dan and Amy would even notice if there were interlopers. I have a feeling they've invited everyone they've ever met.

It's a breathtaking sight as we walk the last stretch to Seaglass. Amy and Dan are leading the way and her long light blond hair is flowing out behind her in the breeze, the glittering turquoise waters of the Celtic Sea stretched out before them.

The staff come outside to welcome them, and more rosepetal confetti rains down as Amy and Dan walk up the stairs.

Later, once the meal and speeches are out of the way, my friends and I head to the balcony so the tables can be cleared for the after-party. The golden-yellow sun is dipping toward the horizon and the festoon lights we've strung up along the outside of the building are starting to come into their own.

Tom is leaning against the railing and I move naturally into the space between his legs. This prompts him to bring his arms around me from behind and gently pull me against him so that my back is flush to his chest. My heart is so full of love for him.

Chas comes over with a pint of beer and throws a wiry arm around his nephew's neck. He's been helping a local indie band set up their equipment on the small stage inside.

"If only you had Kieran here!" Chas exclaims. "I'd be kicking those guys off and getting you boys up there."

Kieran, Mixamatosis's former frontman, moved to Canada last year with his girlfriend, soon-to-be wife.

"I do miss those good old days," Tarek says nostalgically, clinking Chas's glass with his pint of Coke.

"They were great, weren't they?" Dan agrees, patting his uncle's chest affectionately.

"Maybe it's time for a reunion," Amy suggests with a grin.

Chas looks past me at Tom and raises an eyebrow. "Can you sing?"

Tom chuckles and shakes his head.

On his return, Chas was surprised to find me in a serious relationship.

"I thought you were wedded to this place like I am!" he joked, meaning Seaglass.

He seemed happy with the way I've been running things, and I did enjoy moving up into a managerial role, but I'm glad to be able to take a step back again now, even if I'll still be working my arse off until the end of August. It will be good to have a bit more time to focus on the other things in my life once autumn comes.

I can't wait to spend a winter here with Tom. He's going to love having access to so many quieter beaches once the tourists have gone, and I'm excited to get into my garden studio again—Tom thinks I should have heating plumbed in so it's not too cold once the weather turns.

It's going to be good getting the rest of the house back too; being able to wake up and go downstairs to the kitchen-diner.

I never thought I'd be so keen for summer to be over.

Michael walks out onto the balcony, a big smile on his face at the sight of us.

"There he is!" Rach shouts, beckoning him over.

"I heard you're famous now," Chas says when my brother has finished exchanging hugs.

Michael side-eyes him circumspectly.

"Your statue!" Chas explains.

"Oh, yeah!" Michael grins again.

And then he looks past Rach to the other end of the balcony and his face lights up brighter still.

"FINN!" he shouts, wildly waving his arms over his head.

All the lights in the universe blink out and a single spotlight shines on Finn as he makes his way along the balcony to gasps and exclamations from our friends, who very evidently did *not* know he was coming.

I feel myself shrink as everything inside me contracts, getting smaller and smaller. Tom stiffens behind me.

Finn is mere meters away when his Celtic Sea green eyes catch mine and I'm struck by the raw emotion I see in them. Then he severs the contact and stares past me at Tom.

A second later, he's in the midst of our friends.

I tear my eyes away and look at Amy.

"*I didn't know*," she mouths, eyes wide with alarm, shaking her head at me.

And then I'm watching Finn again and the years are collapsing in on themselves, toppling and falling, as pieces of our love story slam into place.

I see him staring at me in the mirror, wearing a holey black jumper and grinning as he told me that I was Olivia Arterton.

I see him up onstage, a smile curving his lips as it dawned on me that he was singing Taylor Swift's "22."

I see him seconds before the first time we kissed, after I'd tried to poke one of his dimples and he'd snatched my finger and bitten it.

I see him standing out here on the balcony, the wind whipping his hair into dark slashes across his cheekbones, minutes after I'd unsettled him by calling him Danny Finnegan.

I see him sitting across a table from me at the Taphouse, telling me that nothing I say is boring.

I see him pogoing around the dance floor with Michael and his friends, and staring at me with gleeful disbelief over my brother's shoulder when he got his first hug.

I see him on the beach . . .

In my bed . . .

On the cliffs . . .

And at Seaglass.

He is everywhere.

How could I have forgotten?

I don't realize that I've stepped away from Tom until I find myself standing alone.

50

THINK I'M GOING TO HEAD HOME," TOM SAYS TO ME AT around ten thirty.

I've just joined him at the bar where he's been chatting to Bill, who stuck around after dinner service for the party.

I've been dancing with Rach and Ellie, and spending most of my time trying to convince myself that I'm not agonizingly aware of Finn's every movement.

Apparently, Dan told him that if he had a last-minute change of heart, he'd be welcome at any time.

Looks like he had a last-minute change of heart.

He and I haven't said more than two words to each other. He went to the bar straight after he arrived to see Tyler, while Dan, Tarek, and Chris trailed after him. Chas went off to talk to some friends and I quickly returned to Tom's side.

I haven't really known what to say and Tom hasn't pressed me, but I've felt his attention repeatedly returning to my face, trying to make sense of the emotions that are clearly raging inside me.

"What? No!" I protest at his words now. "You can't leave! Are you okay?"

"I'm fine. I just . . . I'm a little tired and—"

"If you're going, I'm coming too."

"Don't be silly. Stay and have fun," he insists.

"I'll just get my bag from behind the bar," I state firmly.

He sighs, his golden-brown eyes gazing down at me. "If you really won't let me leave without you, then I guess I'll have to stay."

"That sounds like the best option." I pat his chest with relief and am rewarded with a small smile. "I love you," I remind him.

I feel he needs to be reminded right now.

"I love you too," he replies.

Stepping into his arms, I tenderly rest my cheek against his chest. I may look peaceful to an outsider, but my mind is going haywire.

I catch sight of Chas at the other end of the bar, chatting to the band's frontman. He's up to something. When he comes out from behind the bar and hops up onto the empty stage, my heart sinks.

"What do you reckon to the groom and his Mixamatosis crew playing us a song?" he says into the microphone. "For old times' sake? You've got your old frontman here tonight."

Cheers go up and the crowd begins to chant: "SING! SING! SING!"

This builds to a crescendo and then the whole room breaks out into raucous applause as Dan, Tarek, Chris, and Finn take to the small stage. They briefly huddle together before looking around at the equipment to get their bearings. Finn has his back to the audience as he watches his old bandmates check over the instruments that have been loaned to them and then he turns around and picks up the mic, his eyes scanning the crowd. They snag on me for a couple of seconds before moving on to Tom and then they pass by him to land on Amy, who's standing nearby.

"This one's for the bride," he says with a sleepy grin.

Tom squeezes my waist and bends down to speak in my ear: "I'll be back in a bit."

"You're not going?" I shoot him a look, panicked.

"Only to the bathroom," he promises, squeezing my waist again and casting a look over at the stage. His gaze catches and holds for a moment and I witness his jaw clenching as he turns away.

I return my attention to the stage and find Finn watching me. He lowers his eyes as his bandmates begin to play, and the instantly recognizable melody of INXS's "Never Tear Us Apart" spills from the speakers.

Finn's deep, soulful voice fills the room. *"Don't ask me . . ."*

The hairs on the back of my neck stand up, just as they did the first time I heard him sing. The coincidence isn't lost on me that it's a song by the same band.

It's a stunning choice for Dan and Amy, but as Finn's eyes lift again and lock with mine, I feel that he's singing the lyrics to me.

I am *undone*.

A lump forms in my throat as I stare back at him, trying to control my reaction. His eyebrows draw together as he watches me and the whole room seems to fade away.

I cannot cope with this.

"Don't even *think* about it," Amy hisses in my ear when I manage to wrench my gaze away during the instrumental break.

"What?" I ask huskily, staring past her in a daze.

"He's in your past. Leave him behind."

"That's easier said than done."

"I need to say something to you and I need you to listen," she says firmly, almost angrily, as the instrumental break comes to an end and Finn begins to sing again.

I reluctantly look at her, unable to concentrate fully because his voice is so beautiful.

But no one argues with a bride on her wedding day. Especially not *this* bride.

"When I think about you at your happiest, I think about you that summer when you'd just finished university. You had the whole world at your feet and were so full of excitement and joy for what the future would bring. You glowed. You *sparkled*. The only time I've seen you like that since has been when you're with Tom."

My head prickles as her eyes well up.

"Don't do it, Liv," she begs me as the song comes to an end and everyone cheers. People are looking over at her, but Amy is ignoring the fact that the song was dedicated to her. She doesn't even look the band's way because she's still speaking urgently and directly into my ear. "You'll end up on that same godforsaken roundabout that you've been on for years. He'll jump on for a bit, tear your heart into shreds, and jump off again. I can't watch you do it, not when you seem to be so close to finding lasting happiness."

She pulls away and gives me a hard stare as "Fire" by Kasabian begins to blare out of the speakers. The boys only played the one track.

But *am* I close to finding lasting happiness? How long can what I have with Tom actually last? What if his heart simply gives out one day when we're walking along the beach? I could *literally* wake up tomorrow and find that I've lost him.

Behind Amy, I see Tom emerge from the bathrooms. I bow my head, blinking furiously and trying to compose myself. I don't want him to see me upset.

"Please, Liv," Amy implores.

I nod curtly and walk toward Tom, stepping straight into his arms.

"I think I'm ready to go home now after all."

He hugs me tightly, cradling my head against his chest, and maybe it's the beat pumping from the speakers and reverberating through my body, but I prefer to imagine that it's his heart thudding against mine.

THE FOLLOWING MORNING, on the anniversary of my parents' deaths, my resolve weakens. I'm sitting across from Tom at the breakfast table and I've just told him that I'm going for a walk on the cliffs.

"Do you want some company?" he asks evenly, scooping up some granola with his spoon.

I clear my throat. "I think I need to go alone."

He respected my need for silence when we got home last night. I fell asleep in his arms and woke up in them, so I'd hoped that would be enough to reassure him.

But from his expression, I can see that I'm nowhere close to doing that. I have a feeling he can see straight through me.

I brace myself. "I need to see Finn," I confess.

His eyes are disquieted as we stare at each other for a moment, and then he nods and looks down, placing his spoon back in his bowl.

"I love you," I whisper. "It's only that I feel we have unfinished business."

"Won't you always have unfinished business?" he asks directly. "Unless you actually go all in and have a proper relationship with him, won't you always wonder what could have been? And if he hasn't been available for a relationship so far, what makes you think anything has changed?"

"I don't believe anything *has* changed," I reply edgily. "He's got a girlfriend."

"From the way he was looking at you last night, Liv, I think she's long gone."

My heart jolts.

He roughly drags his hands down his face with apparent frustration.

"Go," he says raggedly. "Do what you have to do. I'll be waiting for you when you get home."

"Thank you," I whisper, reaching out to press my hand to his. "I'll come home and then we'll walk up to Michael's together."

We're having lunch with him today.

I feel terrible as I gather my phone and keys, but if I don't see this through to its conclusion—and I fully intend that this *will be* its conclusion—I'll always regret it.

I can't spend another year, let alone the rest of my life, without proper closure.

51

CAN'T SHAKE MY GUILT AT LEAVING TOM BACK AT THE house as I climb the coast path by the beach, with the ocean and the islands of Bawden Rocks on my right-hand side. I hope that he'll be able to forgive me.

I texted Finn a few minutes ago: I'm going to the bench.

He replied: I'm already halfway there.

He knew I'd go today. How long would he have waited until I came? It doesn't bear thinking about.

My chest contracts when he comes into view. He looks over his shoulder and sees me, and I'd think he was made of stone if it wasn't for his dark hair thrashing in the wind and his eyes slowly tracing my steps toward him.

His lips are set in a straight line, but as I close the distance between us, he gives me a small smile and gets to his feet.

"Hi," he says, opening up his arms.

I hesitate—I don't want him to hold me—but I can't refuse to give him a hug after all this time.

My head and heart are all over the place as we embrace. I intend to keep it brief, but as I begin to withdraw, his grip tightens momentarily.

And then he releases me.

"How are you?" he asks as we sit down on the bench, a foot apart from one another. "I like your hair."

"Oh, thanks." I tuck it behind my ears self-consciously. Before yesterday, he'd only ever seen it long. "I'm okay," I reply, but I sound indecisive. "How are you?"

He looks out at the ocean, his temple throbbing. "I've been better."

I shift on my seat. "Where's Brit?"

He shrugs. "Probably in LA, cutting holes into my clothes. Which is ironic," he adds sardonically, "seeing as I'd finally stopped wearing moth-eaten T-shirts."

His words make me feel so many confusing things.

"Have you broken up?"

"Yep," he replies flatly.

"Why?"

He hesitates for a moment before casting me a sidelong look. "Because of you."

"Me?" My stomach somersaults. "How have I got anything to do with your relationship?"

"I told her I was coming here and she was not at all happy about it. She said if I came, we're done. So I guess we're done."

"Finn, no," I say determinedly. "You can fix this."

"I can't. It's too late."

"It's never too late. Not if you fight for her. You can go back, you can call her right now and convince her you don't want to be here, that you regret coming."

"But that would be a lie," he says dully, returning his gaze to the sea.

I stare at him, my pulse racing.

He turns once more to look at me.

"Do you love him?" he asks.

It's hard to witness the wary trepidation in his blue-green stare, but I force myself to maintain eye contact.

"Yes."

Time seems to stand still for a moment, and then he buries his face in his hands.

The memory of his shattered expression and his eyes filling with sudden tears is burned into my retinas. I suspect I'll take that sight with me to my grave.

I reach out and touch his back. His body heaves beneath my palm and then it begins to shake. I can't bear to witness his pain, so when he turns to me I allow him to clutch me desperately.

A moment later, I lose it too.

"I love you, Liv," he sobs. "I don't love her the way I love you."

"You're not supposed to!" I cry. "That's not how love works. I don't love Tom the way that I love you either. It doesn't mean I don't love him as deeply or as passionately, it's just different. I don't love him any less."

He lets out a ragged breath and inhales just as shakily, and then he lets me go and rubs at his eyes with the heels of his palms, trying to dry his tears. I dig into my jeans pocket for tissues, passing one to him and keeping another for myself. We both blow our noses loudly.

"What if I moved back?" he asks, turning to look at me with red-rimmed eyes.

I stare at him in shock and note the hope flitting across his face at my response.

"You don't want to live in St. Agnes," I point out shakily.

"I would," he states firmly. "For you."

"But you wouldn't be happy," I argue.

"I would." He repeats himself in the same tone. "If I had you."

"Finn!" I exclaim, shaking my head with despair. "Don't do this. It's too late."

"You just said yourself that it's never too late. That I should go home and fight for Brit."

It hurts hearing him say her name—what does that tell me? I am nowhere close to being over him.

"What if I stayed and fought for you?" he asks.

I swallow, steadying myself. "I don't want you to," I reply adamantly. "I want to be with Tom. He . . . he has a heart condition," I find myself confiding. "It's potentially fatal."

Three seconds pass.

"Are you serious?"

His question doesn't come from a place of compassion or concern. The tone is that of someone asking, *Are you fucking kidding me?*

"Why the hell are you saying it like that?" I demand to know.

"Well, it's just typical, isn't it? You're drawn to pain and suffering. It's why you excel as an artist."

"If you're suggesting that I'm staying with Tom to fan the flames of my own creativity, you're out of your fucking mind."

"I didn't mean it like that."

"I'd never forgive you if you did."

"I'm sorry," he says abruptly. "I don't mean it at all."

"I love him, Finn," I say resolutely. "I don't love him because I'm drawn to pain and suffering. What I feel for him is pure and clean. I love him because he's strong and steady. Because he chose St. Agnes. Because he chose *me*. He has never wavered." I reach out and take his hand as his eyes fill with tears again. "I'm not sure I ever said thank you," I say huskily, my own vision going blurry. "I don't know what I would have done without you all these years. I'm so grateful to you, Finn. You helped me through the hardest time in my life—you have been *so* important to me. A part of me will never stop loving you. But I choose *him*. And you've got to let me go."

"You've only known him for a short while," he says hoarsely. "How are you so sure about him?"

"I don't know, but I *am* sure."

"Do you mind if I wait on the sidelines in case you turn out to be wrong?" he asks, trying to make light of it, but his pain cuts straight to my core.

"Don't wait for me, Finn," I implore him. "I plan to be with Tom for a very long time."

Maybe for the rest of my life. And if not the rest of *my* life, then hopefully for his.

THE LAST OF my tears have dried by the time I return to Beach Cottage, but I can still feel the remnants of saltwater tracks on my cheeks. I wonder, surreally, if Tom will see a pattern in them, and then I wonder if Tom will see them at all.

What if he's left? Why would he stay?

Because he told me that he would, I remind myself.

When I say something, I tend to mean it. You don't need to doubt me.

When he first said those words to me, I remember thinking that I could fall in love with him.

And I have. I love him. And I trust him. He'll be here.

My heart rate begins to stabilize as I stand on my doorstep, trying to compose myself before getting my keys out of my pocket. The downstairs apartment is quiet as I unlock the front door and enter the hall. I think our guests have gone out.

Our guests. I notice how right that feels. Tom and I are a team now. I know that he'll be at my side with every step I take.

I open the door to the upstairs apartment and my chest expands at the sight of him sitting at the top of the stairs, waiting for me. His expression is wary until he reads what must be written all over my face.

"I love you," I say as tension slips from his shoulders and he stands up, giving me a small, relieved smile.

I pull the door shut and go to him.

As we clutch each other on the landing, our hearts and bodies aligned, something inside me settles. Since Finn's return, the inner restlessness that used to plague me has risen again.

Once, it could only be soothed by sculpting, but being in Tom's arms again reminds me of the first time I pushed my hands into cold clay after the death of my parents.

It feels like coming home.

EPILOGUE

ONE SUMMER FROM NOW . . .

"Jesus," Tom mutters, wiping sweat from his brow with the back of his hand.

"It was hot like this the last time I came to Florence."

He grins across at me. "Are you happy to be back?"

"Deliriously."

We've just come from the Galleria dell'Accademia, where I wanted Tom to see the original statue of David.

It's the anniversary of my parents' deaths today, which is partly why I chose these dates for my long-awaited return to Italy. I texted Finn a few weeks ago to let him know I was going away. I didn't think he *would* return to St. Agnes this year—he's back with Brit and as far as I know they're happy—but I didn't want to risk it.

He replied: I hope you have a good time. And that was it.

It probably hurts him that I never went to see him in LA. It's not that I didn't want to. After our argument that day in the Chapel Porth car park, when Michael insisted that he didn't want me to stay in St. Agnes because of him, I began to reevaluate things. I *had* been sticking within my comfort zone.

Michael would be fine if I decided to go away occasionally. I just needed to do it.

Tom and I eased in slowly with a few mini-breaks here and there—including the trip to London after Amy and Dan's wedding. And now we've ventured abroad and are planning to spend a few days here in Florence before heading to Pietrasanta to visit the town and the nearby marble quarry.

"Gelato?" I ask Tom.

"Hell, yes."

We stand and wait at a counter in front of a brightly colored selection. He chooses peach, which is the same color as his T-shirt. I press a kiss to his shoulder and smile up at him.

"Thank you for coming with me."

"Where are we going next?" he asks with a grin.

TWO SUMMERS FROM NOW . . .

I come home to find Tom sitting in the room that used to be my parents' bedroom. He's staring out the window at the palm trees, with his back to the door.

I quietly knock on the wall, surprised that he didn't hear me come up the stairs.

"Oh, hey!" he says, jumping up.

I hate startling him like this. I live in fear of giving him a shock that could cause his heart to stop. But it seems to be ticking along okay at the moment.

There was an occasion a couple of months ago when he felt lightheaded. He'd just created a Surfers Against Sewage–inspired sand-art piece that spanned a hundred square meters of Perranporth beach—Rach had asked if he would do it to help raise awareness for the cause. She'd arranged for an official photographer to come.

I was terrified when Tom reached out to steady himself on my arm after he'd finished. I followed him around like a lost puppy for days.

I'm scared that the large-scale pieces take it out of him, but I'd never ask him to stop. I respect that he has to live his life the way he chooses.

"You must've been deep in thought," I say, after he bends down to give me a kiss.

"I was," he agrees.

"Anything to tell me?"

"Actually, yes, there is."

His expression is serious, but he doesn't look worried.

We go and sit on the sofa in the upstairs living room. The downstairs apartment is currently occupied by a couple of artists.

"I've been to see a doctor," he tells me.

My smile slips from my face.

"It's okay." He reaches out to take my hand.

He hasn't been to see a doctor in all the time I've known him.

"I've decided I want to get diagnosed."

I squeeze his hand. "Why now?"

"I'm ready," he says gently. "But also . . ." He takes a deep breath. "Also . . . I think it could help us."

"How?"

"When Cara and I got a mortgage, we were urged to take out life insurance policies. I decided to go one further and take out critical illness cover."

I'm wondering where he's going with this.

"If I'm diagnosed, I'll be due a payout, Liv. A big one. We could potentially buy into Seaglass. If you'd like to."

My head spins. Buy into Seaglass? Chas has been looking into bringing in an investor. He doesn't want to step away permanently, but he's finally accepted that he's *not* as young as he feels and could actually be in serious danger of taking himself out if he doesn't slow down.

So he decided that, rather than sell up entirely, he'd try to see if he could find an investor he'd like to work with.

And I suspect he would love to work with Tom.

Tom is head chef now—Bill left to open his own restaurant

in Redruth. I love walking into the kitchen when Tom's at work, shouting for service and plating up salads like a pro. Just like the bar staff, the kitchen crew move and flow around each other as though they're water. Service is an art form in itself.

I only work part-time at Seaglass during June, July, and August these days, because I need the other nine months of the year to sculpt. I was invited to attend the International Sculpture Symposium in Vietnam back in January, along with thirty other sculptors from around the world. It was such an incredible experience, getting to know other sculptors and watching them in action. We each created our own pieces, which have now been erected in a sculpture park for the public to enjoy. My sculpting career is going from strength to strength, but I still love working at Seaglass with Tom. It's a perfect combination.

"What do you think?" Tom asks. "I want it to be something for both of us."

I nod and climb onto his lap, my eyes filling with tears. "I think that I love you. And I would love Seaglass to be ours."

It already feels like it is anyway.

THREE SUMMERS FROM NOW . . .

I sit five rows back with Amy, staring at Finn's head. He's in the front pew, his grandfather on one side of him and Liam on the other. Tyler is sitting next to Liam.

Finn's grandmother Trudy passed away a couple of weeks ago after a massive stroke.

Tom offered to come with me to the funeral, but he understood when I asked if he'd mind if I went alone. This is the first time I've seen Finn in three years.

"THANK YOU FOR coming," he says to me after the service.

He saw me standing with Dan and Amy in the churchyard and came over, his nose and eyes tinged red from crying.

"Where's Tom?" he asks.

"I thought it might be better if I came alone," I reply.

He gives me a small nod.

"How's Brit?" I ask awkwardly.

He shakes his head and glances at me, then looks away.

I take it that means they're no longer together.

"Are you okay?" I ask quietly as Dan and Amy step away to give us some privacy.

"Not really," he admits. "My granddad's distraught. I don't know how he's going to cope without her."

"He'll have Liam to keep him company."

Tyler moved into a house with some mates a couple of years

ago. He now works as a mixologist at a bar in Newquay, where he lives. We trained him well.

He swallows and nods, then meets my eyes. "Congratulations, by the way. I heard the news."

"About what?"

"What do you *think*?" he asks with a frown.

"I'm now a member of the Royal Society of Sculptors?"

He shakes his head. "No."

"Buying into Seaglass?"

He sighs. "No, Liv. The *other* thing. But congratulations on those things too," he adds with a small smile, and my chest pinches at the proud look on his face.

"I was going to text you about the other thing," I say seriously. I was hoping he wouldn't hear about it through the grapevine before I'd had a chance to tell him. "And then this happened."

About three weeks ago, I woke up in bed to find that Tom wasn't beside me. He called half an hour later to ask me to come down to Seaglass.

When I arrived, he was standing at the main door and he beckoned me up to the balcony.

Down on the beach he'd drawn a geometric pattern on the sand—a series of triangles with one octagonal shape on the top. He creates sand art every few weeks or so—even more often in the winter when there are fewer people around—but in the last couple of years he's taken to drawing abstract shapes and patterns, finding them to be even more relaxing than representational pieces. He's done a couple of commissions for charities too.

I smiled at him. "That's cool."

"Does it remind you of anything?" he asked me, a secretive smile on his face.

I looked again and suddenly I saw it: it was a perspective drawing of a diamond solitaire.

"It's a diamond!" I exclaimed.

And that was when he pulled the ring out of his pocket and got down on his knee.

I clapped my hand over my mouth, staring down at him in shock as his eyes shone with tears, and then I was a goner too.

"Will you marry me, Liv?"

I nodded, because I couldn't speak, and then he was back on his feet and slipping the ring onto my finger.

"Does he still make you happy?" Finn asks me softly.

I nod, my heart squeezing.

He opens his arms ever so slightly to me and I find myself stepping into them without even thinking. He still feels so familiar.

"I'm so sorry about your grandmother," I say into his shoulder.

He gives me a fierce squeeze and lets me go. "How's Michael?" he asks.

"He's good," I reply with a smile, brushing away my tears.

"Maybe I'll pop over and see him tomorrow."

"He'd love that."

"Will you come to the wake?" he asks me.

"Would you like me to?"

He stares at me for a moment, seeming to think about it, and then he smiles and shakes his head. "It's okay. Get home to Tom. Give him my best. And take care of yourself."

I walk away with my head down, tears dripping from my nose, and then I lift my chin and once more look ahead to the future.

FOUR SUMMERS FROM NOW . . .

"Kids?" Tom asks me over breakfast.

The question comes out of his mouth so casually that it makes me laugh.

It's the sort of tone he uses when he's making breakfast.

"Omelet?"

"Bacon?"

"Granola?"

And now: "Kids?"

"Are you asking me if I want a side of kids with my toast?" I reply.

"Yeah," he says with a smile, tapping my nose with his spoon.

It's June and we're in the downstairs kitchen, having decided not to rent the apartment out for the month. It's still booked throughout July and August, but we wanted to keep it for ourselves for at least part of the summer. His parents are coming this afternoon and we've got plans for a barbecue. They've been to visit on a few occasions, and last Christmas we went to Norfolk to stay with them. Tom's mum is quite fussy and his dad is fairly stoic, but their love for their son is evident. I like them a lot.

"Do *you* want kids?" I ask, casting him a sidelong look.

We're sitting next to each other on the bench seat at the dining table.

He nods. "I do. And I was wondering how you felt about IVF."

My chest hurts at the reminder that he refuses to biologically father our children, but I love that he's open to other options.

"Would it bother you if we used a sperm donor? Would you rather adopt?"

"I would love to adopt," he says. "And maybe we should consider that for babies two and three."

"How many kids do you *want*?" I ask with alarm.

"Oh, a whole houseful," he replies with a small smile that turns into a wide smile when he sees the panicked look on my face.

"Fine, I'll settle for two or three. And to answer your question, I would love to bring a child into the world who has half your lovely genes. And if you'd like to experience pregnancy and birth, then I'm on board."

"I love you," I whisper, blinking back tears.

Who is this man I've married? This man who made sure that my name, rather than his, was written on the deeds of Seaglass because he wanted me to have security even *before* we tied the knot?

He still runs the kitchen, and Chas is still going, but I've stepped away a bit. I won a major public art commission, which has kept me busy. I was up against four other sculptors, so it was a really big deal for me.

In the last year, I also made the decision to let go of my parents. Their bronzes, I mean. I still think of them every day, even if I no longer walk out to the cliffs on the anniversary of their deaths.

It was cathartic to sculpt Mum and Dad, though for a long time afterward I couldn't talk about their *Gone* pieces. I've had people inquire about them as they're on my website, but I've always said that they're not for sale. But the last time an art collector called me to ask about them, I hesitated. I felt that it was time to release them into the world.

Tom and I put some of the money toward keeping back the month of June for ourselves, and I have to say, every minute we spend downstairs together in this glorious kitchen feels worth it.

"So what do you reckon?" Tom asks.

I nod at him, deciding to use the rest of the money from the sale of my parents' bronzes to fund IVF. They would have liked that.

"I reckon yes."

FIVE SUMMERS FROM NOW ...

I sob into Tom's shoulder when our third round of IVF fails.

"Come on," he says huskily, holding me tight. "Let's go for a walk, get some fresh air."

We head up the coast path past the Drifty, walking single file along the narrow track. He lets me lead and I'm sure it's so he can keep an eye on me. When the track begins to level out, I look down to our left at Trevaunance Cove and Seaglass. The tide is in and the water is more aquamarine than ever, waves lapping at the creamy-white sand. I glance at the bench as we pass, remembering seeing Tom sitting up there five years ago, half-hidden by brilliant yellow gorse flowers.

The flowers are out in force at the moment, as well as the purple heather. Cornwall is in full bloom and its heart is singing, completely oblivious to the pain in mine.

I'm feeling fragile not just because my period came this morning, but because Amy called earlier to tell me that she's three months pregnant with her second baby, and also that Liam has moved to LA. The boys' grandfather passed away in June.

I was in Manchester at a statue unveiling and couldn't make the funeral, but I sent Finn a text to tell him that I was sorry. We're rarely in contact these days, but I was sad not to see him. I heard that he's dating another singer-songwriter, but I don't know if it's serious.

What I do know is that as time has unfolded, he's had fewer reasons to come back to St. Agnes. And now, with both of his grandparents gone, Tyler settled in Newquay, and Liam moving to LA, it may be years before I see him again.

I try not to think about him too much, but as Tom once pointed out, we will always have unfinished business. I guess I'm still trying to come to terms with that fact.

"Maybe we should put our names down for adoption sooner rather than later," I say as we reach the top of the hill.

The view is incredible from up here. This is a land of hills and valleys, high cliffs and crashing oceans, and I love it for all its melodrama.

I did adore the Maldives too, though, when we went just before Easter. I've seen more of the world alongside Tom than I ever thought I would after my parents' accident.

"Just because it's such a lengthy process," I add.

I walk a few more paces before glancing over my shoulder, wondering why he's not answering me.

He's standing still, his hand on his chest, looking pale.

"What is it?" I ask urgently, my insides flooding with dread.

And then he just goes down.

"TOM!" I scream, running back to him.

I'm scared he's hit his head on a rock because the path is strewn with them, but heather cushioned his fall.

"Tom," I say urgently, slapping his cheeks to try to wake him up. He's out cold. "Tom!"

I know that in cases of fainting or blackouts, there's every chance the heart will restart itself and reset its own rhythm, but he is not moving and when I anxiously press my fingers to his neck, I feel no pulse.

"Oh God, Tom, no." I look around frantically to see if there's anyone who can help me, but I can't see a single soul, so I pull out my phone and dial emergency services, throwing it to one side and hoping to God there's mobile phone reception as I begin to perform CPR.

Placing one hand on top of the other in the center of his chest, I begin to push hard and fast.

"Tom, please," I implore, tilting his head back and pinching his nose, delivering two rescue breaths before continuing with compressions.

Up ahead, a man appears over the hill, coming from the direction of Trevellas Cove. I scream out to him, "HELP ME!" and he picks up his pace.

"Can you get the AED—the defibrillator! It's outside the Surf Life-Saving Club," I shout when he's nearby. I snatch up my phone and swear at the sky. "AND CALL FOR AN AMBULANCE!" I scream after him as he runs away.

I look down at Tom in time to see him open his eyes.

"Tom!"

He gazes up at me, sunshine reflected in his golden-brown depths.

"Oh, thank God. Are you okay? Tom?"

"What happened?" he asks me.

"Your heart stopped. It just stopped."

"I felt it flutter."

I press my face to his neck and weep, my hand firmly on his chest so I can ensure that his heart stays strong. I want to sculpt this chest one day, this heart I love so much, this heart I fear could still be taken from me.

He raises his hand and weakly pats my back, and in the distance, after not very long at all, we hear the sound of rotors whirring. He turns his head to look at the sky, and we both watch as a red-and-white search and rescue helicopter creeps ever closer.

"That's ironic," he murmurs under his breath.

Tom saved hundreds of lives when he flew a helicopter just like this one.

"You're a bit late, buddies," he adds for my benefit only as the door opens and a winchman is lowered down. "My wife already saved me."

He's trying to keep his tone light, but I'm so shocked and terrified I can't even smile.

"You still need to go to the hospital and get checked out," I tell him.

He doesn't argue.

"Fuck, Tom, you scared the shit out of me!" I cry.

"I love you," he says.

The winchman is almost upon us.

"I love you too," I reply.

BUT THE NEXT time his heart stops, he's alone.

SIX SUMMERS FROM NOW . . .

He is gone.

And I am lost.

SEVEN SUMMERS FROM NOW . . .

He sits down beside me on the bench and reaches over, gently taking my hand and staring out to sea. I don't know how I have any tears left, but still they keep coming.

"I'm so sorry, Liv."

I fold over and begin to sob, and then I'm in his arms and all I can think is, *Here we are again . . .*

"I'M LIVING WITH ghosts, Finn," I tell him a while later, once I'm capable of using my voice.

Mum . . .

Dad . . .

Tom . . .

I even feel to some extent that I'm living with the ghosts of the children we never had.

I can't cope when families come to stay anymore. I'm seriously considering selling.

"Come to LA with me," he says quietly, tucking a lock of hair behind my ear. "Just for a break. Come with me, Liv. I'll sort your ticket, your accommodation, everything. You won't have to think about a thing."

He still looks more or less the same, if a touch older. His hair is a bit shorter, a little less wild, but only marginally. It's still dark and disheveled. His Celtic Sea green eyes are as beautiful as ever, his eyelashes just as dark. I'm sure his dimples still exist, though it's been a very long time since I've seen them. His chest has filled out, more in keeping with the thirty-five-year-old man that he is than with the slim twenty-something rock star I sometimes still picture when I think of him.

And lately, I've been thinking about him a lot. He reached out to me after I lost Tom. He just wanted to let me know that he was there for me if I needed him.

"Wouldn't I stay with you?" I ask him, thinking about his invitation.

"I didn't think you'd want to stay with me," he replies, his eye contact steady. "But I'd love that."

"Your girlfriend wouldn't mind?"

He stares at me for a moment. "I haven't had a girlfriend in almost two years."

"Oh." I barely hear the word coming from my mouth. "Do you have room?"

He lets out the smallest snort of amusement. "Yes, Liv, I have room."

"Can Michael come?"

"Of course he can."

WE FLY ON Saturday, a week later, and Michael loves every second of the plane journey. He was delighted when Finn and I called on him to ask if he'd like to go to LA on holiday.

"Yeah! Ace!" he replied.

I've been much more aware of the way he tries to protect me since Tom died. We've watched many movies on his sofa and eaten a lot of lunches together. He invites me to his social club dances, but the one time I went I felt too sad to stay for long.

The sight of Michael and his friends on the dance floor could barely bring a smile to my face. My thoughts were consumed more with Finn than Tom that night.

FINN LIVES IN a four-bedroom vertical house in the Hollywood Hills. It's four stories high, but only a couple of rooms wide. He doesn't have much of a garden, just a long, narrow swimming pool with a living-wall backdrop. My favorite part of his house is the roof terrace, which has a view right across the hills toward Downtown LA.

So this is what a publishing deal with a major label gets you. I'm blown away.

Finn's bedroom and study are on the fourth level, accessed via a small central elevator. Two further bedrooms, which Michael and I have taken, are on the third floor, and on the second is a kitchen and dining room. The living room takes up most of the ground floor and opens right onto the pool. The fourth bedroom is down there too.

Michael is desperate to go swimming. I'm tired and not at all in the mood, but I hate to disappoint him. When Finn sees my conflicting emotions, he steps in, suggesting that I "sit on the edge with a glass of wine while the boys muck about."

They soon have me laughing out loud with their antics. It is just the tonic I need.

I've been going through life on autopilot for the last year and a half. When I woke up on Valentine's Day, only six months after Tom first collapsed on the cliffs, and saw that I didn't have a message explaining his absence, I began to worry. And then I heard an ambulance coming down the road.

I got to the cove in time to find him being carried off the

beach on a stretcher, but it was already too late. A tourist had found him collapsed on the sand, right in the middle of a geometric pattern of hearts that was fanning out across the beach. He must've been just about to call me.

LATER, ONCE MICHAEL has conked out, Finn and I take our drinks up to the roof terrace and sit on one of his outdoor sofas, facing the city. The lights across the hills are twinkling in the darkness, and the air is pleasantly warm and smells of the jasmine planted in pots at one end of his terrace.

"How are you feeling?" he asks me.

"Okay," I reply. "I'm getting there. Thank you, though. I think this might be just what the doctor ordered."

"It's my pleasure. I'm glad to have you both here. Finally," he adds with a wry smile.

"I hate that you always see me at my weakest points. It's not fair on you. How many more times are you going to have to prop me up?"

"Liv, you're the strongest person I know. Give yourself some credit."

He reaches across and squeezes my hand. I let him hold it until I feel too edgy and then I extract myself.

He swigs from his bottle of beer.

"How are Liam and Tyler?"

"They're good. Tyler was over recently. They attended a few gigs together."

"Where does Liam live? I thought he might be here with you."

"You've got to be kidding me. Live with that little twerp?"

"I thought he was something like twenty-three now," I reply, laughing.

"He is. That means he's more than capable of standing on his own two feet. He's in Glendale, near where I used to live."

"You're a good brother to them, Finn." I mean it sincerely.

He looks amused. "After I called him a little twerp?"

"You're a good brother," I repeat seriously.

The boys' grandparents did an incredible job taking care of them when their mother disappeared. But they could only do so much. God knows what would have happened if they hadn't also had Finn checking up on Tyler and Liam, taking them out and bringing them over to LA every year so they could spend Christmases together, away from the dark memories.

"And you're a good friend," I add, reaching over to take his hand again.

He stares down at our hands contemplatively. Then he lifts his eyes to meet mine. Our surroundings are lit only by the glow of far-off buildings and streetlights, but it's enough to see his face in the darkness, his eyes shining.

"I still love you, Liv."

I almost pull my hand away, but when I fail to act on instinct, it stays there, our fingers entwined in the space between us.

"I'm well aware that you're grieving for Tom. But I need you to know that."

My heart is in my throat. "How can you still love me after all these years? After everything I've done?"

"What have you done?" he asks with confusion.

"I married *another man*, Finn!" I raise my voice, anguished. "Didn't that *hurt* you?"

"It fucking killed me," he replies gruffly, letting go of my hand to rake through his hair.

"So how can you still love me?"

"I will *never* stop loving you. I've already told you that. I'll love you until the day I die and then some."

I stare at him. He stares at me. He's deadly serious.

Five seconds pass before his expression softens and he twists so his whole body is facing toward mine.

"Do you think you could ever see a way of us moving forward again?" he asks earnestly. "I don't mean now, but when you're ready. I'll wait for you, Liv. I'll move back to St. Agnes if you can't imagine spending time both here and in the UK. But if you don't still love me, please tell me now—"

"*Of course I still love you,*" I cut him off in a whisper, waiting for the pang of guilt to strike.

It doesn't come.

And I feel that Tom is there with me, in that moment, giving me his blessing, wanting me to be happy.

And maybe I deserve that. Maybe I've been through too much. Maybe it's time to give Finn a chance, a proper chance, to give *myself* a chance. To give *us* a chance.

Maybe it's *our* time.

I STRUGGLE TO go back to Beach Cottage after that week in LA. Michael was ready to leave. He missed Timothy and all his friends.

"But you can stay," he said casually as I was helping him to pack, as if it really was that simple and I didn't need to accompany him on the flight home.

So I left with him, but now, as I stand in the kitchen-diner, surrounded by too much space and too many memories, I decide not to leave it long before flying back.

ONE MONTH LATER, I return to LA and this time, when I walk into Finn's house and it's just the two of us, the atmosphere feels loaded.

"Are you happy with the same room as last time?" he asks me, pulling my suitcase to a stop in front of the small lift.

"Sure," I reply, struggling to meet his eyes.

He seems on edge too.

But by that evening, we've both relaxed into each other's company.

We're sitting on his sofa in the ground-floor living space, halfway into a bottle of wine. Outside the glass doors, the swimming pool is lit up a brilliant blue, casting flickering shadows onto the foliage growing out of the wall behind it.

"I'm sorry it took me so long to come here," I say, feeling a sudden need to apologize.

"Please don't, Liv. Let's not dwell on the past, okay?" he says gently.

I nod at him. "Okay."

"Michael" by Franz Ferdinand begins to play out of his surround-sound system.

I laugh. "Do you remember—"

My question comes up short.

"What?" he presses.

I shake my head. "I was just thinking about the first time you played this song to me, and how you belted it out to Michael in the car." I give him a small smile. "It's hard not to dwell on the past."

"That's not *dwelling*," he replies with a bemused frown. "That's reminiscing. It's okay to *reminisce*." He chuckles. "One of my favorite memories is the look on your face when we played '22.' You were gobsmacked."

I fall about laughing, and we continue to reminisce, polishing off the rest of the bottle. We don't talk about any dark stuff, and why should we? We've both made decisions that have hurt each other. That doesn't mean they were the wrong decisions. I will always cherish the years I had with Tom.

Grief wells up inside me at the sudden thought of him. I excuse myself to go to the bathroom.

As I stand there at the basin, staring at my reflection in the mirror, I wait once more for the guilt to strike.

And once more, it doesn't come.

I take a deep breath. It's okay. *I'm* okay. Forward now, not backward. I made that decision once with Tom. I can make it again with Finn.

I *want* to make it again with Finn.

He isn't on the sofa when I come out of the bathroom. I hear the clink of glasses knocking together upstairs in the kitchen. I follow the sound and come out on the first-floor landing to see him over by the sink, his hands braced against the counter, our empty wineglasses set to one side.

He seems depleted, standing there.

"You want to call it a night?" I ask, going over to him.

He looks over his shoulder at me as I approach, his expression weary. "I thought maybe you did."

"Yeah, I guess."

It's the early hours of the morning in the UK.

He turns around to face me, resting his back against the counter.

"You seemed upset," he says quietly, the muscles in his jaw tensing.

"I was. But I'm okay now."

We stare at each other, and neither of us speaks as the seconds tick by. And then he holds his hands out to me, palms up, in a small, sweet gesture, his face alight with tentative hope.

I smile and step forward.

He pulls me flush to his chest and it feels so right to be close to him again. I rest my cheek against his shoulder, my nose pressed against his warm neck, and breathe in, the scent of him so comforting. Lifting my head, I bring one hand up to cup his jaw.

He stares down at me through his long lashes, his blue-green eyes still tinged with trepidation. They *have* aged, I realize, and I don't mean the fine lines spanning from the outer corners. He's lost some of his sparkle.

I want to bring that sparkle back. I want to see him smile again, dimples and all. At that precise moment, it's what I want most in the world.

I bring my other hand up. And then I push the tips of my thumbs into the slight indents where his dimples should be.

He jerks backward with amusement. "How many years have you wanted to do that?" he asks, laughing.

"Too many," I reply with a grin.

Out of the blue, I experience a strange rush of emotion that passes through me with a whoosh, making me feel giddy and breathless.

"I love you so, so much, Finn."

The apprehension on his face melts away at my words. "I love you too," he whispers, his eyes gleaming.

I step up on my tiptoes, but he meets me halfway.

Our kiss is slow and deep and achingly familiar. Everything about it feels right.

I think of Tom, but only briefly. Mostly I'm able to stay in the moment with Finn.

We move at the same time, my legs coming around his waist as he lifts me and turns, placing me on the kitchen counter.

I reach for the hem of his T-shirt and tug it up and over his head, and then his hands are sliding my dress along my thighs. The heat between us is sizzling. I need this. I *want* this. And from what I can feel as he tugs my body against his, he needs and wants this just as much.

We don't take it slow. I don't think we're capable of taking it slow. It's fast and urgent and leaves very little room for rational thought.

It's perfect.

And afterward, when our sweaty limbs are still entangled and our bodies are limp and barely capable of staying upright, I slide off the counter and into his arms.

"Take me to your bed, Finn. And don't let me out of your sight for the next seven days."

"I won't," he promises.

THE MAN STAYS true to his word. Over the next week, we reconnect both emotionally and physically, sewing together the seams of the pieces we gave to each other years ago.

When I told Finn that Tom had never wavered, I could have said the same for him. He has never wavered in loving me. The pain of his childhood meant that he couldn't choose St. Agnes, but he always chose me.

I was the one who didn't choose him.

But now I do. I choose *us*.

ANOTHER SEVEN SUMMERS LATER . . .

I wake up to my husband singing "Here Comes the Sun" to me. And then I realize that he's not singing to me, he's singing to Maggie, who's nestled snugly into the space between us.

"You should be in your own bed, you naughty monkey," I chide in a sleep-drenched voice. "Who said you could come in here?"

"Daddy," she replies with a cheeky giggle.

Finn reaches down to tickle her ribs and she squirms violently and squeals with laughter, her dimples coming out in force.

"Shh!" My eyes are wide as I look over my shoulder at the bassinet beside our bed, but her little brother is out cold. I stare at his insanely long dark lashes and then turn back to our daughter.

"His awake?" she asks in toddler speak, wriggling up in bed to sit against the bedhead. "Give me the baby," she commands, opening her arms.

She's not quite two and a half.

I stare across her to Finn, who's regarding me with amusement.

"You heard the girl, give her the baby," he says teasingly.

"The baby is asleep," I reply pointedly.

"Give me the baby," she says again.

Finn and I almost laugh. Almost.

"No, he's sleeping," I repeat firmly.

As was his mother a minute ago.

Maggie climbs over me and peers in at the bassinet, her little shoulders deflating at the sight.

"Oh," she says with a sigh, wriggling back down into her snuggly position.

"Do you want to carry on sleep?" Finn asks me.

"Bit late now."

"Sorry," he whispers. "She was pretty determined."

He finds it hard to say no to our daughter. But then, he finds it hard to say no to me. He's always been a total softy in that respect.

The door bangs open and Lennie barges in, his foam sword aloft.

When I discovered that Finn's grandfather's name was Leonard, I begged him to let us use the name for our son, born to us four and a half years ago.

He wasn't sure about it at first, but he came around to my way of thinking.

Maggie—Margaret—is named after my grandmother, and I love that her name sounds a little like Aggie, where we live.

Lennie is going to be starting school next month so we needed to choose where to base ourselves for the foreseeable future. Cornwall is where three of our children's uncles live— Liam moved back from LA a couple of years ago, missing his hometown, Tyler's still in Newquay, and Michael is only up the road. Even Finn has found himself missing St. Agnes when we're not here. He says it's different now that we have kids.

We're creating our own memories and almost all of them are happy ones.

A few years ago, we returned the house to its original configuration and moved ourselves into the master bedroom at the end of the corridor, overlooking the garden.

We still have a home in LA, although not the vertical house I stayed in when I first started going there. After having Lennie, we moved farther out to a larger plot with a more child-friendly garden. We love spending time there too, with Finn's American family, and we will continue to do so on school holidays. But *home* home is St. Agnes.

So we have Lennie and Maggie, and the little guy in the bassinet who has just been woken up by his older brother is called Eddie. He's named after no one but his sweet little self.

Tom remains in my heart. I still think of him often. Sometimes, I desperately miss hearing his low laugh or seeing his golden-brown eyes staring across a table at me. Sometimes, I miss the way it felt to be held in his arms. I will always love him.

I haven't sculpted him and I don't think I ever will. When Arabella passed away a few years ago at the grand old age of ninety-nine, I didn't feel inclined to sculpt her either. I feel I've left my *Gone* pieces behind and have moved on to creating works of art that come from a place of joy and awe. I pour my heart and soul into everything I do—I don't want to spend months working on something that doesn't inspire me, so I try only to take on commissions that I care about.

I thought it would hurt too much to keep my investment in Seaglass once I'd lost Tom. When Chas decided it was well and truly time to retire at the age of eighty-three, Finn offered to buy him out.

I thought twice about letting him. I'd been thinking about

selling up and moving away for years, but somehow all this time had passed and I was still here.

So I gave Finn the nod and now he and I own Seaglass jointly, although we have staff who run it for us most of the time.

Beach Cottage and Seaglass and St. Agnes will always remind me of Tom. And I'm glad. I feel close to him here and I *want* to feel close to him.

But they remind me of Finn too. They are part of *our* story.

I've had two epic love stories in my life. I don't feel like a tragic widow.

I feel lucky.

"Come on, let's go for a walk on the beach," I say suddenly, collecting Eddie from his bassinet.

After God only knows how long, the five of us burst out the front door and set off down the hill toward Trevaunance Cove. The road carves down through the vibrant green hills and the sea seems lit from within as the early-morning sunlight filters through the water.

We arrive at the cove to see that last night's storm has washed more sand up onto the beach and the stream has carved out a tree in its wake.

Once more, Tom is here with me.

But I no longer see an apple tree in its last stages of life.

I see a tree.

In early spring.

And summer will come around again.

SEVEN SUMMERS PLAYLIST

"Sweater Weather"
The Neighbourhood

"Figure It Out"
Royal Blood

"Need You Tonight"
INXS

"7"
Catfish and the Bottlemen

"Go with the Flow"
Queens of the Stone Age

"Ready to Start"
Arcade Fire

"Space & Time"
Wolf Alice

"Michael"
Franz Ferdinand

"22"
Taylor Swift

"Smokers Outside
the Hospital Doors"
Editors

"The Boys of Summer"
The Ataris

"Sold"
Liily

"Stars of CCTV"
Hard-Fi

"'Tis the Damn Season"
Taylor Swift

"Stay"
Rihanna, ft. Mikky Ekko

"7 Minutes"
Dean Lewis

"Never Tear Us Apart"
INXS

"Fire"
Kasabian

"Saturn"
Sleeping at Last

"Here Comes the Sun"
The Beatles

ACKNOWLEDGMENTS

After all these years of writing, I still experience major pinch-me moments and most of them are down to you, my lovely readers. I adore hearing from you so please say hi if you haven't already on social media @PaigeToonAuthor. You can also sign up to my newsletter #TheHiddenPaige at paigetoon.com for news and extra content.

Word of mouth is so important in helping an author's stories to reach readers, so I really appreciate every single person who has taken the time to recommend my books, be that in person, in print, or on online—thank you so much.

I have enjoyed every moment of my publishing journey with Penguin Random House and it has been a dream to work with the teams at Century in the UK and G. P. Putnam's Sons in the USA. Especially big thanks to Venetia Butterfield and my outstanding editors Emily Griffin and Tara Singh Carlson—I absolutely love working with you all.

Huge thanks also to the following people at Century: Olivia Allen, Hannah Bailey, Charlotte Bush, Claire Bush, Briana Bywater, Emma Grey Gelder, Rebecca Ikin, Laurie Ip Fung Chun, Rachel Kennedy, Evie Kettlewell, Jess Muscio, Richard Rowlands, Jason Smith, Jade Unwin, Linda Viberg, and Selina Walker, and to these lovely people from Putnam: Sally Kim, Ivan Held, Samantha Bryant, Sanny Chiu, Brennin Cummings, Ashley Di Dio, Hannah Dragone, Tiffany Estreicher, Ashley Hewlett, Aranya Jain, and Claire Winecoff.

Thanks also to my copy editors, Caroline Johnson (UK) and Chandra Wohleber (US).

Thank you to Monique Corless, Amelia Evans, and the PRH foreign rights team, as well as my publishers from around the world for everything they do to bring my books to a wider audience—it makes me so happy to hear from readers who have discovered my books via translation.

Thank you to my dear friend Lucy Branch. Ever since our boys brought us together at nursery many years ago, I have admired your passion for art and sculpture. Thank you for sharing your knowledge and helping me to understand what makes Liv tick. (Note: Lucy is the UK's leading conservator specializing in bronze, as well as an author and the host of the podcast *Sculpture Vulture* —check her out!)

Thank you to remarkable sculptors Hazel Reeves and Laury Dizengremel for being so generous with their time in helping with my sculpture research—I would have been lost without you.

Thank you to author Hilary Standing for allowing me to read her stunning memoir about her experience of having a sister with Down syndrome before it had even been sent to her agent. I laughed and cried and was fully invested, and when this book is published, I will be shouting about it from the rooftops!

Thank you to singer-songwriter Kal Lavelle for her help with research relating to the music industry. I first discovered Kal when I was writing *The Longest Holiday* and I kept playing her beautiful song "Shivers" on repeat. Fun fact: Kal went on to cowrite another song, also called "Shivers," with none other than Ed Sheeran. I so enjoyed chatting to you, Kal.

While the chances of her ever seeing this are super-slim, I'd like to thank Taylor Swift for the inspiration her songs have given me. I had a vague idea for this novel, but it burst into life after listening to the lyrics of "'Tis the Damn Season" and within days I knew exactly how the story would pan out from beginning to end with heartbreaking clarity. I haven't deviated from that idea at all. I hope that if Taylor ever does come across this novel that it makes her feel just a smidgen of how her songs make me feel.

Thank you to . . .

. . . Carol Bruno for the chat about sand art in Portugal that first gave me the spark of an idea.

. . . Craig Scott for bringing Seaglass to life with his vivid descriptions of the service industry.

. . . David Moore from the Edinburgh College of Art and Dr. Darron Dixon-Hardy from the University of Leeds for indulging my random questions relating to sculpture and aviation respectively.

. . . Christopher Ryan from the National Trust at Chapel Porth for help relating to the beach and tide times.

. . . Jo Carnegie for the coffee foam anecdote that I warned her I would steal.

. . . Alison Cross and the team from Cornwall Hideaways, plus the owners of the real Beach Cottage, and also Damien Anderton and Rob Pippin for their help relating to St. Agnes itself.

All the locations mentioned in the book are real, with the exception of Seaglass, which is heavily inspired by a bar on the beach at Trevaunance Cove called Schooners. If you ever make it there in the summer when it's open, please snap a pic from the balcony for me! I found writing about St. Agnes really quite daunting, as it's such a special place; I knew I wouldn't be able to do it justice. But I hope this story makes some of the locals smile, even though I've used a little artistic license here and there.

Also, a belated thanks to Bethany for her help with *Only Love Can Hurt Like* This Bury St. Edmunds research.

Thank you to these incredible authors: Dani Atkins, Sophie Cousens, Lizzy Dent, Giovanna Fletcher, Zoë Folbigg, Carley Fortune, Ali Harris, Emily Henry, Colleen Hoover, Catherine Isaac, Abby Jimenez, Milly Johnson, Lindsey Kelk, Christina Lauren, Caroline Leavitt, Lia Louis, Jill Mansell, Mhairi McFarlane, Annabel Monaghan, Beth O'Leary, Louise Pentland, Jill Santapolo, Mia Sheridan, Emily Stone, Heidi Swain, Adriana Trigiani, K. A. Tucker, Lucy Vine, and Jo Watson. Whenever one of your names pops up in my socials or email relating to my books, I fan girl. Thank you so much for all your support—it means the world to me.

Thank you to my parents, Vern and Jen Schuppan, my in-laws, Ian and Helga Toon, and the lovely friends who always take the time to read and give feedback on early drafts of my books: Jane Hampton, Katherine Reid, Katherine Stalham, Femke Cole, Colette Bassford, Rebecca Banks, and Kimberly Atkins.

Last but not least, thank you to my family, Greg, Indy, and Idha Toon, for the behind-the-scenes stuff that nobody else sees but which I appreciate with all my heart. I love you all so very much.

SEVEN SUMMERS

Paige Toon

A Conversation with Paige Toon

Discussion Guide

Excerpt from Someone I Used to Know *by Paige Toon*

BOOK
ENDS

PUTNAM
—EST. 1838—

A CONVERSATION
WITH PAIGE TOON

What inspired you to write *Seven Summers*?

The seed of the idea came from hearing about a sand artist who creates works of art on a secluded beach in Portugal, a country I've visited every year since I was young. I imagined a heroine who resides in a tourist town and lives for her summers, when a boy she loves returns for his annual vacation. She sees a future with him, until one year, he appears with a wife and child in tow and all of her dreams are crushed. Distraction comes in the form of a mystery sand artist. I liked this idea, but I didn't love it, until I listened to the lyrics of "'Tis the Damn Season" by Taylor Swift and felt inspired to take the story in a different direction. There's a line in the song that really appealed to me, about how she won't ask him to wait if he doesn't ask her to stay. In *Seven Summers*, Finn is the singer-songwriter who returns to his hometown for the holidays and, if he and Liv are single, they spend the summer together. But the words they eventually say to each other are slightly different. He doesn't ask her to wait; he asks her to leave. But she *can't* leave—and he won't stay, so I had to construct reasons for why. I decided to set the story in Britain rather than my initial idea of Portugal because I felt I'd identify more with a British character.

How was writing *Seven Summers* similar to or different from writing your previous books?

To begin with, it was much harder. I had so many other things going on, including writing and filming a writing course for Domestika, plus an *insane* amount of book research to do for topics that I knew next to nothing about. For the first time since giving birth to my son sixteen years ago, I had to ask for a deadline extension. The writing was coming steadily but slowly, and then suddenly it took off at breakneck speed. I always feel a deep emotional connection to my characters, and this was especially intense in the last two weeks when I was writing until midnight and waking up at 3 a.m., with my mind racing and my fingers itching to get going. That kind of fervor wouldn't have been sustainable for a longer length of time, but I loved feeling so engrossed during that fortnight. I'm sure it's part of the reason that I feel so attached to this story—it's my favorite book I've written to date.

Which was your favorite scene to write and why?

There are so many that I loved writing, but the romantic moments are always my favorites—the first time Finn and Liv see each other in the bathroom, their first kiss—and Liv and Tom's. The first time the characters take things to the next level. . . . And I loved writing the moment Finn returns at the end of "This Summer." But another favorite scene is Michael overhearing Liv and Finn arguing in the car park, and the words he says that make Liv realize that she's only been seeing things from her perspective. I adore Michael.

Why did you choose to set this story in Cornwall? Was Seaglass inspired by a real bar and restaurant?

I've already set two books in Cornwall (*The Last Piece of My Heart* and *Five Years from Now*), but it's so stunning—with its dramatic cliffs, white sandy beaches, and turquoise waters—that I keep coming back to it. One of the biggest challenges in writing *Seven Summers* came from trying to do justice to the town of St Agnes, a place I had only been to briefly on a research trip. Usually with my novels, my lead character is visiting the location where the book is set, so she doesn't need to know it inside out like a local. But Liv had lived in St Agnes for years, so writing about the town from her perspective was particularly challenging. All of the places mentioned in the book are real with the exception of Seaglass, which felt like a character in itself. I didn't want to feel constricted by reality, but it is heavily inspired by a bar on the beach called Schooners. Look it up on Instagram—it will definitely give you Seaglass vibes.

Were Liv and Finn inspired by real people? If so, who? And if not, how did you come to create these characters?

My characters are rarely inspired by real people. Their personalities grow as the story idea develops: before they're fully formed, I'll know where they've come from, what they've been through, what their passions are and their hopes and dreams. I've written about rock stars before (*Johnny Be Good* and *Baby Be Mine*), but I didn't want Finn to be a typical bad boy musician. He has empathy and depth and kindness, which I think is incredibly sexy. He and Tom are so different, but Tom has a manliness and strength that I found very appealing. I always fall head over heels for my male leads as I'm writing a book, but never have I adored and fancied them both equally. I think my readers will be torn as to whom Liv should choose at the end of "This Summer." But for me, it was an easy decision—because I knew there was more to the story to come.

Summer is a season commonly associated with freedom— perhaps freedom from home, from school, from the need to wear layers. How might have Liv's romantic journeys with Finn and Tom differed if she'd met them in winter, or another season?

The beginning of summer feels like such an optimistic time. People are generally on a bit of a high, more open to adventure and possibility. In winter, we tend to retreat into our shells a little more, and this is certainly how I imagine Liv to be, even though we never actually see her during a winter. I think when Liv meets Finn, she's open to all the fun life wants to throw at her, so she's happy to get to know him and see where things go. She would have been a bit more introverted during the winter months, and of course, she wouldn't have been working at Seaglass, so their paths wouldn't have crossed that often. As for Tom, I think it's all about timing. Liv is ready to open her heart up again, and that could have happened just as easily in the winter with him being her houseguest. I can imagine them walking hand-in-hand along deserted beaches and snuggling up together in front of a log fire.

What kind of research did you do to write *Seven Summers*?

SO much. I'll say this now: I will never again write a book about so many things that I know nothing about! Usually there are maybe three big topics that I need to get my head around, but the research with this book felt endless. As you'll see from my acknowledgments, I spoke to lots of people—

from famous sculptors to an award-winning songwriter—and I also did a ton of Internet research. I knew very little about sculpture, so writing from the perspective of someone who lives and breathes art was a major hurdle to overcome, as was trying to do justice to a character who has Down Syndrome. I've learned so much, and I hope that Michael is as rich, complex, and nuanced a character as he deserves to be. St. Agnes in itself was incredibly important to understand—its complex history, landmarks, festivals, and the surrounding area. I needed to know about Liv's degree and her art training, her job at Seaglass—both managing a bar and restaurant, and working at one. Tom's job and art took time to understand, as did Michael's role at the National Trust. Then there are all the little things that impact the story like tide times, moon phases, and which wildflowers are in bloom and when. The research was hard, and only a tiny percentage of what I've learned has actually made it into the story, but it all helped me to connect with the characters, and I hope the book is effortless to read.

Music runs throughout this novel. What is your relationship to music? Do you play an instrument?

I do play the piano, although not well and I'm pretty much self-taught. Music has always been important to me—when I was a teenager, I used to write songs and I even wondered at one point if it was something I'd pursue as a career. Now it just really inspires me. I usually write while listening to music, and I always listen to music when I'm out walking—sometimes a lyric will capture my attention and story ideas will form. I got the entire idea for my sixth book, *One Perfect Summer*, after hearing Adele's "Someone Like You."

Finn and Tom are two very different love interests that come into Liv's life at different times in her life. What draws Liv to these men and why is each connection so powerful?

She's physically attracted to both, but with Finn, there's instant chemistry from the moment they lock eyes in the bathroom mirror. I adore Finn's sweet, sexy side. He's young at heart and he's so into Liv. Tom's more of a grown-up. After the tragedy Liv experiences, I don't think she realizes how much she wants someone to take care of her and protect her until Tom steps into that role. He's strong and kind and caring—and it helps that he's also drop-dead gorgeous.

What lesson, if any, about love and distance do you hope readers will take away from *Seven Summers*?

I'm not sure that I'm teaching anyone anything about love that they don't already know, which is that sometimes it all comes down to timing. You can meet the right person at the wrong time, and it may never work. You can stick it out and hold on, but at what sacrifice? What might you lose if you spend years waiting for the time to be right? On the flip side, there are people who settle because it feels like the right time, even though the person they settle for wouldn't have ticked all their boxes at a different stage in their life. There's nothing wrong with that: sometimes our expectations are too high, but people change and grow and adapt—and often they grow together.

Without giving anything away, did you always know how the story would end?

Initially I planned to write a different book entirely, but one of my editors (I have two: Emily in the UK and Tara in the US) had reservations about the idea. I ran this idea past them which was still in its early stages, and we agreed to have a Zoom meeting five days later to flesh it out. But during those five days, this story took off for me in a huge way, everything about it, even the title. I vividly remember telling my editors the entire story in-depth from beginning to end, and we were all in tears, which was pretty special. I haven't strayed from that idea at all—when a story comes to you that quickly and that intensely, you know you're onto a good thing. These characters mean so much to me—Liv, Finn, and Tom will live in my heart forever.

DISCUSSION GUIDE

1. When Finn and Liv agreed to spend the summer together if they remained single, how did you feel about the reasoning behind their promise to each other? Did your opinion change as the story unfolded?

2. If you could rename Finn's band, what would you call it?

3. Have you ever felt a strong connection to a stranger? If so, what do you think drew you together?

4. When Liv's mother first learns of Finn and Liv's budding relationship, she tells Liv to be wary of him because of his family's past. Do you think her mom's warning was justified?

5. Liv felt like she needed to protect her brother after their loss, but Michael ends up supporting her in many ways as well. Who do you think was protecting whom? Do you have someone in your life whom you protect just as much as they protect you?

6. Many of Liv's life decisions are influenced by loss. Is there an event in your life that you feel has influenced many of

your decisions? Would you have made different choices than Liv?

7. Liv comes into each relationship at very different points in her life. How do her non-romantic priorities affect her romantic decisions? Have you ever struggled to choose what passions to prioritize in your life?

8. If you were to make a playlist capturing Liv and Finn's relationship, what are a few songs you would include and why? What songs would you include in a playlist for Tom?

9. What do you think kept Finn and Liv coming back to each other? Do you believe that someone can meet the right person at the wrong time?

10. How did you feel reading the ending? Do you think Liv made the right decision in the end? Would you have done the same?

Keep reading for an exciting excerpt from

SOMEONE I USED TO KNOW

by Paige Toon

PROLOGUE

T HE FARM IS VISIBLE AS SOON AS THE TAXI CRESTS the brow of the hill.

"There it is," I say to the driver.

"Hard to miss," he responds good-naturedly.

When I left at five thirty this evening, it was still light, but now, at almost eight, the fields are blanketed in darkness, save for the occasional glowing window from neighboring farmhouses—and our place, which is lit up like a giant Christmas tree.

Jamie really went all out with those fairy lights, I think with a mixture of guilt and envy.

I wish I'd done more to help him set up. This is my parents' joint seventieth birthday/retirement bash and I haven't even managed to stay for the duration of the celebrations. The party kicked off at three, but I had to take Emilie back to the Airbnb in Harrogate after only two and a half hours, and she took ages to settle. Hopefully she'll stay asleep until we return. The babysitter, Katy, seemed competent, but I wouldn't wish our screaming fifteen-month-old on anyone.

"Would you be able to come back for my husband and me later?" I remember to ask the driver.

"Afraid not, I'm clocking off after this. My mate could probably do it, though. What time are you thinking?"

"Midnight? Could he also take our sitter home afterward? She lives a few minutes away."

I wait until the return journey is arranged before getting out of the car, wincing a split second before my black high heels connect with mud. But the soles of my shoes hit only grit because, as I now remember hearing, *Jamie was out here all morning, sweeping the whole courtyard and the length of the drive.*

Jamie, Jamie, Jamie . . .

My brother, more of a son to my parents than I am a daughter, it often seems, yet he is not my blood.

He *has* done an incredible job, I acknowledge, as I pay the driver and get out of the car. This place has never looked better.

Festoon lights crisscross from one side of the courtyard to the other, reflecting in the darkened glass of upstairs windows and casting a warm glow onto the sandy stone walls of the farmhouse and barns. Tealights in lanterns sparkle atop brightly painted metal outdoor tables, and colorful bunting sways overhead, dispersing the ribboning smoke from cigarettes below.

A scan of the crowd confirms that my parents have retreated inside along with their friends. They never were ones to outstay their welcome where the younger generation was concerned.

My gaze comes to rest on Theo, who is sitting at a sky-blue table with Jamie and a girl I don't recognize. His dark hair falls just shy of the collar of his black shirt and a lit cigarette is resting all too familiarly between his long, slim fingers. He brings it to his lips and inhales deeply, his face flaring briefly to reveal a sharp jaw and a perfectly straight nose.

I'm snapped to attention by the taxi doing a U-turn. Moving out of the way, I track its headlights as they sweep across the field, illuminating the small wood in the lower paddock. The white trunk of a solitary silver birch tree shines back like a beacon before it's enveloped once more by darkness.

Technicolor synths and drumbeats explode from the outdoor speakers as Cid Rim's "Repeat" featuring Samantha Urbani kicks into gear.

Jamie has hijacked the music.

I smile and set off toward the courtyard.

Jamie sees me first, bouncing to his feet and almost bumping his head on an outdoor heater. He's fairly tall at five foot ten, but his hair—black, short at the sides and wild and curly on top—adds at least another three inches to his height.

Arms open wide, a huge smile lighting his face, he hollers at the top of his voice, "SNOW WHITE!"

It's the nickname he gave me years ago in the dead of winter, when my skin was, admittedly, as white as snow—especially compared to his warm brown complexion. That was as far as my resemblance to the fairy-tale princess went: my hair back then was long and light brown, not ebony, and my eyes are hazel rather than brown. But at the time, before I could rustle up any sort of comeback, he warned, with a perfectly straight face, "Careful, don't be racist."

Theo shoots his head around to look at me—along with every other person in the courtyard, thanks to Jamie bellowing—and quickly stubs out his cigarette. He gives me a cheeky, guilty grin as I approach.

"*I quit! Absolutely-one-hundred-percent-for-good this time!*" I mimic his words of only a few months ago.

"I only had one," he replies in a huskier voice than usual.

"Sure," I say dryly.

"Okay, maybe this is my second." He smiles up at me with his best puppy-dog please-don't-be-mad impression. "You've been gone ages!"

"I know," I reply grumpily, indulging his change of subject.

The girl at the table freezes theatrically, her big bright eyes boggling up at me from behind a thick coppery fringe. "*Leah?!*" she asks.

Out of the blue, I'm hit with a memory of a mousier, plumper, younger version of her.

"Hello!" I cry as she jumps up to give me a hug.

I rack my brain wildly for her name.

"*Danielle,*" Jamie mouths helpfully at me over her shoulder.

How could I forget?

"Danielle!" I exclaim, drawing back to study her as Theo grabs a pastel pink chair from nearby and swings it around to face the table. "I need a drink," I murmur meaningfully.

"I'll get you one," he replies.

"What took you so long?" Jamie demands as I sit down.

"Emilie was *wired*. I swear someone fed her a bag of sugar."

"She did eat two pieces of birthday cake earlier, plus all your dad's leftover icing," he tells me casually.

"Bloody hell! Why didn't he stop her?"

"I don't think he noticed."

"Why didn't *you* stop her?" I think to ask.

"She looked happy," he replies laughingly, palms up.

I roll my eyes long-sufferingly at him and smile at Danielle. "How *are* you?"

Danielle, Jamie, and many of the other twenty- and thirty-somethings here tonight were fostered by my parents at some point in their lives. I left home for university in London when I was eighteen and made the city my home, so there are people here that I hadn't met before today. Others are more familiar to me, like Shauna, who was with us for two years and who still lives locally.

Some flitted through briefly: Danielle stayed only a few months while her mum was in rehab. And then there's George, who left a scar on my heart that still takes me by surprise, considering the relatively short time I knew him.

But Jamie hurtled into our lives at the age of thirteen and never left. He turned thirty recently and although he hasn't lived at the farm in almost a decade, he turns up nearly every day to visit my parents. They'd be lost without him.

Mum and Dad have finally retired from fostering, but they will never retire from parenting, and that's what they consider themselves to be to every young person who ever walked through their front door: parents. Those who came to them left knowing that this place would always be open. Fostering wasn't a job to my parents, it was a vocation. It's why they've stayed in touch with so many of their former charges, why so many of them have made the effort to travel here tonight.

Of course, there are exceptions.

"I should check on Mum and Dad," I say to Theo when he returns with my drink.

I find them in the living room, in the midst of their friends. My parents are fit, healthy, and active, but neither looks young for their age. Dad is head down and deep in conversation with some of his fellow stallholders from Masham market, his hair now entirely white and as wild as ever. Mum appears more polished with her makeup still intact and her neat light-brown bob clipped back at the sides. She's been dyeing her hair for years, but the lines around her eyes and mouth betray her age. They seem to have expanded even in the few months since I've seen her.

She's talking to Veronica, our closest neighbor and the mother of Becky, my old school friend.

"Have you only just got back?" she asks me with surprise.

I nod reluctantly and raise my glass to clink hers and Veronica's before taking a sip.

Mum tried to convince me to put Emilie to sleep in their bedroom, but the thought of waking up a teething toddler in the dead of night and expecting her to transfer to her cot after a twenty-minute taxi ride . . . She would have kept us awake for hours.

We *could* have stayed here, but . . . *nice solitary Airbnb vs full house* . . . No contest. It seemed worth sacrificing the return journey time for the peace and quiet.

"Never mind, you're here now." Mum pats me on my arm.

She doesn't do "I told you so," *Supermum* that she is.

I'm not even being sarcastic.

"I hear you're moving to Australia?" Veronica chips in as my father excuses himself from his friends and comes over.

"That's the plan," I reply with a smile at Dad as he throws his arm around my shoulder.

"As long as neither of them gets a criminal record before their visa application is sent off," Dad teases, repeating Theo's joke from earlier.

He gives me a kiss on my temple, the smell of whiskey on his breath. The weight of his arm is familiar and comforting.

Oddly, I miss him, even though he's standing right next to me. Is this what anticipatory homesickness feels like?

"How's Becky?" I ask Veronica, feeling bad that I don't already know the answer.

"She's really well," Veronica replies warmly as Dad lets me go again. I shoot him a smile, hoping he doesn't stray far. "Did you know she's expecting?"

"No!" I feel a pang at my ignorance. "When's the baby due?"

"Late August, so he or she will either be the youngest in their year, or the oldest if they don't grace us with their presence until September. Becky doesn't mind either way; she's just glad it's not Christmas."

"I bet," I say with a laugh.

Becky's own birthday is overshadowed by Christmas. Emilie was also born in December, but she was an accident, so her date of arrival was down to the luck of the gods. I have no idea if Becky and her husband were trying for a baby or not.

"She was so sorry she couldn't be here," Veronica continues. "She would have loved to have caught up with you. She and Robin are in Canada at his sister's wedding. I have a horrible feeling Becky's going to like it there so much that she'll also decide to emigrate."

"Oh, no, she *won't*," Mum says dismissively, trying to reassure her old friend.

Her reaction makes me feel guilty: my parents are gutted that we're moving abroad.

"I would have loved to catch up with her too," I say, and it's true. Once, my high school bestie and I were inseparable, but now an entire year can go by without us exchanging a word. It's not that we meant to grow apart, we just did.

"She and Robin sent a lovely card." Mum nods at the crammed side table.

"Jamie read them out earlier," Veronica adds.

"You missed the telegrams!" Mum realizes with dismay.

I stare at her and she has the grace to look awkward.

So, not only did Jamie read out all the messages sent by those who couldn't make it—something that surely should have been my responsibility—but I wasn't here. Did anyone even notice my absence?

"There was one from George," she adds, and my jealousy is immediately scrubbed out by another emotion I couldn't even begin to describe.

"George Thompson?" I ask with barely contained disbelief.

Mum nods, blissfully ignorant of what this news is doing to me.

In a daze, I walk over to the side table and pick up card after card until his handwriting leaps out at me, immediately recognizable with its small, neat letters and left-handed slant.

Dear Carrie and Ivan,

I saw the article in the paper and felt compelled to write. I'm sorry it's taken me so long to get in touch, but I wanted to say thank you for all that you did for me. I've thought about you often over the years. I'm doing okay and hope you are too. You look well in the picture.

Wishing you both a very happy birthday and a (hopefully) relaxing retirement.

George Thompson

His handwriting has hardly changed in almost thirteen years, yet he sounds completely alien.

Suddenly I see him clearly inside my mind: long legs, high cheekbones, chestnut curls, dark eyes . . .

Every hair on my body stands on its end.

George saw the article?

The local rag ran a piece about my parents and it was picked up by one of the nationals. But where did he see it, the local or the national newspaper? Somewhere online? Where *is* he?

I turn the card over, searching for a return address and finding nothing.

"Hey."

The sound of Theo's voice causes me to spin around. He looks at the card and then at me, with my rabbit-caught-in-the-headlights expression.

"Oh, yeah," he says flatly. "Jamie read it out earlier."

"I heard." My hand is shaking as I return the card to the side table.

"Thought he was gone for good." His tone is quiet, uneasy.

"I thought so too." I swallow hard and turn back to him.

"Theo Whittington!"

We both start as Alfred, an elderly farmer from the surrounding area, interrupts from a nearby huddle. The old man hobbles over to say hello, unaware that we're having a "moment."

"Now then! How are you, lad? I swear you look more like your father every time I see you."

"Hello there," Theo replies amiably, somehow managing to sound cheerful.

I step closer to his side and take his cool hand in mine as Alfred persists in making small talk.

If there's one thing Theo hates, it's being compared to his father.

He squeezes my hand, *hard*.

LATER, IN THE taxi, I take the middle seat because I want to be close to my husband.

He climbs into the car beside me and buckles up, slipping his arm around my waist as we leave the party lights behind us.

He's on edge until we pass by the imposing stone gateposts and gatehouse of his former home, but once that obstacle has been cleared, he relaxes and pulls me close.

"You look so beautiful tonight," he murmurs in my ear. "I like this dress on you."

It's black with long sleeves and a hemline that skims my knees.

I tilt my face up and he dips his head, giving me a gentle kiss. I lean into him, wanting more, and he doesn't disappoint. The smell of his cigarettes lingers as he kisses me, deep and slow, but I don't mind the taste on his tongue as much as I did the last time he started smoking again. Maybe it's something to do with the nostalgic feelings that the evening has dredged up. The past seems closer somehow, more tangible, within reach.

I push my fingers into his dark hair, feeling heady. I've consumed so much wine in the last couple of hours in my attempt to make up for lost time that I realize I'm actually quite drunk.

Theo's hands slide along the curve of my waist and I breathe in sharply, a thrill darting through me.

The car jolts to the left and right in quick succession as the driver corrects his line.

Theo tenses and breaks away, giving the rearview mirror a dark look. He takes his arm out from behind my waist and places his hand on my knee.

I'm figuring that's the end of our make-out session for now. These winding country roads are dangerous enough without giving our voyeuristic driver additional distractions.

WE'RE STAYING ON the outskirts of Harrogate, a few miles away. I've been checking my phone intermittently throughout the evening and Katy has obliged me with repeated "all is quiet" texts. I let her know we're on our way back and she opens the door straight away to our light *rat-a-tat-tat*.

"Hello!" she exclaims in a loud whisper, her long blond hair swinging in a thick high ponytail as she steps out of the way. "Did you have a good night?"

"Yes, thank you. How was she?"

"Perfect!" she replies to my relief, hopping on one foot as she pulls on a trainer. "Not a peep! I checked on her a few times, though," she adds hurriedly, shoving her toes into the other shoe.

"Thank you."

Theo plies her with the wad of cash we counted out on the return journey. "I'll see you to the taxi," he says. "We've already paid the driver."

While Theo walks Katy outside to the waiting car, I kick

off my heels and go to look in on Emilie. Our daughter is fast asleep, sprawled out on her back with her arms spread-eagled like a starfish. It's hot in here—it's only March, but the heating has been turned up too high—and a few strands of her dark-blond hair are plastered to her forehead. I can't resist carefully brushing them aside, holding my breath as she stirs. She falls still again, so I crack open the window to let in a whisper of cold night air and quietly leave her room.

Theo is standing inside the front door, looking uncertain.

"You okay?" I ask.

"Yeah," he brushes me off.

"What is it?"

He hesitates, shifting on his feet. "I didn't like that taxi driver."

"Why? Because he was perving on us?"

"No, more than that. I have a bad feeling about him."

"Are you worried about Katy?" Now I'm concerned. Theo's instincts are usually correct, and although he can be overprotective, Katy is only seventeen. The thought of anything happening to her . . .

He frowns and then shrugs. "I'm sure it's fine. I asked her—in front of the driver—to text us as soon as she got home, so he knows we'll be checking up on her."

"Good thinking."

"Emilie okay?"

"Out cold."

He gives me a small smile, his twilight eyes framed by dark lashes.

I slide my hands up and over his toned chest to rest on his shoulders. It's more of a reach than usual—he's still got his shoes on. I'm tall at five foot eight and Theo is a little under six foot, so when I'm wearing heels, we're almost the same height.

He leans down to kiss me.

George was taller . . .

I push out the thought and focus on the feeling of Theo's hands skimming my waist. He pulls me against him as our kiss deepens, and I want him like I haven't wanted him in ages. I'm tugging his shirt out of his trousers when he stills my fingers.

"Let's wait until we hear back from Katy."

I sigh, but nod in agreement, resting my head against his shoulder. I like that he cares. When I first met him, it seemed as though he cared about nothing and no one, but how wrong I was about that. It's *because* he cares that he had to build a fortress around himself.

My heart hurts for the boy Theo used to be. And once again my thoughts are pulled toward another boy and the pain *he* suffered . . .

© Greg Toon 2022

ABOUT THE AUTHOR

Paige Toon grew up between the UK, Australia, and the United States and has been writing emotional love stories since 2007. She has published sixteen novels, a three-part spin-off series for young adults, and a collection of short stories. Her books have sold nearly 2 million copies worldwide. She lives in Cambridgeshire, England, with her husband and their two children.

VISIT PAIGE TOON ONLINE

PaigeToon.com

 PaigeToonAuthor

 PaigeToonAuthor

 PaigeToonAuthor

 PaigeToonAuthor

PAIGE TOON